99 Waves

Persis Gerdes

Journal of Experimental Fiction #18

JEF Books/Depth Charge Publishing
DeKalb, Illinois

ISBN: 1-884097-18-9
ISBN-13: 978-1-884097-18-8

ISSN: 1084-547X

The Great Wave off Kanagawa is a woodblock print by the Japanese ukiyo-e artist Katsushika Hokusai. It was originally published sometime between 1830 and 1833, and is used here with great respect and appreciation.

jef

The foremost in innovative fiction
www.experimentalfiction.com

The Journal of Experimental Fiction is
catalogued through EBSCO

99 Waves

Persis Gerdes

I can't help feeling tense, shaken up and like hell about the movie I saw with you last night. How am I supposed to overcome so much violence? I feel it inside sometimes. Not just sometimes, a lot of the time. Wading through the shit I get so weary. Then something happens. It's like something connected with what we keep avoiding, what you never want to talk about. Then you say something that just pulls the trigger, and I go berserk again! I get so crazy sometimes, but not the cool way people used to talk about.

I'm here, I'm here! I'M HERE! It's just like in high school when I felt separate from everyone. Maybe I'll never grow up. Maybe the evolution that people call growing up is really just forgetting your dreams and your original reality. Becoming mature may be just becoming part of the crowd: faceless, a faceless mutant.

Whose voice am I speaking in? My voice or someone else's, like yours is in my mind or is it in yours? So how could you forget three men being beaten to a pulp while they slept, just because their hair was a little too long? Did you only remember the captivating desert scenes with horses, cattle and the occasional Native American? I suppose it's easier to remember the beautiful things. I really want to tell you how I feel, but how can I without causing another fight? I'm sick of it. I'm a man, and I'm expected to accept violence, to not be bothered by it. I'm supposed to be rough and tough so that I could kill you or anyone else if I had to survive. The American dream? Irrelevant.

You and I have been together for about six months, and I love you so much I can't stand it sometimes. But you and I are completely different people. I can't even voice my opinion sometimes, or you'll shoot me down. I can't really please you. Every woman seems to want a man who's the strong hero type. A knight in shining armor that you women have been brainwashed into believing will one day come and save you is supposed to come instead of me, sweep

3

you up and carry you away. I'm not that guy, baby, but I don't want to tell you that because I don't think you even realize that you think that way. If you did see it, I'm not sure you'd still want me.

Well, I've thrown out a few ideas to you, but as I suspected, you seem to be coming from left field, and I just can't cope with any of this anymore. Maybe I should just check into a nut hut or a booby hatch like good ol' Jack, 'cause I think my head has flown over the cuckoo's nest for the last time. But then again maybe it's this planet that's totally blind. There is no direction in any of our lives any more, except how quick we can profit or get pleasure. A lot of good that's doing all of us.

***

"How come you always shut up so tight whenever we get into some tiny disagreement?" you ask me with your eyes squinting.

"I don't know, Mary. Why don't you try and answer that question?" That'll keep you from nagging me for a while, and maybe it'll help you figure a few things out.

"Good night," you say curtly.

"Good night, dear."

You turn over, look at me and say, "You know this isn't going to last much longer if you think that every little scuffle is cause for an argument."

"How can you say that to me? I don't understand."

"Yes, you do. This just won't work if you think that every disagreement is an argument. I mean how else can people communicate?" You open your arms in query.

I sit up fast. "So you think that the only way people can talk is by arguing—constantly?"

You just lay there, close your eyes and pretend you don't hear me. But you can't do that to me. I just asked you a very important question. So what would I like you to do? What would be the best thing you could say to me right now? In order for you to feel worse for what you just said and did and for me to feel better—no, that wouldn't be right. I guess I really want you to feel good, but not at my expense. I'd like you to sit up next to me and put your arms around me and tell me that you love me no matter what I believe in. I'd like you to stop contradicting me all the time and quit looking for faults in everything I do and in every theory I have. Each one has taken me years to develop through disputes and struggles. Each one has come through years of careful considerations and calculations and is now refined and polished. Yes, I know most of them appear quite out of the ordinary, but I'm amazed that many of the problems that continue to exist on this planet have not yet been solved. These little ideas are just some simple solutions.... My arms are wrapped around my legs while my shoulders curve comfortably. I wish you would take just a few moments and remember the sandy beaches we enjoyed when we were just friends—and I wanted you to be my lover. You seemed so intensely involved in what I had to say then. But now you keep negating things I say before I have a chance to fully explain. Why? Why, why do you just lay there?

"Hey, are you asleep or something?" I touch your arm.

"No," you squeak.

"Then will you please answer my question?"

***

Morning breezes push white sheers over the bed and cover two bodies pulsating with energy.

"Hey, I can't see your face." I whisper and pull the white from your face. "Oh, that's so nice, but help me—I need to see your face!"

"Why?"

"Because." I try and pull you closer.

"Tell me."

"Because I want to know who I'm making love to. Now get this stuff off...." I get a little rough when I pull the curtain, so you say, "Ow, watch out what you're pulling." You hold the curtain with both hands and stop me from taking it off. You wrap it around so tight, then pull it off slightly so all I can see are your breasts. I pull them and suck them till I'm hard. I tickle you slightly as I do this and you squeal, saying, "Hey, who do you think I am anyway?"

"I know who you are...."

"Yeah, I'm Gladys from next door."

No, I can never mistake this part of you. You seem to dance with the sheer white around you. It slowly slides off your taught shimmering skin. You show off your beauty, and I enjoy you lavishing yourself in self-love. I'm so stiff all I can think of is home, my home inside you.

***

"Ooh," you take a long sexy sigh and I want to crawl back inside. "It can't be that late. I'm still tired. Besides it's Sunday, or Saturday, and I need my sleep." You put your pillow over your head. I grab it off.

"Hey you," I smile, "what about the party? I thought you were gonna help me." I've been holding the clock since I first looked at it. I try to put it up on the top of the bedstead, but it falls off and into the garbage instead. The alarm jams on, so you start to yell, "What the hell are you trying to do to me!"

"I—I—I'm sorry, honey, I—damn it, where'd it go? Ew, what the hell did you put in here?" I get it out and shake off my hand and then wipe it off with a used tissue.

"TURN IT OFF!"

"I—I'm trying to, damn it, what's wrong with this thing? Oh, I think it's broken or something...."

"Oh, quit your whining and give it here." You yank it from my hands look at it and shut it off. "There now wasn't that easy?"

"I—how did you do that?"

"I swear, William, you must go out of your way just to irritate me." You look at it closer, squinting because you can't see the nose on your face without your glasses.

"It's five thirty." I stand up.

"This says... oh my god, it's five thirty?"

"Yup."

"Where are my glasses?" You look around frantically.

"Next to the bed where you left them." I point to the night table.

"Where?" you say, patting around. I leap over the bed to help, but I kick you instead and you fall on the floor, hitting your head on the wall.

"Oh, honey, I'm so sorry, I didn't mean...."

"Ow. Oh, I know you didn't mean to, but will you please just give me my glasses?"

I slip them on your face and kiss your nose as I do. "I'm really sorry."

"That's all right. I'm sorry I was so crabby getting up."

"You should keep track of these, you know."

"I know."

"You know you're blind as a bat without them?"

"Well, I'm not that bad."

"Yes, you are... you remember last week when you put my pants on and walked around all day wondering how you lost all that weight?"

"Well—"

"Well?"

"A—I do set my glasses here every night, or every night since I moved in here."

"Yes."

"Well, I set them here, but I always seem to forget

them."

"Well, it's only been a few weeks. Maybe you should let me hold them on my side of the bed, and then I'll give them to you in the morning."

"I'll think about that one."

"It'll keep you from thinking you're skinnier than you are."

"What do you mean by that?"

"Oh, when you put my pants on, well, it must have been quite a shock to find out you're just as plump as ever...."

"What?"

"Oh, come on, you know I'm just kidding. You know I think you're perfect. You'd probably be ugly if you lost any weight."

You look bewildered. "Are you kidding me?"

"No, but I seriously think we have to get our little asses out of here so's we can get the party stuff."

"Okay, okay, but I bought a bunch of stuff for the party yesterday."

"That's right. Did you get the chips and dip shit I asked you to get?"

"Well, I got some...."

"Some? Okay, okay, we'll get more, but what about the keg of beer, did you order that?"

"I—I got some of that too...."

"What do you mean? No, don't tell me!" I run through the halls and tear open the fridge. Bright light blasts me as I find you didn't get what I asked you to get at all. "MARY!" I scream through the house.

You run into the kitchen, "What is it? Are you all right?"

"You know I'm okay. Tell me what it is that you bought us here, Miss California?"

"Now, now, William, don't get m—mad. Didn't you

just look into the fridge?"

"Yes, I did but all I could see was a bunch of rabbit food. I asked you to get party food, and this isn't party food... so I'm asking you what is this?" I'm so pissed that my head burns. I just bring a woman in here, and what do I get? She tries to make everyone healthy—AT A PARTY?

"But, William, you weren't really serious about all that greasy food you asked me to get now, were you?"

"YES! This is my apartment still. Remember you said this was a temporary situation, until you got an apartment of your own. These are my friends and..." You are crinkling up your face and it's turning red. Your eyes look really wet and red and then you run down the hall. "Mary? I'm sorry, come on, where are you going?" I follow you into the bedroom where you pull out your suitcase and begin packing. "Now look, we can work this out. It's just that my friends expect certain things when they come to a party, and I think I've really tried to be open to your ideas in the past, and, and Mary, you can't leave now, people are going to be here any minute and, and, you didn't get any beer?"

"Yes, I did," you sob between words. "It's in the fridge—didn't you see it?"

"Uh, you mean those bottles in the fridge?"

"What did you think it was? Root beer?"

I try and stay calm as I ask, "What did you spend all that what was it a hundred dollars I gave you?"

"Well, I got the veggies and dip, and I did get some potato chips with onion dip for it. Then I bought some foreign beers and some soda and some hard liquor and then, ah, well that's about all. Besides why don't you like veggies and dip? The last party we went to had all kinds of veggies and stuff like that."

"Mary, the last party we were at was at Jack's house, and you know he's rich. Where's the receipt for all this stuff anyway?"

"I threw it away."

"You threw it... oh, never mind. I'll just look again and get more of whatever we need. We really could've used that keg."

"Don't you and your friends like foreign beers? They're more exotic."

"Most of my friends are really into the American thing. Don't worry. I'm sure it'll be drunk."

"Just like your friends?"

"What'd'ya mean by that crack?"

"Only kidding."

"I know. So listen up, Girl, stay here and chop up all those veggies and answer the door while I'm at the store."

"What time are people supposed to come?"

"Around eight o'clock-ish."

"Sure, I can do that."

***

It's about eight thirty Saturday evening the 20th of January, and I'm cutting up these stupid vegetables that you promised to cut up. But you're still in the shower. I haven't even taken mine yet, and god knows when you're gonna get outa there. Slice down through the top of this mushy thing. Why do they call this a mushroom? Mushroom. A mushy room inside of this little thing? No, I can't see anything in there. A room where one day some guy was locked into a room cutting veggies all day and night while watching toads jumping around outside through a tiny window. The toads laid eggs. And then the eggs grew trunks, so the eggs turned into little round umbrellas. So the guy tries to sit on the biggest one, but he falls down because it was too mushy. Stupid stupid, stupid. So what the hell am I supposed to do with a carrot? Mom used to peel them. But I sure as hell ain't gonna go through all that, red bleeding knuckles left from scraping the grater so you never knew if there was blood in the bowl along with all the other strange objects you were forced to consume. I'll just cut off the tops—oh yeah, and the bottoms. Top and bottom, top and bottom, top and bottom, top and bommon—no bottom. Which is the top, and which is the bottom? The top sticks out of the ground, and the bottom sticks into the dirt, so maybe to the plant the top is the bottom because it always looks the shittiest. The bottom always looks like it should point up, like me when I wake up in the morning.

What's taking her so long? People are gonna be here any minute, and I have to take my shower and change. She spends a hundred bucks on bottled beer and veggies and... I look into the fridge. Now I see what she spent the other fifty on... A BOTTLE OF WINE? I'm not cutting another plant. Most of them are cut up into a nice neat pile, and if she wants them any other way she's gonna have to do it herself.

"I cut the veggies!" I call to her as I reach the bathroom door.

"What?"

"The veggies are cut, and I have to take my shower now. Can you do whatever-it-is-you're-doing in the bedroom?"

"Well, the light's too low...."

"Come on, Mary. It's 9:00, and people were due an hour ago. So you're just going to have to get out or forget it."

"All right, all right, I'm coming. Just give me a minute."

***

I switch the water off and open the curtain. I grab the towel from the rack and dry off. I hear voices from the L.R. Sounds like Freddy and his girlfriend, maybe.

I dress fast and zip a comb through my hair. I'm outa here. Oops, my clothes. I grab 'em and throw 'em into the linen closet. I neaten up the room and head out.

11

"Hey, Freddy, my man. What's happenin', bro?" I grab his hand and shake it hard. Then I pat his back a couple times. We're real tight bros. Kate's talking to Juanita.

"Nothing much. Long time no see." We laugh a bit and start our mindless party talk.

"Jeez it's good to be away from the ol' institution and that so-called proper way of conversing." I mock the accents.

"Ya, man, I work real hard at talkin' like a white boy," says Freddy with a laugh.

"I'll bet. You pull it off better than I do."

"A, excuse me but the final 'do' is improper because—" says Mary.

"No, it isn't. We changed that line in the third rewrite."

"Oh, yeah, then you speak so, so well, gentlemen, even for school teachers."

"Why, thanks ya, Mz. Mary, ma'am. Youse speaks very't'wail yoselfs, ma'am, a yeahza."

"Anyway, I'm in social studies, so I don't have to correct people too much, just in their papers or things like that," says William.

"And since I'm in music, I just correct their notes," says Fred.

"You are 'really' sly, my friend, real sly."

"Just call me Freddy the fox."

"I feel sorry for Jack sometimes, having to be so perfect in everything he says." I scratch my head.

"Don't. He loves being the king of language. He goes around correcting people all the time. Why, I wouldn't be surprised if he corrected the principal or the dean sometime."

"Yeah, well..., what time is it anyway? Don't you want a beer or something?"

12

"I've got a beer." He lifts his bottle. "Your lovely lady friend was very gracious to my fiancé and I." Then he whispers, "even though she didn't know us or trust us at first because we're black."

I give him a glare, "I'm real sorry, I just didn't think of you as being black or anything, I just told her your names."

"I understand, but we are black, and there's nothing to forget or hide about it."

"I wasn't...."

"Never mind, it's just something we were talking about earlier today."

"Excuse me, Freddy. I have to talk to Mary for a minute."

Mary hears me and looks up from talking to Juanita. "You need me, dearest?"

"Yes, darling. Come with me, please." We walk down the hall. The door shuts behind us.

"What did you say to Freddy when he and Juanita came?"

"I—ah—I don't know exactly. I didn't know them if that's what you mean."

"That's what they said. I thought you met them at Jack's party."

"No, they weren't there." The door sounds with three accurate knocks.

"Yes?" I ask.

"Someone's at the door. Should I let them in?"

"Sure thing, Fred. You probably know them."

After a few minutes of silence between us we exit into the kitchen and find a few people standing around.

"Hi, everyone!" I call out. They greet me, and I invite them into the living room, pointing out the hall closet and refreshments. I'm standing in the kitchen overseeing everything still as I hear a few taps on the window near the door. I peek out the curtain and see Jack waving a bottle of champagne at me. I yank the door open and forget the incident with Mary for good.

"Jacko—Jacko—this is really great, come on in." I shake his hand vigorously, take his coat and introduce him and his girlfriend to Mary, who is standing by the door. I take his hat finally, so he's had a chance to show it off a bit and demonstrate his etiquette by removing it when he sees the ladies present. It took a few times before I figured out the lapse in time. Each time I see him he's wearing a different hat. Tonight it's a purple derby, to match his tie. Thank god he's not wearing a suit coat. The moment I introduce him to Mary is when he removes his hat and bows to her. He takes her hand in his and kisses it. We are all amazed, especially Mary, who is smiling wide-eyed.

"Willy, you should have told me your lady friend was so lovely."

"I, ah," I feel really stupid and a tiny bit jealous at her attentiveness to him. "I thought you met already."

He's still bowing when he says, "No, sir, I know I would have remembered this lovely lady if I had ever met her before or laid my eyes upon her elegant beauty."

"Ah, Jacko,"

"Yes, Willy?"

"Where'd you get this gem anyway?" I twirled his derby.

He finally rises to the compliment. "It is a gem, isn't it, but it was at Lord and Taylor, I do believe. I have so many hats I can't remember where I purchased them all."

"I'm Matilda," says a squeaky voiced goddess next to me. This must be Jack's latest.

"We really did meet at your last party," says Mary.

"Come to think of it I do remember meeting you. And I never forget a face, especially the lovely ones. It seems Willy here always gets the most delicate creatures to escort him."

"Oh, brother," barks Matilda. "I'm just his live-in shadow. Say does anybody have a wine glass around here for some of this here bubbly?"

"Of course, of course, I bought some too. Though I'm not a true connoisseur, but I spent a lot for this...." Mary hastens away as if escaping the paws of Jack and babbles about everything possible to Matilda. So that is where she spent the last fifty or so.

"This was the most expensive bottle I could find, so I figured it was the best, after all this is a special occasion. I'd better get out ten or no, maybe twelve, in case some others come before we're finished pouring," babbles Mary.

"Who is here by the way?" asks Jack.

"What special occasion?" asks Matilda.

Mary and I begin to speak almost simultaneously, "Fred and Juanita" and "Fred and Juanita just got engaged last night."

"I didn't know they were your friends, Jack."

"Stop it, Matilda, I told you they might be here. They're good honest working ones, at least Freddy is. I don't know about his girlfriend or whatever she is."

"She is actually my fiancée, as of last evening," says Fred from the doorway.

"Why, Freddy, I didn't know you were standing there."

"Well, Jack, surprise, surprise. But don't worry— since we seem to not be wanted here, we may as well leave. Oh, by the way, Juanita is doing her post-doctorate work at Harvard where she has her medical degree already."

"Oh, really, what is she doing her post-doctorate work in?" asks Jack with a lump in his throat.

"Brain surgery and you better hope you don't need any, right?"

The air is so dark it's hard to see through all the

tension.

"Freddy, the girls were just getting out the glasses to toast your engagement. You said something about it earlier, but it went over my head. Congratulations, Man."

"Thanks, William, but I really gotta go."

"No, no, please don't go."

"We're not going to stay where we're not wanted. Juanita, come on, dear, let's go, we have better places to go, places where people with more class are." Fred walks into the other room and gets his and Juanita's coats.

"Now wait, Fred, please don't go. You don't have to leave."

"Why should we stay?"

"There are a lot of stupid people in the world, but hey, whose house is it anyway?"

"Well, yours, I guess, unless you rent it. But how can we stay in a place where people hate us because of our skin color?"

"First of all I really don't think they hate you, do you, Jack and Matilda?"

"Well, no, of course not. We just don't know you very well."

"You don't trust them either, do you?" I ask.

"Well, I, ah…" Jack turns red.

"Jack, tell them," demands Matilda.

"Tell them what? You got us into this mess, and I'm sick of defending your foul mouth. I'm not going to bail you out this time."

"How dare you talk to me that way. You were the one that said that if that ignorant colored boy was here you'd leave, so why aren't you?"

"I did not."

"Yes, you did."

"Did not."

"Did so."

16

"Just a minute you two! The house rule is to take all fights outside. Now march!" I point to the kitchen door and reach to open it just as the bell rings again. The two leave, and fifteen more enter. Some of them greet me, and some of them don't. I can't remember who all came in. I'm just concerned that the two outside don't get violent as I suspect Jacko does. He's got the temper of a scorpion, fast and sharp. People are mingling happily in the kitchen as I continue watching the scrap outside. Then I remember that I don't remember if I remembered to turn on some tunes. I jog into the living room and flick the switches. A bunch of people shout and wave between words, "Hi, William, great party!" I think they're probably wondering if I'm ever going to join them or serve them any food or booze. I grab Mary's arm and ask her to serve the people while I keep my eye on the two outside. With all these teachers I'd hate for one of my dimwit neighbors to call the cops on those two outside. As I enter the kitchen, Matilda taps on the window and then opens the door a crack.

"Could you please call me a cab?"

"Is Jack still out there?"

"Uh, yes...." She turns around for a moment. "No, not anymore." Her voice squeaks and turns around every vocal pothole it can manage.

"Are you sure?"

"Of course, I'm sure. Now are you going to call, or should I go down to the next block or wherever it is and call myself?" still squeaking.

"Would you rather stay?"

"No, thanks," she says as sweetly as possible.

"Where will you go?"

"Home," still sweetly.

"With Jack?"

"He won't be there now."

"Oh, I guess it's none of my business."

17

"No," she pauses, "no offense."

"None taken." I call her a cab, and in about twenty minutes she takes off.

I grab a beer and hear hard rock changed to reggae, classical is next and it's changed to jazz and then changed to new age. I down my entire beer before grabbing another and enter the crowd.

I walk around from person to person greeting and gabbing and greeting and bullshitting, mostly about school. Something about the Bears who are beating the Vikes again. I grab a handful of chips and scrape up the last bit of onion dip, but my chip cracks on the side of the bowl. I hate that. Why in hell didn't she get dip chips when she knew we were having dip? She spends $50 bucks on champagne and fifty cents on food—party food, that is. What's this? Looks like she put out another tray of the carrots and shit. It looks nice. What happened to the bowl of them that I cut up? They couldn't have eaten them all up yet. I'll clear some things away and look in the kitchen. I didn't ask everyone over to talk shop. I pick up a few ashtrays and dump one into the other so I can leave one here. As I casually make my way into the kitchen. Some idiot's unlit match blows up from someone's still lit cigarette. I jump when it explodes, and the whole thing falls onto the floor. I'm so clumsy! I'll bet everyone's looking at me. Shit! I walk into the kitchen to get a broom or something. Hope I don't light it on fire. Oh well, maybe this'll give me a little more attention. Funny, isn't it, how the one who gives the party isn't always the one people come to see?

Mary is in the kitchen talking to some guy I don't even know. I feel kind of stupid walking in on them, like I'm interrupting something.

"Oh, hi, honey," she says, trying to be nice, I'll bet.

It really seems sometimes like people really hate each other. They spend half their lives trying to find someone who has similar interests to them, or someone they're forced to deal with because of work or school or something stupid like chance. Who the hell is this guy anyway? I go to the sink minding my own business, getting a rag to clean up my mess before I burn the house down. *My* house that she's flirting with some guy in. I don't answer her. She didn't ask me a real question anyway. I won't be patronized. Maybe it's really nothing. Maybe it's just paranoia left over from all the acid I dropped in high school—I do regret it. I almost wasted my entire life. I guess that was the only way the government could pacify the riots of the students back then, by shipping in all kinds of drugs. And we all thought it was our own idea.

Maybe it's that movie from the other night that keeps dragging me back into my past, over and over. A man isn't supposed to get queasy from violence. A man is supposed to stomach all the slicing of flesh and blood and thoughts and beliefs that this fuckin' world dishes out. Is it only women who can long for something better? Is it only women who wish for something as wimpy as peace? Maybe it's us wimps who are too damn lazy or chicken to do the real work that it would take to actually have world peace. Maybe it's us wimps who are supposed to stand up and take responsibility for ourselves and show the so-called macho ones how to be real men! I guess that would include not blaming someone else for how we feel—how I feel. I reach my arm around her as a little surprise and touch her gently. She startles for a moment.

"Who's your friend, Mary?" I'm workin' real hard on controlling my feelings. I think she knows from my long silence and my washing that clean towel out about fifty times. Fifty. There's that sweet number again.

"This is Alexander, William; Alex, this is my boyfriend William. I thought you two met before."

"I don't think so, Mary." I'm short with her, but I

try and recap it by being ultra-polite, "I'm really glad to meet you, Alex. Glad you could make it to the party. You two must be pretty good friends."

"Whale ah've known Mary for a few yares now, right, Mary?"

"Why, yes, Alex. I thought I told you he was coming, William."

She looks pretty nervous trying to climb out of this mess. I'm on to you, girl, and I think
you know it. You better consider coming out of this private conversation and help me, and I better not have to say that to you out loud. It better be your idea too. But instead, Alex the Southerner makes his squeamish exit before he sees my collar get any tighter.

"Ah, yo' don't mind if I mingle, do yo', Mary?"

"Why—no—Alex. Make yourself at home."

"I didn't know you had a boyfriend Mary, you should've told me."

He darts out and he sounds a little pissed too. I guess I don't blame him—too much.

"I—I'm really sorry," you say with your hand on my shoulder. But I can't look at you. I don't know what to think. What were you trying to do?

"Look at me, William." You speak so sweetly, sometimes, but I just can't. "It's not as if you found me kissing some guy. We were only talking."

I reach to get my mug for beer, still pretending you're not here. I open a bottle and pour the gold foam. I toss the bottle. You do have a good point. You weren't kissing him, not when I came in at least. You were talking, and laughing, real close. I look at you for a second.

"That's it? Just a glance?"

"Guess so." I'm real cold, but I don't want to tell you what I think of you now. There's a party goin' on out there, sort of. I better get back in there and see if anyone needs a beer. I start to walk out of the kitchen with my beer, but you hold onto my arm. I try and pull away, but you're holding on real tight. So tight, I drop my beer and barely catch it again. Beer flies all over the walls, and my mug, the really great one I've had for years and years, slips out of my hand 'cause I didn't catch it tight enough. It slaps against the corner of the cabinet, smashing into chunks. I cut my hand as I try and gather the pieces.

"William, I'm so sorry. I know that meant a lot to you. Here, here, let me clean it up. Oh no, let me see your hand. I'll get a wash cloth or something, I'd better clean that up."

You really do love to mother me.

"Leave it alone. It's okay. If you wanna help, then help me pick up this ceramic."

"Your beautiful mug."

"Yes, my beautiful mug. Do you know where I got this thing?"

"Your Grandpa Sweeny."

"Ya, and d'you know where he is right now?"

"Six feet under? I don't know—let me wash your hand, William."

"That shows how much you know. *Man*, Shit. Why in hell did you have to be in here with that nerd? That guy's a gnat! I needed you so much out there, and where did I find you? Shit, my mug. I used to have two, a matched set, but some other jerk broke it at a party a few years back."

"You know sometimes I think you're two different people. You control yourself so much that one little thing triggers your, your—I don't know what."

"Quit analyzing me. And this isn't just one little thing, ya know. There. Now all the pieces are here so I can put it back together later. But I'm outa here." I storm out. Who needs her anyway? She gives me too many heartaches. Here and there, up and down. I feel like I'm always in front of an audience, and I never know what to do next. The living room's filled with smoke and people talking and people listening to music and people listening to nothingness. Why the hell do we do this? Sit around and pretend to talk to people we really don't want to talk to? Is this socialization? Is this discussion? Why? Because we don't have anything better to do except pretend? No one really changes anything. We all just putter around with our pretenses of importance. I think sometimes I'm the worst.

"Anybody need a beer or something?" Doorbell rings. Good, maybe we'll breathe a little air into this room. Shit. I scratch my scalp. Who in hell do I think I am by putting all this on my friends? My friends who don't even ask how I'm doing. I turn around to see who the bitch— no... it wasn't her fault—really. Except it was her fault in buying all the stuff I didn't ask her to buy with my money. But no one could have foreseen the mug breaking—I suppose. I'll just have to try and think differently about it or else I'll be just like everyone else—stacking up anger.

"H-hey, Sascha! Oh, baby, I'm glad to see you." I give her a real hug. Boy, she feels so good. What a woman. Too bad she never cared about me. I'll bet she gives better things than hugs. But no, I can't think that way, I've got Mary, I guess. I pat Sascha on the back. She knows that means to cool it. I feel great now—like a cliché of adult rebirth.

"So how the hell are you? I see you got my message."

"Ya, ya, I got your message just today when I got back from the airport."

Sometimes I think she leads people into asking her where she's been. But she's so good hearted that I'll give her the benefit.

"All right, where were you?"

"Oh, I was just giving a seminar on some of the new

American stock market methods."

"Oh really? Where?"

"At some of the European business colleges. Pretty boring stuff if you know nothing about it. But I get paid a lot of money for doing it."

"I had no idea you were an expert on the subject."

"Well, I guess I do know a few things."

"Yeah, huh, right, just enough to be flown to Europe to give seminars. I'll say you know just the right amount," says Mary from beside me. I almost forgot she was there.

"Oh, excuse me, Sascha, I'd like you to meet Mary." The two shake hands. Sascha looks at Mary with a strange radiance. Sometimes I want Sascha real bad when we're together, but when she's gone, I just don't think about her or miss her, hardly.

"Well, Mary, in answer to your comment, I really don't think I know all that much—not as much as a few other people I know. But I do know how to get the info across without boring people. I'm also very precise, and European businessmen want that."

"You're always smiling," I say half consciously querying and scratching my head. "Hey, let's introduce you around. You want a beer or something? Mary bought wine." We walk off into the kitchen, leaving Mary.

***

We've been sitting around talking for a while. Sascha on my left and Mary on my right. Sascha always makes me feel so good. No, not good, great. Like I could do or say anything and it just wouldn't matter what anyone else would say or think. She's like a guru to me—and a lot of others, too. So strange because of her line of business.

"I didn't see that movie. I tend to steer clear of violent movies like that. I rely heavily on the ratings and critics in that category," Sascha responds matter of factly.

"I saw it, and I was floored. Some people think it's

like a release of tension—like what they say about girly magazines, you know, that they keep us men from going out and raping every woman in sight. As if none of us has integrity." I don't care anymore when I can't talk right. I'm drunk. I just rattle off whatever the hell comes into my head. I just don't fuckin' care now.

"But I really didn't remember that movie, or what was in it," Mary says.

"Mary, how in the world could you forget something like that?" asks Freddy.

"I—I don't know... wait, now wait...." Mary looks at her hands.

"Yes?" Freddy responds.

"Let me just ask you this.... What were the names—just the names of all the movies you saw in, oh, say... 1982?" asks Mary.

"1982?"

"Right."

"1982."

"Yer stalling, Freddy, ol' pal," I spout.

"You, my friend, should stop drinking for a while." he snaps.

"Wait, I know, how about *Clockwork Orange*? That came out in about '82, didn't it?"

"I think that was '78," says Sascha.

"What about, um... *Eraserhead*?"

"No, I'm sure that was before '82," Sascha corrects.

"Well, that doesn't mean I didn't see it that year."

"Freddy?" prods Juanita.

"What, what? Is it time to go?"

"No, silly," she giggles delicately. "I just think that this game has been proved."

"Proved?"

"Sure, don't you see what Mary's trying to show us?"

"Oh, yeah, sure," and then whispering, "*What?*"

"Come on, Freddy, don't you try none o' your bull now with me."

She knows when to turn it on and off and to any other station she wants I see.

"All right, all right, I concede, Mary. I guess I can understand why you wouldn't remember what was in that movie," I smatter unwillingly.

"Thank you, William. And just to show you there's no hard feelings, I'd like to change this rather heavy subject and turn to Sascha to ask you, Sascha, what kinds of haircuts people in Europe are getting these days."

Sascha, shocked, chokes a bit on her wine. "Haircuts? You want to know about haircuts? Oh, William, she is a real whiz kid. But are you joking, dear girl?"

"What's wrong with that? I think haircuts reflect an obvious spiritual and humanistic trend in any society. You know, are they wearing all that short business yuppie look or are they wearing it in several shades of green and purple, like the kids are here?"

Sascha looks at Mary for five long seconds before responding, "Hell, I don't know. I really didn't pay that much attention to people's haircuts. But I'll bet it's about the same as here. Ah, I'm kind of dry, and I know we're running short of booze. Anyone want to join me to the booze store?"

I begin to sober up when I realize we drank all that $100 worth of booze already. I will never let a woman do my shopping for me again. But going out for extras... it's probably all right.

"You drivin'?" spouts Ruban from an invisible corner.

"Sure, I guess so. You wanna come?"

"You got that cool Alfa Romeo outside?" He peeks out the curtain.

"How'd you know?"

"I saw it at the parking lot at the school a few times and I saw you pull up tonight. I never drove in one before."

"Sorry, but you're not driving this one either."

"Oh, ha ha... I didn't mean nothin'."

"I know. So, anyone with a taste for the finer life—*hand over yer money*! Savvy?" Sascha holds out her hand.

"You sure can be rough when you want to," I say timidly.

"That's right, and don't you forget it. Now hand it over."

Several people hand over wads of green and grey. Ruban collects some, and so does Sascha. There are only about ten people left, but most of them give to the cause.

Sascha writes down a few choice words, shoves the paper in her pocket and walks out. Ruban dashes out behind.

People mingle. I sit staring at Mary, who seems to be moving closer to her friend, the weasel, who keeps looking at me and then at the woman he's talking to or with and then at Mary again. I fade in and out. I hear people talking about the school, and then I doze at the fashion sections. I perk up a bit when a tat of political mash strokes my ear. I pull myself together for a bit and trudge off into the kitchen.

"Oh, shit, sorry."

Fred and Juanita are kissing.

"No—no sweat, we were only talking... you want to join us?" Fred wipes his mouth, Juanita straightens her hair.

"No, thanks. I think this conversation is strictly private."

"No, really, it's ok," says Fred.

"Really, like I say, I like the way you folks talk, but I don't think I speak that dialect. Wouldn't mind though—

she's gorgeous Fred, you certainly got yerself a catch."

We all smile till Juanita says, "Wait a minute here, fellows. You did not fish for me, and this smile did not come easy. Fred can confirm that information for you."

"I—I'm sorry, I really didn't mean to insult you, I was try—oh, forget it, I guess I was really outa line."

"That's okay, William, I think you were actually right on the mark. *She just thinks she tried to get me when I pulled out all the stops. I planned every sly and teasing move,*" Fred whispers.

"Freddy, how can you say that?"

"Because it's true. Now hush up and tell him why we were talking so sweetly."

"What?"

"You remember—now tell him."

"No, Fred, that's your place. I'll ask my sister, and you'll, oh, come on now."

"I—well, I guess you're right then. I'd like you to be my best man, William."

"No, me? I would be honored. Hey, but I thought you had a brother."

"Well, I do, but he's really far away and kind of broke now."

"Can't come?"

"Well, I don't think so. I just didn't ask him yet."

"But why not?"

"That's right, William. That's what I asked him," says Juanita.

"Aw, come on. You can understand why, can't you?"

"Not really."

"He's a proud man, and I think he'd probably do just about anything, 'cept steal, but he'd probably hitchhike out here if he was asked to."

"What's wrong with that?"

"Come on, William, would you ask your brother to hitchhike five thousand miles?"

"Well, no, I suppose not, but then I would rather not have him get hurt when he found out he'd missed my wedding—and wasn't even asked to come to the service."

"That's about what I told him." says Juanita.

"Well, I s'pose you two are right, but I wish I could solve this a little more easily."

"Have you tried talking to your mom about it?"

"His mother passed on last year, Will."

"Oh, I'm sorry. You had told me about that, of course."

"Well you would've been absolutely right, I sure depended on her for advice when she was younger. But in her last few years she was a bit slow. At 96 that strong black woman was so
solid and clear on who and what she was."

"Ninety-six? She must have been pretty, well, pretty well along in years to have had a boy as young as you."

"Yes, they called me the love child. They thought she was way over the hill to have a baby at sixty-one years of age."

"Sixty-one? Are you sure, I thought that was almost impossible to be that old and have a baby."

"That's what the doctors said too. But my mama, oooh, she wanted me powerful strong. And I knew it, too. Papa, too, Mama used to tell stories of him goin' up an' down the block boastin', his chest puffed out to here, so proud to be a papa again. No one believed him. No one at all. 'Course it was touch an' go for a while. The doctors wanted to do this test and that one, but Mama wouldn't have it. Papa even tried to talk her into a few. But such a strong woman, she said she would not put her faith in anything but the almighty. And, I guess it paid off."

"I guess so. Well, listen now, you two, I don't think

we had any kind of proper salute, or, or, toast or anything like that for your engagement and so forth, did we?"

"Sure we did, didn't we?" asks Fred.

"No, well, I don't exactly remember, I mean... sure we did, William, earlier, didn't we?"

"Now you two don't try and be modest, come on out here."

"But, William, you can't,"

"And why not?"

"We haven't got any booze."

"*Sure we do!*" blasts Ruban, "and here it is!" The cork pops open, and everyone's glass finds a space under the falls of foam.

"Wait, *wait*! Everybody, before you drink, I'd like to propose a toast to Freddy and Juanita, the happiest couple in town! They're getting married! But, but, when?"

"Oh, uh, when Freddy? When are we getting married?"

"Don't you remember?" He's shocked.

"Oh, oh, of course I do, do you?" Juanita smiles.

"May, dear, May 28th." Freddy encircles his wrist in hers.

"Well, then to May 28th, the most perfect day of the year. Drink, drink everyone." As I tip my glass up, I feel the cool bubbles rolling down my throat and effervescing up into my eyes. I see Mary staring at me staring at her bubbles and I know what she is thinking of me: *Thinking of him with those same bubbles of slight bitterness and wicked dizziness thrills me as I know it does him.*

We're all laughing now, trying to clink our glasses while Sascha and Ruban parade between us filling our glasses as they're emptied. Behind me I feel a little tickle, like William sort of, but I turn to find Alex knocking at my door again. He smiles, and I return the favor. But I feel William's eyes burning my back, so I tell Alex I think

William's calling me, even though I thought I saw him staring at Sascha early on in the evening. But I bid Al adieu, bowing head long, practically climbing through the crowd. I climb away from him because of how tipsy I feel. I locate a chair.

As I bid adieu to the murmurs of crowds around me,
numbness encrusts my senses.
Is my zipper zipped?
Are my buttons buttoned?
Does saliva slip from my lips?
From my slitted eye all that lies before me
is the shimmer of a round box, unopened.

"Mary, Mary? I think she's had it. I should probably carry her off to bed." I think that's William's voice.

"No, you don't. I'm fine now. Just taking a little nap." I pull myself together in a snap—with a quaint rhyme at that. I draw myself up and sit very straight. I smooth my hair back and wipe my mouth, as daintily as could be expected, and then some.

"I'm sorry, Mary, I thought you were asleep. You've been sitting there for over an hour."

"William?"

"Yes, dear?"

"Come on, now. You sound like some old married man like that. Besides, I wish you'd shut up a bit so people would stop staring at me. I was just dozing a bit."

"I think you've had a bit too much to drink."

"Well, if I did, I didn't have a drop since I sat down here."

"That's true."

"And I'm not driving anyone home, am I?"

"Alex has his own car, doesn't he?"

"What? Of course he does, er, what should I care anyway?"

"It's pretty late now anyway and lots of people have gone. They have to work tomorrow."

"On Sunday?"

"Some. And some even want to go to church."

"People that were here tonight?"

I look around and spot Ruban talking to Freddy and Juanita.

"Hey, so, Freddy, when's the day?"

"The day?"

"Ya, ya, you know what date are you goin' to join up in this matrilineal brigade."

"Say what?"

"I think he means what is the date of our wedding," says Juanita.

"Oh, 'scuse me I din' mean to speak dat a way to you, I mean maybe is none of my business," Ruban says.

"No, no, of course not, Ruban. You're invited. It's just that I never heard of it being put quite that way before. Have you, Juanita?"

"No, Freddy, I haven't."

"Well, hey, man, I'm so happy for you bot' I mean…" He grabs the two of them and bear hugs them at once.

"Let's have another toast."

"No, Ruban, please? We've had too many toasts." Freddy smiles.

"All right, all right, just clink the glasses, I just love to clink the glasses."

"I'll bet you do." I smile from my chair.

"*Here, here!*" shouts a drunk from behind the background, the background of walls and interior settings and painted scenes on painted trees. It's the invisible drunk coming to drink us away by reminding all of us of what we abhor and ridicule when we are not the same way, or shall we say, not in the same sense of humor?

"What are your plans for the future?" I ask trying to sound very smart for such a question.

"Well, we're going to get married, and then I'm going to finish school. And Freddy will keep working at the high school like he has for the last ten years.... Are you up for tenure yet?"

"Jeez, I'll have to check on that, dear. Good question."

"How long have you two known each other?" I ask before I think. And then I insert the largest extremity into my somewhat large orifice. How wonderful it is to be under thirty years for yet another year. I can still make a fool of myself and people won't tell me.

"That sounded pretty crass. I'm sorry."

"No, it didn't. Did it to you, Juanita?" Juanita gives him a look.

"What I meant was, well, probably not anything that important anyway, I guess I was just curious."

"What are you going to do after you get married? B-besides finish school. You know, have kids, work on any special projects or go and live in a foreign country?" William asks.

"They're going to change the *world*!" yells the same anonymous drunk in the shadows.

"Who the hell said that?" asks Freddy.

"It sounded like your friend, Mary. Where is that creep?" Will turns around.

"I don't know. I've been right here the whole time, haven't I, Freddy?" Even though I was thinking of talking to him earlier, just for a bit. But I knew it would've been a fatal move. I'm starting to feel much better now after that nap. Everyone else begins to look around and end their search for Alex, poor guy.

"Anyway, I don't think anyone could do that," says Freddy.

"And why not?" asks William.

"Well, I guess we all do alter the course of history in a tiny way, but not anything major," Freddy admits.

"Why not?" asks William trying to be calm.

"Well, I really don't know why, but we don't. Unless, unless you mean like some of the really big changes that came from some of the movements, you know, the Jews, the Germans, the Russians, and back to us U.S.ians. But, hey, does anything ever really change?"

"You could say that we're very lucky to be Americans. At least I feel I am," says Juanita.

"Well, I hate to say this, but it's a common error for us to say that we should consider ourselves lucky. Because we really aren't that different from any other country with a dictatorship."

"No way, man! You can walk down the street, and you don't have to worry about whether you're gonna get home or not," spills Fred.

"In some parts of the U.S. you do, depending upon your race or what ghetto you're walking in," I say.

"Yeah, but I don't think you can compare the U.S. with what's happening in South America, South Africa and what still happens in the Middle East, namely the torturing of Palestinians," says Sascha.

"Look at the swing in things."

"Swing, William?" asks Ruban.

"Yeah, you know, the sixties compared to now. We had some major changes come out of that era, but some people think nothing changed at all," says William.

"Well, plenty happened, but a lot stayed the same, and so many people took to it like a fad or something. Look at men's hair styles," says Sascha.

"Right, right, like in the sixties it meant something

to have long hair," says William.

"It meant you weren't part of the establishment," says Freddy.

"Right and that you weren't gonna conform to the war or racist scene."

"But then with all the drugs an' shit, everyone wore long hair to be cool," says Ruban.

"Just like now," I say.

William whispers, "Mary, I think we're headed into some talk about the same thing we argued about the other day, and I don't want to do this."

"What's going on you two?" demands Sascha.

"Well, ah…"

"William doesn't really want to talk about this kind of stuff," I blurt out. Shit, is he gonna be….

"Mary? How? Why. You really know how to…."

"I'm sorry, I—"

"What's going on, you two?" asks Ruban.

"Nothing's wrong. I just think we should talk about something else," says William.

"But this is interesting," says Ruban.

"Well, I think this is just too heated a topic, and I, well…"

"It's not heated yet, William, and so what if it gets that way," says Freddy.

"I just am so tired of arguing every time." William looks down at his hands and crossed legs.

"Don't worry. You're among friends," says Sascha softly.

"Yeah, man, we all love ya!" yells Alex from his hiding place. But I wonder how he heard her, maybe X-ray hearing.

"Not if he stays around," says William.

"He's pretty drunk. He'll probably pass out soon," Sascha murmurs. William stares sternly at her.

"I'll call a cab," she says as she rises.

After a few minutes the issue is settled when Fred and Ruban escort Alex out, rattling and sputtering like a car on the verge of collapse.

"So how would you go about changing things?" asks Sascha point blank.

"Sascha, isn't that kind of—" I stammer.

"Oh, come on, you two. Can't we just talk without getting all scared and, and squeamish? Let's really talk now."

"I—er, well, how would you go about changing things?" asks William.

"Well, I d'know, I don't think things are so bad around here. I have a nice job, people love and respect me. I make lots of money—" says Sascha.

"You have Alfa Romeo," says Ruban.

"Right, right, I have an Alfa Romeo. So what could I possibly want to have changed? The present world situation suits me just dandy fine. In fact, if things did change, I think I'd go nuts, absolutely nuts."

"Well, I for one would like people to stop treating me like a third class citizen all the time," says Freddy.

"Freddy, please?" asks Juanita.

"No, this is a farce, I can't see what it will take to change the minds of people so that there's more than one black or black couple allowed. Do you know, Juanita? William? Sascha? You with your perfect world, well, perfect for you maybe. You're a gorgeous white chick with everything it takes to succeed in this world, and so you just happened to luck out here. So what about us—less fortunate folks? We is just scrapin' ups za pot mamza. An we dun finished wit dis here bullshit!"

"Yes, yes, I know that. I guess I wish I could make everyone as happy as I am, but I don't know how. What would you do to change things?" Sasha looks down.

"I'm sorry, I didn't mean to take this anger out on you. You're certainly not to blame, are you."

"I hope not, Fred."

"Well, what about in other ways, you know like social issues like, like, pollution, and war. What about them?" Will sits up.

"What do you mean, William? Do you want ideas on how to change these things?" I ask.

"Sure, sure. Like even the basics, like what we're eating or drinking out of. Or, or, this is good, like how do we see at this time of night?"

"What're you talkin' 'bout, man?" Ruban scratches his head.

"Don't you get it?" Everyone looks dumb.

"What are we supposed to get?" Juanita turns in her chair.

"Well, I don't know about you all, but I'm a night person. I get up in the morning because someone decided that morning was the only time children could learn. I'd rather do my thing at night." William smiles.

"Then get a night job." I smooth my hair.

"That's what I'm saying. High schools aren't open at night, are they?"

"Then become a janitor." Sascha takes a sip of wine.

"Come on, now. How many people would rather be working at night?" William reaches for a chip but finds an empty bowl.

"I would." Juanita reaches for her glass.

"Well, you have that option." Freddy looks stunned.

"How do you know?"

"Because you're going to be a surgeon, and, well, people get hurt at night, too." Fred pulls his climbing sweater down.

"Well, they usually just have interns on staff at night and have the regular surgeons on call. And then

36

during the day you schedule the surgeries when it's convenient for the patient." Juanita sets her glass carefully on the table.

"Don't you see? We've gotten ourselves into this rut of everyone working in the daytime because our mothers or fathers didn't want to wake up in the middle of the night because they were in the same rut." Will grabs his empty beer bottle.

"What about before electric lights?" I set my glass down.

"Well, of course it probably started then, but we had fire, and I'm sure someone had to stay up and keep the fire burning or watch out for bandits." William leans back in his seat.

"But you made the connection of our parents being the promoters of early bedtimes, right?" Sascha pulls her knee length red hair over her shoulders till it completely covers her yellow silk blouse.

"Well, yeah, that's a theory. I'm probably a bit off in that instance. But if you had a kid and you had to get up early so you could get to work on time for the only job you could find, wouldn't you kind of ignore your kid when he cried at night?"

"No, I don't think so, William. First of all because I think that no kid should be crying through the night. And if he or she is, I'd bet it was probably something wrong. Babies don't just cry for nothing." Sascha sits rigid.

"Actually very few infants would naturally get colicky if they were nursed instead of fed the myriad of phony formulas now advertised as nutritious," Juanita crossed her legs.

"I thought you were going to be a surgeon." Freddy scratches his head.

"Well, I am. I've just done an awful lot of research on the subject."

"I guess so."

"SIDS is even less common for nursing babies." Juanita switches her legs.

"This is really interesting Juanita, but do you think there's a connection between more or less people working at night than during the day?" William grabs his empty beer bottle again and shakes it a bit. I guess he forgot it was empty. He does that sometimes, picks up his glass or bottle or can and checks the contents but replaces it and forgets to get another one before checking it again. He may have taken the last sip half an hour earlier, set it down and then during a conversation without looking at the bottle, lifts it, shakes it, and replaces it again.

Juanita looks down.

"I don't know, William, I don't think I quite understand the question, 'Do you think there's a connection between more or less people working at night than during day?'"

"Oh well, I see your point. Um, I guess I was just trying to ask what the...."

"What the hell I was talking about SIDS for?" Juanita purses her lips.

"Juanita? What did you say that for?" Freddy tries to whisper.

"Don't you try and hush me. We're at a party, and I know William was getting all excited about what he wanted to talk about, and so was I, and I just wanted to share something I knew, but I guess because I'm a woman."

"Don't give me that cop-out. Um...." Freddy looks at everyone staring at them. "Let's go in the other room for a moment. Will you excuse me, William?"

"Juanita's right, Freddy, I wasn't giving her a fair shake. I was really excited about this, and, well, I think I tried to not be rude, and well, I'm sorry, Juanita. I guess I just never get the chance to talk about this very much. I got too excited. I asked a very dumb question. Can we start over?"

"Sure." Juanita smiles. "I am interested in what you were talking about."

"And I really want to hear more about that thing you were talking about, that Sam's or Steve's or...."

Juanita laughs. "SIDS, William. It's really serious, and I shouldn't laugh when I say this because it's so sad when it happens. It's called Sudden Infant Death Syndrome. You've heard of it, I'm sure, like when newborn babies die in their sleep."

"Oh, I didn't know, I couldn't quite figure out what it was." William excuses himself to get a beer and offers a refill to everyone, but I get up and do it instead so he can hear more about what Juanita's talking about. I clear the clutter as I go. I find an old tray he's had on top of the fridge for a while. I wipe it off with a wet sponge. It smells foul. I throw it away and search for a new one down below. What a mess. I'll have to clean this out sometime soon. Looks like no new sponge. I'll have to buy another one. I grab some paper towel off the roller and wet it down and add some soap. I wipe off the tray again, dry it and toss my scraps in the trash. Now let's see here—who wanted what? I grab out a few, no five bottles of beer and the bottle of wine that's open. I bring everything in and serve it while they're all listening to Juanita still. I set the tray and bottle down on top of it for later. It's getting uncomfortable in here. I open a window to clear the air.

"That's really interesting, Juanita. Maybe you can give us an update later on about some research you've read." Sascha pulls her hair back and takes a sip of wine. "But getting back to the other topic, William, I was wondering if you thought about the fact that if we split up our time more, between the night and day so that it was about equal, then don't you think we'd be making all these electric companies richer off the night shift?"

"I sure as hell don't want no nuclear power plant in my back yard." My mouth hangs open for a few seconds before I realize what I'm doing.

"I don't either. So we turn to sun power." William takes a big slug from his beer bottle.

"It's not profitable. There are very few, if any, that I can recall." Sascha scratches her head so slightly anyone else might miss that she'd done it.

"What do you mean, Sascha? Very few what?" William grips his bottle.

"You know... companies. I mean companies in the stocks."

"Companies?" Fred looks at Juanita squinting a bit.

"Yes, yes, companies selling solar power equipment." She waves her hand in a circle like she's playing charades.

"Solar powered companies on the—" I'm interrupted.

"Not solar powered companies, Mary, companies that sell solar power equipment." William loves to correct me, I think.

"No companies on the market, Sascha?" Ruban sits up in his chair.

"Right, right. No companies that I've heard of, unless they're selling it from a company that sells something else primarily."

"Can they do that?" I'm feeling doubtful of her words.

"Well, technically not, but well I don't know everything."

"But even if they weren't selling it in the open market like stocks or something, it doesn't mean they aren't some small company out there somewhere." William shakes his bottle slightly again before setting it down.

"Right, well that's precisely my point, William. It hasn't been profitable enough yet to have people invest large sums of money into it."

William rises up and grabs his bottle. "Well, maybe it's not because there's no money to be made, but then maybe it would mean the public would become independent of these large multinational corporations. Who'd want to invest in something like that?"

"I guess we have to get the money circulating from somewhere." Freddy picks up Juanita's hand and strokes it a few times. "Right, baby?" He looks at her. She smiles and tilts her head.

"If we have to, I guess." She smiles.

William blows lightly into his bottle till we hear hollow ringing. "So abolish money."

Freddy spits his beer out before laughing. Juanita smiles and shakes her head. Ruban says, "You crazy man? What you been drinkin' there?"

Sascha looks irritated. "Thanks, William, that's a good way for me to lose everything I've got. Aren't you going to say anything?" She looks at me.

"What do you want me to say?"

"Tell him he's never gonna get anywhere with a stupid idea like that." Sascha pulls her hair back pompously.

"I don' know. I guess it depends upon where he wants to go."

I smile at William. He grins back. Freddy jumps up to get a towel for his mess. He quickly wipes it up and returns to his seat.

"Well, for one thing, how do you think we'd eat or have a place to live and sleep?" Ruban lifts his bottle from a puddle. He grabs a sheet of paper towel from the roll Fred left on the table.

"Oh, man, it's so simple that it probably sounds

ridiculous." William lifts and sips his beer, then holds it as he speaks. "Imagine you're walking along in the best place you could possibly imagine. You're being what you really want to be. Like me, I'd probably be a painter. Now you walk to the store and go inside and find folks who just like being part of a food scene. So they have all this food and stuff that they had delivered from the area farmers and small manufacturers. So the store owners, or whatever you want to call them, store all the food and stuff on their shelves. Then all they have to do is keep inventory of what everyone takes. Like see yourself now. You go to this small but jammed store full of fruits and veggies and dry goods and nuts and dairy foods and maybe meat, if you eat it, and you know, pretty much like a regular grocery that we have here today, because it's real clean and neat, but it's different. It's not run just to make money. It's run just cause all these cats want is for you to come in and take as much as you want or need. So you take some of this and some of that and you bring it to the counter and the counter person puts it into bags, and while she or he is doing it, she or he writes down everything that you're taking so they can keep their inventory, and then you go home, if you want. Along the way you see folks farming, or like maybe you hear little kids singing in one of the schools or just talking away. So you, you walk on down the street, and what do you see but a couple of dudes arguing and pushing a bit. They're about to really have it out, but you don't really give a shit because it's between them. So if they beat each other up for a while, then maybe they'll straighten out their problem, whatever it is. And if the fight gets too bad, then a couple of people will probably tear them apart. So? So what. Eventually they end up on the opposite side of the street or the same side, if they take the time to work it out. But the point is nobody gets involved unless the fight gets out of control or if somebody else gets hurt. We're all human, so we all work together to keep things cool.

"So you keep walking down the street, and you're feeling the bricks and cobblestones down under your feet. This town has a strange architecture, filled with geodesic domes of varying sizes and grass-ceilinged roofs—all kinds of things. Some construction is going on, too. You stop and watch the men and women work together on these unique homes. But the workers aren't like any you've ever seen, because they aren't doing it for a living or a buck or because their parents wanted them to, but only because they chose this work. They don't work for money, but because they love the work. They're real artists in their trade. In the distance you see some kind of Indian tribe moving behind some trees. Some are singing and some are working. But they have their own perfect space to do with as they see fit.

"People don't steal here, because they don't need to—they get whatever they need or want, and they don't need to take it. Everyone earns their way, though. You don't see anyone slouching or begging, and there's nobody watching over anyone, unless it's like a parent or teacher helping or something. Everyone has been brought up to trust everyone else. It was really hard in the beginning stages, though. But once they got going, it was easy, like something everyone always wanted but never knew how to get it."

"You're talking in past tense, William." I sit up a little.

"Oh, yeah, I guess I am."

"Sounds really nice." Junaita smiles.

"You seem to have most of your bases covered." Freddy scratches his head.

"Well, I, ah, I guess so. I mean I've put several years of thought into this."

"Almost sounds like a fantasy world or something." Sascha taps the corner of the table with her drink.

"I guess it is in a way."

"How say you?" Freddy furls his brow.

"Well, I, at the risk of sounding corny or something, it's like when I think about all the different problems this world has and all the people who're being hurt every day, I just sort of imagine all these solutions."

"But they seem to make sense." Sascha holds her glass firmly without looking at anything but the glass.

"Well, as I said, I've been working on this for years."

"That's obvious. But the problem is getting from point A to point B." Sascha still glazes the glass with her green eyes.

"You mean point Z, don't you?" Freddy leans over to grab some Corn Curlys.

"Well, yes, I suppose so." Sascha looks squarely into Fred's face, with a corrected authority.

"I don' know, I don' think anyone's gonna buy that." Ruban scratches his shoulder.

"It does sound pretty hard, doesn't it?" William leans down over his knees and shakes his bottle between his ankles.

"You weren't actually thinking of trying this, were you?" Fred sits up quick.

"Well, I think life would be a lot easier for everyone."

"You're crazy, man. There's absolutely no way you're gonna change the minds of billions of people. No way!"

"Like Christ or Mohammed?" Sascha throws her cape of red behind her.

"Don' you dare." Ruban pulls his arms close to his sides.

"What? Please don't get excited, I was only making an observation, not an actual comparison. But you have to consider the fact that humans have made major changes

44

over the years, and it has never been easy for any of us, but things have progressed quite nicely, haven't they?"

"Don't patronize him." I cross my legs. "Now, we all know that there're too many governments and powerful people who would just as soon as have us all tortured to death for even talking or thinking about something like this. And then don't forget about all the mercenaries and Bible thumpers who would totally misconstrue this kind of a thing. And then don't forget about all the millions of people who think their lives consist of whatever their jobs are, and they don't even really know who or what they are, let alone what's best for them or the difference between their asses and holes in the mud."

"Mary, I think most people have probably just learned to adapt to whatever the planet has presented to them." William shakes his bottle again.

"Bud, I think most people are too afraid to make these kinds of change. They may think you are from the devil or somethin'. You are not a worshiper of the devil, are you? But if you are, then maybe you will not say." Ruban's fingers climb down his pant leg till he unconsciously, or so it seems, straightens his pant.

"Ruban, you've known me for a long time. Don't you think you would've noticed something else? Besides I'm not proposing a war, but peace for everyone. It would actually be more of a natural way than what we are forced into now."

"You mean like God's laws?"

"Well, I don't know, but I guess you could call it that. But look at the most positive aspects. Ruban, wouldn't you like to be something other than a teacher?"

"Well, I've always wanted to really know my people down in South America."

"And what about you, Mary, wouldn't you like to be living or doing something else with your life?"

"I don't know, I suppose so. I like living with you... er, I mean..."

"I didn't know you lived here." Sascha looks at me, and I smile.

"But it isn't that simple, William. We have an entire world that's filled with people who hate one another because of their skin or hair or age or sex or whatever. You think you can just go up to everyone and say, 'Hey everyone, I have a better idea. Forget what you're doing now and do it my way'?"

"Well, that's not exactly what I had in mind."

"There have always been bad apples screwing things up for the good ones. Ya know what I mean?" Fred grabs William's bottle from his hand and offers refreshers to everyone else. Then he walks off into the kitchen.

Everyone is quiet until Fred comes back. William takes a sip from his bottle and thanks Freddy.

"That's exactly why the plan I've come up with would have to be carried out to the letter. But it's true what you said about all the people. People may not take too kindly to such an overhaul like this. I know we would have to contend with the FBI, the CIA, gangs and gangsters, and, yes, all those people who are convinced that the world will absolutely come to a violent end.

"We all seem to play into that scenario, and I know that I'm not always the most positive person to live with. But we just really have to need to somehow change the patterns that we've set up for this planet. Most people will do the right thing if they're given half a chance."

"How can you say that? What about all the criminals and child molesters and, and...?" I clutch my glass.

"Well, don't you think the child molesters are criminals?" Juanita yawns.

"Oh, that's irrelevant, and, oh, I'm sorry, Juanita,

but I just don't understand how William can say that people are or could or *would* even consider changing, when it's so much easier to just take advantage of others."

"Do you really think that some people are just born bad? Don't you think that something in their childhood may have put them on that road? And then what about the chemical imbalances that doctors are finding?"

"Oh, William, isn't it about time people stopped blaming their lives on their parents or society, or their bodies?"

"Well, but are you a criminal? I mean, I know you're not, so how can you understand what they're really thinking? How can you know what their real motivations are? I think that if you take each person, you'll find something behind their anger and greed and bitterness. That's precisely the way and means that can drive everyone into getting rid of these ridiculous systems that don't work. We only want to be happy. We don't want to struggle or hurt others or take from others, or keep people in the gutter. I think we all just want to be safe and secure and well, just to know that we can all get by, and happily, with full stomachs, warm hearts and fine minds, and of course, free spirits. But nobody on this planet is truly free. How can anyone be free who is afraid?"

"So what you're saying is that with your little plan everyone is just all of a sudden gonna be happy and blissful? Sounds almost like a cult or something. To tell you the truth, I kind of like the struggle." Freddy sits back straight in his chair.

"Freddy, how can you say that? Wouldn't you like our children to have a real future that they can create? Remember, William is not the first person to want to really do something about the situations we live in. I know of one man who was killed because he had a dream." Juanita looks sour.

"Well, I guess you're right about that. But I do like working hard on my teaching. I work damn hard to prove what kind of man I am." He holds his head very high.

"I'm glad you're a friend of mine. But I thought you just said about an hour ago that you didn't like being treated like a second-class citizen?" William shakes his bottle and foam
sticks its head out.

"Well, I don't. But I am proud to be black, and I don't want to melt into some pot and die because nothing matters anymore. You know what they call that, don't you? Stasis. That's what they call it—unmoving, or dead."

"Who said anything about dying? Did anyone here say things wouldn't matter anymore? Look around us and everywhere you look you see ways our parents and grandparents made mistakes. This planet is just not going to be able to take any more of it. We already have a hole in the ozone layer, we have almost every single lake, river or stream polluted with our lovely but of course, 'necessary' waste products. Oil rigs are causing massive accidents and destruction." Sascha pulls her hair forward. "What will any of this matter if we all just kill ourselves with the poisons we eat every day? We don't even hardly remember what food tastes like anymore without a ton of salt or sugar or 'flavor enhancers' in almost every food you find in a package. Do you really think that a positive future would mean death? *Wake up, man!*"

"Well, I, er, well, I guess I see what you mean. I just think that there's no such thing as a utopia. And especially without a government of any kind. That alone scares me."

"Well, I can understand that. We've been brought up to not trust anyone. Our parents have told us since we were infants, 'Stranger Danger.' So, anyone who is different fits right in that category." William takes a big swallow and sets his bottle down for a second before picking it up again

48

and shaking it.

"Hey, man, you haven't lived where there was no law except the law of the street. That's when Darwin's theory of eat or be eaten really holds true."

"I think that there's a way to get rid of that kind of life."

"Right, think whatever you want. But until you step into that street and meet the cutthroats and beggars and sleaze, and become a part of all those lives who don't know nothin'
'cept the law of the street, you can't change a fuckin thing."

"Freddy!"

"I'm sorry Juanita, but he don't know what it's really like."

"That's exactly why I need your help."

"I ain't no scapegoat or dog's ass for no one, man, I don' care who you are. I have a good future as it is, and I ain't gonna get killed before I turn eighty, unless of natural causes, that's the unnatural law for me, because I'm a black man. Did you ever wonder why you see so few old black men? We get killed usually before we're forty or fifty years old. That's something I have to live with. And this kind of a jack ass idea of yours would really put me under the trigger."

"All right, all right. relax. I don't want you to do anything you don't want to. I can't do this alone anyway. It's just a dream, as you say, anyway.

"Freddy, I think we should get going. I have an exam on Monday, and I'll probably have to study all day tomorrow."

"Sure thing, Juanita. Uh, thanks, William. Sorry to sound so hard. It is a good idea, though. Well, anyway, I'll be talking to you about the other thing."

"Right. Thanks for coming. Please don't be angry. And please don't tell anyone what we talked about here.

That goes for everyone here. I don't want anyone who I don't know knocking on my door."

***

William is at home with the telephone and all the other household machines turned off. He hasn't answered the front door to anyone. It's been a week since I've talked to him and shown that side of myself. I wonder why he's cut himself off from all his friends. I never thought that part of me would come out again. Maybe I wasn't that bad. I mean, I agreed with him for a good part of what he said. I didn't tell him about everything I thought. How could I? To think that he wants to ruin my future in the stock market! It's like he really knew what I was thinking or something. Maybe he doesn't want to be near me anymore. I'll bet Mary sees him every day. He was probably playing a game to see if I'd take the bait. I think he thinks I did.

Peacock feathers fall from rockets. Blue and turquoise morsels of pigeon sweaters clothed in white sapphire beads. Dribbling waves of extortions. Militant women surge up through the ranks of heavy artillery thinking of their one goal. Speak to the Earth, our mother from birth. She's the only mother we've ever really known. We come from her as chemicals to matter and energize. Stinging shocking rifles false fire among us, tripling our casualties. You and I are not separate anymore, even though we have been fighting against each other for centuries. We find after all the destruction has maimed everyone we love and hate, that what we thought we fought was not each other but ourselves.

***

You grab your purse and keys from the rack by the door and look over your shoulder to see that the little red light on your answering machine is lit. You slam the door and hear echoing steps as you make your way to your Alfa Romeo. The pale lavender shines like water on flowers you can smell or hear as the engine roars down the street. Something about this car, and the sheer excitement at surprising him makes you squeeze the accelerator hard, while your flaming red hair flows across the rear of the lilac trunk, from your topless car. Stop light? No, not now. You screech to save your license. One more will throw you in the slammer, even though you could buy your way out of everyone. Your daddy's words of warning, warning, warning you not to buy something that could go so fast. Just join the air force or become an astronaut or buy a REAL race car. A real race car was sitting in the lot when you bought this beauty and you seriously considered what daddy said. Yellow light flashing, flashing, flashing. Downshift, smooth as silk gliding over freshly shaven legs and oops someone is going to try and beat the light by zooming through but you have the big end of the stick and you peel out faster than daddy thought a rocket could.

Just about there and you begin to feel that part you felt was missing from who you are and who I am as though I am who you are and talking to you in that way was leaving you in part to let you become who you'd really like to be. Who you are as I am and we are whoever the Big G said it was. It's all right I'm not crazy, just scattered. I love me, I mean you and I don't want anyone else to know because they may become repulsed. Nobody is really supposed to love yourself, or myself, or ourselves. Love people, to some degree as long as you can keep one eye on them at all times so they don't stab you in the back, the back, back, back. Or love your parents, without showing it too much 'cause they can't really handle it—too intense for most folks over forty. Love your children until they become a pain in the ass, and then love them as far as their teachers say or as far as they obey you, but never for who they are, especially if they become drastically different from you. Because they really become what you hate in yourself. Love

objects and, of course, activities and money and power. They're the safest of the lot. Some people even love to kill. The greatest paradox is when they love their country so much they kill for it. Imagine that—killing for a piece of sod. Question is, how is that sod going to pat you on the back? With an earthquake maybe. Make sure of course that you only love the good guys. If you love a bad guy,
then you will become a bad guy. And once you become one of them, you may as well be dead. All you have to look forward to is the life of a bad guy. Slithering, sliding, sulking slow slaughter, sailing somewhere between burnt sesame seeds that never open and strange filthy illnesses.

I slam the car door and grab my purse from the open seat. I walk toward the front doors. Adrenalin pulses through my veins as each step seems to echo louder and louder, thunder shatters a light fixture. Imagine, imagine if I could really do that, or rather, when I will do that. It's okay, it's okay. He doesn't hate me. I was agreeing with him. But it could have been a trick. Maybe he was trying to trap me into letting him know who I really am and where I come from. I gotta let go of my self. No, no, I gotta get hold of myself. All these codes and symbols people learn from the mass medium and I just can't get a handle on it. I wonder if any of them fit into this strange subconscious world of chaos. I know he doesn't hate me, I—I'm just getting so paranoid from all the heavy vibrations of this planet. I'll have to just spend the rest of the evening meditating. I really have to surface from all this. But I'm so ecstatic about the possibility of finding.

"I'd like to speak to William Colin, please. Could you please tell me what room he's in?"

"Ah, yes, let me see, he's in room," replies a grey-faced lady pulled down low from time and rejection of the positive forces. She peers over her paper, examining me. I look around nonchalantly so she can see that I'm not a threat, till I look right into her eyes, long and hard, mesmerizing her for about ten seconds. She stops her investigation and blushes, but huffs, "I'll have to see if he's in the lunch room or not. Maybe he's in his classroom. Just a minute please." She walks over to a hefty red open ring binder. She opens it displaying the shiny silver toned rings, with pages and pages of writing and typing filling the 3″ rings till they can barely hold tight. She takes hold of the tab with the letter C and opens the pages, smoothing them down as she goes. She whispers, "Cab, Cad, Can, Cain, Cedar, Chaps, Chapman... ahh, Colin. Now let me see, it's ten thirty in the morning.... Now why would anyone be at lunch now anyway, silly me.... Nobody has lunch before eleven. Hummmhummmhummm, well, he should be in his room now. Yes, he should be in his room now." She begins to speak to me somewhat directly.

"I have a very important meeting in about an hour, and it is downtown, so if you could please just tell me what room he's in? Could I just go and see him. Please?" I smile so sweetly, but I know I sound firm. She's got something that I want, and she's enjoying being the ruler/oppressor. I think she must get her kicks this way most of the time.

"Well, I'll have one of the hall monitors bring a note to him. What did you say your name was?" Her nose is still up and her brows are arched high above her nose. This must be her only power on this planet—to judge people, or stop them from where they want to go. I coldly tell her my name. As she writes, she tells me to sit in a chair next to a student who doesn't look terribly pleased to be here either. The old office lady didn't even look at me but just pointed to the chair, pointed down with her skinny finger. I feel like knocking her glasses off her face. Calm down, calm down, I tell myself. Peace, peace.... I will see him, I will see him.

"Sarah?" The old lady calls to a girl standing just outside to come in. "Take this note to Mr. Colin's homeroom, please."

After the girl leaves and the lady sits back down at her typing table, I stand up and look around at the walls, which are covered with student oriented things: newspaper articles, PTA meeting schedules, contests, outstanding student lists, etc. But I saw these while I was sitting in the chair and looked around for a moment to make her think I was interested. Instead, I quietly slipped out after the girl. I follow her up the stairs to Wil's room. As she hands him the note, she looks up at me with a funny expression. I stare back at her with authority. Her eyes turn to the floor and then to Wil, who responds to the note and thanks her. Just as he's about to close the door, I keep it from closing and say, "Surprise?" in a very little voice.

"Yes?" you ask, not looking up from your paper. I peek in and see your classroom is empty. You are still looking at your papers while I walk in. You look up while speaking and it seems assuming to see a student. "I just told Sarah that I couldn't see—but how did you—" You smile, thank goodness.

"Why have you been avoiding me?"

"I haven't been avoiding you—really."

"Yes you have. But why?"

"To tell you the truth, I've been avoiding everyone."

A hard angry knock shutters in the room. The woman from the office stands as firm as an insecure cop.

"I thought you told Sarah that you didn't want to be disturbed by this woman."

"It's all right, Miss Walgamuth, she's a friend."

"Please to make your acquaintance, Miss Walgamuth." I hold out my hand but I know she won't respond.

"But I thought you said...."

"Well not exactly, but it's all right. You didn't call the police again did you?"

"Oh—why did you have to bring that up? Of course I didn't. But I thought of it. You know, young lady, this is against the law. I could've called the police, and you could've been thrown in jail."

"But you didn't this time because of the trouble you made last time right, Miss Walgamuth?"

"No, oh...."

"That'll be all now. Now go back to your work. Did you leave the office unattended—again?"

"Uh oh, don't tell Mr. Spatz, will you?"

"Of course not. Now run along, see you later."

She trottles off, her heals clicking down the linoleum halls.

"I hope you're not offended."

"By you? Yes, of course I am. By her—infuriated! But only at first. But now, I don't really care. I did like how you handled her. You used some pretty chauvinistic plows."

"Did I? I just don't like her doing that."

"So the thing with the police before, was that pretty serious?"

"Sure. She thought one of the school board members was an intruder, and she called the cops. The principal was so pissed that he had the office closed for about half an hour while he yelled at her."

"Sheesh. Well she teed me off, but I've had my share of insults. I just had to bite down a little harder than usual."

"I wondered why you always wear a silver bullet around your neck."

"Oh well, the chain is gold. But yes, I have bitten down on this bullet a few times. It reminds me of the buildings back home."

"Buildings? What do you mean? Some buildings made of silver?"

"Did you know you speak so much more clearly

when you're here?"

"Here? I think you're avoiding the question."

"What? Which question?"

"The one I just asked you."

I sit down before saying, "Really though, William I think the first unanswered question was yours."

"What? You're still doing it."

"Who are you avoiding, anyway?"

"Well, this time I guess you deserve to be direct. I've ceased to avoid you now—as you can see."

"That's only because I had the balls to sneak in here, out from underneath her nose." I stand up and lean over your desk. I look out the door as if looking at her when I speak of her.

"Hu, hu, ha, ha. You snuck out from under her nose?"

"Yes. I knew you'd try and avoid me. Why?"

"Well, I, ah...."

"I was supporting you and your ideas, but you shut me out. Why? What've I done wrong?"

"It was... wait, I think someone is—" You whisper the last few words and then tiptoe out to catch Miss Walgamuth outside the door. "Yes, Miss Walgamuth? Was there something else?"

"Humph!" She trots off again clicking her heals more loudly than before.

You shut your door completely. "Should've seen her face—beet red." You sit down.
"To tell you the truth, Sasch, I've been avoiding everyone that was at that party."

"But why? I mean I can understand your avoiding the really disagreeable ones, but me and...."

"And who? There wasn't anyone really who agreed or even considered the possibility."

"There was Juanita, and Mary."

"Well Mary and I have been arguing about this thing for a few months now, so I don't really think of her as being in my court.

"As far as Juanita, well, I don't really have the opportunity to talk about or to or with her anyway, so that was a treat. In fact I guess I really have nobody to talk about these ideas anyway. So why should I talk to anyone?" You lower your head and fiddle with your papers.

"That's right. Mary wasn't exactly seeing eye-to-eye with you. But I'll bet you saw her afterwards."

"Well, she's living with me, though, even though I really didn't ask her to."

"You didn't want her to? It was a real shock to me to hear that she'd moved in anyway. You've always been so old-fashioned about those things."

"Yeah, well, don't mention it to her, but she needed a place to stay, so I let her. But we were in love anyway, so...."

"So, why don't you marry her?"

"Well, well, I'm not exactly sure she's the right one. You know how it is."

"How is it?"

"Well, I just hoped that I'd find someone who I could share some of my strange ideas with—without being shot out of the water. You know?"

I really want to say how I feel about you now, but I can't. Sometimes I think you know. You must have sensed that you and your wisdom are not the norm of the planet Earth. I crave the meeting of our minds. But you have yours, and I can't push you. I sigh and look at the floor waiting for you to tell me again how much you love her. I brace myself once again and hope it won't hurt as much this time. I don't ever want to possess you.

"You know, William, I care very deeply for you. More than I'd care to say."

"Yes, I know, we've been friends for a long time."

"Stop, I mean, that's not exactly what I meant. It doesn't really matter now because you're in love and thinking of marriage. I think we should change the subject. Now as far as the subject from last week's discussion, I am more than interested in your ideas. I have another meeting downtown pretty soon, but I'd like to get together this evening, or so—with some others who are also interested and see, just let's see what we can do about this thing." I look up at you, longingly for a few seconds, and you try and innocently to avoid my unspoken words. I stop looking at you for a moment and wait for a response. You drop your pencil on the floor and quickly retrieve it. I have been standing back from your desk. I'm beginning to feel weak in the knees from your silence. I return to the seat in front of you. You click your pen on and off, on and off, on, off.

"I don' know. I think it's possible. I didn't think it would actually be probable. We'd need a lot of people that we could actually trust, I mean completely—total hush, hush. You know if the Feds or any other government agency got a sniff of this, well, you know—we'd be eliminated, or worse, set up with drugs or murder or god know what all crimes they'd probably frame us with."

"Yeah, I know. Freedom of speech as long as it agrees with the system. It's like they don't teach about a truly free society in the schools. They teach how to be good citizens regardless of what the self-elected government wants."

You slam your hand down on a bug. "Yeah, I know." We are both silent again. We hear the breezes through the windows from this slightly chilly day. You get a chill and get up to try and find the cracks. You reshut a few windows. One that looks really open is stuck, but you can't budge it. I walk over and open it and then close it tightly, and easily. You have a strange relationship with

58

your environment, I think before sitting down.

"When can we meet?" I ask getting up and working my way to the door, while eyeing my watch.

"Well, I don't know. I guess we can talk about it soon."

"Yeah, there're a lot of wars going on now. Our poor planet."

"Too many have access to the bomb." You drop your pencil again.

"How about tonight?"

"Ah, I guess, sure. How about seven o'clock?"

"Good, that'll be good."

"Don't tell anyone until we've talked."

"What about Mary?"

"I don't think she'll be around tonight."

"Can you trust her if she is?"

"I really don't know. I hope so."

"Well, a little discussion can't get us into trouble, I don't think."

***

William walks out of the ancient fortress of stone late, after everyone else is gone, he hopes. He quickly makes his way across the large lot to his car. There are a few cars left. He knows the owners of two. He pushes the key into the slot, turns, click the door opens. CREAK. "I forgot to put that oil stuff in again. Hope I can shut the door this time, without having to use that wire." SLAM, SHUT, EEEERRRREEE. "Shit, I don't think I'll be able to open my door now. Maybe Mary's right, maybe I do need a new car. She still gets good gas mileage though. Uh oh, looks like Ruban is on his way out. I'd better high-tail it outa here." The engine starts right up. He takes off in a spin, balding tires screeching. Ruban runs out after him, takes a hold of the little yellow bug. Wil slams on the brakes. Ruban trots to the window.

"I'm in a real hurry man!" yells William.

"Oh, no, I been thinking 'bout what you was saying. Can I come over and talk some about it?"

"You what?"

"I wanna talk about your ideas more."

"Oh, what the hell. You got your car here?"

"Ya, I kin' follow you."

"Come on, then, I'll meet you back at the house."

***

I pull into the driveway, and there's still space for my car. Wil's yellow thing is sitting, waiting. He's probably still mad at me for what I said. He didn't answer the phone all last week. He was always too busy to talk to me at school. What am I gonna say to him? I just... what a strange feeling I have about these' thin'. I know I'm supposed to do something here for this thin' I hope he likes the beer I brought for him. I walk down the still frozen sidewalk. My steps are hard and loud. Bubbles in the ice pop and crack as I cross. The smell of this winter air is so hollow. The vines on Wil's house are cold and grey, like the cement below. I think my English is really getting good. Good thin' I don't teach it. He answers the door before I knock.

"What took you so long?"

"I brought you some Corona. Hope you like Corona."

"Come on in." William smiles and holds the door open for me.

We're very quiet till we get into the living room. I sit down and pull out two beers. I open them and hand one over to him. I pull a lemon from the bag and ask for a knife. He asks why I brought lemon. I tell him what it's for. He offers to put the beer in the fridge while he gets a knife. He takes the lemon with him as a sort of second thought. He comes back with the smell of fresh yellow all over and a plate with some oddly cut lemons in a pile. We each take a piece and squeeze it into our beers. We are quiet for a while.

"You said you were in a hurry. Did you take care of what you needed to take care of?" I set my beer down on a coffee table nearby.

"Well, I, ah, yeah."

"Hey, man, how come you cut the lemons dat' way?"

"What? Isn't that the right way?"

"You're such a riot man, din't anyone show you how to cut a lemon?"

"Well, no, I was told that food prep is woman's work. And so now, here I am, unable to do really simple things."

"Yeah, I saw how you cut the vegetables at the party the other night."   "Say, did you come here to insult me or to talk about my ideas?

"Oh, I'm sorry. I didn't mean nothing by it. I just think it's funny."

"Well?" He looks at me kind of bitter. I must have really insulted him. Great, now I can't even talk to him. He must think I'm some stupid Mexican or something. Why in hell did I say anything about the way he cuts vegetables? That was really stupid. He's waiting for me to say something now. I have a lump in my throat now.

"Listen, I really feel bad about how I put down your ideas last week. I really wasn't thinking when I answered you. But I've been thinking, and I think they're really good ideas. I'd like to help if I could."

"Why did you change your mind?"

"Well, I had a long talk with my mother and father about what we talked about."

"But you weren't supposed to tell anyone."

"Well, I didn't tell them who. Besides, my parents are really trustworthy. They would never ask nothing about this to anyone. They know better than this. They told me about my people in the jungles of South America."

"Whereabouts?"

"I think near Guatemala or Peru."

"But they're on different parts of the continent. Are your parents sure about where they come from?"

"Well, my mother comes from Mexico, but my father's family had to move around—to get away from the Spanish explorers. He really didn't remember if they started in Peru or Guatemala."

"Well, you knew this before didn't you?"

"No, no. He said that our family was from a tribe that was part of the Aztecs. When Pizarro killed our kings and forced many of us into slavery, many of us ran to the jungle for safety. Those that survived have been living with the family for about four hundred years now."

"Wow! That's really incredible."

"Not any more. They are killing off all our trees and coming closer to where our tribes are hiding. I think I can trust you, from what you said last week and because I have known you for about a year now."

"That's right. You came to teach about a year ago. But this is a real problem that some people are just beginning to consider—the killing of the rain forest. But they haven't really thought about the people who are trying to live there. I saw a report the other day about satellites and how there are hundreds of fires burning down South America, now more than ever before."

"They can see that from the satellites?"

"Yeah, and it's really scary to me."

"This is what is killing my people."

"Well, I guess that if we just kill each other off, then it won't matter anyway. Maybe the Earth can just start over fresh."

"But my people have done nothing to bring this

upon them."

"Some so-called spiritual people say that all things that come to people are brought upon us because of our pasts or our present thoughts."

"I don't understand."

"I don't know, but I can see it for some people but for others—I don't know—like the people who came across the lands first. I don't think they were trying to conquer all the peoples and gain wealth by killing off all the animals and digging up the planet they always respected."

"There were head hunters...."

"In South America."

"Yup, real cannibals. And there were some tribes in the North who had kings and slaves and wars and things like that."

"Really? But I thought they were primarily peaceful people."

"Well, to some degree. But these were only a few tribes. Most had a real respect for others. They thanked god that they had food to eat and praised the animals for giving themselves up for food."

"How do you know all this?"

"I have a minor in anthropology."

"How come you didn't know about your own family?"

"I knew there was some connection for a long time, but it was just a feeling. My parents didn't tell me much."

"Weren't you curious?"

"Si, but that does not mean that I would ask. They showed me about some of the old religion—but just a little. I guess they were afraid. But now my talk with them has opened many doors. They seem to have some hope that you may be the one their leaders spoke of."

"Me?"

"They spoke of someone who would help this world

become united as it was before the demon greed came upon the land."

"That's pretty big."

"They want to meet you. I think you must be a good man to think about these things. I don't know if you are the one they talked about, but you still have many good ideas. They are right, I have been trained too much in these schools. They always told me right from wrong. The wrong things in the Catholic religion that tried to tell our people that the old ways were evil and not to be done. They told my people about hell and guilt and many things that the white people already knew about. But because we were so innocent, we knew nothing about these things. They threatened us with death and torture and slavery. Then they told us that our heaven is not on Earth but after we die. So much incredible bullshit was shoveled into the mouths of these honest and loving people. But they could not kill us. We kept alive and in hiding."

"Both your parents came from South America?"

"My mother came from Mexico—I said that."

"Yes. Yes, you did."

"I know they were oppressed too and forced into the Catholic religion. It's a good religion for some people. But religion should never be forced upon a people."

"I agree."

"If they do not decide by themselves, then how can it ever really be theirs?"

"You're right. But what do we do with this?"

"I thought you would have some ideas."

"Well, let me ask you this. How do you think you fit into this thing?"

"I—I don't know. I think I want to hear more of your ideas. If there is a change, a real change, then maybe my people can all go back to the jungle, where they want to be. But it can't be forced. We can't do what they did."

"Go back to the jungle?"

"No, no, the explorers."

"Well, you know...."

The phone rings, and William goes over and answers it. I go and get fresh beers. I come out and he sounds mad, "Who told you? Alex? He was drunk. We had to throw him out. I should've known he was a friend of yours. Look, I have someone here now and we're talking. But how can you possibly.... How would you be able to.... How do I know you're on the level, man? You were involved in some.... All right, all right, come over and we'll talk. But I'm not sending my buddy home. Okay, then, I'll see ya." He practically slams the phone down. "OOOH, he really pisses me off. He's just such a pushy asshole."

"Who was that? If I may ask."

"You know, sometimes you have an accent and sometimes not. What gives, man?"

"Well, it comes and goes. When I am with white people it seems to disappear completely. When I am with my people, it comes back. Of course, then I'm just talking in my first language. So but who was that?"

"That, oh, that was just my brother."

"So I will meet him?"

"I don't know if you'll really want to if I tell you about him."

"I've always wanted a brother. You must be so happy to have one."

"Not this guy. He's an embarrassment to the family. In and out of jail for god knows how many things. Why don't you have a brother? Do you have sisters?"

"No, my parents don't have a big family. These stupid American doctors took out all the parts for my mama to have more babies. But they didn't tell her until years later when my parents wanted to find out why they could not have any more children."

"Well, but maybe she was sick or something."

"No, no, they did this to many people who were poor or part of a minority."

"But isn't that illegal?"

"It is now, but I don't know if it was then. We didn't have enough money to find out."

"Couldn't you go to legal aid or something?"

"I don't think they had legal aid back then."

"Well, I'm sorry, but my brother's not too hot anyway. He's broken my mother's heart."

"But he's still your brother. He comes from the same blood as your mother and father. He doesn't have to be hot. He's more than any friend will be. And I'll bet you, that he will someday change his ways—if you show him that you love him and encourage him."

"I suppose you're right, but he has done some horrible things in the past."

"Why did he call just now?"

"You remember that drunk that was here at the party?"

"Sure, sure."

"Well, that guy told Kent enough to give him some ideas about what we talked about the other night."

"Well, you see, he's interested in this, and I think we need all the people we can get."

"I can't trust him."

"He's your brother. Of course you can trust him."

"Trust him to stab me in the back, sure."

"I don't understand."

"You don't know what he's done."

"No, I don't. You can tell me if you like. I really won't tell anyone."

"What about your parents?"

"I—they—we didn't talk about who you are. They respect my privacy. They only gave me some advice.

They're my parents."

"Right, right, of course, I'm sorry, that was really unfair."

"You have such a hard time trusting people don't you."

"Well, I don't know of too many people who I can trust. Do you?"

"Si, of course I do. I know people who I've been friends with all my life and they have never broken that trust."

"Well, I... I don't think I know of anyone who I trust like that."

"You must be very sad inside."

"I guess it's that sadness that you speak of that has pushed me towards the big project that we came here to talk about."

"Why don't you tell me what your brother did to you?"

"Well, maybe later." Wil looks at his beer bottle and shakes a few times. Foam pokes up beside the lemon and starts down the bottle.

"After you meet him, tell me what you think of him. Maybe you can tell if he's worth my trust. I think you're a perceptive type of person. So tell me what you think, and then I'll give you the dope."

"What do you want me to look for?"

"Lies."

"Well, I will try, but I may just think of him as your brother and forget about any other feelings I may have."

"Just do your best—I mean if you don't mind. Are you hungry?"

"Oh, yes, I am feeling a bit hungry. You, too?"

"Sure, let's order a pizza." They order a sardine and pineapple pizza and turn on the basketball game. They drink a few more beers before the phone rings.

"YEEllo? Mary, dear, I was wondering what happened to you. Oh, yeah, I forgot about that exercise class that you have. Well how's it going? Good, good.... So what's up now.... Oh, just a sec—Ooh, Oh, you're out with your girlfriends? Well, that's nice. Oh, me? I'm, oh, wait— oh no... NO, honey, I'm watching a basketball game with Ruban. Yeah, yeah, I know you don't like it much.... So stay out as late as you want. Sure I love you, but I want to watch the game. Get this: we're also waiting for my brother Kent to come over.... Yeah, I know what I told you. No I won't let him in the bedroom near your jewelry.... Well, apparently he's a friend of your boyfriend.... You know who I mean, the drunk from the party? Yeah, they know each other and so Alex told Kent about what we were talking about.... I didn't think he heard any of it either, but I guess enough to tell Kent about. Maybe he was just spying for Kent. No, it'll just be Kent, not Alex, so don't get all excited that you could see him or something. Anyway,... anyway, anyway. So Kent is coming over to talk about it. No, I don't know how long. Maybe. We'll see. I know you want to meet him. Listen, I gotta get goin'. I can't leave Ruban here feelin' like a dope. Well we've been talking for about twenty minutes. Yes, of course I love you. So I'll see you later all right? Yeah, you have a good time too. Don't stay out too late.... And hey, if you bump into Alex, send the drunk my hellos.... I turned it on when I got home... 'cause I left early and we didn't talk about, you know what was going on tonight.... Come on now, I really have to go now.... Bye, ya, me too, bye." His hand sets the phone down so fast I thought he was pissed. He goes into the kitchen and yells, "Hey need a beer?"

"Ah, yeah, si, por favor."

"Here ya go. You know you don't have to be so damn polite around here. We're not at the prison camp now."

"It's just the way I was raised. In school I have to work especially hard to speak correct English." I mock the correct English part.

"It's strange to me to think that you even have to do that. I mean you have a college degree and all."

"A college degree can be given to someone from a different country who speaks very poor English."

"Ya, I know, but you're not from another country. You're an American citizen."

"Well, I went to a, well, a ghetto high school, and well, everyone spoke either Chicano, or some Mexican, you know. A lot of immigrants and migrant farm workers. The kids who didn't stick around long enough to learn English. It was just to get by, and the government didn't really care. We were in a sort of school. You know, government regulations and all."

"Where'd you go to college?"

"At St. Francis, a city college in Los Angeles. It was a real place for me."

"What do you mean?"

"Well, the majority of us were Chicano and, well, I felt like on top of the world, when I was in there. Until I stepped outside."

"So where did you get your bachelor's?"

"At Northeastern Illinois University. And boy did I have to kick butt to get outa there."

"Pretty tough?"

"Yup."

"You did all right I take it."

"Of course, graduated with honors."

"That's great! No wonder you were hired here so easily."

The doorbell rings. Wil gets up and gives the pizza guy a twenty for the pizza and beer.

"Here's your free quart of coke, pops."

"Pops? I'm not that old."

"A little inside humor. Nothin' personal, mack. Hey, thanks fer the tip." He trots off.

We completely demolish the pizza and beer, without benefit of napkins or plates. The game is going pretty well and we totally forget our original purpose. The game is over after about thirty minutes. We are silent for a few and talk a little about the game.

"So how do you think you can be part of this little plan we were talking about?" You shake your bottle, which is empty.

"I'd like to hear more about your ideas. Most people think our planet is going to end in a major war or something."

"There has been a growing number of people that think we can really achieve world peace. I think that in itself is a reason to begin moving in this direction. Now ten years ago, most people had made up their minds that the world was going to end or at best that you could never achieve world peace. But things are changing."

"You really think we have a chance?"

"Well, sure. I want to have kids and I want them to have a good future and not have to deal with all the mistakes their parents made."

"But isn't the U.S. having peace talks already?"

"I don't know, really. I was never at them. And they are always taped, so we really don't know what goes on in them. I do know that there is a group of people, and this is true, that feed the American public all kinds of trash about how Russia has been cheating and has been building more missiles and doing all kinds of strange shit. Or that that new régime is just a front or a way to trick us into believing in them. But this little group of men who are trying to keep the defense budget big by lying to the public will get their day soon enough."

"Get their day?"

"Sure, the truth is bound to come out that the checkers for Russia have never caught them cheating, you know, and shit like that."

"Never?"

"Not once."

"Wow, man, I remember all that about the cheating of Russia, too, and I believed it, too. Where'd you hear about this?"

"I was at this seminar by these teachers who work for one of those big universities on the East Coast somewhere. I'll dig up the info for you later."

"But all this time I thought we heard the truth from the news." I scratch my head.

"Did you really believe that?"

"Well, I know one thing for sure. This is the best country in the world. We have a strong government, freedom of speech, freedom of the press. This I know because I studied it in school."

"Well, I hate to break it to you, but that's precisely how they keep us, all the little kiddies and adults, in line."

"What do you mean?" I'm confused.

"Citizenship, my dear fellow teacher, citizenship."

"I still don't understand."

"Why was your mother sterilized?"

"Not because of citizenship."

"Well, I don't know about that. But there are plenty of ways our sweet and innocent government reinforces racism and poverty. Do you think that if we didn't work our butts off, we peons down here, that the government would lift a finger to stamp out racism or poverty, or crimes against people or the environment?"

"Well, I don't know. I think we all have to do our part."

"Right, right, but if we invest time and money in a

group of people who are supposed to help us stay in line, then I think it should do it, or they should do it for everyone, and not just a few."

"Well, yes, but as you said, the government is just made of people, and we can and are all wrong sometimes."

"Right, Ruban, and that's why no group of people really has the ability or the right to govern another group."

"You'd have chaos and violence in the streets."

"Like it is now?"

"William, it would be worse, much worse than now."

"No, well, maybe at first it would be pretty scary, but once people got on the right track and were self-motivated, well, then there would be no problems."

"People are self-motivated now. And there is still crime. It really has nothing to do with the government. There will always be crime."

"As long as we continue with this line of thinking and not trusting."

"In what? Each other, humanity, a higher power?"

"Sure."

"Which?"

"All three, Ruban. I think it will all work out."

The doorbell rings, and it is Kent. They are mumbling to each other, and I can see Kent through the sheer curtains of the kitchen door window. William lets Kent in, and I go and sit down in the chair in the corner and turn on the tube while they're settling things a bit. After a few minutes they walk into the living room. William introduces Kent to me, and we exchange the usual greetings. I offer a beer to Kent and William as I know they're still uncomfortable with each other. They don't want one yet, so I just get myself one. While I'm out there, William yells to me to bring one instead, no two, or three, whatever. I grab the others and walk cautiously out into the other room.

They're talking sort of nicely, though Wil is obviously tense. He grips his bottle and shakes it every few seconds. I'd better get some kind of towel so when he gets the full one he doesn't spill it all over. His brother is sitting back in his chair looking confident when I return again.

"Well, here you are. This is what you asked for, isn't it?"

"Sure, right, have a seat, Ruban. Kent here was just telling me about what he's been doing lately."

"Really, what have you been doing?" I try and be nonchalant.

"Well, I've been doing a little of this and a little of that."

I sort of nod my upper body. "That's sounds interesting." What do I say now, that doesn't sound equally as stupid? I should probably just try and listen. The doorbell rings again.

"Expecting anyone else?" I ask.

"No.... Oh no.... I forgot about Sascha."

"You know, Wil, I agreed to meet with you, even though your friend was going to be here, but TWO others, well I don't know if I can handle this." Kent folds his arms and furls his brow.

"Well, if you recall, you did call me, so if you'd rather leave, be my guest. But I'm going to answer the phone."

"You mean *d*—"

"Ah, I mean *door*." William walks out of the room and answers the door—just as he said. Sascha and Wil are talking quietly in the kitchen, leaving me with Kent, who I don't know what to say to. He obviously feels the same about me. Sascha's voice is raised for a few seconds, but I still can't make out the words. I wonder what they're talking about. Almost sounds like I'm hearing it from under water. I hear the door open. Maybe she's leaving. Then the door closes again and I can still hear her voice. Now it's really quiet in there again. I wonder what they're talking about. Did he see her earlier today? I know he wasn't taking calls from anyone yesterday because I called and that's what Mary told me. So why would he have plans with Sascha already? Footsteps—a few come but then stop again. Kent is yawning. He gets up to go to the john, I guess, unless he's going to the living room I mean bedroom to check on Mary's jewelry. I'd better do something. I can't follow him or he might haul off and slug me. If I ask him, he'll say "none of your business." I know that type. And if I go in after he's gone in.... I hear the door shut. I tiptoe over to the door. He's in the john. But just to make sure.

"Hey, you two," I peek into the kitchen, "What in the world is taking you so long? You having a love scene? Or a lover's quarrel?"

William gives me a dirty look.

"I get the picture. Hi, Sascha. Vroom, vroom." I make her smile as I pretend I'm driving a car.

"You planning on buying one?" She broadens her smile.

"Sure, as soon as I payoff a mortgage and my car loan and payoff a lifetime of bills."

She begins to walk into the living room. William slowly follows.

"Where's Kent?" Wil holds his forehead in place.

"I think in the john."

Wil gives me a fast look of disgust, like I'm supposed to be babysitting. I throw up my hands. "I guess we all came here for the same thing." I say.

"To go to the john?" Wil looks down with a tight face.

William sits down and looks at the half empty pizza box. "You want some pizza, Sasch?"

"Sure, what'd ya got on it?" She's so beautiful yet

she can talk like a hick.

"Sardines and pineapple. You want a beer to go with it?"

"Are you kidding, who in the world except a famous duck would eat a pizza with sardines and pineapple. That's the worst."

"Do you at least want a beer?"

"I don't know, Ruban. I'm not sure if I'm staying." She looks at William, who looks at the floor and then at his shoes.

Kent walks out of the john and walks straight outside. Then walks back in.

"Where'd you go?" William asks while walking into the kitchen. With Kent's loud voice
I can hear him.

"I went out to my car to get this here bottle of champagne."

"Did I hear champagne?" Sascha asks as she walks into the kitchen. I follow her.

"You sure did, pretty lady."

"You didn't tell me your brother was a pig, too, Wil."

"Now why did you say that? I was only trying to be nice."

"Well, you called it as you saw it, and so did I."

"Why does that bother you?" William gets glasses out of the cabinet.

"Because it makes me feel like I'm just something to look at and that I probably have nothing important to say."

"I didn't say you had nothing to say. I just said that you were pretty. Were, because after that comment, I'm not so sure."

"You are the most despicable man I've ever met. And you call yourself William's brother?"

"Hold it, hold it, Sascha, what's come over you? I've never seen you like this before. You don't usually lose your cool. I mean. Is he really worth it?"

"Thanks a lot, guys. I come in here friendly, bring a bottle of the bubbly, compliment a woman and then all I get are insults. I don't get it." Kent looks out the kitchen window for a moment, keeping the curtains closed completely except for a crack.

"What's up, Kent?"

"Think they're following me again."

"Oh, great, what are you up for this time?"

"Nothing, nothing. Look, I parked my car down on the next block, but when I was running with the champagne, I think they saw me."

"Get out of here then. You think I want to be connected with a crime? Especially with what we're talking about?"

"But I'm telling you, man, I'm not in trouble."

"Then why?"

"They, well, they want to tag something on me real bad. I'm underground now."

"Did you break out of jail again?"

"No, no, man, I haven't done nothin' for years. But thanks for giving these folks a good vote of confidence in me. I paid my time and I'm clean."

"Then why?"

"Don't you know this country yet? They're worse than the Chilean Junta's secret police."

"Then what are you doing now, why are you back here?"

"Yeah, and why are the cops after you?" I blurt out.

"Well, listen," he lowers his voice and turns his back on Sascha and me. "I've been involved with a lot of ecology groups. And I'm actually doing undercover work for them."

"ECOLOGY GROUPS? YOU?" William's mouth

76

opens wide.

"Yes, but don't announce it to the world."

"I—I'm sorry, I didn't really introduce you, did I?"

"I think you did to me," I tell him.

"Well, this is my dear friend Sascha. And she is most definitely not just a pretty face, in fact sometimes I forget that she has one." Sascha smiles, scratches her head and slowly puts out her hand.

"I'm sorry for being so jumpy. I don't really know why it bothers me so much. I know most women are brought up to be just that, beautiful for men, and so a compliment like that would put most women on cloud nine, right?"

"Ah, well, I don't know anymore. Some women like it, and some don't. But I guess until women are giving compliments like that to men without the whole world thinking that she's a slut, then it's pretty touchy for both sexes." Kent shakes her hand, short, firm but gently.

"Nice shake," she says at him.

"Kent here says he's been working with ecology groups."

"Yes, I heard."

"You heard?"

"Sure, you were only about a foot away. So have you been to South America yet?" She picks up a glass from the counter and then sets it back down again.

"Well, Peru, ah, but just for a short time. Listen, may I have a word with William, please?"

"Anything you're gonna tell me, you can tell them, too."

"That's all right. We'll go into the other room, won't we, Ruban?"

"We will? Oh, sure, we will, and then you can tell me more about your car." This is great. Now she wants to be alone with me. But maybe not because she just gave Wil a strange look.

"Sure, Ruban, we'll talk about my car again."

We walk into the living room and sit down. Sascha jumps up and goes into the other room. I hear her say, "Excuse me."

She comes back with the bottle of champagne and two glasses. She really thinks of everything. Now if I could only get her to think of me. She quietly and carefully unwraps the foil and sets it on the table. Then with the cork screw on the table—how'd that get there? She open the, hey, wait that's champagne, why is she using a cork screw?

"Wait a minute, por favor, may I help you?"

"I can do it myself, Ruban."

"But señorita, you need no cork screw. That is champagne, no?"

"Oh, yes, of course. I must be thinking of something else. But I've gotten it stuck, I...." She tries to pull the cork screw out and ends up pulling the top out till it pops and explodes foam into the air. I grab the glasses and fill them with the bubbles and run to get two more from the kitchen, dash back out to help catch the fountain. Most of it is on the walls and floor. Kent and Wil come out all excited and try to help, though we have everything under control, or rather, the situation has us under control. We all grab something and wipe up the spill. Sascha looks very embarrassed.

"Don't worry about it, Sasch. It could've happened to the best of us."

"Could've, but it didn't. I'm really sorry, Kent, I know that was expensive champagne. I'll go out and buy another."

"Don't bother. I brought it back from the West Coast. I don't think we could find it here. I will take my half a glass though." We look down and find the four glasses that were once filled with foam now have less than half a glass of champagne each. But at least that is some.

"What was it you wanted to talk to me about, Kent?"

Kent slumps down on a chair and says, "Well, the things I wanted to talk to you about—the things Alex told me a little about, well, I just thought they may be better talked about in private. But I can see now that that is probably very unlikely."

"Well, these are my friends and, well, Kent, they were here first. Besides they're just as interested as you are."

"Yeah, but I'm your brother, and I want to help plan this thing, too."

"I don't even really know if I can trust you."

"Shit, man, did I ever really do anything to you?"

"You, um, well, I can't think of any... hey, wait a minute, you took my baseball that Grandpa Whitey gave me—signed by Babe Ruth himself. And you didn't even ask first."

"What? You're talking about kids' stuff. That was when we were about eight or ten years old."

"Well?"

"How can you talk about something like that when you know my really dark past started way after that. Besides, I only took it to show some of my friends. You were too greedy to let me when I asked you."

"You still took it, didn't you?"

"Ruban, I think this family stuff will get solved with or without us. Why don't we go and get another bottle of something?"

"No, don't go. I think we're about finished. Besides, we could use a referee in case this gets out a hand." Kent takes the last sip of his bubbling drink. "Remember, Wil, I did give it back, didn't I?"

"All right, all right, you never did anything really

against me, so I guess you're right. But you did rip off one of my friends by selling him some really bad pot."

"I didn't know it was bad. Besides I gave him his money back, didn't I?"

"After I beat you up."

"I think we can trust him, William."

"What? Thanks, Sascha." Kent smooths his hair back.

"How can you tell?"

"Same way I can probably," I blurt out while scratching my head.

"Now can we go and get that drink?" Sascha begins to stand up and get her things together. I'm feeling a little dizzy.

"While you're gone, I'll order another pizza."

"But not pineapple and sardine. I'm a vegetarian, remember?"

"I thought you were too, Wil." Kent looks at Wil with a question in his head.

"Sure I am. I just don't consider fish, animals. They're really like vegetables, you know."

"Not in my book." Sascha opens her jacket and checks her pockets.

"You're gonna get sick from that pizza, Wil. Believe me."

"I've had it before. I know what I'm doing. So what do you want, half pepperoni and half veggie?"

"How about a small veggie and a whatever size you want of the meat kind? That way I don't have to have meat on my side at all."

"You won't if we put half on one side and half on the other."

"No, well, William, I'm pretty strict and I can always taste the meat on my half when people do that. And frankly, I don't want to get sick again. So please?"

"All right, Sascha. What time is it anyway? Whew, only about nine. That's good, the pizza place I usually order from doesn't close until eleven on a weeknight."

"Hey, Ruban, are you going with?" Kent is looking down at me.

"I don't feel too well. I don't think I can get out just yet."

"Go and get some Alka-Bubbles or something. Medicine cabinet."

"Sure thing." I start to get up but I can't and sit right back down, almost missing the chair. Geez, now Sascha is gonna think I'm a real wimp.

"Well, I'll get goin' then. I hope you feel better, Ruban."

That's nice that Sasch hopes I'll be feeling better. I smile and wave slightly so she knows I understand.

"Maybe we'd better get him onto the bed so he can rest a bit."

"That's a good idea, Kent, but what if he throws up? I don't want that on my bed."

"Then what're we gonna do?"

"Well, I'll get him some bromo bubbles and then we can see how he does out here."

"In that uncomfortable chair?"

"Well, we can get my sleeping bag out and set him up right by the hall so he's comfortable and somewhat close to the door."

"All right. I guess that'll do. Where's your bag?"

"On my closet shelf in my bedroom. I'll get the seltzer."

I lay there sort of hearing what they're saying and slipping in and out of it. I'm trying to wait until I can at least get some relief for my stomach. Seems like someone like me who's been raised on hot spicy food could take a little beer and pizza.

81

"Here's the bag." Kent says as he unrolls it and puts it where William said. "I knew that pineapple and sardine pizza would get to one of you. Too bad, buddy."

"Here's the stuff. Now I'm not real good at this, so, just open your mouth and I'll try and pour it in." I try and open my mouth, and Wil does pour it in and spills half of it on my shirt. But I get enough in to make a difference. The two pick me up and drag me and lift me and turn me and scrape my side on something, and I end up on the floor. They roll me over like a log, and I end up with the light in my eyes and the pillow under my feet. I hear them talking about something I can't quite make out. It sounds like they're talking about the plans to change things. I feel like my senses are fading.

I walk onto the port where my papa boarded a ship bound for America with my mama. Except that she's not there. He's by himself and going the other direction. My short fat papa with his dark skin, balding head and mustache. He's wearing a nice suit, but he's carrying his jacket because it's so hot today. I walk up behind him carrying our luggage.

"Where's Mama?"

"She'll come later. She said she'd meet us in Mexico City when we get there next week."

This is the trip they'd always wanted to go on. The cruise that I'd always wanted to buy for them. The vacation I'd been saving up for them. But how did I get on board, I wonder as I walk down the corridor to our cabin. Then I remember that the world had changed. Everything and everyone is now doing exactly what they really want to. But nobody is doing it for money or revenge.

After we unpack our things, papa takes a shower and says he'll meet me on deck in about an hour. He shouts this from the shower. I yell my acceptance of this plan, and walk out of the room. I begin to look in my wallet for money, but then I realize there is no money anymore.

I don't need it here or anywhere. Why would people want to serve me on a cruise ship? Wouldn't everyone want to be served? I guess not. I know I like serving my parents and taking care of the children I teach. I probably still need time to understand the extent to these concepts. That tree was so beautiful when we first bought it, no got it from the store, or green house I mean. It was nice to not kill a tree for Christmas this year. It sat in the room so bright and proud. I wonder if that was what began to kill it: the lights and ornaments, or maybe the cats. I never did like the idea of keeping a box of feces in a corner for cats to plow and add more to, let alone their night time practices of pawing anything that looks alive or delicate. That poor tree. What did I do? People will think I'm crazy to feel this way over a plant. But why should I care what they think? It's high time more people worked on saving the planet. But I guess now we are. So I should feel happy.

I walk outside, carrying the potted tree. I'm sure that this beauty will begin to grow again and feel the sun's warmth, and then for generations to come we'll appreciate this beautiful piece of life. I dig an ample hole in the ground. I then gently pry it from the pot. I set it in the rocky dirt and cover it over with the loose flesh left, flesh, being the dirt, the covering, the skin of the Earth. I cover it with the blackness and hope that it will find peace and contentment and of course enjoyment in allowing its roots to be free to expand and discover the more boundless regions of the underground, than this tiny pot can hope to allow.

This morning I looked outside and saw that it is dry and, if alive, fading fast. How can I save a plant who's decided to die, to pass on, to become part of the flesh, of this planet. AHA! Is that what the scriptures spoke of? The flesh of the planet?

Perhaps this little creature has found more peace because it is now of the flesh of the planet. But it doesn't, well, yes, it does make me feel a little better about what I did. But then how can I know that I actually killed that little plant. DAMN, how could I have forgotten it for those few weeks, or however many it was. Maybe I did water it wrong. BANG! OW! My fist should never be used to say what I feel. OOoh, my right hand too. But what can I do, cry on the elevator? Ow, that really hurts. Why did I plant it there? It should have been next to the big tree on the side of the house. It's such a mighty fir tree and yet I wonder how in the world it got to be so big when the other three we planted in the yard are dead or dying. Well, I guess I can feel bad all day, or I can try and put it out of my head, and my heart for now. Writing it down like this helps. But it sure hurts to write with my hand so sore. I wonder when Papa is gonna be done with his shower. He's been in there for an hour.

The walls are fading and turning into trees. Like a story I once read to a bunch of kids. But why do we see things just so. Do we change into objects in the sun or sprout flowers when we're feeling good? I'm in a small boat crossing over the lines of waves cemented into place by radar from an interplanetary being. I see stars soaring through the moon whose holes have become tunnels. But this cannot be our moon, It has a lavender haze over it and follows a strange pattern that is not any orbital pattern I've ever studied. Is space the final frontier? If it is, then I know many people who should be explored.

"Are you ready for dinner?"

"What took you so long?"

"I told you I'd be out in an hour."

"That's true, but I thought you would come out first."

"You didn't go on deck?"

"For a short time and then I decided to return—yes, return and retry and retreat and retrap and reshape and repair and restrip and retype and rerip and reiterate and retrospect and rent and reap and read and rest and then I forgot what the question was."

"What was that you said, Son? You on drugs or somethin'?"

"Me? How would you, How could you, How say you, How may you, and How pay you bills and Steve's and Julian's, and—"

"Cut the crap kid and let's go or better yet, you stay here and contemplate your navel while I rip open a bifstek."

"Wait, Dad, I'm sorry I just got a little crazy. Do you realize what has gone on here in the past few months and how we were able to actually change the planet's perspective around?"

"You only need one question mark. Besides it's been twenty years, and I'm not really your dad. And your mama isn't coming to meet us. In fact I don't know what you're doing in my bedroom anyway, or why you're calling me 'dad' or 'papa' or whatever the hell you're doing. Did you escape from one of those institutions or something?"

"No, I didn't escape. I was put here to go on a cruise that I've been saving for for most of my life so that I could give you and Mama a real treat. A honeymoon that you never had."

"You weren't put here. You boarded this ship, and you followed me to my room. And I thought you'd get the hint when I told you I'd be out in an hour, but NO! You couldn't leave me alone, and you're going to follow me around until I take matters into my own hands. And for another thing, THIS IS NO DREAM! YOU'RE JUST NUTS, NOT THE WORLD!"

I run out of the room and down the hall, which turns into a street and bends and folds, and I can't see in front of me. What did they give me anyway?

"Hey, he's sweating like crazy. What's wrong with him?"

"Ruban, you all right?"

"Yeah, hey, Ruban, can you hear us talking?"

I try and mumble something to them. They who I can't see and who are trying to talk to me in the dark, through the line of nothingness that is another dimension. But I can't hear them completely, and I don't know who they are or what they're trying to do. "Leave me alone, you're just shadows, just ghosts."

"No, Ruban, it's William, can't you hear me?"

"Willeeyum? Who's Wubbumn?"

I hear a door open and steps coming toward me, but I can't hear completely and can't see anything. Why are they doing this to me? Why can't they leave me alone?

"What's wrong with him? Ruban?" A woman is speaking to me. She sounds sweet and almost familiar.

"He sort of passed out, and we gave him some stomach stuff 'cause he said he felt bad. But now he's been mumbling to himself, and he's sweating up a storm."

Someone touches me, my face. I cringe and try and get away, but I can't move. I'm held down in place by something. I need to fight and run away and try to get away from these voices in the dark.

"Maybe it was something he ate. What did you give him?"

"I don't know, yes, yes, I do, the bromo bubbles. I'll go get the package." I hear him run away and come back. "Here it is. Let's see, what, what's in this stuff. Pesssimmismsetria snuchumkakovance, vardiostashionsta, blautabuuka, miliovantru, iliosmapdack, slimeysvalionsack, dickadackarackapackafoo, slushoil, hydrophaliopinoil, man oh man, I don't think I'm ever gonna buy this garbage again. I wonder how many other things there are in all this garbage they call medicine. Most of this I can't even pronounce. But wait, I think this is penicillin. What if he's allergic to penicillin?"

"He should have an arm bracelet or something."

"No bracelet or nothing. Well, I don't know. Should we call the paramedics?"

"No, mmmmmbulingstat oratistancktinpionoinfonic sblaastion." I don't want to go to the hospital. It's probably just the sardines or something.

"I take it that he doesn't want to go."

"I'm not sure of what that means. It could mean that he's like dreaming or something." Kent's low voice sounds like gravel when he's bending down.

"Well, I don't think he's sweating any more. Let's put a cool cloth on his head just the same." Sascha's long hair falls on my face for a moment. I'm getting hard. Great, they're all gonna know how I feel about her. But maybe not, I have a blanket on top of my lap. Or is it a sleeping bag? Well, I, "OWWWH!" Someone leaned back on me, on my balls and prick, and, oh man, I hope I'll have kids after this. I curl up real fast.

"Just leavemealonenow," I say as clear as possible.

"What did you say?"

"I a saidleave me alone nowUnderstand?"

"Ruban, this is Sascha."

"OH, Sascha." I'm grinning.

"Wow, I guess he likes you, Sascha."

"He likes my car."

"MMm, Lambrignivroom...." God, I feel so bad, so sick to my stomach.

"See what I mean. All he can think of is my car."

"Sascha, red hair, mmmmm." My pants are getting real tight.

"Are you allergic to something?"

"No, noIjusthadtoomuchbeer,oooh."

"What? I can't make that out."

William looks over me and says, "I think he said he had too much beer or something." My eyes are part open and trying to see, but I can't get them open any more.

"Ruban, do you think you got sick from the sardines?" Kent gravels near my ear.

"OOOH, sardines," I start coughing and feeling like puking from the thought of that trashy pizza.

"It's the sardines. We'd better just leave him alone for a while."

But now I have to get up and get this out of my stomach—oh no, I'm not going to do this in front of my friends. I try and lift myself up, holding on to the wall and feeling my way.

"Look at him, he's getting up."

"He's probably gonna be sick or something. Why don't I get a pan or a bucket?" William runs into the kitchen.

I make my way almost to the john, and I feel like a ghost. My stomach begins to eject this trash, and I try and run or something.

"COME ON, WILLIAM!"

Just as my mouth is letting go I feel some cold metal under my chin and William says, "It's all right, Ruban, take a seat, I got ya covered. Go in the other room, you two!" He knows how embarrassed I am from all this. He's a good guy. "I got you into this mess, and I'm gonna try and get you out of it." He holds my arm and helps me slide down the wall. He sets the pan on my lap and walks to the john. He brings back a towel and wraps it around my head and face. He leaves again and brings back a wet rag and dabs off my forehead a bit, then puts it into my hand. I'm not sure where I am in relationship to everything else. I think I may doze off again. I wonder if this fish was bad or something. Maybe just some of it was, like just mine. After

a while I start to feel better and pull myself up the walls
again. I can just barely open my eyes and see the light of
the john ahead. I climb into the light and set the pot down
on the floor. I open the spigot and slide water over my skin.
I can't quite see myself because it's so bright in here. I dim
the lights so I can adjust easier. I fill the sink with the clear
stuff and cork it. I fall face first into the miniature tub.
After a few, I pull it up, then dump it again. I set my
heaviness down on the terlet and with the rag William gave
me I drag some more fluid onto my neck and arms and face
and hair. I rest, rest for a few. "PHEw... that was awful. I
know what I'm never gonna eat again."

"What's that?" asks a sweet voice.

"Oh, excuse me, I'm really sorry about that I, er,
um...."

"Don't worry about that. We all go through it at
some time or another. This is the other time. We were
pretty worried about you, though. Thought you may have
had an allergic reaction to something or other."

"Maybe the sardines." I talk away from her and then
wipe my face about five more times. "'Scuse me please." I
walk into the bathroom, now that I'm able, to some degree.
I shut the door. I am really feeling lousy. I don't feel like
going out there again to face them, yet I want to go out so
they don't feel like jerks. They probably haven't talked
much about the plans. If they did—I mean who could with
a sick man lying on the floor? They're probably just waiting
for me to come out. But who am I to think that people
would center their lives around me? They aren't my
parents—that's for sure. But they are my friends, and I
know I couldn't just sit around chatting while a friend was
laying there sick. But I guess some could. Like generals and
presidents and kings, they could all sit around chatting, just
expecting people to die for them. After all, it isn't the
country anyone ever fights for, it's the ones in charge. It's

like people rooting for a football team because it's their home town team, all the while knowing not one member is from the home town. Kind of like saying your family is bred for royalty or the upper class, and all the while telling the poor that they will get theirs in heaven—for their good deeds. How do they know? Maybe they just believe in it. After all, if they didn't, how would they be able to keep their position? Why am I thinking about this crap? Why should I care about this stuff? Because a part of my family is dying because some people think they're in the way—in the way of progress, in the way of wealth.

***

"I'll go and check on him." I walk up to the door and tap lightly.

"Yes?"

"Ruban, are you all right?"

"Is that Kent?"

"Yup. Do you need anything?"

"Oh, no, it's all right, really, I'll be out shortly."

"All right, but let me know if you need anything, all right?"

"Sure, thanks."

I walk back into the living room and Sascha and William are talking quietly and close. "Am I breaking something up here?"

"Ahm, no, really, we were just talking about some ideas. You haven't really heard the plans yet, have you?" William sits up.

"No, I haven't. Oh, sure Alex told me a few pieces of the puzzle. But that's why I came here: to hear the full story. Are you ready to let it out?"

"How's Ruban doing?"

"Pretty good I guess, William, but I don't know for sure, until he comes out of course."

"Sure, sure, I understand. Well tell me, er, I mean

us, what you do remember about it, and then you can ask some questions. Okay?"

"Sure, well, I know that you were proposing some kind of World Peace thing. But how you were trying to do it is a mystery to me, except, except, something, like that you needed people to trust, and that's when things got a little sticky."

"Well, Alex told me he was pretty drunk and that he wasn't sure about everything, but he and I'd been talking about things like this for a while."

"Why was Alex such a jerk?"

"He's not really, it's just—well, he was expecting to pick up where he'd left off with Mary. He didn't know you and she were together or nothin'."

"You talk like a street rag."

"What's that?"

"Oh, just slang term for runaways, pimps, pushers, dropouts and, you know, general riff raff."

"I don't talk like that all du' time you know."

"Sure, sure, well, anyway we really have to start working on this project."

"Don't worry about me. Come on, quit that. Are you my mom?" Ruban walks down the hall with Sascha holding on to him so he can walk a little better. But he tries to keep his distance. Just like any other man, who'd want the guys to know he needed help from a woman? Not me, that's fer sure.

"Come on, there, Sasch. If the man says leave him be, I think that's what he means."

"I'm only trying to help." She looks down for a few and slowly loosens her grip on him. He gives me a look like "thanks, man." I sort of half smile. I know these women will never understand what we men have to go through. How could they? A man's world is completely different than a woman's. Women all just want to be like men or somethin', but they won't, and they never could. Even those weirdos who change into men, they'll never understand.

"Well, now that we're all comfortable let's talk a little more about what we discussed the other day."

Everyone finds a seat and moves around a bit till they're settled. Like a house, four houses settling, and waiting for someone to move in. 'Cept, I got someone in here already.

"Why don't we just try and imagine ourselves at some kind of coffeehouse watching some music or theater. Some girl brings us our coffee and—"

"I'd like some cappucino please." Sascha smiles.

"And ya, er, I'd like some mocha. Ya, mocha." I sound pretty exotic sayin' that.

"Just give me some seltzer water, with lime, not lemon."

"Well, sure, I'll go for it. So we're at a place where people can come in and rest and refuel and watch some good tunes. The place is dark, and hardly anyone smokes anymore. It's just become so uncool, shall we say, so people can really breathe in this place. The ones who do smoke sit nearest the door so the smoke goes out easier. Some people are playing Go, and Chess, and some strange games that are part of the future. We're sitting around, and there's this really huge stage. It's kind of rounded, or circular, and people come out. The curtain behind them is blue and turquoise and very sheer. Two people walk out with purple faces and hair and costumes. They come out from opposite sides of the stage. Then they come towards each other and do this wild dance toward and away from each other."

"Sounds really beautiful, William. It reminds me of my childhood. Oh, I mean, a dream I had." She looks at her hands.

"What are you talking about, Sascha?" What a strange woman she is. No wonder she's alone. Beautiful, but she's way out there. Who would be able to handle her?

"Nothing, Kent, the dance William was talking about. Is that okay with you?"

"Sure, sure, I know it sounds nice. But so, William, what's the point anyway? You leading someplace with this here pretty story?" I was beginning to fall asleep. I'm glad Sasch made a fool of herself.

"Well, I was trying to describe what a future place, a future world would be like."

"Well, let the art scene take care of itself. You can write down all the buutiful dance exercises you want when we get to that point. But now we need to hear about the government the schools, the taxes, the wars, you know, the nitty grutty."

"Don't you mean 'nitty gritty'?" William tries to correct me once again.

"No way, that statement, 'nitty gritty,' is a cliché, you hear? I don't talk in none a' them clichés. What I said was 'nitty grutty.' Got it?"

"Sure, Kent, I guess."

"Good, now, let's get down to business. What kind of governments we talk in about here?"

"No government except the natural ones."

"You don't mean dog eat his neighbor do you?"

"Not exactly. I think we've progressed way beyond that. We don't have to kill everyone in the world to prove our strength do we?"

"Well, we gotta get through, you know."

"Does he mean 'get by'? Do you mean 'get by,' Kent?" Ruban still looks dazed.

"Sure, sure, I just don't like touse you know—"

"Clichés, right?"

"Right, Sasch. Good work."

"Well, anyway, how many people do you know that would rather be doctors or writers or artists or something like that?" William picks up his bottle and begins to shake it a bit.

"You still shakin' yer bottle, bro?"

"Oh, yeah, sure. I, ah, forgot about that."

"Well, anyway, yeah, I for one would like to be a scientist or somethin'."

"You? You never did very well in science."

"That don't mean I didn't like it or was good at it. I'm a firm believer in what the mind decides it can do is what it really does."

"That's a good attitude for the work we're going to be doing."

"Right, Sasch. So but imagine a world where people are doing exactly what they want, and I don't mean like violent things or nothin' like that because people don't need to do that anymore."

"Why not?" I think he must be crazy to think that someone wouldn't want some extra power or something.

"Well, if we were all getting what we want in the way of food and clothes and goods and all that, then all we would have to worry about is being the best at whatever we were doing, right?"

"Makes sense on paper, but it sounds a bit simple. How would anyone get what they want, trade or something?"

"No, because that would be really hard to trade corn for a horse or a meal for a painting. I mean it could work, and maybe we would have to start out that way, just until people started to trust and stuff. But the main goal is to just trust completely and just take what you need or want and know that everyone else is giving and taking as much as everyone else."

"William, do you realize what you're saying?"

"Yes, Kent, I do. I gave it a lot of thought since the party when your friend was here, and I've come up with a sort of parallel that we use every day."

"And that is?" Sascha pulls her hair back with her hand as she leans back.

"Well, think of driving down the street. Imagine the sharpest curve on a two-way street you can possibly think of. Then see yourself and another car passing each other, right?"

"So?" I look up and see Ruban with his eyes half shut, before looking back at William.

"See each time you pass someone on the street, safely, both of you have done something fantastic."

"Fill me in, will ya?"

"Are you getting this, Ruban?" Sascha looks over at him.

"Oh yeah, sure, I get it, two cars passing on the street without crashing is miraculous right."

"No, that's not it, it's—"

"Yes, it is, Kent, that's exactly it. You see every day you drive, you trust the person who passes you."

"I don't trust no other drivers."

"Maybe not to a very high degree, I mean, you look where you're going and...."

"I mean it, I am constantly looking where ever I go and I make sure nobody is in my lane and all."

"Do you look at the signs?"

"Of course."

"Do you look at the traffic signals?"

"Sure, but...."

"Are there other cars on the road when you're stopping?"

"All right, all right, I see your point. I trust them for at least a little while when I'm looking at other things, right."

"Right."

"So what's that got to do with not trading or

something?"

"We just have a little ways to get to a society where we don't need someone else to take care of us or make our decisions or even make laws."

"You mean we'd make our own laws?"

"That's what I mean all right."

"Well, I know it's a real crappy system we live in, but doesn't human nature like lend itself to failure."

"Why do so many of you people think that way? I mean, that simply is not true. People are made to succeed. It's just that when you're little and you watch all that garbage on the telly and then you grow up believing what the system tells you. They want the people to believe that they could never do it on their own. They feed all the kids with the garbage of bad guys and good guys and that way they keep them scared so that they follow the system. Do you see that?" Sascha turns a little pink after her speech.

"Wow, Sasch, I never really thought of that. I remember all those cartoons about bad guys and good guys, and I just thought that was how the world is so I believed it." Ruban is really awake now.

"Yeah, that's right, I mean it's gotta be right. We have a society that's developed from fear. We always feared the biggest animals and then the biggest gods and then we feared the biggest kingdoms, and then we were taught to fear religion and the Christian god, and then now we're taught to fear the bad guys on the street, and the government and...."

"We fear the big corporations and the government agencies and we fear diseases and we fear each other. This is amazing! We fear everything in our lives, and then we wonder why we're always getting sick!"

"Right, Ruban, the whole system is built around fear and protecting ourselves from danger. So what you're trying or wanting to do is to somehow take all the fears away. Like letting the society relax and just be happy or something? Well, that's really nice, William, but it sounds like fear is not just a disease, but it's a cancer that nobody really wants to treat."

"I think you may be right about that. So that's where we come in. We have to start helping people to see and think of a positive future."

"Right, right. How?"

"I don't think we really have to worry much, though."

"Why, Sasch?" William looks at her strangely.

"Because, if you look at the changes we've made in the past fifty years or so, I'd say that a big change like the one you're probably proposing is going to happen anyway."

"How can you say that? Our country is sending more troops to all kinds of countries, like I think I read recently, our current Prez sent some to Panama, which puts us in the present tense."

"Sascha, I thought you were just talking about how bad we do things. And how we're kind of backward with our thinking."

"Well, sure, I'm sure things are happening slower here than on other planets, but that doesn't mean it's not going to happen."

"On other planets? How would you know that? Are you one of those people who's seen people from other worlds or something?"

"Oh well, I, ah, sure, I saw some people from other planets. But I don't want to talk about it, and I don't want that fact repeated to anyone, do you all hear me?"

"Sure, Sasch, we understand. I didn't know."

"So getting back to this other stuff—maybe we will get there eventually, but at least we can sort of help it along, right, bro?"

"I think so, Kent, although she might be right."

"I think it would be better if we started working on it now instead of waiting for it to happen—it can only be better for everyone."

"Well, how do you think things could be different?"

"Well, I'd be a scientist like I said before. I'd like to work on things like ways to heal the environment after all the garbage our parents and grandparents have put this Earth through. I already have a few designs for ways to eliminate some really bad toxic chemicals and radioactive wastes and things."

"You do?" William looks surprised.

"Well, sure, I can show you the drawings some time."

"Why don't we imagine ourselves again walking down the street, and we all go into this wonderful smelling diner. We can just feel the love that goes into this place. These people really do something they enjoy. We all sit down and have a great meal and then we get up and thank her and leave. No money needed, because we're all just sharing everything. We walk down the street, that's paved with stones, not blacktop or cement to trap the earth in. We hear the sounds of kids playing, and the Muslims singing their morning songs to Allah. There are Jews walking to morning Temple and Mormons in their horse-drawn carriages. And maybe there are villages made up of just one religion, but this town has several.

"There are other people who walk to their jobs and go to their businesses and what not. The kids are nearby in the school yard. This school has a combination of several types of education, like Montessori, open classrooms, religious classes, traditional, and whatever else people can and will be thinking of at that time.

"There are people who just write all over buildings, and they are really beautiful. They're not dirty and looked down upon, It's considered an honor to have your building decorated by an artist. Of course, I guess you'd have the choice to say no, but when those artists are given the time and space, they're good, really good. Then if a wall gets filled up, someone comes over and whitewashes it, so they can start over again."

"How would you keep law and order?" I scratch my head.

"Well, first of all, the laws would be kept and decided upon by everyone in the village, so that's the first part. Second, everyone keeps laws they decided upon. Also, since we've taken away the need to steal and cheat and be greedy, then, well, that's a big portion of the crime right there. The only ones left are the violent ones. Now, I know that some people are born with the problems of organic imbalances and things like that, but those things can be treated. Also the little kids wouldn't be poisoned all the time with chemicals from their foods or air, so that would or will change a lot of how people feel. Then we could start parenting classes for every new parent and every parent who wants to adopt or have another baby. Also, we would have to check parents who have been abused themselves and see how they would treat a child by taking care of a child with observers but without their knowing it."

"That sounds awful sneaky." I wonder about some of his motives.

"You have a good point there, but there are other ways to find out what people might do in situations. I guess the hardest would be sexual abuse. But I think over time if we train all parents in several parenting techniques and what works and what don't I think it will help tremendously."

"Where would you train them?"

"In the hospitals or in their homes as part of the prenatal care. And then there would be some follow up work, like parent groups from the different classes to help with stresses and stuff."

"I think that's a great idea. Why didn't you tell Juanita the other night?" Sascha picks up her glass and takes a tiny sip.

"Well, she was talking about some other things, and, well, I don't know. I didn't think she would really be interested.

"I think that everyone, or well, maybe not everyone, but most people could use someone to talk to that isn't necessarily their friend."

"You mean shrinks or something?"

"Yeah, Kent. I think it makes life easier to be able to talk to someone who isn't in love with you or your best friend, you know to kind of just listen and give advice when you want it and, well, you know what I mean. That in itself would probably help those people who would normally be criminal minds, don't you think?"

"But, William, if you think of it, that would mean that the shrinks of the world would be sort of like running the world." I'm quick, real quick.

"Kent? Are you serious?" William gives me that strained look.

"Yeah, I mean it. Think about it. If everyone had a shrink to talk to then some would have to double up some you know, but then think of what the shrinks would talk about."

"You might be right. One other idea I had was to rotate people into different jobs, so that everyone has a chance to do everything. Wouldn't that be great?"

"Only if you want to, but, William, every new idea, starts to sound like more controls on everyone, instead of the free society that you talked about the other day. I think things would be better if we left them alone. They'll settle themselves, really."

"Sascha, I think a lot of things will be settled if we

leave them to the money-hungry, power-hungry people on top. Sure, they'll end up just leveling everything with bombs and pollution and poaching and who knows what else." William grips his chair and then gets up to freshen his beer.

"There's a lot of different types of therapy, you know. The one I like the sound of the best is logotherapy, because they use really positive ideas, like say the problems of the past that you are hurting from and then trying to find meaning from each of them."

"Ruban, I had no idea you knew about that." Sascha looks at Ruban with a gleam.

"Well, sure, I read that kind of stuff all the time."

"What, self-help books?"

"That, and just mainly, non-fiction."

"That's nice, I sometimes like reading that stuff, but mainly fiction. Science fiction." Sascha takes another tiny sip from her glass and sets it down on the table so carefully that it's like she's practiced that move every day for the last ten years. William comes out.

"Like say two guys are in a bar, and they both love the same woman. So they drink a bit too much when they find out their problem. The dark red wood of the bar gleams in the light as these two begin yelling at each other. The bartender asks them to go outside. So one of the guys pushes the bartender away from the bar. In our present society we would have the bartender try and defend himself or call the cops and wait for a while or start a big barroom brawl. But in this other society, I think that the other guys who have their senses who are just in there for a few should stand up and talk some sense into the two jokers. If they don't go, the others throw them outside. They push the two down the street to a fighting pin, and they tear into each other. They begin ripping each other's head off, but so what? They both want this woman, and as men go, I mean, guys don't want a fair argument all the time, not when emotions are involved. The woman is standing by the side now watching them, and she's like fretting and shit, and so she just doesn't know what to do or say. She does love one of them more than the other, but she doesn't want to hurt the one she doesn't really want. But if they had just gone to her honestly and asked her who she wanted most, then she could have straightened it all out. So, so what? They fight until they drop, and then they wake up in some strange place wondering why they did something so stupid, especially when they feel so lousy from the drunk and fight and insults they gave to the bartender."

"What about the bullies, you know like gangsters and rednecks and secret agents, you know, gangbangers, who force people to do whatever they want?" Ruban is really feeling like talking now. He's got most of his coloring back.

"Well, I think we'll try and get rid of them before hand and try and help them to not become like that."

"Them who?"

"Well, you know the kids who start out as bullies and grow up that way. I think they're probably just lonely and don't know how to make friends or something. So we can help those kids who're acting out. We won't have any slums, so people won't become pimps or pushers or gangsters. And then we won't need the police, now will we?"

"Well, I don't know. What if we were in your so-called perfect world? You're going to have to allow for the bad apples. Not everyone is going to conform to your little programs." Ruban picks up a glass that's in front of him, assumes it's his and takes a swig. His face goes sour as he realizes that that glass has been there since before we got here, and maybe longer.

"Yeah, I know you're right, Ruban. I know it won't be easy and that most people will hate the ideas and think of ways that make them sound worse than the ways we have now. But I just think that if we start the ball rolling, not anymore Band-Aids on the same ideas over and over and over and over. We need to level things off. And it'll happen in either a violent way like most people want, or it can happen in a gentle way, like I think our planet and the powers that be would prefer.

"Say if we were walking down the street later in the day, and everything is deserted because the town is having a meeting that evening. We hear some screams, which is a real big shock because of the incredible peace compared to most places we call big cities in our current society. We run to where the screams are coming from, and when we get to the alley where they're coming from, we get real quiet. We see two guys with a woman on the ground. One guy is holding her down, and the other is raping her. We run down and grab the guys. The one holding tries to run, and the other one is knocked off by us. Sascha helps her, making sure she's all right. She covers her up with her coat and then runs into a house to get help. You call the ambulance."

"Why don't I call the cops, too?"

"There are no cops here."

"But we'd need them for something like this wouldn't we?"

"No, Ruban, cops are just people, people doing a job as they see fit. As they are told to follow certain laws made by another group of people, people we don't know and who don't know us."

"But this blows your own theory out of the water doesn't it?"

"No, not really, Sascha."

"What is your theory then?" I ask because I am not understanding this now.

"If you try and put it into words, it's basically that we humans are now capable of very high thought and philosophical and mechanical reasoning, so we can and do overcome the animal urges that supposedly we all have in our instinctual beings."

"No, how? I don't understand." Sascha asks nonchalantly.

"Through proper nurturing and training by some general accepted world-wide rules."

"How can you do that if you have Muslims living in the same village with you? I heard about a woman who was in a grocery store in India or Pakistan and because she was wearing shorts or something like that, she was raped, right in front of everybody, and nobody lifted a finger to help her. How are you going to get them to accept a set of rules that doesn't apply to anything we know to be true?" Ruban crosses his arms.

"That's really a good question, and that one I don't have an answer for right now. But I'll work on it. One thing that I know is that in many countries like that, and every country we know of, there is a ruler, or group of rulers, and they control the people and the people's beliefs, by media and propaganda. We have to stop telling all the children how to fight and hate people who are different. That goes for all the countries. I don't know how we'll manage all this, but it needs to be done, somehow."

"You're talking about totally controlling everyone's mind," I blurt out.

"No, not really, it's quite different, really. I think it's actually the opposite of controlling. When you free up the minds of the masses, then you get a natural harmony, just like how the trees and plants live with each other. Those that scientists say are the lowest form of life, or one of the lowest, are possibly the highest. They don't intentionally kill each other. They just live and do their best at being what they are. I think that's how people were intended to live, and that's how we can develop."

"I think I need a better explanation please." I am feeling like I'm from another planet with all this stuff.

"Well, you see, if our brains weren't so cluttered with all these stupid beliefs that our parents and teachers and television have given us, I think we would be more self-directed. We would be free to let our imaginations wander and grow in really positive ways. We will become a race of super beings. Uncontrolled by any superior race or government or police or situation because all restraints will be off."

"Do you really think people will buy that? Don't you think they'll probably laugh at the ideas?" Sascha turns her head away.

"Well, I've tried to share my ideas with other people for quite a long time now, here and there, of course, and I know they have laughed and thought I was crazy. So I guess you're probably saying that I should give up or something?"

"Well?"

"Well, I can't. I have been driven for so long to work on this. Every problem does have a solution. I've walked along the beaches and watched the waves play on the shores, wondering why I'm so obsessed with these ideas—this kind of fantasy world I live in. But I'll tell you that some of the ideas I had ten years ago and didn't tell people about have now been adopted. And so I could just let it go, but then again, I can't—I really just can't walk away from a situation in this world without wondering how it could be and how it will be different later on when people come to their senses."

"Well, I don't know, pal, but sometimes I think everything is possible." Sascha hugs William.

"Even the possibility that something is impossible?" I had to say that. I don't know why.

"I don't know either, but look, if this were possible, this, this, fantasy sort of thing you have here, then how would you really go about making it happen?"

"Well, I haven't put an awful lot of thought into that idea yet."

"One thing that's absolutely certain is that we must have a lot of people behind us who are tight friends, and people who are willing to take a chance. I think that for the sake of their children and their future also, we really gotta do something about all this and quick, because it is too late already."

"I thin' you're right man, even though I don' know how this will work, there's got to be changes, in a big way."

"You're right, Ruban. But, William, if you had all these people, how many would you need to pull it off?" Sascha pulls her hair from in front of her face and rests her elbows on her knees.

"I don't know." William stands up and looks out the window.

"I think we need people in every country to...."

"Every country?" Ruban blurts out.

"Sure, I can see that. You'd have to in order to have a real change." I counter the negative.

"But where are you gonna get that many people? And people you can trust?" Ruban throws another wrench into the works.

"Well, I don't know, but I'm open for suggestions."

"Well, I do have a lot of connections with the underground—all over the world. I spent time in prison, and I spent time with all those ecology groups, and they trust me. I know I can count on tons of people for favors." I brag just a little.

"No criminals." William the whiner I used to call you, until you kept growing and I didn't.

"They're part of this too, aren't they?"

"Yeah, but I need to trust the people who would help. Most of the criminal types are just out for a buck. Until we get some of those programs going, I just can't trust drug addicts or crazed murderers. I can't take that kind of chance."

I scratch my head again and lean back on the couch. Ruban hands me a beer with a piece of lemon in its mouth. I squeeze it into my bottle till it foams up. "Listen man, I have people I can trust. I can talk to some of them who I thinks would be most interested and see what I can get going."

"But, William, won't it be total chaos if we take down the governments?" Ruban looks bewildered. Maybe he thought William was thinking of something else, or that some of the ideas would be refuted or put down. But some door is opening for all of us.

***

The night is cool. It's close to midnight. We've got about a million people working for us with their watches all set to go. We're taking small sections of each country tonight and then a little more each night, till we have it all, and then till we have freed them all.

The time is now. Search lights flow across dry dirt looking for us, looking for us, looking for us, us, who they will never know. Kent is around the side. He passed the guard station, and he's now waiting in the shadows. I breathe a mist of frost into the air and feel my heart pumping loud enough for the whole country to hear. Without notice, we rush in. Kent takes the guard down. He's gagged and tied and now stripped by Kent. Kent puts the guard's gun in his new holster and steps back into the shadows to kneel and drag the guard into the dark of the small building.

Sascha is up by the lights now with Ruban and about fifty others. They're waiting for me to switch off the electricity from the fence and floods. I see the break I need. Two soldiers are up on the roof looking down periodically and then back at each other in perfect formation. The lights pass each other, the guards look at each other, and I dart under their noses to the doors. I crack the lock with my special pick and then check around to make sure nobody heard. I slither inside and close the door gently. Windows capture some rays as they pass by. I use that to search the walls for the switches. How did he even know that this is the right building? What if I'm spinning my wheels? What if the blueprints were wrong? I look right out the window and see a few signals. Good, Sascha has the search light guy down. Quick, quick, where in hell? Oh, yeah, this must be it. Five other guys find a way in and take down the other night guards. Now this has got to be it. I can feel something where Kent said it would be, but no, what's that? I switch on my squirt light 'cause I can't feel the right switches on the walls. Where, where? What's that? Light out and I'm in the shadow again waiting for the, oh shit, someone's coming in. I sidestep them, but I'm sure they'll head for the lights. A flashlight goes on. I'm in the corner by the metal cabinets, waiting, waiting, waiting, My heart's going to explode.

"Anyone in here?" A voice I don't know talks to the dark. I touch the cabinet and "BUMP!" Shit! "Hey, who's there?" He heads over to the light and "OH, humph, ER! Ah, ooh.!" He's fighting with someone! Who's there? I hope I hope, I hope. "Hey, Will," whispers Kent.
"Come on, did you switch it off or not?"

"No, I can't find it."

"There, it's there on the left wall like I told you." I'm standing in the darkness with my squirt on the wall and there, yes, it's exactly where he told me. I scoot over, trying to avoid the man on the floor and the furniture, "Oh no, ow."

"You okay?"

"Sure." Click, click, click, click, bam. "Done." All the lights are off now along with the electric fences, so the others are going through the whole camp and gathering the troops and loading them onto the trucks and taking all their guns and keeping them quiet. We all have our masks on, so none of them can point us out until we get them out of the country. I hear an army of trucks moving through the yards. Each truck is at a barracks entrance loading. Five of our guys are at each entrance and exit. Some have gone inside each and grabbed the guns at gunpoint, searched the men to make sure they aren't carrying any weapons.

Kent and I walk to the different buildings and see how we can help. One of ours yells, "All right, all right, surprise inspection get up, get up, and get dressed. Come on out and load up into the trucks. Come on, Come on, MOVE IT! MOVE IT! MOVE IT!" They all look rather stunned and not sure what's going on. They try and whisper to each other but they're stopped by our guys. "OUT, OUT! GO, GO, GO! Onto the trucks, up onto the trucks. Come on, move IT!" The trucks are being loaded somewhat slowly, but quick compared to what is going on.

"Hey, what's going on here?" A captain, or *the* captain, is awakened while we search his rooms. I explain to him that we have a special plan for him and his men. I hold his shoulder down a few seconds while I suggest to him that he follow orders very carefully. He spits in my face, and I click my gun for effect. Kent hears me and yells at me to stop, telling me how valuable the captain might be later on. I stand back for a minute. Then, I push his face down into the pillow with my hand and say, "You have a choice. Either put your clothes on and get into the truck, or leave your clothes off and we'll throw you into the truck. I suppose your men will love to see you naked."

"What if I don't get into the truck?"

"This isn't an option, if you value your life. NOW GET GOING!" He slowly sits up and puts his clothes on. He reaches for the gun that we've already stashed. I lift up the gun he's searching for, and he sighs and then swears at us some more. He'll probably try a few more Nam tricks, so we tie him and gag him along with the other upper echelon. What if they try and hop out of the back? What if somebody has a gun or knife hidden in their clothes or in a truck or someplace only they know about? I yell at a couple of guys who are standing around to search the men again and to search the trucks and everywhere these guys will be. No glass or metal chips or anything that could possibly be used as a knife should be left near these men. The men are tied to each other and allowed one at a time to go to the can.

"Hey K., better search them as they get on the trucks." I walk to the next group and tell the next one of ours to do the same thing.

"But W, we just searched them before they got tied up. How could they possibly do anything else?"

"I've seen some pretty fantastic things in my life, and getting another weapon behind your captor's back is not too difficult an idea to think of."

"Well, I guess."

"Please just do it."

Each group searches again and groans a bit with each because of what it entails. A pile of locks is pulled out of a hardware barracks, and one by one the trucks are locked, if even the canvas backs are roped and pulled shut and locked in some miraculous fashion. One guy yells, "Hey, how we supposed to breathe?"

"Air gets back there—you don't need to worry." Kent answers. I bring Kent aside and ask him about all these guys and if they will be safe. This is kidnapping, and I don't want anything to happen to them—just in case. Kent

110

reassures me and sends me back to the front truck.

"Is M taking care of sending those missiles into space?"

"Yeah, right out there into the blue yonder where they belong."

"Great I'll radio ahead to the ships that we're on our way, right on schedule. I know there'll be a few slip-ups, but maybe, maybe we'll just pull this off without too many more hassles. I wonder how the rest of our people are doing in the other countries."

"I don't know and right now I don't care, except for this group, so if you don't mind, I'd like to get going."

"Sure, sure, K, I'll mount up. I can't wait to take off these masks—this mask, rather, as I'm sure you'll agree."

"Right, right. See you up front."

I walk up to the front truck and check all around to see that the men are all in the trucks and our guys are locking the doors. I step up of on the running board and look over everyone. One of the flood light sets was turned back on earlier, for us to use, but now the morning lights are beginning to pierce the gloom of the night. This is our signal that time is a-wastin'. I grab the loud speaker from the front seat and order the men to get going. It's time to move out. Soon the trucks are ready.

Ours begins and speeds out through the gates down the highway near the desert and on to the docks. All around the world similar things are happening. People are banding together and overtaking soldiers in every country in the world. This is going on, and I don't know how my brother got all these people together in such a short time. It's pretty wild to imagine what is really taking place.

We pull up near the docks, where a monstrous cruise ship is waiting for us. Our people are armed and waiting for the signal to open the doors. It's still slightly dark out, and the front is quiet. I talk to the captain and ship hands and make sure everything is ready. I give the signal to open the doors.

"Now, you men and women may try and escape or try something stupid. Let me tell you that you have nothing to worry about. You have no reason to be afraid of us. We are not going to hurt you. Please do not try and escape because we will use force to keep you here. The reason for all this will be explained later on this afternoon. Consider this a vacation, and you will do quite well. But before that you must follow directions.

"First of all, you must get off the trucks quietly and safely so none of the others are injured. Then you will be taken into the ship. Now, if nobody tries to be a hero, we'll be all right. Well, get going, people!" They unlock the ropes tied to the chains and unstrap the ropes. Then one at a time the U.S. military is taken out of the truck and sent down the path to the ship. Since they're all tied together, they can't escape. The most they can do is try to scream. One guy yelps pretty loud. One of ours goes over and threatens to hit him with the butt of his gun. Alex scratches his face under his mask. He's probably sweating as much as I am. He clicks his gun to make sure the soldiers are listening and on the right track. All the commanding officers are unloaded from their special truck. They are sent up separately from the remaining soldiers in order to keep their plans to themselves. You cannot be too safe with these people—each of them trained to be sneaks, heroes, killers, saboteurs, and always ready for death, even those who aren't. Good traits, for wars, but soon my friends these traits will be obsolete. The gags that were put on before the drive are loosened a bit, but not enough to allow audible sounds. Otherwise, the soldier who tried to yell out earlier may have signaled the ear of someone in the warehouses nearby. The plans have obviously been worked out very carefully. I'm glad Kent came into the group. Without him, none of this could have even been started yet.

I follow the commanders up the ramp and into the ship. We enter the large room where they are to sleep. Two men accompany me and proceed with untying the captives. They then loosen their own gags. They give me some real dirty looks and begin asking questions. I still have my mask on, along with the others. Just in case. At least until we get on out to sea.

"Jim, how could this have happened? Aren't we supposed to be a maximum security camp?"

"That's what I was told."

"No civilians were even supposed to know about us. That is unless these aren't civilians. Say, if you aren't going to answer any of our questions now, when will you?"

"Tomorrow, when we are under way and you are all fed and rested."

"Fed and rested? It sounds like a luxury tour all right. When's dinner?" the fattest one asked.

"Well, it is supposed to be a cruise type vacation for you all." I scratch my mask again.

"Say, who's putting you up to this? Is this some sort of real vacation? Like somebody is playing a very nice practical joke on us? Come on, you can tell us. If this is a reward for something, I'd like to know."

"Well, I told you as you were all getting off that it is supposed to be a vacation."

"Then why did we get gagged and tied?"

"And separated from our men?"

"Because this is supposed to be a forced type of vacation, and our officials knew that you all would have to be dragged to it."

"No, it isn't." The captain stands up from the chair he'd been watching me from in the corner. "That don't add up. If we was on a vacation, I would have been notified. And, you wouldn't have used guns. It just don't add up."

He crosses his arms and stares at me, cold and hard. I get a chill down my back. This is a man who has killed probably hundreds of men, because they were the "enemy." He's probably tortured men, women, and children, and walked away, no, ran away from screaming dying people, in order to save his own skin. He is a captain, of a brutal army: a group of hired killers, torturers and destroyers of land and animals. Though I don't hate him, I know that he sees me as an "enemy."

"Think what you want, men, but you are here to have a good time, and to rest and recuperate. We are not enemy terrorists or Russian spies. We are Americans, just like you, who want to see things a little differently, just like any man who goes in to kill soldiers or civilians, except that our aim is not to kill, but to bring out a change that will never have to be fought over again." I know I've thoroughly confused them and probably talked too much, but so what? They have a taste, and I have answered some of their questions, for now. The three of us walk out. They check all the window, or rather, portals, and doors. They check their bugs and two way mirrors, because these are the ones we will have to be most concerned with.

One guard is posted in the next room with the two-way mirror, and the other is posted outside the doors and windows where he passes back and forth.

After the doors are locked and we leave, one begins, "Geez, I wonder what they're gonna do with our missiles and tanks."

"What about our guns?"

"What about our soldiers?"

"Maybe it is a joke or something."

"Aw, shut up, Ralph."

"Sir, I wonder if this is just some sort of test. After all, these are top soldiers."

"I know, I know.... Why do you have to keep

reminding me?"

"I don't know, I guess it's because I expect so much from them."

"So did I."

"I'm sure they did their best. Given the circumstances and all."

"And all, and all what? They didn't guard their posts. Period, that's it. These top men and women did not maintain position during something as easy as a raid. What gives here? I can't just give up unless I know. Because, Lieutenant, if this is not a joke, and if it is a joke or test as you said, then we're in a heap o' trouble, and so is the United States of America."

***

"So, Kent, where are all these people from, anyway?" asks William while leaning over the rail. The waves smash the side of the ship as it moves along. The city lights can be seen in the distance. The two brothers sip beer from cans, holding them as tight as possible.

"I was wondering when you and Ruban are going to have to leave the ship."

"Tomorrow, but then does that mean you don't want to answer my question?"

"Yup."

"Are they criminals?"

"I don't know that for sure. But I know that, no, that they aren't now. Let's just say that in some circles they never were. They just did their jobs—extremely well."

William scratches his temple. "Are they mercenaries?" William looks at the sky. Kent, startled, looks at William for twenty long seconds.

"I can't lie to you, big brother."

"So they are?"

Kent continues to look out.

"Your silence tells me what I want to know. I don't

know what to say to you."

"Then don't say anything. Just know that all these people have helped us with our dream because they wanted out of what they were doing. They see this as a vacation on a luxury cruiser."

"We can't pay them what they're used to."

"This trip is payment enough."

"They don't want extra money?"

"It's not part of the deal we made."

"What if they try and turn around and take over the situation?"

"They can't. I've taken the precaution to make sure that none of them are together enough to try something like that. Besides, did you ever think that maybe, just maybe, you're not the only one who has had dreams and desires for some kind of resolution to this mess we've called living?"

"You talkin' high class now, bro—"

"I—I am? Sure, that's nice. Well, anyway...."

"That's great, if it's really true. I—I just can't take that kind of risk. These soldiers that we captured must be rehabilitated into thinking in terms of peace and the ending of world conflicts instead of always playing the super hero game. I just hope the shrinks can help us, or them, rather."

"If we can make them soldiers see that the big change is already happening, and that they don't have no choice, then I think they can overcome their own problems. I imagine it must be pretty lonely, knowing at any day at any time you might be called upon to mutilate and murder somebody you don't even know just because your "superior" has a beef with their "superior." Or, that you may be called upon to die at any time. Even in basic training. They lose their identity and become part of a crowd of faceless people—all with the same hair, same clothes, same title. I don't know how they can be so gullible as to listen to those crazy ads."

"Yeah, yeah, I know, man. You don't have to convince me about all that. You know I almost signed with the Air Force once."

"You, William? No."

"Yeah, really." The night air hangs down over them till they feel like they're inside of a gigantic glass jar. The sounds bounce off the sides and echo off the boat. They are a tiny boat inside a bottle. Put together piece by piece until the little people are placed with tweezers onto the deck so they can talk forever, forever in the night's salty breeze. Cool it feels to them, but not cold. Fresh and stale because it is as old as the Earth itself, and yet only as old as the old man that put them inside their closed container. They travel through the limitless reaches of space, but only as far as the ocean will travel until it hits a shore or breaks on the sharp rocks of a continent. Or until the storms stretch their bow so thin that it shatters into a thousand tiny bits of wood, flesh, metal, blood and plastic.

"I hope we can rehabilitate all these people all right. I wonder what's happening around the world."

"I don't know but I think you were right in not allowing any communications between the different groups yet. It would be easy to trace, once one is found. I hope the idea works. I hope all the plans worked."

"Well, hey, let's have a little faith. I'm sure all the people you screened are good and reliable and especially prepared in this kind of spy type stuff, so, hey, it'll be all right."

"Thanks for the vote of confidence." They look over the edge again as footsteps come closer in the dark.

"Seen any whales out tonight?" Ruban speaks through the dark.

"I didn't know there were whales in these waters." William shakes his can of beer. "Is that you, Ruban?"

"Of course. Who did you expect?"

"Whales do come round here quite a bit. The Pacific Ocean is home of many whales and the coasts are also the paths of many migration runs for cetaceans."

William shakes his beer slightly and then takes a swig. "I thought it was just the California Grey Whales that come through here."

"Nope, nope. Say, I was wond'ring when you're planning to leave the ship." Ruban rubs his forehead.

"I think we'll probably leave tomorrow. As long as Kent has everything under control—you just can't trust these military guys yet."

"Well, I think the people who've helped us so far will be able to keep them under wrap. We have every room guarded—I think we know what we're doing."

"Good, good. I know they're trained. It's just that we can't make a single mistake. Besides, if your people think they're on a vacation, aren't they going to want to relax at some point?"

"That's where the shrinks come in. You know what I mean?"

"I think so—the guards relax a bit when the shrinks work, right?"

"Right."

"But what if somebody goes berserk and belts a shrink?"

"Then he calls someone, or, or, better yet, we have all the shrinks' rooms monitored during the sessions by a handful of guys, so if one small thing happens, the shrink doesn't have to do a thing. We just get there on the double. Meanwhile, the other thousand guys are resting or enjoying the amenities."

"Sounds like a good plan, Kent."

"Thanks, Ruban. When are the shrinks supposed to be coming on anyway?"

"We're supposed to meet them on the yacht St.

Mary, tomorrow 0700."

"What's that mean in plain English, William?"

"It means seven o'clock, Kent." Ruban feels proud.

"You're right, Ruban. At 7 a.m. we pick them up. Then after you've briefed them—"

CRACK! SMASH!

"Shit! Let's go!" yells Kent.

The three run toward the noise and find the mercenaries with their guns on four soldiers who tried to break out.

"Apparently they didn't see us under their portals, so they just tried a little escape. Where'd ya think ya'd go, huh, to the sharks?"

"It's all right, K, we've got things under control now." A black man with his blue uniform starts to push the soldiers into the room.

"Yeah, we got things under control all right. Now get back in there, you feces!" The second guard pushes the soldiers into their rooms.

William pulls Kent aside and whispers, "I want to talk to each of the guards separately tonight."

"What, W?"

"You heard me. Starting at 0600 sharp."

"W, I thought you said this thing wasn't supposed to get into a power struggle." Kent's arms are firmly on his hips. His face is full of disgust.

"Look, K, I don't mean to sound that way, but we can't be treating our captives disrespectfully if we are to expect them to trust us."

"Disrespectfully? What the hell do you think we're trying to do here?"

"We are trying to make a change," says Ruban from behind them.

"Thank you very much, sir. I'm new here." Kent crosses his arms and begins to walk away.

"But, Kent, you can't have an attitude like you're some superior being. You can't treat these people like trash we're getting ready to toss out."

"If you think for one minute that I'm gonna ask these guys to become pussies for you, you're wrong man, 'cause they won't."

"You're unbelievable you know that? I thought we had an understanding here. I thought, wait, wait. Now let's go get another beer. We're brothers and I'm sure we can come to some sort of an understanding here, somehow. Ruban, do you mind?"

"No, no. But I would like to be there for part of the talks with these guard guys, okay? I mean you said tonight at 6 o'clock, but does that really mean 6 in the morning, since it is nighttime, or does it mean tomorrow night? And didn't you also say that we were going to leave after we picked up the shrinks sometime tomorrow morning? Or were we going to stay another night?"

"Woah! Did I say all that? Well, I'm glad you caught it all because that means I can unscrew everything. Tell you what, Ruban, I'll tell you about what our decisions are either in an hour, at say 2 o'clock, or at breakfast at 8 o'clock. Which is it?"

"I don't know, until I get there. But I'll see you at one of those times in your office, or in your office before breakfast."

"Well, I suppose that's all right."

William and Kent go to the bar and talk for a while, and then Kent finally agrees to start bringing in the off-duty men now. So, one by one they come in, and they are interviewed. At 2 Ruban comes in to join them. After a couple more minutes, Sascha joins them.

"What we are trying to do here Sam, is to bring about a peaceful change."

"Ya, ya, I know dis. Kent hera toll me all 'bout dis."

"Why were you a mercenary?" Sascha folds her hands.

"I was once a soldier for da German army an' I din' like da way t'ings were done. I wanted to twy an' do t'ings difwent."

"You still killed people for a living didn't you?"

"Sometimes, when necessary. Besides, Kent knows all dis bout me before I come to help you. Why you ask all dis 'bout me now?"

"Why did you decide to join us?" William diverts the question.

"I vas zick of twying to do all dis for jus' za money. Alzo I thought it would be nice to be on wacation for da time. It iz werey nize, sank you, Kent, for inwiting me for dis cuise. I vant
to be helpful. Iz there something I have done wrong?"

"What we want from you now, is for you to be fair to our captives. And not too rough. Most of the guards here have done or have similar backgrounds at you, but you can't look at these people or anyone else again as a job for you to execute. Get my drift?"

"Sure."

"We also don't want you to overwork yourself. This is a cruise ship, and we have enough people on board to cover every soldier two or three times over. So there's no reason to be abusive in your actions or your language. That means no hitting, slapping, punching name calling or plain insulting. These are people just like you who probably don't like the military any more than you, and they need to be shown how to get out of that mentality. All right?"

"Vell it vill be nize to haw the peaceful world. Have I done anysing vrong?"

"No, no, we're just talking to everyone and making sure that they have things straight."

"Vell, Kent did tell us all 'bout this tings, before ve

accepted zees positions. So, may I go back to vork?"

"Just one thing—wasn't it part of your deal to make this a sort of vacation?"

"It is, it is. I eat anysing, I sit still and relax and enjoy the sun. I don't climb through jungles or vorry 'bout killing anyone. All I do is keep deez people in their rooms or under control. If I am good to zem, dey vill remember and twy an learn more—maybe yes?"

"Maybe yes. Good, thank you. You may go now."

"Bita." Sam walks out of the cabin and the others continue talking until about three ante meridiem.

"How many more are there, Kent?"

"Well, there were roughly a thousand, give or take a hundred, and we've seen maybe a hundred—five to ten minutes each, well, you know I don't think it will be easy to finish this job, bro."

"You may be right. Do you think you can come up with another idea?"

"Well, how about a large group, or better yet maybe ten different groups, so that everyone has a chance to talk."

"Do you really have a list of people there, Kent?" William lifts a cup of coffee and looks inside before taking a sip.

"Yes. Why, did you think I didn't care about this project?"

"No, I didn't say that, I just didn't know you had put so much work into it. I'm impressed. That is a good idea, by the way, to have group discussions. I take it you mean after Ruban and I are gone?"

"Sure, unless you want to do it now."

"No, no, I think you all have the idea. In fact I think your idea will probably work much better than these isolated interviews. The people will be able to discuss their feelings and feel like they have an important job, instead of just something to keep them occupied. It'll be good."

"How did you enlist all these people, Kent?" Sascha scratches her left eyebrow.

"Well, let's put it this way. I have some connections."

"I'll bet," says William.

"Major connections." Kent smiles.

"If I'm gonna go with you tomorrow, I'll have to go an' get some rest now."

"Sure, Ruban, go on ahead. We won't be too much longer anyway." William gets up to show Ruban to the door.

"Are you staying on the ship or going back with us tomorrow, Sascha?"

"I'll have to stay here, Ruban. But I'll probably see you in a couple of months when we all get back together. Good night, Ruban."

"Buenas noches, señorita." Ruban smiles and then exits.

The door closes and Ruban's footsteps can be heard fading down the hall of the boat. Kent begins to jeer, "I think he's got it in for you girl."

"He's sweet. Don't make fun of him. There are so many American guys that could take some lessons in manners from him."

"Well, well, I think we have something here," says Kent.

"Cut it out, Kent. You were always such a kid about these things. Ever since I can remember, you were always so skittish about love and romance."

"Shut up, Willy. You were always so dull and serious, and look what that brought you."

"What do you mean where it brought me? At least I have an honest job."

"Right, as a science teacher or something. Well, you know what they say about teachers—those who can't, teach."

"I teach history, and sometimes math, and those aren't exactly things you can do much else in."

"Wow, you're even worse than I thought."

"Ya, well, at least I finished high school, and college, and I have a master's, and I have a wonderful woman who loves me, and I have a house and a sort of a car."

"All right, you two, don't start goin' crazy on me now. Don't we have work to do?"

"Ya, bro. I thought the whole idea in this was so people could be free with their opinions and not have to be tied to the stake for not fittin' in the American dream."

"All right, that's right, that's great. Let's not really get into it. I don't want to have to bring you outside and show you who's bigger, do I?" William stands up.

"Sit down, Willy. I think I should tell you that since I was away, I've gotten myself into shape, good shape. In fact I'm so shapely that I got myself a black belt in karate. I think you should also know that I've beaten guys twice your size. But I will tell you you're still my big brother, and I'm not about to prove it one way or another. So sit down, please. Sit Down!"

Sascha sits back in her chair again and reminds them of the line of guards that they already called for the evening. There are three left waiting. William sends a message to the ones who have appointments set up for the evening and informs them of the plans for the next day. Then they call the next customer into the room.

***

Propellers slowly start to turn. Then, rapidly they set the copter into motion. William and Ruban are quiet for a long painful hour.

"What's up, Ruban?"

"Ha, ha, I don't know, what's up wit' you?"

"So, Ruban, do you have much to do to get ready

when we get back?"

"Probably pack again."

"Again?"

"Ya, my parents don't want me to go."

"What? But I thought they were all for our plans."

"They are just afraid for me. They think I will get hurt."

"Well, you do run the risk—you know that it won't be easy?"

"That's what the training was for, right?"

"Training is, of course, to prepare you for what might happen. But that doesn't mean we can know what will happen, right?"

"Ahh, well, they don't care how much training I had. They just don't want me to go."

"Great, great. That's just great, just great."

"It's okay. I thought 'bout this for a long time now. I know I have to go. Hey, I want to ask you about all those army trucks you took with you on the boat. Why did you bring them along?"

"I didn't want the police to trace us at all. I even had our tracks covered after we went over those dirt roads and at the base itself."

"This is what I thought."

The two are once again very quiet for a very long time. Until "William! A whale!"

"Wow, I think I see two!"

"I hope none of those pirates or Japs paying those pirates goes after those babies."

"Are those babies?"

"Figure of speech."

"But I thought the Japanese stopped whaling?" William brushes hair from his eyes and then puts his hand back on the wheel.

"They were supposed to, but because the American

Eskimos say they need to hunt whales for their diet, and because the U.S. government doesn't want to interfere anymore—thank goodness—the Japanese use the Eskimo whale quota to increase theirs. Iceland, Korea and Norway still murder whales too. It's such a sadistic thing to do. You agree?"

"Sure, Ruban. I didn't know you knew so much about all this."

"Did you know it takes at least an hour and sometimes up to two days for a whale to die, depending upon the way they are killed?"

"Wow, what do they do that takes two days? Throw stones at it?"

"No, no. This tribe found in the North Atlantic called the Azores take tourists out to watch them sacrifice whales with little spears and long lines. They stab them over and over and over and over and over and...."

"I get the picture."

"It's sick, really sick what these people can see in killing something as great as a whale. Like little children playing as though they are big supermen or something."

"Ya, ya, Ruban, I heard somewhere that Ben Franklin once said that, until people, except that he said men, because of when he lived, but he said that until we stop eating flesh, then there will be war."

"Is that true?"

"I don't know for sure because I didn't see it in his autobiography, but I do know he was a vegetarian for most of his life."

"We have a long way to go, William."

"I just hope this work we're doing doesn't take too long for people to understand."

"How much more hours do we have in this helicopter?" Ruban takes a sip of his soda.

"I don't know. I have to go way around the bases

and airports in order for to avoid suspicions."

"Can I take a short nap?"

"A siesta, you mean?"

"Si, si, ha, it's okay?"

"I'll set my watch for about an hour until or if I get tired out. Then I'll need you to help me stay awake."

"We brought some coffee?"

"Of course, could you kindly pour some for me before you fall asleep?"

"Si, amigo, anything for the pilot of my life."

"Ha, you got that right."

Ruban fills the special rider cup with coffee. Then Wil says, "Don't say that in front of anyone, though. They might think I'm strange or something, you know what I mean?"

"Que? Oh, si. I understand, hahhahaha, no way, José."

***

I sit quietly waiting for my children to finish their meal. They are plump and happy children. We have no poverty or disease since the white people have gone away. Our villages share what we have and need and we always have enough. Some people went back to the jungle life, and some like us, didn't want to, we like living together with others. We don't need to fight about the leaders or punish the followers because we all are leaders and all are followers. We live by God's laws, by the old ways, not the religions that were forced upon us.

The sun is lowering and we all make ready our nice clean faces and happiest thoughts. They skies are turning peach and lavender. We all join on the top of the biggest hill in our town. We make a circle and join hands—some don't want to touch hands, and we don't force them. We think about our oneness throughout the world. If the baby cries we comfort her and sometimes we sing "God Bless This

Earth," to the little ones. Then after we are quiet, we light the big candles and the big fire in the middle and talk about the good things and the bad things that maybe need changes and how we can do things together to help things get even better. We want to build a new school for the children—but they will learn the old ways first and then the new.

Many things are the same as they were a hundred years ago. The food we eat, the way we grow the food, the clothes we wear, and now back to many of the same religions—though we all follow our own. The ones who sacrificed long ago, they don't do that no more. We don't have wars either. We just try and do our best for our families and children. We are like all the people of the planet now.

It is good for the old people to talk about the old days before the big change. The old people talk about it with fear to remind the little ones why it is important to not be lazy or to hurt another. They talk about how bad people can be when they try and control others, or when they use money to live instead of living from the land that God gave us. They tell us of the simple-minded people who didn't care if they murdered someone else. The soldiers and criminals who were taught and forgot who they were—thinking they had to kill or be killed for their country or their family or their drugs.

The old people talk of all the blood and violence that they had to see. But they tell the children of the excitement and happiness that happened when the big change finally happened. The old religion told about the big change, but it didn't tell when, so many people had to suffer before it came.

We are quiet now, and the really hard things that come from just trying to do the best you can are forgotten for a while when we all come together. We try and think on these problems. Many people try to help the ones who have big problems, but we all know that nobody can do our work for us. If a farmer is too tired to get up and water his plants, how can they grow? If a painter wants to paint and give his paintings to one who will love them, he has to be very careful and make them as beautiful or different as they can be. If the store wants people to use the things they keep for people, then the store must be kept clean and full. Not to let the little animals to eat the food or to let the sand and dirt from the rains fall and stick to the packages or things.

***

"Well, Mama, this is it."

"No, Ruban, it is not. You are not to go. It is not too late to change your mind."

"Papa, this is very important to me. Mama, can't you see?"

"No, no, don't talk to your mother that way. This is not important to anyone except for you. You're not doing this for our people, as you say. You are doing this to be some kind of hero!"

"Papa, Mama, you two were the ones who thought this was such a good idea. If you didn't think this was good before, why did you tell me this thing now?"

"All we talked 'bout was the man who you did not know very well and wanted to know if we thought he may have good intentions. We thought he must be good because of the ideas you told us about, but no, not this. This is plum loco. Can't you see that? You don't know what you're in for down there."

"I have a plane to catch. Please, please give me your blessing."

"The only thing you have learned in this country is independence. You never learned God's commandment to honor your father and mother."

"Yes I do honor you, but, but I can't explain

anymore, but I do honestly believe that I am being guided by the great spirit."

"If you go now, then you are turning your back on your mama and me and this will break our hearts. But then we will have to turn our backs on you—our only son, who tries to be a hero." The couple walk into their bedroom and close the door. Ruban can hear his mother weeping along with his father.

Ruban feel a sharp pain in his chest and a big lump in his throat that water and breath can't quench. His eyes are brimming when he lifts his bag and walks quietly out the door. As the screen door is slowly released from his fingers, it swings back through the front entry and hits the wall in the foyer, knocking down three dingy coats. Then it flies back to the outside wall and waves back and forth, slower and slower until it finally putts to a stop. The cab door slams and the wheels scream as the driver floors it.

***

William meets Ruban in the men's room at the airport. Wil walks out of a stall, and Ruban immediately walks in after. As the toilet flushes loudly, Ruban lifts the tickets, passport maps and traveler's checks from the toilet paper roller they were wedged into with an envelope. He quickly checks them and places them in his coat pocket. Ruban exits the stall, washes his hands, walks outside and to the nearest airport bar. He sits two seats from William. He orders himself a drink, sips it for a while and then looks over at William a few times.

"You going to Mexico?" William sips his stein of beer.

"No, little bit further. I go to see my papa. You?" Ruban moves one seat closer to William so they can talk quieter.

"I think we're being watched."

"Will the trip be safe? Maybe my parents were

right."

"We have no other choices now. Things are getting into full swing across the continents."

"I keep my eyes open, look behind my back."

"Watch your back."

"Is there something on it?"

"No, R, you're kidding me, aren't you?" Ruban smiles. "Have a good time, buddy."

"FLIGHT NUMBER 327, SOUTH AMERICAN AIRLINES, NOW BOARDING!" "That's you, buddy. Safe trip and Godspeed."

"Gracias, amigo. Phone my mama and papa and tell them I'll be all right, por favor?"

"Sure."

***

You are sitting back in your comfortable chair, waiting for the plane to take off. Your belt is a bit too tight, but it refuses to adjust. A very large African-American woman with a lovely dress and sweet perfume asks you if you're going home or just vacationing. You smile as if you don't understand. You put your headphones on and adjust the sound. The stewardess demonstrates the safety equipment. You don't really care about anything right now except your destination and how you will make contact with your party. When the flight attendants come around to offer drinks, you ask for a gin and tonic—in Spanish. It's a South American flight, so you figure the attendants must know the native, or rather the current tongue.

A lovely lady brings you your drink. You pay her and smile. "Gracias, señorita."

You settle back in your chair for a long nap. What better way to spend five or so hours from LAX?

You begin to hear children laughing. You see a little brown boy scampering through the forest. The area is a lavishly painted scene filled with lush greens of unlimited quantity and quality.

You begin to chase the children. Running and running and trying to find the children you are hearing laughing and chasing through the trees. You look ahead and look behind and try to remember when you last were there. You remember running between these same trees and trying to run away laughing, and then you remember that you are a boy running after someone, someone... until you hear a gentle beating, thumping, drumming, humming and beating, the same as your heart beat, beating so fast and so hard that you see the drummer, and you don't see your own being till you stop and listen and watch as several people sit in front of a half hutch built with twigs and leaves. People all sitting around humming with the drumming and all brown and golden like you, but you, for some reason, you feel strange waiting and wondering what you are supposed to do, wondering what you're going to do and when you're going to do it.

A very old man, deep with lines and full of life has very long, shiny grey hair. He begins to laugh and then dance wild and free. He sings with the others but not with the others, till finally he comes closer and closer then he claps loud and hard and screams in your face all at once. He now stares straight at you, in you, through you. The music stops at the same time as his clap. He reaches his hand out to you, and with a gentle smile he is now reaching to you through the trees where he is held in place by the thick green brush and brown trunks. You move slowly away, as if ascending from him. His face grows sad.

"Mr. Alvarodes? Mr. Alvarodes, we're about to land. Please fasten your seatbelt."

"Wh—QUE? Que?" You look around to see if you are still in the jungle or being overcome by your dream. There is nobody who even resembles the elder. But the woman who sits next to you looks at you very strangely.

"Landing... you know, down?" the American waitress points down and out the window and then smiles.

You walk off the plane still half dazed. You look around for a hotel upon your exit from the tiny airport. You had been told that this was the largest airport in the country, but this is like a stopover airport in America. You smile at the uniqueness of everything. You are stepping out of the doorway when you turn a bit to catch the man staring at you—the same man from your dream. You look away, but the burning from his eyes pierces your back as you pass.

He is following you and begins to walk faster than you as you are trying to make your way to a nearby hotel. The elder comes closer and grabs your hand to stop you. He yanks your arm, saying, "How are you? We've been waiting for you." He is speaking a strange dialect that you mysteriously remember.

"Who are you?" You use your plain Spanish. The elder does not answer you just yet, but instead holds your arm and begins to pull you along. You do not want to struggle, but you have an odd sense that you must run away from this person of your dreams.

"I am from where you are from."

"How do you know...?"

"Shshsh, we are being watched. Come, and I will tell you all you want to know."

"Cut out the pulling, though, this is beginning to hurt. Say, I'm carrying some very important papers and things. I can't walk that fast."

"Shshsh, be still. Your things will be safe. We must move fast." The two hop into the taxi and close the door. One other man steps into the other door.

"Who's he?"

"He is part of us. Do not worry. There is jaguar in the forest, hungry for meat, for the slow ones are always the best food."

The taxi shoots off through the city streets. You try and memorize them as you go along. The other man has bad teeth and a big smile when you look at him. He stares out the windows to see if anyone is following.

"How do you know who I am? I was supposed to meet somebody down here. Where are you taking me?"

"SHSHSHshshsh, we have time to talk when we are safe. Do not worry. Your dreams are not a lie."

You are very quiet for a long time and are wondering where you are going and who these people are, but amazed at the same time at your incredible luck, if it is that.

The driver is instructed to drive up and down several winding streets till the path of gravel begins. Then he drives more slowly for fear of car damage. The road is long and dusty and narrow. An old wagon is being pulled by a donkey that a young girl is hitting with a tree branch. The back of the truck holds a pile of something that may be manure, but you're not sure. The cab waits for the wagon to pass as you stare at the beautiful but filthy and quite sad young woman. After an hour on the old road the driver stops the car and says, "Listen, but I can't go no further, people, I might lose my cab. It'll be three hundred pesos por favor."

"Pay the driver," says the elder to you as he exits.

You are surprised, but you pay anyway, with your traveler's checks. The driver has to look up on his sheet how many American dollars goes into the pesos and vice versa. You compute it at the same time. You get out of the cab and see nothing for a second, except for the cab turning round and puttering off down the dusty road. You look around and see only the trees moving slightly where you hope the others went in. You yell, "Hey! Where'd ya go?"

The elder's companion pokes his head out of the wall of trees and beckons. You follow.

You begin talking as you enter. "Where are we going anyway? I wish you would talk to me." You notice that you are doing something very odd. You're talking nonstop, just about, to people who you do not know, and you are also filled with horror and its opposite at what you do not know lies ahead. You think about the madmen you have heard about in these woods. You see imaginary soldiers pass by as you think of the photos you saw of South America in one of the news magazines. You think you do not know where you are, but you know exactly where you are and you know how far you have to go.

The two ahead begin to strip their city clothes from their bodies and throw them up in a tree. They have left on loin cloths. They pull their hair out of the ties so their hair falls free in front of their shoulders. You follow their steps carefully, but you leave your clothes intact and pull up your nap sack on your back. You're glad you're wearing boots instead of gym shoes through these sharp bushes.

Very quietly you begin to hear a low rhythmical beat. You think at first it's your heart from all the movement under and over the brush, keeping up somewhat with the others. Your steps begin to follow the beat and begin to speed up, trying to keep up. They begin to trot, and you begin to run, faster and faster, barely keeping the two in sight.

A deeper fear comes over you as all the stupid movies you've ever seen flash before your eyes. "Mama, I hope you were wrong. But what if these people are cannibals, or what if they still follow the old religions of sacrificing people? Maybe I'm next."

You stop. All around you is the jungle. In front of you is the low hum of voices calling for you to come, come, come. Behind you, you cannot tell where the end of the jungle is or where the road starts or where your path ends, except for right behind your feet. You draw up all the

energy you have ever had or known and from all the dreams
you have ever felt that brought you here. You listen to the
cool quiet jungle with its gentle but constant bird calls and
rustles of slight breezes. A tingling sound settles in the
furthest background till you concentrate on it. You smile
when you begin to smell the same sound that you see and
feel the trickling waters in the distance as it flows down
sparkling rocks someplace where you will surely be
sometime, someday, soon. You continue to climb in through
the brush after the two new old friends you are making.

The drumming drowns the buzzing as it is fast
pounding louder, playing with many voices humming,
strumming, singing. The sounds progress louder and louder
and louder and it begins to hurt your ears until, suddenly, a
hand grabs you from behind an invisible door while the
crash of the loudest drums halts all sounds, except the
occasional bird call and fluttering leaves. A friendly face
peeks out. The hand releases you, Ruban. Your face lets go
of fear as your eyes lay on the face of your brown friend of
your dreams, a lovely maiden adorned with golden brown
skin and warm green leaves. She motions you to follow.

***

William sits with his arms folded around his folded
legs. Mary sits across from him. Several others sit in a circle
with them.

"When do you think the best time would be to
discuss this with your co-workers?" William looks at the
woman, Phillis.

"Well, since most of the militia has been kidnapped,
or whatever, there has been much less spying. And yet,
there has been more. I'm wondering if there is a way to get
them all together under some special heading. In other
words, William, I really don't know, but I'd take some
suggestions."

"Um, that's great. How about like during a union

meeting?"

"No, there's too much publicity for them. Besides we just had ours a couple of weeks ago and we're not due for about five months. Would you like to wait that long? Not everyone shows up usually, unless they have a complaint anyway."

"How about a bar or coffee shop where everyone goes to hang out or something?" Mary sits with her ankles crossed and her hands in her lap. She lifts her tea cup with two fingers and curls her others, on her right hand, up, while her left stays in her lap.

"How about someone's graduation party?" Phillis delights at her idea.

"How about at some sort of convention or something?" a young and very pale man quietly suggests.

"Is anybody's anniversary coming up?" Mary asks.

***

"Shshshshsh! Everybody, he's coming!" whispers a loud voice. A hundred people hide in the darkness. The door opens. He flicks the light on. "SURPRISE!" everyone else yells.

After twenty minutes of greetings, thanks and congrats, the champagne bottles are cracked open and served. The first glass grabbed is by an older man.

"I'd like to propose a toast to a man who's been the backbone of this fine company for as long as it's been in existence. With his brains and motivating power behind several of our best inventions, and today TWENTY YEARS with the company, here is one of the true great geniuses of our time, RALPH NUDABAKER!" The owner raises his glass to Ralph and then takes a big gulp with all the workers.

"Here! Here!"

"Speech, Speech!"

Ralph says a small quiet speech, with bubbling

laughter brimming from every word. The group talks and mingles and every so often someone shouts and gives a speech about something great while more and more beer and wine and the last of the champagne are poured into the empty glasses. The laid out food is eaten quickly. After an hour or so, the owner, president, and other company officials discuss going home. They talk of their wives and husbands who may be worried about them. They allow the majority of the group to stay, leaving the one who the party was in honor of to lock up the shop after everyone's gone.

The commanders announce their decisions and orders to the group, which suits the group fine.

After about half an hour, the man of the hour begins collecting a small crowd who choose to hear a new idea for his latest invention.

"This thing would be so great, none of you would have to have such dangerous jobs anymore. Instead, you could do what you always wanted to do. We will soon all have homes and businesses that are self-sufficient."

"How could that be?" yells a man from the rear.

"Solar power and wind power together in a compact unit, scaled to the exact size needed for a home, apartment, etc. This little baby will furnish all the power needs of any home or office. We can build them in many different sizes and adaptations to fit any size structure."

"Wait a minute. That means you're taking our jobs away. That's our livelihood. Then what're we supposed to do?"

"Just exactly what you want to do."

"And what exactly is that?" says a plump blonde leaning against the shiny yellow painted cinder blocks and rubbing her cigarette into the wall.

"What you do on the weekends—bake."

"You nuts, man? Or, no, you just a pig, that's what you are! Damn, he's gone senile in his old age, and here I was celebrating you." She lifts her leg to balance on the wall.

"Frances, that's not what I meant."

"Right, because I called you on it."

"No, not at all—haven't you all heard about the military that's being eliminated—all over the world?"

"Yeah, yeah, what the hell's that got to do with anything?"

"I can't believe that you all don't know what's happening here."

He looks around at the calming crowd. They're becoming increasingly curious, mumbling to themselves about his record as a trust worthy person, always sweet and kind. "The only reason I said baking, Frances, is because I know how much you like doing that—you told me yourself you always wished you could open a bake shop."

"Yeah, right, so like where am I gonna get a couple o' grand to open up a shop like that. You gonna give it to me, I s'pose?"

"Well, soon enough, you won't need it. I'd like to tell you all something that's very important, that you might as well know about so you can be prepared. It has been well known in the scientific community that a major change will have to come about in the very near future in order for our planet to survive. But I think you all must already know that, don't you?" A few mumble the affirmative in response. "Well, a very large group of people has apparently taken it upon themselves to bring that change about."

"They must be commies, or pinkos!" a very large man yells in a deep voice.

"No, no, no, no, NO! Not in the least and never at all. No, sir, no way, never can you ever not ever can you ever call this group a bunch of commies. NO! In fact, they are, in all my studies, a lot more American than most people in America. They have taken the basic principles that our country was founded upon and developed them and formed a plan to help modify the more violent behaviors of other countries and to help educate those Americans who were in fact ignorant to many of our founding fathers' ideals. Yes, yes, yes, they are such a fine group, such a fine group indeed! OH, yes, indeedy! And that's what's going to happen. We are moving toward a completely free world, where people learn and do take full responsibility of their actions without blaming or leaning on some ambiguous and small group of people who we'll never meet and who don't give a damn about our feelings, to decide what we can and can't do or what's good or bad for people they don't even know." Ralph stops for a few and rests, while everyone else looks around perplexed. They mumble to each other, and then someone speaks up.

"Ah, excuse me, sir," begins Phillis. "Are you saying that the whole world is really going through a big change?"

"Yes, yes, yes, yes, I am."

"And, ah, are you saying that there'll be no more commies?"

"That's right."

"No more pinkos?"

"Wait, wait, wait a minute—Do any of you know what a pinko is?"

"A homo?"

"No."

"A yellow-bellied rebel!"

"Ah, I don't know what that means, could you please tell me, Mr. Woodjakowski?"

"Oh, urn I think it means somebody who don't want to fight for our country."

"And what's wrong with not fighting if there's no reason to fight?"

"Oh, um, I dunno. Why don't they want to fight?"

"Haven't we grown up enough to learn to use our

words?"

"Are you patronizing me?"

"Aha!" Ralph smiles. "That is very good. I may have been, and that was uncalled for. I apologize for that, sir. Let me rephrase that question. I think we are a very advanced society, don't you?"

"Wael—I s'pose so. Sure."

"Well then, advanced cultures are normally measured by the capacity for communication, aren't they?"

"Waael, geez, I dunno, I s'pose so. You're the scientist 'round haer, s'pose you tell me. What's it mean to be aye advanced society?"

"How kind of you to ask, yes, yes, how kind. Well, sir, I think that the most advanced society ever imagined are those who are able to communicate without their voices. The only sounds that leave their lips, in fact, are songs, songs of a thousand different types, styles and structures. This society is able to construct things with their minds and without moving their hands or any object. They can create paintings and art with their thoughts alone, or enjoy the beauty of the movement with their hands. This society does not know the meaning of violence except in the form of friction, which has been only used during the act of making love."

"Woah! Man! Ah likes the sounds of that already! Where do I sign on?" People snicker, and the room begins to lose focus.

"Wait, wait, wait, now, I'm not finished."

"Come on, now, you guys. Let's hear the good old doctor out."

"Thank you very much, Mr. Saxony. As I was saying, the other part is this society's movement. Did I tell you they don't need cars, or busses, or trains, or planes, or bikes, or even horses. But they get around, yes, they do, they get around better and faster and safer, than even with

141

an airplane." The people mumble. "For these people, and I hate to say this almost because you people, who are kept in the dark about everything, will probably not believe me. But, let me remind you of my reputation. Let me not brag in saying this either, but I do have many connections within the scientific community, and remember, most of the information that we get, we are not allowed to tell the general public, because the Pentagon does not allow it. You never get the whole story unless you see it for yourself. But this society, a society on another planet who our government actually has had contact with, and who claims was once as undeveloped as our world, can transport itself, because they, each and every one of them, can fly." Everyone mumbles and groans and queries and shakes and laughs and cries and whispers and wonders and looks at each other and looks at Ralph and doesn't know what's true or what's fiction. After a long time of noise in all forms except explosions or rivers, the crowd is suddenly silent.

Everyone looks at Ralph and waits quietly.

"Now that, sir, is a very advanced society. And, mind you, we are probably a thousand years from that. But maybe not. Who knows, maybe only five hundred years from now we will be that."

"What in hell is the point of all this discussion?"

"Good question, Miss Smith, very good, in fact. Well, you see that there are societies who are extremely advanced. And the United States has been at the forefront of most of the important advances that our world has made. But somehow we have taken a nose dive backwards. It may have been all the greed or all the brutalization, or all the weakness of those who were afraid to stop fighting for fear that they would be called a coward instead of strong enough to trust in the other person and discuss things like the more advanced individuals."

"I don't understand a word of what you is sayin',

Mr. Scientist, sir. You is talkin' about some people in some cloudy sky and some other people who was afraid to fight but they didn't fight or that they were afeard a being called yeller so they didn't fight or sum such bull. What're we standin' here fer?"

"All right, then, in plain English, the world as we know it is going to end. We are all going to go through a BIG CHANGE. After we have gone through this change, nobody will be fighting wars, or throwing garbage anywhere they want, or beating up women or children or men. There will be no more big corporations, no governments, and in fact, there will be no more money. Instead, everyone will be required to be responsible for only themselves and their families. We will all just do what we want, so long as it is helpful or giving, to others. There will be no more jobless, shiftless, lifeless, faceless people, because we will all be doing the most important thing that we can think of. And, here is the important part: you all have the chance to begin now on your project to help us get to that place in a better way. You are all invited to help me produce the first free home/office/apartment solar-wind power machines, never ever thought of or produced anywhere. Sound exciting!"

"What 'bout them criminals?"

"Well, we will have to work together to help modify their behavior. They will simply not be able to commit anymore crimes. And, with a society without money, they have no reason to steal or cheat or squander money. The violent criminals will have to go through complete treatment, intensive, until they are taught how to live peacefully in a peaceful society."

"Then, are us Americans the only ones who're gonna do all this?" Phillis sits at a table looking up at Ralph.

"Ya, I know that since they started talking about the secret missions that the military is all on, I been keepin' my guns loaded and by my bed at night," the very large man says.

"In order for the plans to work, every country must participate. It's like a dream, but we can start that dream now. We can set into motion something that the world over will remember our generation for. We can disassemble the nuclear time bombs, so our children—your children can have a future!"

"Ain't that there disassembling stuff?"

"Yeah, I mean I don't have no nuclear bombs laying around," Phillis lifts her cup.

"Well, without seeming to be a fanatic, I can tell you that our government has broken thousands of laws and treaties. Just now some of them are beginning to come out. Imagine all the fish you eat. Now realize that pollution and radioactive waste into those oceans, rivers and lakes that you fish out of. There is so much more. All you have to do is read some of the scientific journals, the daily newspapers and the environmental magazines and you'll getting just a portion of what is really happening to you and your future—your children's future."

"You know, doctor, you're gettin' pretty serious here. Is there some other problem?"

"No, no, no. You're good people, and I know things will turn out all right. Everything is up to you now." He walks away into his office and continues to work on his current invention.

The outer conference room, where the party is being held, is very quiet. Its inhabitants talk among themselves for quite a while. They are unsure as to whether their dear scientist has gone mad or is serious. In the corner sits a very quiet woman who is nearing retirement, close to the age of the scientist. She stands up and says, "I heard that the fluoride they put in our drinking water doesn't do a thang fo' our teeth, but that it's poisonous."

"What?" The largest man, who had been sitting,

stands up and walks over to Flora and looks down at her. "Poisonous? I thought that it was supposed to help our teeth. Who told you that?"

"Mah dantist. He toll mah that it din't help our teeth at all. Not at all."

***

The moon splashes down on the rippling sea while many—twenty or thirty soldiers at a time are brought to separate rooms, where doctors of psychology, psychiatry, and therapists in the fields of psychotherapy, logotherapy, sociology, behavior modification and many others patiently await them.

***

"Each soldier is spoken to individually in order to assess the damage to each psyche and determine the treatment in order to return each of them to their natural state, before the fear was set in—before the violence need was injected into their brain patterns.

"In the therapy, each soldier is taught how to see his/her self as a complete and whole individual.

"They are guided to consider and dwell upon ways they may eventually learn to give to others, instead of to kill.

"Each soldier is shown how killing and bombing does not lead to peace and harmony or self-satisfaction, but to shame and horror.

"Many have felt a sort of masochistic movement to feel the need to allow their bodies to be killed or mutilated instead of another's, not knowing that it is their presence that perpetuates the chain of war, fear, anger and a somewhat retarded ability to communicate that seems to be an inherent trait in those who control or attempt to control the lives of others.

"One of the first methods is to show one group many, many hours of films, in color if possible of actual war footage of every war photographed or filmed. This group should see at least ten hours of non-stop violent footage.

"A second group, consisting of the same numbers of men and women as the first group, should watch at least ten hours of spiritually uplifting films, comedy, fantasy, positive future

films, etc., all without any violent clips, whatsoever.

"A third group shall watch no movies or videos or any music of any kind, as a sort of check on the general psyche of an average soldier's group. Please note however, that all soldiers

used must be pre-battle groups or all single battle groups, but not a mixture.

"All three groups will experience their basic film footage as mentioned above at the same time. Following this, they are given thirty minutes of time alone. Following that thirty minutes, the three groups are brought together in a large conference room. They are allowed to mingle about and talk and even fight if they so wish. During this time, they are secretly taped. After this segment, which will consist of three hours, the video tapes are shown and discussed. The soldiers are allowed three ten minute breaks during the first viewing time of ten hours and one break between each of the other segments consisting of thirty minutes each.

"The purpose is to help the soldiers begin to question their motives and their purpose as hired killers. We hope that they will begin to question their current careers, their morals, their god, and even their country." She set the piece of paper down on the desk and awaited their responses.

"Excellent work, Dr. Scrimshaw. I am duly impressed." Kent hands her a cup of tea.

***

You begin to take it apart. Every single piece can be dismantled. No violence necessary? You can't say that because how can you help it when they're attacking you? Every day they attack you. They want to examine you, talk to you, probe you and prod you. What do they want? When will they stop? You become afraid and angry. You are afraid when anyone asks you why you feel so strongly. You wonder why they don't feel the same way or, then again, maybe they're lying. You are afraid of them because they appear to think differently. They are either stupid or evil. Maybe they're of the devil, come to haunt you. You must be the only good thing in the universe. You and those who think exactly like you. Those who act like you are the only ones who are sane or good or normal. All others smell different or dress different or talk different or believe different or look different or walk different. They are wrong; you are right. You and those who look like you, act like you, smell like you, think like you, believe like you, talk like you, walk like you are the only right ones, the only good ones, the only clean ones the only ones who need to live. Those who are like you hate those who are not like you because you hate them, too. Hatred gives you energy. Hatred gives you power. Hatred makes you feel like a god. Hatred gives the energy to do your god's work. Revenge gives you energy. You take revenge on those who are different.

***

The moon splashes down on a black rippling sea. It's your time to go and see one of the shrinks. You still don't know exactly why you're on this ship. But you're here, and, like it or not, you're a soldier. So you follow the orders of the enemy in order to avoid being killed, except you never give out any information of any kind. They don't seem to you like they're gonna hurt you. They just have this funny way of thinking that there's something inside of you that needs changing.

You've been looking out the window for some time.

You feel like a prisoner, except that you don't feel trapped. In fact you feel less trapped than you did on the base. You want to talk to your commanding officer. You've been told repeatedly that you will talk to him in a few days.

You walk down the outer corridor of the deck, in line behind several other guys—some your bunk mates at camp. You don't talk much. One guy tried to slip you a note, but it got grabbed fast by the guard. You see that they're onto that sort of stuff pretty easily. That other guy should have been more cool and looked around better before passing a note. You wonder what it said. You wonder if you'll ever know.

You think about the fact that you've had ample food, alcohol, exercise, including a weight room and pool, and smokes, when you wanted them. Somehow you think they're out to get you.

You are finally brought in to see the shrink. The same guy everyday so far. You wonder why they're trying to make you think about these things. He tells you he wants to know why you joined the army. You tell him it is none of his business. You know then and there that for sure they are trying to crack you, but gently at first. You don't know what's next.

For the first week you tell them just your name, rank and serial number, just like you were trained. But then this guy starts talking about freedom. He starts saying that all the ideas that our forefathers had, like fighting for freedom, may not be necessary anymore and are, in fact, ludicrous. You start to get angry and tell him that if we stop having an army, then we'd be taken over by foreign countries that will make us slaves.

Then he asks you another question, a sort of stupid question, you think, but then now, you can't stop thinking about it: "What if all their governments disassembled to nothing along with the U.S. governments, until no military, no police, no small person or group of people was in control of all the people anymore?" You tell him that it would be anarchy, total chaos when everybody would go crazy. So he asks another one, like how insane can it be—he calls himself an analyst. He says in answer to your anarchy response, "Then it would be the same as now? Violence, wars, crime rampant in the streets?" You say what you can say, which you don't want to say: "Yes, I guess."

***

I walk into the room where the shrink is waiting—again today. He asks me if I want something to drink, wine, beer, anything? I ask him for a beer. He asks me what kind. I tell him I haven't had a Moosehead for a couple of years. He says he's from Wisconsin, too. I just nod. I'm still waiting for him to try and brainwash me or something. I'm still standing, so he asks me to have a seat and make myself comfortable. I sit down and keep my back straight and steady for the chance I will have to escape, or to keep him from trying to brainwash me into becoming a stool pigeon or something. I wonder what my family thinks happened to me. I wonder if the government did do this or if they told my family that I was kidnapped. I wonder if they know who these people are. He calls room service and asks for two Moosehead beers. I am used to calling room service to my room. Nothing else to do for a lot of the time except stay in my room and eat. I suppose I don't get out enough.

He sits down in a ruby velvet chair near me and just sits real quiet like for a while. He asks me, "Are you feeling okay about being here?"

"That's a stupid question." I shouldn't have said a thing. Maybe that's his cracking point, underneath his sly niceties he's evil.

"Why?"

"How would you feel if you were kidnapped?"

"Were you kidnapped? I thought the government

told all you about all this—maybe I shouldn't have said that. But let's take it another step. What about the fact that you are being treated so well. If I was kidnapped but treated pretty nicely, I think I'd wonder what was really up the sleeve of my captor. I'd probably feel like you do, but then maybe not."

"Yes, you would because you wouldn't know what was really goin' on. You can't trust a kidnapper. Who the hell cares if you're treated right? When you're kidnapped, that means without your consent or any permission. You're a prisoner." He sits there for a while thinking about something, thinking about it I hope. Maybe I got through to him.

Then he says, "I guess you're right. I'd probably like to be doing something else." He's quiet for a while again. Maybe he's thinking about how to free us. After all, he didn't kidnap us. It was those other guys.

"Ya," I say," I'd rather be with my family."

"I guess I would probably feel the same way. Is that where you were when they took you?"

"No, but I...." Shit, maybe that's another ploy or something to get me to open up. I'm not talking anymore. The beer and wine come and, boy, oh boy, they bring a sixer. That's not all for me, I don't think. Besides, I can't get drunk anyway. That's when they try and crack you. That's when you tell all sorts of army secrets. Except that I don't know any secrets because I'm just a private. That's what I'll tell them, that I don't know anything because I'm a private. They don't tell privates any secrets—no privy info—savvy? Why do they even waste their time on me? I suppose that's what all prisoners in prisons for no reason wonder the same thing: why me?

"I think I have a bottle of wine left in my fridge here... yes." He reaches into the small white box and brings out a corked bottle. "You can have as much of that beer as you want, or save some for tomorrow."

"Is that when you're gonna try and brainwash me?"
I say half under my breath.

"I'm not trying to brainwash you. I wouldn't know
how. But if you must know, my specialty is un-
brainwashing people—such as you. That's why I'm here."

I don't look at him. I look at a spot on the wall while
I open a beer.

"You remember hearing about all those cults and
things?"

I don't look at him.

"Well, I helped un-brainwash hundreds of them. It
was pretty hard work to get these young people, and some
older folks, too, to let go of what they thought was the
answer to their dreams—but whose only intention was
selfish."

I look at him like he's nuts without saying a word.

"You think I'm crazy? Well, you're the one
following the cult."

"I ain't in no cult, mister. I'm a prisoner of yours
and whoever is running this show here. And I want to be let
go now!" I stand up as I say this, and point my fingers and
look at him because when he's done trying and I get
rescued, he's dead meat!

"Many people who are under the influence of a very
strong cult don't understand that it's for their own good to
be taken as a temporary prisoner. But it really is for your
own good, you know. You see when the Big Change comes
about, you're going to have an easier time than some people
who are older and more stuck in their ways of violence and
fear. But you're young, and there may be some hope for
you."

"Listen mister, I don't know who you are or what
you are or what the hell you're trying to do to me but I
ain't buyin' it, not one bit. I think you're pretty low

down—it's against the law for anyone to kidnap anyone! I'm an American citizen, and I have my rights to do as I please."

"Including murder people?"

"I never murdered anyone."

"Oh, good, not yet, then. Well, I'm glad of that. But I guess you will someday, then—that's why you're in, isn't it?"

"No, I'm going to fight to protect my country. I don't have to stoop to—"

"You mean you're going to be paid to murder people you don't even know?"

"War is war—if we don't do it, they'll do it to us."

"Is that what they told you?"

"It's the truth. How do you think we got this free country, by just talking? People had to fight for this country, for our freedom, you know what they say now: Freedom isn't cheap, or something like that."

"You're right, you're right, absolutely, and I can see that now we do need to keep fighting, always, till everyone is dead or at least till we've blown up half the Earth, right?"

"Oh well, I mean, er, yeah, or unless or until they stop fighting. Yeah, they gotta stop it first."

"Right, right, they should stop fighting before we do. So let's get our guns together and just start fighting. I mean you and me, let's just start shooting at each other right now. I'll go get the guard's gun and one for you too, all right?" He gets up and starts to go to the door. He's nuts.

"Why should you and I kill each other?"

"I don't know, I guess we should just go and kill everyone on the boat, right? Let's go. I'll get some guns and we'll just go and kill everyone."

"Wait, wait, man. You can't be for real. I mean, we can't just go and shoot everyone."

"Why not? Don't we need to save the country? Don't we need to keep fighting until they stop?"

"Well, that's not how we have a war."

"How is it then?"

"Well, we have to get an assignment and orders and all."

"Oh, who assigns the orders?"

"The general and then the captain, and you know all the other people in charge. Then they tell us soldiers what to do."

"Oh, so as long as somebody else tells you what to do, then you'll do it?"

"Right, I mean no, I mean—if a commander tells me to do something, then I have to do it."

"Have to?"

"Or I'll get shot."

"So you're basically owned by somebody?"

"Sort of."

"Like a slave?"

"Well, no. I mean I signed a contract."

"To be their slave or they would kill you if you don't abide by it?"

"Well, no, I mean, shit what in hell you tryin' to do to me?"

"I'm trying to find out what you are and how things work for you."

"Well, I'm not sayin' nothin' more. This is what they was talkin' about prob'ly you're just tryin' to confuse me. I know who I am, and I'm a soldier for the U.S. Army, and I'm proud of it."

"So you're admitting you're a slave?"

I don't say a word.

"A hired killer?"

I don't say a thing.

"A murderer?"

"Hey now, I never killed no one!"

"Right, right, not yet, but they're teaching you how to kill anyone they want you to kill, maybe some guy you don't know, or some woman, or maybe a little kid, or how about a dog who gets in your way, or better yet, don't look at any of their faces, just blow up rows of houses. But you're being paid, and you're fighting for your country, because god knows if you didn't kill these people, then they would come over to the good ol' U.S. of A. and kill us right?"

I wanta beat this guy to a pulp.

We sit without saying a word for a long time. Then he begins again.

"You don't belong to a cult, do you?"

I shake my head no.

"That's right, because cults convince their people that the most important thing is the religion or the group, and there is no group that you hold allegiance to, right?"

I shake my head no, still staring at the floor. Then I look up at him in amazement. That's so strange. Maybe he's right. But he's just waiting for me to give in. I look away.

"Cults expect you to do whatever they say, no matter what. And the army doesn't say that now, does it?"

I look down on the floor where there's a large crack.

"Remember all those guys who used to dress up like Indian monks and try and catch people at the airport? Well, I helped to unbrainwash some of them, a lot of them actually." He wrinkles his brow for a second, and when he sees me looking, I look away. "Those poor people, those lost people, who thought it was the way to help their life get off to a good start, they were told they would have spiritual enlightenment, but all they got was hard floors and little food. They had to give up their freedom, except for when the head guru gave them permission. Some of them got killed for leaving. But the real kicker is that they were told always that they should not listen to anyone who told them that what they were doing might be wrong. They were told that if someone tried to tell them they were wrong, then that person was probably a spy just trying to wreck their life."

"I knew a guy from high school who was in one of those cults, and he was just like you say. He was so skinny, and he worked his balls off." Shit. I wasn't gonna say nothin'.

"His parents and siblings must have been pretty upset."

I don't say a word.

"Oh well, it's all right. I know you've been trained to hate me."

"Hey, man, one of my best buddies is black—so there, I don't hate you 'cause you're different. I just don't see why you have to keep hassling me."

"You mean you're not racist?"

"No—I even have a Jewish friend back home."

"I'm sorry, I didn't mean to...."

"It's all right. I guess a lot of soldiers are that way. But I don't know if they really are because we all do everything together, you know, black, white, yellow, you know."

"What nationality are you?"

"American, blue blooded."

"I thought it was red-blooded American, as the saying goes."

"Just thought I'd put in a little humor, you know?"

"Yeah, right, haha. I'm Norwegian-American-Earthling."

"Earthling? What's that for? Aren't we all from Earth?"

"Sure, but that doesn't mean any of us remember it. I think it's probably the most important element of being here. I mean after all I went through—in the Vietnam War, or massacre, if you were to give an honest description. I was a Marine."

"No way. Not you. Why, you're nothin' but a...."

"Maybe you think so now, but you wouldn't have thought so if you'd seen me fight my way through the jungles and bombs of Nam. I killed a lot of people." He pulls his sleeve up and shows me his tattoos, with the dragon showing he was in a place that was a nightmare. I look and see how old they are, how old he is.

"You've seen some pretty heavy action then I guess."

"Pretty heavy. That's why I'm so determined to unbrainwash as many soldiers as possible. I don't want you to have to go through what I went through." His eyes are sunken and empty as he looks out the portal. He looks too old to have been in Nam.

"Are you sure it was Nam you were at? Not some other place that was just pretty hairy?"

"Why?"

"Well, if you pardon my sayin' so, you look a bit old for the battles over there."

"I'm only forty-five."

"Forty-five?"

"I know, I know, I probably look about sixty or so. But after a man kills someone, anyone, and then more than one, and then he wants to stop..., but if he stops he gets shot by his commanding officer, or else the so-called enemy."

"But they were the enemy."

"No, they weren't, we were trying to fight a war for other people, in the name of freedom, democracy and peace. Haven't you done any reading of the facts?"

"I've had classes about all this, you mean given by the military or something?"

"Well, sure. They'll tell you young ones anything. Don't you know I was brainwashed, too, and they're trying to do it to all the young boys now by showing them all kinds of violent cartoons and making soldiers into heroes."

"But can't you see that if people weren't willing to fight back in the beginning of this country, we wouldn't have what we have now. Don't you see that?"

"That is true, and I do agree that those people did do a great thing for us, but that's precisely my point. Things have gotten out of hand. People are fighting now just to fight. They fight for some nebulous country whose views and ideals are so scattered and contradictory that the only ones who push it to the hilt are the ones on top, so they get as many young men to fight for them as possible. Why don't these heads of state fight their own battles? Put them in their places. If they're so tough and powerful, let them do the fighting. But they can't. The power they have is power over people, the power to have millions of people murder and maim and lose their lives and souls for them. I was brainwashed just like you."

"Fuck you, man, I wasn't brainwashed, I went in with my own free will and everything. I been waiting for some action for a while now."

"Yeah, yeah, that's how I felt. But when I got over there it hit me. I realized that maybe it wasn't my free will. The media is a very powerful tool that our government has. When we got there, it was all blood and fire on flesh and guts, and you just never knew who was shooting at you, if you were lucky, and then when you saw the little boys and girls who were taught to fight for their lives. It all became so clear. I was just some idiot that the government had trained since birth to be their dumb little pawn. Their toy that they could dispose of when they were finished with. Either way, all you are is a dumb pawn. Someone to do whatever they want, and they don't even care."

"I'm nobody's pawn."

"Oh, I'm sorry, you don't answer to anyone?"

"Well, my captain and drill sergeant and, well...."

"Exactly. You do whatever they say, because that's what they trained you to do."

"But I went in under my own free will."

"Oh, really? Did you ever have any guns as a child?"

"Sure, every kid does."

"The girls?"

"Well, no, but why should they? They're never going to...."

"You got it. Do you remember all the cartoons with fighting heroes and all the guns and soldiers?"

"Yes, but how can that...."

"All little boys are taught that it's good to fight. Soldiers are taught that they have to beat up the bad guys, so as a kid they give you toy guns so you learn how to kill people and you learn to enjoy it."

"I never wanted to kill anyone."

"Then why are you in the army, Barney?"

***

Hundreds of shades of green shine and shadow in the cool jungle. There is water in a small deep pond fed by a long narrow river. Above it, a bustling waterfall cascades down from a tall mountain of rocks. Plants stick out from cracks. A bird lands near the water, waiting. The beautiful young maiden waits while Ruban stares. She says something in her native tongue that he doesn't quite understand. He looks at her queryingly. She motions him to come. He does. She grasps his hand tightly as they move quickly through the jungle. Then he hears the drumming sounds again.

Suddenly, a curtain of leaves opens up to them. Tthe elder who met them earlier smiles and reaches his hand to Ruban. Ruban enters through the door of a tremendous village. This village is a grand castle-like structure, made of white iridescent stone. It is surrounded by a fifty-foot wall, made of trees, cut down and roped together. The outside is covered with plants so thickly, the wall is invisible. Inside the clearing people dance around a bonfire. They are dressed in colorful feathers and woven clothes. But the women are bare-breasted, so the clothes are short enough to keep their legs cool and of course bare. Most people have their faces painted in brilliant colors. Some look like birds, some look like other strange animals.

As Ruban enters, everyone stares at him with curiosity. They crowd around him. In a friendly way they try to touch him. The elder introduces him to everyone, then they return to their dancing. Ruban is then taken to a small room in the fortress. There is a grass mat on the floor and a small window looking at the villagers. Ruban looks around wondering where the maiden has gone. The elder looks at him.

"Who are you?" Ruban asks in his broken tongue.

"The name my father gave me is Suscawacha."

Ruban stands up quickly. "That was my grandfather's name!"

"Yes, it still is."

"No, you can't be. He would have been over a hundred years old."

"Yes, I am 115 years now. Sit here—we must talk."

Soon a few young men and women enter with more suitable clothing for Ruban. The men help to undress him, though he struggles with this. He continues to smile with boyish wonder at the customs. Suscawacha waves his hand for the villagers to leave them once the women have poured the contents of a clay pitcher into two bowl-like cups, placing one in his hands, then one in Ruban's.

"How could you still be alive? People don't just live that long."

"I am here. I am alive."

"My father, your son, is well."

"I know this."

"He didn't want me to come here."

"I know this also."

"How can you know this?"

"I hear from the wind and the trees." He gestures towards the trees.

"The wind and the trees?"

"The trees speak to each other and tell of families and what any man wants to know."

"The trees?"

"The wind carries their thoughts to each other. This is why the wind changes direction, to carry these thoughts to each other. Then any man who asks can know of anything that is happening on this island."

"You mean South America?"

"South America is a small place on this island."

"What island are you talking about?"

Suscawacha draws a circle on the dirt floor, then a larger circle nearby. He draws eight other circles around the two first.

"This, our mother island, you may call it 'Earth.' Here's our little sister who is still asleep." He draws a small circle very close to the Earth.

"The moon?"

"Yes, moon."

"Why do you call Earth an island?"

"It is apart from its family but joined by the breath and light from its father, the Sun, as you call it here." He points with his stick.

"How do you hear what the trees say?"

"I hear. I ask. They tell me of many things. Many sad and terrible things that men do to our island—our mother. This is why you have been sent here."

"Sent here? I came of my own mind."

"We have been sending thoughts and dreams to you for many many years. Now you are here."

"Dreams? Thoughts?"

Suscawacha nods.

"In a way you were forcing me to come here then?"

"You did not come unless you wanted. You have important mission."

"What is it? I mean I now know you may have called me in some strange way that I still don't understand but what do you want me to do?"

"You will know this soon. First you must remember the ways of your people. We will have celebration for you."

"Celebration?"

"Yes. When the Sun touches the edges of our island, we will come and bring you to see many wondrous things. Things you have been dreaming of for many years."

"But you know the Sun doesn't really touch the ground, or, our island, as you call it, don't you?"

"The warm love of the Sun touches every part he sees. When our island turns, and the Sun moves his light away from us, we thank him for what he has given us today and pray that he will return tomorrow."

***

I sit in my bedroom on the end of the bed and wait for Mary to get out of the john. Why the hell do women always take so damn long in the john? Do they take naps in there or something?

Mary walks in the room wearing a killer black negligee. Every curve and crevice is outlined in sheer luxury and I'm pounding, just pounding. She acts coy, picking up some book from her night stand and lying down so her pretty little bottom is face up for me to enjoy. The book is underneath her just about, and her head is turned away from me. I don't see how she can read that book with her head like that, and I think she's trying to turn me on, which she has, desperately, but I'm still confused. Besides, she doesn't have her glasses on, and if I just peek over her shoulder and... the book is upside down! She really thinks I can't tell? Well, it's my turn. Five minutes and I'm done. I hop into bed, and she's pretending to sleep now. She must be telling me to climb inside. She loves it when I do that. But not this time—I'm so tired I can hardly keep my eyes open. On the other hand, I keep seeing her in that outfit, next to me, waiting for me and, she's just so beautiful, so, so beautiful. I reach over and stroke her arm, just slightly. She gets goose bumps. She may really be asleep, but then she is a pretty good actress. I don't want to play this game tonight. Tomorrow's a really big day. I look over at my desk. My papers are piled up. It took so long to organize that mess this morning. Looks real neat. I feel kind of peaceful, relieved just to look at all that work I've done. Oh, but let me just check and make sure I've got everything I need there. I begin to sit up, but she grabs my arm.

"Where you going, honey?"

"What?" I sound really dazed. "Oh, I have to check and make sure about something here."

"But I thought you did all that this morning."

"Yeah, well, I did, I think, but, come on, you know, I just have to make sure I have my presentation down. I just can't goof up."

"Fine." She snaps at me. I would have gone back to her. I thought she was asleep.

"I thought you were asleep."

"Right." She gets up and goes into the john again. Must be getting close to her period or something.

***

"Good morning, Mr. Colin. You're right on time. I'll let Mr. Sanchez know you're here," says a pretty old lady with white hair turned tightly up into a bun and wearing a

162

very sexy dress for a woman half her age. She gets on the horn and informs the superintendent of my arrival. After a few minutes he walks down the hall from his inner office. I watch him nonchalantly through the glass of the outer office doors he comes toward us. He has a slight limp. He carries a manila folder. I turn away slowly.

"Good morning, Mr. Colin." He reaches his hand toward me as I stand to greet him. "I'm so glad we finally have a chance to meet.

"Thank you, sir, I feel the same way."

"Call me Ron. And may I call you William?"

"Of course, all my friends call me that."

"Well, why don't we get going? I'm sure everything's set up now, isn't it, Wilma?" He looks over at the secretary, who's leaning over, showing her cleavage.

"Oh, why yes, sir, I just checked with Margaret and she said everything looks lovely."

"Good. Oh, and please hold all calls, will you?"

"Yes, of course, Mr. Sanchez."

We walk out the door and proceed down the corridor with the slight squeak of our shoes echoing off the lockers. We turn a corner, and my suit gets stuck on one of the lockers. I practically fall over, just missing a crash by bracing myself against the wall. Ron unsticks me, or whatever you'd call it, and just as he almost gets it off, or whatever he's doing, Wilma comes out trotting down the hall, startling Ron, who tears my suit. My new new suit that I bought for today is torn. They both stand there looking at me and then looking at each other. He looks at her cleavage, and they look back at me and my tear. He sort of straightens my suit.

"I'm sorry for tearing your suit. Are you all right?"

"Yeah sure. It can be sewn." I'm real hot headed now. I feel like shouting, what stupid imbeciles. I could've gotten myself undone if they'd let me, but instead they had to try and help in a stupid way. What am I gonna do? Walk in there with a ripped suit? I have to calm down first and foremost. I have to get a hold of myself and try and relax. Just center myself and look inside and try and see the light and breath, that's it, breath.

"Shall I try and sew it for you?" Wilma touches my arm.

"No, no, thank you. I just feel sort of silly wearing a torn suit into an important business meeting."

"Well, don't you worry about that. I'll just walk in front of you and seat you right away. I'll take off my jacket, and then you can follow, all right?"

"Sure, sounds like a good plan, and thanks."

"For what?"

"For getting me unstuck." I straighten my hair out since I'd slicked it and tied it back for the occasion. I hope people in here are not too old fashioned as far as hair goes. I think long hair is back in style again, anyway.

We enter a large conference room with long redwood tables and cushioned chairs waiting the occupants. If the tables were removed, the room could hold probably two hundred chairs, for a meeting like a school board meeting, like this one, or, no, not like this one, but like a PTA meeting.

"Good morning, ladies and gentlemen," Ron Sanchez says graciously around the room. Several respond in same. "I'd like to introduce you to Mr. William Colin—a math teacher at the Academy. As you well know he will be giving you a presentation this morning. Pardon me if I take off my jacket. No need to be formal here. We're a friendly group, aren't we?" Several look around in a sort of daze. There are two maids or servants at one end of the conference room pouring coffee and assembling plates with rolls and fruit. "Oh, I see that Wilma has taken care of everything. She is a wonderful secretary. I hope you all helped yourselves."

People still look stunned as though there is something wrong, terribly wrong here. I slip off my suit coat still twinging from the tear. I rest it over what I assumed was to be my chair. I thought he—Ron pulled it out for me.

"Did you want me to sit here?" I ask quietly.

"Sure, sure, sit anywhere you like?" He speaks loudly.

Finally a man walks over and introduces himself to me. I thought I had egg on my face or something.

"Hello, William, I'm Stanley Stinabakel. I used to teach high school, but now I'm Vice Principal of West High." He grabs my hand in a hearty shake. "You'll have to excuse the group. This was not planned very well. I mean, it looks real nice, but the problem is that somebody forgot to let us all know what was going on until this morning at about eight-thirty."

"Woosh. I'm sorry if this is an inconvenience for any of you."

"Nonsense. We were all just doing our mindless jobs in our little cubicles." Stanley walks around the table arrogantly.

"Why don't you continue the introductions, Stanley?" Sanchez blurts out, shattering the dense air. Everything seems white and heavy. The faces look taut and puffy. Everyone sits staring at me as if I'm supposed to do some song-and-dance routine.

"Well, then, shall we start with Miss Crabits?" Stanley leans over the table and touches her arm. She jerks away. Her brow furls and her nose wrinkles. Her skin begins to luster as though she just lost ten years.

"Hello, Miss Crabits," I say politely

"Hello, William. Call me Elizabeth, will you?"

"Why of course, Elizabeth." I beam.

"Uh, she's President of the PTA, (and about fifty years old)," Stanley whispers.

165

"Why, she looks twenty," I say half gasping.

"Uh, this is Butch Bright, and you know him of course."

"Yes, the Dean of the Academy, but I never really had a chance to talk with you before now, sir. How are you?" I reach over to shake his hand, which he folds under his arm.

"What's this I hear about some radical new 'teen' project. You been out smokin' that stuff again?"

"Now wait just a minute, Mr. Bright. That's a pretty hefty accusation to be throwing around. I thought you didn't even know Mr. Colin."

"Well, not personally, but look at him. That 'in' look, that long hair, those new ideas. He's a hippie if I ever saw one. And I know what you hippies do on your days off—smoke that pot!"

"I—I'm no—"

"Uh, Mr. Bright, will you come with me, please?" They go outside, and after a few minutes Sanchez comes back in, alone.

"He had no right to say any of that to you."

"I—I'm just so shocked. I really don't know if I can do this today."

"Nonsense, Wil, we don't take him seriously. He's just a fanatic racist military nutzoid. He doesn't know who he can trust. Drives his wife crazy, too."

"Are you going to stay, William?" Sanchez asks me gently.

Well, do you think I have half a chance?"

"Ah, well, what do you folks think?"

"Well, if you want my opinion, I'd say forget the introductions and get on with the presentation."

"Well," said Ms. Stewart, "well said. Does everybody agree?" Everyone either nods or says yes to Sanchez.

"Would you like something to drink, Wil? Perhaps a

sweet roll? We've really gone all out for this special occasion."

"Probably later, but for now all I want is a glass of water with ice, please."

"Bessie, will you get William here a pitcher of ice water and a glass." One of the servers who was fiddling earlier leaves and returns with the items requested. I thank her and proceed.

"Well, why don't you get started now, please," Sanchez says with a pleasant smile.

"Well, of course, sir. Good morning to all of you. I'd like to first of all, acquaint all of you with the very small but well-equipped television station called WKPP. It has been owned and operated by a man called Mr. Sam Dobelson for the last five years. He started the station, but has been unable to keep it financially afloat now for the last two years. So, needless to say, he's now selling it."

"What is the selling price?" asks a man with a small head and a piece of paper he's carefully taking notes on.

"Twenty-five thousand."

"Sheesh. That's pretty high isn't it?"

"No, not when you see all the equipment he's got in there."

"You know a lot about equipment, then?"

"Well, no, but I'm having a reputable serviceman assess all the equipment. Plus, I forgot to say that I did talk him into lowering his price about seven thousand dollars."

"Well, then we really don't know what shape this equipment is in, do we?" says one blonde with very curly hair up high on her head and glasses that look like they're about to fall off the end of her nose.

"No, not exactly, but I do have the man checking the equipment right now, and he's going to call me when he gets the report. Plus Mr. Dobelson said that everything is in perfect working condition and if it isn't, we could knock the repairs off the price of the station or he'd have it fixed for us—our choice."

"That's still a pretty steep price. How did you intend upon paying for it?" asks the man taking notes.

"And what do you want us for?"

"Well, please, of course, the price is perhaps high. But not compared to others I've inspected." I took a sip of iced water.

"Perhaps so, but they have followings. Look at QMAF in Maryland. They sold upwards in the millions."

"Yes, and they had continuous revenues coming in prior to and proceeding the sale and their ratings went up. Now I know that we have pretty low ratings and close to no revenue coming in at present, but—" I'm cut off again.

"So what's your gimmick, William?" Stanley taps his pencil.

"My gimmick? Yes, well, I had thought of one, but not in so many terms as you have here. I mean, all or at least 90% of the programming can and will be done by students of mine, and special programs we can do with other classes and schools."

"The biggest market of all—" Stanley taps his pencil.

"That's exactly what I was thinking." I sit back a moment beaming. Their faces seem to change from one expression to another like a kaleidoscope in the light.

"I see you've been doing your homework." says Ms. Stewart.

"Yes, well, I've been working on this idea for quite some time now. I'd like to answer the second question that was posed to me earlier, about what I'm hoping will come of this meeting." I look around to see if anyone is opposed to my proceeding. "To answer the question completely, I'd like to tell you that, being a teacher, I have always fancied the ideas of students—especially the ones who are having some problems in school." I search their changing moods. "The path I'd like to take is this: There can be videos made and written for students. By having students write, act, direct, edit and produce their own programs, it'll give them an extremely valuable skill. They can further pursue it in college if they wish. But there is a two-fold purpose and effect here—the work they do will serve as an outlet for the wide array of emotional situations that they all go through during high school."

"May I ask a question?" asks the confident looking man.

"Yes, of course, sir."

"Aren't you a math teacher?"

"Math and science."

"Well, then, shouldn't this project be given to the art department or something, a little closer to home?"

"I beg your pardon, sir, but don't you have another full time career besides being on the board?"

"Yes, but I'm still in administration."

"You have a good point, Jack, but it is William's idea. I wouldn't feel right giving the project to somebody else. It wouldn't be right."

"Oh, of course not, sir," Jack says quickly.

"Well, so the bulk of the programming can be created and etc. by students. We can also sell portions of programs to different groups. But within all this, the way I'd prefer you people to help me, or the school district, to be exact, is to help me financially, and of course we would be helping each other. If you could back me by purchasing a portion of the station, then you, or the district would be part owners and operators. This would in turn give you a percentage of the profits."

"Providing there will be profits," says Stanley.

"I've had a contract drawn up, and I took the liberty to make copies for all of you so that you can all examine it carefully, of course. There probably will be alterations in this, so I've called it a rough draft, as you can see at the top there. I have saved enough to put a down payment on the station, but I will need you, the school board, or another backer for the secure commitment. Since I will be purchasing the station with the full commitment for the students, I think that you will want to be a part of this, also. Oh, here is some more data about the station. And, if Mr. Sanchez will permit, I'd like to check in at your office and see if the repairman has been to the station and can give me the information we've been waiting for."

"Oh, yes, I almost forgot that I'd told her to hold all my calls. Go on ahead. I think we've heard enough, unless there are more questions here."

"Is there a mock program set up and a breakdown of costs and possible revenues?" asks the little man.

"Yes, it's in this packet of information about the station. Thank you all for your time and patience." As I get up and pack up, everyone claps lightly, as an honest appreciation. I think my face is flushing.

***

All is black. I need to switch on the lights, but I can't find the switch. I feel the panel. There's a red light, so tiny I can hardly see it beyond the black. Small pieces of material, almost like plastic, but that went out years ago. Metal, cold metal probably, or else wood. They don't pollute the environment as much when they're trying to disintegrate. But then, who cares when these ships get sent off into space for their final runs. Switch, switch, where's the bloody switch? Wait, wait, I've got a pen light—thank you, Suzie.

DOOOOOOOGHGHGHGHGHGHGHG SWACK!

"What in hell? Well, at least the lights outside are on." Now I can see almost everything
on the panel. I look around the screen to see who's opened

170

the switches in the hangar. Ah, above me. "Must be the night crew. Yo! Fellows! Whast new on the front loin?"

"Not much, Captain Place. Heard you wanted to roll a few diggers. Where've you been for the past millennium?"

"Oh, just back home having a baby."

The three men sitting in the window of the flight crew, opposite Cpt. Place, start cheering.

"We didn't know you were pregnant."

"Ya, ya, that's how it usually works."

"Who's your partner tonight?" the first man asks.

"I couldn't get anyone, so I guess I'll play against the computer or one of you chaps. I have a match with Marthy Salis tomorrow at noon. That's why I'm here now—thought I should give 'er a once over... I'm probably a bit rusty."

"'S like riding off a sled. You'll beat 'em no matter what."

"Thanks, Ralph, but I'm afraid I'm very rusty now."

"Well, we're almost ready for you, so you can test her out."

"Say, Cap, what'd ya have, a boy or a Brongo?" asks Hilbo, the second in command at the panel.

"No wise cracks, they're getting old, centuries old. Besides my old man is only half Brongo. So my little girl is a quarter. And she is really a wonderful darling."

"Does she throw fire when she breathes?"

"That's an old wives' tale. Brongos only breathe fire during love making."

The crew laughs and then shuts off their vocal capacity so I don't hear. But I see them talking, probably about Brongos. So ridiculous that prejudices should continue to exist in 1997. Oh well, someday they'll learn. But at least they keep them to themselves. The voices are clicked back on.

"What'd you name her?" asks Ralph.

"Well, we haven't done that as yet—thought we'd wait until she's shown some of her spirit before we find what her name is."

"How long'll that be?" Why is Ralph the only one of the three who speaks to me? Probably 'cause he's in charge and they're shy or something.

"Oh, the midwife says it takes about two months." I press all the switches on and strap myself in for take-off. Ah—it's coming back to me now. "Ready when you are."

"Stand by," the low voice of cliché utters out my speaker like water into a glass. The immense door in front of me slowly opens to display the heavens' matter and energy. I can barely see the Earth to my left as the station walls cover half of it. The sun is behind the Earth, except for a tiny crescent, soon disappearing. I press the final switch to open my power. Carefully, I steer my ship toward the front of the station, checking all systems as I go. "After all, a new mother can't be too careful," I remind myself.

"Ready for take-off, unless, what did you say?"

"Sorry, nothing, just talking to myself. Go ahead, please."

"Five, four, three, two, one, take off!"

I press all the buttons on the front panel under my tips and pull down the throttle till the rockets thrust me forward deep into space. I circle the space station, GRHS18, five or six times to get the feel of the equipment again and then I head out.

"H208, come in H208, are you still with us?"

"Of course I am. Where the hell else would I be?"

"Come on, Cap, don't be hard on Naker. He's just following codes. Besides, you know there's always some risk."

"That was Naker? You never spoke before, Naker. Welcome aboard. And of course I know there's some risk. After all, gents, I'm a new mother you know. And sorry, Naker, these good old female hormones are fooling around in my system here, if you know what I mean."

"No problem, Cap. We know you're human. So are we. So what's your locale anyway?"

"I'm near the outer blaster unit, just spinning her around for a few. Trying to make sure I still have the touch. You know?"

"Sure, sure. Hey, you must have had some labor or something."

"Most births go that way."

"Well, how did it go?"

"One minute—I'm viewing something inside here, like, I've never seen before, I—what is this?"

"The new twister?"

"Twister? Looks like a black hole or something."

"Great, that's what it's supposed to look like. Now fly the ship directly inside, aim for the center."

"Are you sure about this... looks pretty real."

"Believe me, it's simulated. If it was real you'd a-been sucked up a minute ago, and we'd be out the back door."

"I—I gotta pull back for a minute. I can't follow this course. Why did this thing get put in here?"

"It's like a new challenge. We'll program your computer to give you the menu." A few beeps are audible, and then my screen switches to a miniature of what I thought I'd seen. The panel shows a grid of the top, then turns it to the side, then to the end of the funnel. It's a hologram. The computer shows me there are almost limitless levels of skill required—like a real black hole, limitless. "Go on in. You're not gonna realize the magnitude of this beauty unless you let go and climb in."

"Well, where would you suggest I start?"

"Just follow the yellow lights, just follow the yellow lights.... "

I turn the ship inward, holding this creepy feeling back from my judgement, trying to go deeper into myself as I go into this, this, thing. Yellow light to my right, I turn towards it. A splashing glow like a firecracker of olden days shines before me, and into the center flashes another yellow light. I turn into it till an immense hand of blazing pink appears before me opening into a beautiful blue rose. The lines of the hand diminish, creating the edges of the petals till a whisper of yellow hits the screen, speaking to me an another language, another century but not a visual image of a flashing yellow light, but a speaking tone opening and closing its sound. I stare outward not knowing where to move or turn, so I guess it adjusts to flashes of yellow within each petal. Maybe I'm supposed to be using my intuition to know which flash to follow, but I can't figure it out. I head into the strongest flash and immediately they disappear, leaving a very tiny yellow flash from my left blinking ever-so-slowly. But I quickly turn my ship into its direction till it disappears into a blackness I've never seen before. I hold still, very still. Then a sprinkle of lights, none of them yellow, fall across the screen almost waiting for me to begin the chase—but I'm frozen until quite a tiny dot enlarges. It becomes quite bright and then moves across the screen, leaving a flaring tail curled in the loop de loop that fizzles like a sparkler into a single tiny yellow flashing light. I turn toward it quickly. It continues to flash and flash and flash and flash as I come closer or the simulated action zooms forward. But here before me glows a strange-looking ship. This is where the flashing is coming from? But it almost looks dead. How could it have been causing all that strange light? But what am I thinking? This is a hologram—I think.

"GRHS18, do you read me? Come in, GRHS18, please."

Nothing happens. This is real strange. What am I supposed to do? Yellow light usually means caution, or help needed. Maybe they're real people or something. I try and communicate with them first with my signals. No answer. I open the visuals to the ship itself. On board there are people, or things that don't look human, or even close. I press the scanning information to read the health of the crew, because they look hurt or something. They're just large spheres located in sort of cubicles, but not moving. They have openings in the front—I think, to give out vibrations and take in vibrations, but I can't get a reading as to the health of these things. Perhaps they can't be read with our equipment.

"If this is a game, please switch off now, or else give me a reading of the station GRHS18 please, computer, and/or space station GRHS18—"

"Yes, Cap?"

"Didn't you read me before? This is an emergency!"

"Is it?" Ralph says mysteriously.

"Well, I think it is, isn't it?"

"It can be as real as you want it to be."

"So this is the new game or something?"

"From what I heard, it tries to be as real as your subconscious mind believes these visions to be."

"But how can it read my mind?"

"To tell you the truth, it brings forth a myriad of images as you saw already, right?"

"Well, yes... you mean these aren't preprogrammed images?"

"No, not at all. I have no idea what you saw or are

seeing right now. In fact we at this station cannot see what you see. It's all up to you."

"How odd. But how is it that the computer can read my mind, did you say?"

"Well, I think it has to do with magnetics. Your heartbeat and general energy vibrations are altered with each image."

"Incredible. Well, thanks. Guess I'm off."

"You want to continue?"

"Does it possibly alter into the more positive realms, depending upon the person's fear and intensity levels?"

"Did you see anything that you thought was beautiful?"

"Well, sure. I saw a tremendous rose whose petals were tipped in light."

"That tested your sense of beauty."

"Whoosh, this is almost spooky... some machine knowing how I feel about things. Thanks, guys."

"What're ya gonna do?"

"I'll stay on track for a while. What time is it, by the... just a minute, I have a watch right here, but, no, it can't be."

"How long have I been up here?"

"Ten minutes."

"It feels like, it feels like, I don't know."

"That computer has a way of doing that to people."

"Geez, guys, is this the only game anybody plays nowadays?"

"Most of the time, Cap. But I'm sure your opponent will go to the old games if you want."

"Just to warm up a bit. I mean it's been four months."

"Righto. Plugging into frequencies." The tornado shape of the hologram disappears into space, leaving two blue beacons for the "older" games.

Several red lights clustered together hold a tiny opening for ships to enter. As I steer my ship, Alexandra, through the lights, the red lights part. Somehow, this time, this occurrence is a beacon to me that safety is surrounding my life, my aura. Immediately I switch on the rays. A blue groglet appears. I carefully and quickly touch the blue light on my board, but the groglet flies off before I come near. Great way to start a game. I fly in and out trying to build a pyramid of the various colors. I'm also trying to move fast enough to move these odd shapes before they rush headlong into each other, creating a wall between me and my work.

My time is almost up, and I have barely scratched the surface. Far from some sort of container. If I don't finish soon, all my radioactive wastes will be released and destroy some innocent territories.

***

"GI Joe... American Hero!" sings a private while sun-bathing on a blue chaise lounge. His long toes reach into the water, and circles form, creating more and more circles, bouncing on each other and onto the walls of the pool. Two men and two women lie face down on their beach chairs.

"Great diversion, ain't he?" says a burley fellow, whose gut sags the chair low enough to miss the red tile floor by an inch.

"Sure. So where'd you say the captains are?" answers the other guy. The women are listening intently.

"I'm not absolutely sure, because I think they move them every night. But last night I could swear it was Lieutenant Laker walking by our porthole."

"How could ya tell, Jack?"

"I don't know fer sure, Lake, but I thank it sounded like him. So I looks out the window and shore 'nuf it looks just like him, from the rear, that is."

"Watch out what you watchin' there. You ain't one

o' them funny type o' guys now, are ya?" says a woman with black lines for eyebrows.

"Hey, don't you worry 'bout me none. I am totally homogenous, I mean homosapious. Besides I was tryin' ta find the Lieutenant Laker. So it was just like I said, see, Lieutenant Laker."

"Do you say 'Lieutenant Laker' every time?"

"Sure, sure, sorry, but anyway, Laker—there, you happy?"

"Thanks," says the woman in a red suit who hasn't said anything important yet.

"Now let me tell you all. See, I was watching Laker's ass, that's all. Now don't look at me like that, see. Laker is always complaining about his hemorrhoids and stuff. That's why I figure he's got such a flat ass. And I mean flat. Even if I was one of those funny guys, I'd think his ass was ugly. I likes my women with nice rounded asses. But Laker, well, I think God put all of Laker's rear into his front or something."

"Shut up, guys. Here comes the guard."

Three guards who rotate around the captives at the water and who relax among the soldiers, as sort of spies, move closer to the group. The three keep an even eye on the captives—what they feel and do. Commanding officers are still kept completely free from the others, so as not to start a riot or something, like throw a wrench into the deprogramming of the soldiers. Nightly the officers move from one room to another, guided by the soldiers who have them gagged and bound. They'd been in for group therapy and intensive deprogramming sessions. After two months the officers, or most of them, still held on to their old beliefs that America was the best program, has and is the best business, the best form of government, in the world, at least on the American ships. These same ideas were spoken in different languages and with the same energies on the ships of other countries. The continuing fallacy: "our country is the best." Whatsoever the president, congress, prime minister, king, dictator, etc. says and does is, for the majority, absolutely the right thing. Every soldier is certain that some evil foreign power has kidnapped them in order to overthrow their precious government. They feel they must attempt an escape and fight for their country and to the death.

Tiny black and white players wait for my every move. They believe in me completely. They will do whatever my hand and mind commands them to do. I may squash one, or a million, when I am angry enough at my opponent. The only goal is winning. For me to command and be obeyed by those stupid little plastic things that once thought they were free, is my breadth, though they're all expendable. They wait like statues for my word. So when I get mad, really mad at one of those other 'leaders,' and won't do what I tell him, I just command all of my guys to massacre him and his peons. Why not? Anyway, if the idiot doesn't listen to reason, then they should all be killed. If he didn't want to be stubborn and have to do everything differently than I tell him is best, then, well, he obviously want to play some other game. No problem, I'll show him who's better. I'll show him who's bigger, who's got more power. Every one of my guys is willing to do anything I say. They'll get hacked up, shot up, tortured, drowned, for me. All for me. I must be great.

"Have you all read it?" I ask the officers all sitting in neat rows. They look up at me and then around at each other. Nobody wants to be the first to speak—as I figured.

"Come on, aren't you all just a little curious as to who wrote this little gem?"

"He probably did," whispers one to another.

"No, I really didn't." I have excellent hearing.

"It was written by one of your fearless leaders. It was in his memoirs. Found after his death."

"Who wrote it?" a voice shouts out.

"Doesn't matter anyway. There's not one fuckin' thing we can do about it, is there?"

***

"Okay, Ralph, everything's loaded onto the trucks," spurts a small white haired woman of about sixty.

"Great. Let's check the radio. 23, check in please."

"This is 23. What time have ya got?"

"Three sixteen, exactly. Set?"

"Roger, Ralph, we're set."

"Number 16, check in time."

"Ya, I Roger. What time ya got?"

"Three sixteen and twenty seconds."

"Roger, Ralph, I love it. We're ready whenever you say."

Ralph goes on down the line of all twenty trucks and their radios. He considers the fact that in every state and country, the very same thing is going on or has just occurred within the last 24 hours.

The trucks, carrying Ralph's 'baby,' head out for the homes and small buildings, in the dark. Soon they'll be part of a plan to create more light than ever before.

"Ralph?" asks the white haired woman, Ruby, "what about the other countries? Are we gonna do this for them, too?"

"Ruby?"

"Yes, Ralph?"

"Can you keep a secret?"

"Better than a military agent."

"Ruby, this same thing that we're doing here is happening everywhere in the world—everywhere it's dark that is."

"Are you serious?"

"Yup. Everywhere in the world that had lights to begin with. I mean we can't put where they had no electricity before, you know."

"Oh, no, 'course not."

"Things are going to look very different for a lot of people."

"But, Ralph, this doesn't seem to sound like it'll benefit those poorer countries, or the ones where it's hot all the time."

"Well, then, maybe we'll have to build a reading room for them, somewhere close to home."

"A reading room?"

"Yeah, Ruby. You know how hard it is on the eyes to read by lantern all the time."

***

Ralph sits in his bed, full of energy and vigor—though he's been up all night.

"Geez, shouldn't have had all that coffee last night."

He gets up and switches on the television on his dresser. A newscaster reports: "There is something amazing in the air. This morning, over fifty thousand people in the area woke up with something new and exciting over their heads. In fact it was primarily found on their roofs."

Ralph, who'd lain back down and tried to doze, suddenly realizes that it's near nine o'clock—time to be at work. He jumps back out of bed and scrambles into the shower. Under the steamy falls he mentally outlines who he must call and then plans to keep everything very hush hush. Did they remember to cover their tracks from the trucks? Should he have the drivers all turn the mileage back on the trucks? Are the trucks parked in their original spots? But most importantly, are all these people going to be able to keep their mouths shut about what they've done and simply trust? It is an awful lot to ask from people who've known him as only a back room kind of old professor type.

It's especially tricky when their jobs are all at stake and their futures are, hopefully, very bright.

***

"Turmoil is running rampant in the streets. But the ones we fear the most are those who have the guns. The governments are falling apart. They've lied for centuries just to keep the masses in control. I think it's time we had a meeting with the ones on top."

"But, William, are you sure this is the time?" asks Sascha.

"Can you think of a better one?"

William struggles with his sheets, which are practically tied around his waist. Mary is awakened from her sleep by his thrashing.

"No, NO!" William sits up.

Mary sits up and encircles him with her arms.

"It's all right, honey. What were you dreaming?"

"I was, I was dreaming of violence, violence in the future. It's so hard to imagine."

"Hard to realize you mean?"

"Yeah." William sits quietly for a long time. After a while he turns and looks out the window to see the sun just beginning the climb into the sky.

"You have a meeting today with the board again, don't you?"

"Yup."

"Why don't you try and get a few more dreams in before you have to deal with them, huh?"

"Dreams?" His eyes widen.

"Sweet dreams. Dreams of what you'd like the world to be."

"Well, no, I think—no."

"Do you need to go over a few things beforehand?"

"Well, I don't think so. I mean I have all the contracts and program outlines, the bank statements and the, the, the...."

"You're really tired still. What about some yoga?"

"Ya." William crawls out of bed and onto a prelain mat.

He begins a few postures and meditates as well. Then he begins, "Mary?"

"Ya?"

"Would you mind if we just meditated for a few together?"

"Well, of course not." She takes in a big breath and rises part of the way, crawling onto the mat with him. They both move to the lotus position, facing each other. Long deep breaths move in and out of each. They concentrate on their inner light. After a short while, a bright golden and white light hovers between them.

William's mind changes position and floats to a different space, a different country where he is walking around and talking to people who are doing many different things. A minstrel is walking around inspiring people with laughter. How odd a world it really would be if its inhabitants were actually doing what they wanted.

***

You wake up to the sound of drums deep in the jungle. You are still trying to become accustomed to the lack of plumbing and electricity, as well as the 'modern' methods of hunting. You get up off your mat of grass and look out your tiny opening—a primitive window. You hear drums but cannot see where they come from.

That old alarm clock is blaring, blasting my ear drums out. I hear the birds, I know it's morning. So why do I keep this old thing. I slam the snoozer button. But I can't go back to sleep, not for only ten minutes. Those guys were outa their minds. What a noble way of wrecking the day. Wake up with a bugle in your ear and then try and go back to sleep? For ten minutes! Absurd.

But on and on it goes, nobody questions the logic of
something so crazy. I'm going to try and get up. Or maybe
just snooze. If I get up all the way, then I won't need to
snooze. Oh, hell, here it goes again. Slam it down again.
Oops, I missed. I sit up and shut up, or no, that's not what I
was going to do. I was gonna shut it off manually. I do that.
My eyes get their rub down, along with the rest of the head
parts. I stretch slightly. I lie down again. Put my right leg
into the air and stretch it slowly. Relax, relax. Strain and
pain. Set it down, crossing it over, pulling the other muscles
of my thighs. Relax, relax. I go back and forth between the
two legs before letting myself relax again. I breathe in the
prana left over from my forefathers and their bad deeds.

I sit up slowly and reach for my thick beach towel
that's sitting on the chair next to the bed. I fold it up and
set it next to my mats on the floor. I go into the plow
position, meditating on my chakras from the tail bone up to
my head top. At each point I see a spiral of light becoming
larger and larger, pulling in energy from the universe. At
my heart chakra I try and see the sun here so I become
completely at peace. It looks like what I see at night when
I'm just falling asleep. Just below my vision a sun seems to
rise, but it falls below, always below my straight-on vision.
The heart chakra is where my E.S.P. develops.

At the center of the back of my neck, on my spine, is
where my next chakra is located. This has a direct
relationship with my desires, what I want, ask for and
receive. Whatever I accept for myself on a mental level
manifests as a physical experience. We've all been taught to
ask for what we want, nicely, and aloud, and not just in our
thoughts. I see the whirling rays. It relaxes my throat in the
morning air.

I uncurl my legs from over my head, lingering in the
air as my spine poops out, sauntering along down. My heart
barely pumps. I am more relaxed. I turn over to stretch

conversely. With my fingers and palms down, my fingertips touch the top of my shoulders, though they're flat on the ground. I rise up like a push up, but instead I bend backwards, away from the floor, always keeping my belly on the floor. When the tension becomes too great, I slowly lower myself down. I remember when that pretty little yoga instructor had us all doing these poses. Sometimes I floated off to sleep. I look at each chakra, mentally again, but this time I see each color. Red, orange, yellow, green light blue, dark blue, and purple. The dark blue one, for my third eye, will someday show me a world without evil. The attraction of opposites is only to cancel each other out. For only that which is of god will manifest into the only truth we see or experience. The final chakras, at the top of my head, the place where hats and yamakas are worn, shows the brightest light, the strongest energy and receptor of the spiritual light in the universe. Like an antenna, it pulls in all the love and power we will ever need on this plane. The royal purple color, chosen for royalty, probably for our ancient memories of the truths of who we really are. The reasons we are all here. But now I better get on with things. I have plenty to do today.

I walk into the kitchen and turn on the faucet for a long time while I sit on the receptacle in the lavatory. I do have plenty of energy now, but I still have to take my mornings slow so I don't burn out again. I need the chance to take in all the spiritual energy that I can get.

I swallow a great quantity of ice cold water from the kitchen sink after I'm out of the john. Birds are singing, but not quite as happily as an hour or so ago. How can that be? Maybe I'm dreaming.

My horse, Nancy, waits for me to feed her before we leave for work. On our way in, she slows down to sip from a stream. We arrive in town, and I tie her to a pole in front of the building, but very loosely. I check to see that there's

water in the trough nearby. Other horses drink from it. I
pump the well to fill it. The roads are bricks and stones.
They get dirty from the horses every day. I remember what
Grandpa used to say about the big cities of the olden days,
where the streets and sidewalks were so dirty trash would
blow up into your face. Some of the sidewalks that had
started out white got so grey from lack of rain and too much
pollution that you couldn't tell the black pavement from
the sidewalks. We spray our streets down every day, even in
winter. Some of the older or slower folks really enjoy taking
care of the streets and parks. I don't quite understand it,
but I guess some people just love to clean. I'm no slob, but I
have things that are more interesting to me than cleaning.

I guess what Grandpa said about the pollution—air
pollution was part of the whole problem, especially in that
state everyone said was gonna fall into the ocean. That's
where the sky looked grey all the time, even on sunny days
or after an angry storm. I wonder if it's still that way. I
wonder if the people over there ever got the air cleaned up. I
know they stopped the factories, cars and electric plants.
Oh, those people took a long time to get over all that
radiation left from the experiments and daily x-rays as well
as all the bombs they set off when the Big Change was going
on.

I should probably try and find out more about
what's going on in the world today. I could read the
newspaper or watch telly. I could listen to the trees or the
ocean waves.

"Oh, uh, sorry, everyone," I say to a group of people
sitting around a large conference table. I know this isn't a
real problem, but we did all agree to be on time, especially
for meetings. Oh well, so I blew it again. I'm sure everybody
will want to grill me. I sit down in my usual chair. I put my
briefcase on the long oblong table. Who's the chairman
today, I wonder.

"You are," answers Matailda to my unspoken question.

"Sorry, I forgot. It was a strange weekend. I know I have no excuse. What can I say? I won't do it again. Holy people are usually pretty moody. Do you all forgive me?" Nobody looks at me. They didn't hear me at all. "Did anyone hear me?" No one looks up. They all read their notes. "I'd like to call this meeting to order. Listen up, everyone." They still ignore me. This is weird. Are they ignoring me? Did someone slip me some drugs? Am I dreaming? "What in hell is going on here!" All right, I have a gem. I think they're all just kidding. "All right, joke's up now. I call this meeting to order." I wait for two whole seconds, and then I walk out. I get on top of my horse and ride off with her. I don't need this. All I really want to do is create. Other people have a knack for business and service-type things. Not me. Sometimes I wish I did, but really. I want to do something different for a while. I want to, to sculpt from clay or stone, or both.

I trot over to Mrs. McGillicutty's store and pick up some items for dinner and tomorrow. I know that I'm going to be working for quite a long time—on this thing. I'll work well into the night.

In the basement of my house is a very large vat of clay that my grandmother left me when she died. She knew how much I loved playing with it. She gathered little bits of it whenever we passed by a drying spring. She took it home and kneaded it for several hours. She pulled all the stones out of it and saved the gems. Only the finest chunks of clay were saved and stored for me. They've been sitting inside this stone clod vat for almost thirty years.

I scoot out an old table from the webs and twigs blown in from years. I sweep it off. I carefully open the stone lid. It sounds like wind blowing right from it. Maybe Grandma is happy that I'm finally gonna use it. I dig a wet

187

pile from the center. It almost feels alive, warm, and almost moving. I set it down from fear. No fear necessary, no fear necessary. I open the windows. They squeak like screams of death. Where are my thoughts going? I don't think this way normally. Or do I? It must be the clay. I know that when I don't know something then I get scared, or maybe it's just the not understanding something that scares me. I suppose there should be some things that I should be afraid of, like wild bears and sharks. I hear some quiet music in the background. The minstrels must be on their way into town for dinner. Has that much time passed? I think I'll follow them with my horse.

I change my mind and pull out a chair that was stuck in a corner for a good long time, I'm sure several years. I brush it off. I pull the string above the table so the light pops on. I pull the chair under the table. I slam my hand into the clay on the table. What am I here for, to play with my hands? Dad used to harp about what a genius I was as an infant in none other than this stuff—this sloppy, gloppy, hard and soft mud. I catch myself staring at it for a long time. It begins to look familiar. It's Grandpa! Well, I'll be. I've sculpted this hunk of rot into....

"No, you haven't! Now get back to real work. Like I always say, early to bed, early to rise."

"Yes, yes, I know, Grandpa. But I've tried so many times to be good in business. I just don't seem to have the knack for it. I just thought I'd try for a little while, you know, to sculpt like Dad always told me I could."

"This ruddy muck and mire? Your grandmother used to swoon and sway over your talents. Looked pretty average to me."

"Oh, Albert, it was not. Our grandchild always had genius." The clay changes into her likeness.

"Grandma? Is that you?"

"Sure is, Sweetie."

"How did you get here?"

"Oh, I've been waiting for you to open this vat of clay for a long time. It means a lot to me to see you here."

"You mean to feel the light of day?"

"Oh, Albert, hush up. Can't you see I'm having a conversation with our grandchild? You never did respect the proper ways to speak, did you?"

"All right. But I still say business is better for the mind."

"You big lug, business is better, business is better. If business is so much better, how come it never got you anywhere?"

"Grandma, now don't be so harsh on Grandpa. He's doing the best he can. Remember that Yoko Ono song you turned me on to a while back?"

"Yes, dear, you mean the one where she says she wants her man to rest tonight?"

"Right, right. So anyway, Grandma, glad you're here. But I really don't know if I'm that good or even want to go into the arts, or go back to my old job, or back to school or something. I just don't know."

"You are a natural at clay, Plubard. Don't ever give it up and I promise you you'll be successful. Even if you go into something else, never give up the clay. Lay your hands over the clay and feel the coarse weave of energy mixed with elasticity. You need but only ask."

"What do you mean? This mud has some sort of power that I can use?"

"No, but...."

"You mean that it has power—over me?"

"No."

"Other people?"

"No, no, no, not at all. It...."

"It has no power at all?"

"No, it doesn't. You have finally hit the nail on the

head."

"Come on, Grandma, I'm not little anymore. If I were, you'd still be alive, and I wouldn't be talking to you here in this cl-HUUUU? What? Why am I talking to you like this?"

"Because you need to talk to your granny every so often, right?"

"No, no, no, NO. You got it all wrong, Granny. I am. I should be talking to a shrink or something now. I shouldn't be talking to a piece of clay."

"I'm no piece of clay. I'm just using this here to get through to you. Your angle, your talents have always been with things you've had to lay your hands on. And I don't mean the opposite sex either, though you haven't done too badly on that. This is real hard cold advice now. I want you to listen to your old granny."

"I must be crazy."

"No, you're not. Didn't you just meditate this morning?"

"Yes, but...."

"Well, what did you think it would do for you? Help you pick peaches?"

"Well, I, ah...."

"Ya, that's what I thought you'd say. So listen up here. I was saying that all you need to do is put your hands over the clay. That's right. Then feel the warmth. It's just your own power being magnified from the mother Earth, a portion of which lays before you and under you."

"Then what?"

"Then touch the clay and...."

"Touch your face?" I open my briefly closed eyes and stare ghastly at my granny's face. But she's disappeared. Granny?" No answer. "Grandpa, are you here now?" He doesn't respond either. Well, I guess I'm alone again. What did she last say before she so coldly left without saying goodbye?

"What was that you said, dearie?"

"Goodbye, Grandma and Grandpa."

I put my hands on the clay, and it seems to move with me. I move my hands with it as it becomes mounds and indentations. Whatever it's doing or that I'm doing, this thing is becoming really, wild. "Ooh man." I yank my hands away from it. It's really beautiful, in a strange sort of way. The edges are pointed upward into seven different directions. Odd cone type shapes. I dive back in.

Upstairs my phone rings. I dart up to catch it. Voice waves connecting person to person, sound to sound, energy pushed as waves transferred into audible signals. To humans this is a tiny task, our Earth, 2028, May. On the old calendar, that is. But now it's really the year of our world independence. Independence from all oppressions we've ever put on each other.

"Plubard, are you there?"

"Ah, yes, sorry. Who is this?"

"Katrina, you remember me?"

"Oh, sorry, I was just thinking about something."

"Not another of your imaginary sequences, was it?"

"Of course. What else would you expect?"

"Let's hear it then. You know how curious I get."

***

"We've gotten all the soldiers secured into their treatment now."

"What about the commanding officers?"

"Well, they still think we're trying to overthrow the U.S. government."

Yeah, I remember you were having a problem with that the last time we talked."

We've started to show them the videos of the wars they themselves have participated in and all the violence it really held, as well as other wars—same kinds of footage.

Our next plan is...."

＊

Fifty men and women, including many of the commanders, are asked to change into other clothes. They are Russian military uniforms, so they put up a tough fight. Eventually they give in when told nothing would happen to them, and that it was just part of a role-playing experiment.

Soldiers on a ship nearby, a Russian ship of captives, are also given different uniforms to try on. The two groups are required to wear the uniforms for the next two days. While in these uniforms, the groups are secretly traded from ship to ship.

The chosen ones were, of course, the toughest soldiers to crack, and so gave a real fight during the trading. When they are brought in to the opposing ships, the two groups are divided into smaller groups and bunked with other soldiers who wear the same uniforms the newly entering group fought to avoid.

In the morning you wake up and find yourself on a different ship. You had no idea of it at night because your head was covered and you could hear only strange walking, jumping and ship-type noises. You didn't know you were jumping to get to a different ship. You look around. You're still wearing the wrong uniform. But everyone else is, too. These guys don't look the same as you remember. They must be from a different camp or something. They must have been trapped and forced to wear these stupid uniforms, too, you think. You try and gently strike up a conversation with one of the guys. When he responds, he seems to be speaking a different language. It's Russian. You're sure of it. You've been really captured and put on board with them, you think. You can't understand why they would put you with these other guys and not in the brig.

One guy stands up and says something you don't get at all. You try and talk friendly and curiously, like you don't understand either. You don't want your head smashed in. These guys stand up and talk to you fast and hard and mean. They mean business. But you're alone in there, and one of these guys starts to yell at you, like he's demanding something from you. You tell him you don't understand what he's saying.

There's a knock at the door, and all three of them are startled. One guy answers it. A friendly sort of man walks in and asks them several questions, you think. You're waiting to get taken out of there. You hope you're going to get taken outa there. You hope they put you in the brig. The guy who walked in there has a large grey streaked beard.

"I'm Dr. Scott. I'm the logotherapist for this group of men."

"Why am I here? Take me out of here before they kill me, please."

"I'm more interested in how you feel about this situation you're in, in here."

"But I don't know what situation I'm in here. I think I'm on an enemy vessel, but I'm wearing the same uniform as these guys. Why don't you just put me in the brig with the rest of my crew?"

"Why in the brig? You're not here because the Russians have captured you. They haven't, you know. I'm surprised they didn't tell you that over there. No, we're just trying to demonstrate the fact that the Russians are just like us Americans, like you. These guys thought the U.S. was trying to take over Russia."

"What the hell is going on then?"

"As it was explained to you before, a major upheaval is in the works. We are trying to help you personally overcome your need to kill and control all people and things that are unlike you. You need not defend yourself. But most people have these same feelings."

***

"Well, it was a challenge."

"You mean you got it?"

I gleam with pride. "Of course. Did you think any less of me?" I get up and grab two flutes from the cupboard. My hand slips and knocks over the bottle of champagne I just bought. I grab it and pull it out of the long brown bag.

"Guess we'll have to wait a bit to celebrate. But at least you didn't spill it. That's good, isn't it? Remember last weekend when you'd gotten the glasses out after you'd opened the bottle and then did almost the same thing?"

"Don't mention that, will ya?"

"Sure, sure, but I kinda figured you'd get the gig, so I went out and bought a bottle for us, too." She opens the freezer and pulls out a perfectly chilled bottle of France's best. What a woman.

"What kind did you get now?" I ask with a vivid smile and my arms around her.

"Oh, just a bottle of the best I could get—Dom Perignon."

"Man, oh man, you did this for me?"

"Of course. I knew you'd get it. "

I hold you very close and kiss you deeply. I put my head on your shoulder. I gently touch my lips to your neck several times. Your body begins to tingle in my arms, and I grow warmer by the second. "It takes a rare woman to trust in my work. Thanks." I run my hand slowly down your spine. You pull away a bit.

"Let's not put this stuff to waste here now." You grab the two glasses, and I grab the bottle before we walk down the hall.

***

"Plubard, you know that you're chairperson today,

194

don't you?"

"I know, I know."

"Well, are ya gonna be on time?"

"I hope so. I know how mad everyone gets when I'm late."

"It really doesn't matter what everyone else thinks. They all have their quirks, too. But I was wondering if you prepared for the agenda on the board?"

"Well, I took notes last week, but I don't exactly remember where I put them."

"You can use mine. I can be your secretary this week."

"Great idea, thanks. But only if I can be yours when it's your turn to run the meeting."

"Well, sure, thanks. Should we meet someplace or just have a coffee at Jelopie's cafe?"

"Let's go to Jelopie's."

"All right, should I pick you up in my carriage, or do you want to just meet there?"

"We can meet there, unless you'd like to drive. I know it's a new carriage, and you've tried to get me to see it a few times now."

"I'll pick you up at three, no, make that two o'clock. And if you're not ready, then I'll force you to get ready. Got me?"

"Sure, sure. I understand. You don't want me to be late."

"Smart you are, very smart."

"The only problem is that I'm working on something here, and I really need the space for it today."

"What's the matter? Did you forget to clean this week?"

"Oh, that, too, but I really think it'd be better at the cafe anyway."

"To meet?"

"Yeah."

"But you know you have problems in getting to places on time. I mean, I don't want to hurt your feelings, but you must be aware of the fact that you run on a different clock, don't you?"

"All right, then we'll meet at three, and you can pick me up at three sharp."

"But that'll only give us two hours to work on this thing."

"That should be enough. And if it isn't, then we can let the meeting run later."

"No, we can't."

"And why not, Katrina?"

"Because, Plubard, the Jewish people in town need to be home before sundown for their Sabbath."

"Oh, yeah, I remember that. We had a big meeting a long time ago about taking less time or starting earlier."

"Well, we'll just have coffee and really work hard on the text of the meeting and then go over to the next village for supper."

"Let's go to the Whimsical Room, can we?"

"Where all the comedians hang out and perform?"

"Yeah, I could go for a good laugh. How 'bout you?"

***

Ruban is interrupted by a group of young men painted and oddly dressed. They bring in a tray made of leaves and twigs. Four strong poles are connected below each corner. The four men carrying it set the contraption down in front of Ruban. They signal to him to climb aboard. But he, scared, runs out toward Sascawacha, who tries to avert him. Ruban steers round Sascawacha, who then quickly trips him.

"What do you run from?"

"Let me go. I ain't gonna be no sacrifice for no god of yours."

"You are not a sacrifice. You are a human being."

"Where'd you really hear all them fancy words from? You some swindler trying to force these people to do weird things?"

Sascawacha looks shocked at Ruban, who is still trying to get up from his fall. "Why would you think these things? We were coming to bring you to a feast being held in your honor."

"What?"

"Yes. You were to be brought to the center of the feast to be honored. Why would you think you would be sacrificed?"

"The platform, the platform. It's just like one I saw in a movie as a kid."

"Oh, hohohoho. We are very sorry. We have offended you."

The other men come out of the hut and speak with their leader in their native tongue. Then they all start laughing.

"You don't have to laugh at me. My folks didn't want me to come anyway. They were afraid that I'd be in some serious trouble if I came down here."

"That is why we met you at the airport. The wind told me of your coming and warned me
of the perils you would face if you tried to find me on your own. You need not worry now. You have a special purpose. Now come with me, and you can walk to the feast. You will be honored here. You will see."

Ruban struggles to his feet, and Sascawacha helps him but continues to hold onto his arm after he is up.

"I ain't your dinner, so let go of me will you?"

"Yes, young one. You are my great-grandson, but you don't know that very well yet. Why would I want to kill our tribe's chances of survival?"

"I don't know. But then, why the big frying pan

deal?"

"That is a platform we use to carry our guests, our honored guests, for ceremony."

***

Throughout my life I've had this feeling, this obsession that there is some way to help people to see the future as the opposite of what the imprisoned, starved, tortured and crazed author of the Book of Revelation would have us believe. If I were stuck in hell, or what sure seemed like a hellhole prison with no chance of survival, I'd probably be pretty pissed off and wish with all my might that the world would come to an end with me, especially the ones on the outside. I'd sure talk mad about my oppressors, too, as he did. I would imagine that most people
might feel a touch upset if they were treated as badly as most prisoners of war are. The anger inside them for their oppressors may be the only thing keeping the corpses alive. I wonder what the masses of oppressees felt for their guards and torturers before they were released. Most of the great teachers have taught forgiveness, and then some people are quite gifted in that area, even as prisoners, and do spend all their time trying to forgive those who are torturing them. I wonder what our world would have developed into by now, if Revelation had been written by one more similar to the great teacher he professed to know. Perhaps Christianity would have become something less violent, and all the nations who claimed it as their religion would have been fair and just and forgiving and loving to all its inhabitants.

Right now we live in a world where child sexual and physical abuse, rape, incest, bestiality and taking freedom from anyone those certain societies think shouldn't have it is as acceptable as driving a car. In fact all countries and religions and governments seem to accept violence against other peoples as acceptable behavior. We look at the criminal as the problem. But unless we devote our lives to

198

creating a peaceful world, aren't we in fact accepting the behavior of criminals as—normal?

"Ah, excuse me teach, but did you write this stuff?" asks Sam the punk.

"No, it was written by a famous writer, composer, inventor and humanitarian."

"Who?"

"Hey, I thought this was a science class," says a brown-haired blue-eyed girl whose glowing skin causes all the boys to become gentle in her sight.

"Ah, why yes. It is, Miss Sanders. But we are going to begin a new series of projects, which may be used as a portion of your grade. It must include some aspect of the scientific future of our planet."

"Scientific future? What's dat, teach? Science fiction?"

I lean back in my chair and pause for thirty long seconds. "Possibly, but it won't entirely be fictional. At least my future won't be."

"What do ya mean, other project?" asks a very large boy in the back row who's in all the sports clubs or teams or whatever they're called.

"Good question. Let me try and make that more clear. This was a surprise for you, really, and since I now have the reality in my hot little hands, I can tell you and I'm sure you'll be pleased."

"What, what?"

"Calm down, I'll tell you. Well, to put it straight into your hands, with the help of the school board, I have just acquired a small television station, with lots of video equipment." The room roars with ruckus.

"Hey, hey, now. I don't want the principal to come in here. I'm glad you're all as excited as I am, but it's not going to be easy for me. It'll be more fun for you. But you have to remember that this is a science class, so anything you do for the station as a TV show or part of one has to be related to science, in some way, however small."

"Ya, man, like the science of how music tames the average woman's body, ya!" spouts the punk.

"Well, you know, I like the idea of the science of music, but I know you and I would get in trouble if the word—s-e-x—entered into it. I'd probably lose my job and the station."

"But it's in all the biology books, ah, ya."

"You know this is no joke here. Have you ever heard of another school that was even given the IDEA of having a student group who puts on their own programs? Their own station?"

"So what's yer point, man?"

"I think this will be really great for all of you as well as for all my other classes, you know, to really see how it's done. This'll show you how to write real scripts, and it'll show real producers, directors and camera folks work."

"What about the actresses?" asks a girl in a sort of reclining position.

"Ya, that's it. You will all be in your own productions as well as every other part you'll need to fill. I'm gonna pass these sheets out to you. Take one of each of these. Here, here. Now this is a list of areas you can choose to work in.

"The whole class or separate groups can work on one show as part of the final project. But you each have to come up with an original idea on how to teach some area or concept of science. Give me at least five ideas of what you can do by Monday. One of the most important elements is that it must be a real scientific concept or experiment and that it must be interesting to you. You need to make it really interesting. So interesting that you can assure me that your friends will watch it, enjoy it and be thoroughly impressed."

"Monday? You mean we gotta work on this over the weekend?"

"Come on now, it'll be fun. You'll see, once you start working on this and get some ideas going, you'll probably come up with ten examples. You may start by looking at what we've worked on so far in the term, as well as in the chapters ahead. Use some of those ideas if you want. Maybe there's something you don't quite understand and you want to explain in a better or more interesting way than the book or I have been able to do for you. Let me remind you of one other thing. It won't be easy, but you'll love it. I guarantee."

"Ya, fun, fun, ha ha."

"However, if you really don't want to work on the TV program or two, then you may start working on the two- to ten-page research papers instead. But once you sign up for either project, that's it. You cannot change your mind. So think hard about this proposal."

RING, RING, RING! Shouts the bell for class changes. Everyone tears out of the room, gabbing as they go. I slip my papers and books into my briefcase and snap it shut. I wonder if this will be a real waste of time. They're only giving me a year to try it out. I wonder if there are a lot of repairs needed at the station. That guy never called me back that I can recall.

***

"How's the experiment working?" asks Kent.

"I don't know yet. The guinea pigs aren't as afraid of their adversaries as they used to be. But you know they don't speak the same language, so they can't really get along too well with the others," answers Dr. Trotchky.

"Should we exchange any more men, do you think?"

"No, I really don't think that's a good idea. Not just yet at least."

"Maybe we should return them to their original

posts first."

"No, no, no not yet. I think it will lose its effect if we stop the experiment too soon." Trochky folds his hands nervously.

"I'm sorry, Kent, but I overheard your discussion outside. May I join you?" asks Sascha like the wind.

"Come on in and share with us your observations about the experiment, will you? Oh, and shut that door so nobody else can hear what we're discussing. We don't want any nosy note-takers do we?"

Sascha gives Kent a very strange look before closing the door and sitting down with the other two.

"Why don't you have some comfortable chairs, or a couch in here, Kent?"

"Because, Sasch, the shrinks took my couch for their office. har, har har. No, but really, I never had one, and I don't usually get visited by so many wonderful people at one time."

The three are quiet for a long time, trying to calm down and collect their wits about them. The doctor is nervous in the presence of Sascha and Kent. Sascha is nervous from Kent, and Kent is nervous in front of Sascha and the doctor. The three try and pick little bits of wood or stone thoughts, like little children who try and make sense out of this messy world. Many a mother, while staring at her once-clean children, wishes the entire world were made of asphalt and cement. Nothing should be left for the messy digging of the little imps. Nothing should be left to claw or scrape or take things apart with, like sticks or shells or feathers. The entire world should be paved and stabilized into a neat package of predictable thoughts with only a notepad-size list of acceptable responses for each feeling or expression. The mothers of the world would only have to clean their children once a day. Then, all the clothes would snap on and off so that at the end of the day they could be hung on the balcony, clean and white and unfrayed for all the neighbors to inspect. The mothers could then close their curtains so they wouldn't have to worry about the clothing until the next day, when the perfect routine would begin again. No thoughts but clean, clear, unscrambled ideas that the TV or tabloids would allow.

"Why are we here, Dr Trochky?"

I look at Sascha and sit up straight in my chair. I remember my little boy, who wanted desperately to become a soldier, because his so-called friends and uncles were or wanted to be at one time.

"It does hurt me on some deep level to try and unbrainwash these men and women, even though it is for world peace."

"We're trying to decide what the next step is in our plan, Sasch." says Kent answering the question that I couldn't.

Three clicks mark the door.

"Come in?" answers Kent.

Sascha slowly moves the door open. She pokes her head through the tiny opening.

"I, ah, thought Kent might be alone now, but I can come back," a small woman, Dr. Swenson, politely responds.

"No, no, please come in, Dr. Swenson." Kent stands up quickly and opens the door wide for Dr. Swenson to come through. Kent pulls up a chair for her to become part of the half-moon around his desk.

"You know Dr. Swenson, don't you, Sascha and Dr. Trochky?"

"I'm pleased to meet you." says Sascha, holding out her hand to the doctor.

"We are talking about what our next plan will be. Do you have any ideas, Sascha?"

"Well, I do have some information that should be

exciting for you all to hear. I do want to caution you all in a way because I have had a small fear recently, and that is that what we are doing may in some way become a cult, a worse cult than any we have ever heard of before."

"That's really a scary thought Sascha, but I think we all have it to some degree. I guess we all just have to be very conscious of our individuality and our freedoms. Cults are usually run by one person or a very few. You may say that most or all governments are forced cults. These cults start at the time a child is born, with continuous brainwashing through the media, their parents, music, and schools. Trying to make drastic changes in any government can be punished by death, as in any strict cult I have ever heard of."

"That's an astounding concept to examine, Dr. Swenson. I think you've cleared that up for me, so that I can go on with the other topic I mentioned earlier. Anyway, unless anybody has anything else they want to add before we go on?"

We all look at each other to get the sparkle of recognition and reassurance we each need. Nobody responds, so she continues.

"It is very exciting for me to tell you about this young soldier, Pete. He is in the infantry and, well, basically he explained to me that his original intention for going into the army was to learn the ins and outs of the military, and war, and then by this, he wanted to somehow learn how to prevent wars."

"Doesn't make much sense, really," says Dr.Swenson.

"I know, but at this point I think that what he's saying is that he's really interested in world peace. I think he may be able to help us with the rest of the soldiers."

"I can't understand why he didn't tell one of us before." I spout out.

"Well, Dr. Trochky, maybe he just felt more comfortable with Sascha."

"Oh, I suppose so."

"I think that we all need to get every doctor or technician into a meeting, for say, this evening, say after dinner. We need to figure out what our next plan of action should be." Kent picks up a pencil and taps the eraser up and down on his desk.

***

One bulb shines on a large black machine. Two men lean over a dark pile of metal pieces, twisting screws and tightening bolts. After tapping, the younger man adds the small part to the pile below. The two barely speak.

"I t'ink dat's it."

"Ya, ya, let's try it out. I'll get the filaments."

The older of the two lifts a cloudy piece of glass from a box. He places the block into a large opening in the side of the cold machine. The other, shorter man flips a switch. He then slowly turns a knob, which begins to heighten a faint hum corning from the center of the machine. The balding other man flips pages in a tiny notebook. He moves his head closer. From another box, he removes a cellophane-covered scoop and a tiny scale. He sets them down near the now-purring engine. He watches the table a moment. The scale shakes slightly. He removes it, holding it while seeking another space. He locates a tiny typewriter stand and rolls the three pieces nearer to the light. He sets the impatient scale onto the grey plane. With metal baskets around the wheels, it sits still and doesn't roll unless they turn a red knob on the top. What better way to judge the accuracy of finite granules?

The younger man continues to tinker down the machine while he awaits the deposit of additional materials.

"Almost have it?"

"Yes, yes, as soon as I find that other box of

phosphorus."

"It's right here," the younger one points to the glass jar.

"Yes, yes, of course, everything is usually where you left it."

"No, no, everything is usually where YOU found it."

"Don't tell me your mother read you the pussywillow book to you too."

With a smile, the young man says, "It's still on my bookshelf where I keep my other very stimulating books from my past."

"Posh, Captain, posh."

The younger man lifts a cardboard box and sets it at the older ones feet. He pulls out his Swiss army knife and opens the box with it. Among the white peanuts sliding around, there lies a green can. They carefully lift it from its nest and set it gently on the ground. The two men kneel down and examine the closure. The younger notices a few pieces of tape holding the top shut and cuts them with his thumb nail. There is a set of opposing thumb holders that we assume direct and allow the opener to pop the top off. Each man takes a side. With gentle strength they simultaneously pop the top off. The lid flies up and down with a wobbling clang. Tiny green particles glitter in the faint light.

"So, my fair beauties, I finally have you." The older man rings his hands and smiles with disgusting glee.

"How long?"

"It's only a matter of seconds now."

"I'll set the machine."

"Good."

They move to their appropriate positions. The older man measures the granules in the scale with musical accuracy. Each particle hitting the metal bowl clings and sparkles as it is stared at along with the corresponding lines of measurement. Each particle seems to take seconds to leave the scoop and reach the metal bowl and pile of shimmering green partners.

The body protects itself from millions of highly dangerous germs and viruses every single minute of every single day. But what is usually neglected is the fact that pain is also removed from our body by our body. But is it because this removal is merely an instrument or action of our mind, therefore a result of thought? Perhaps our body has a mind of its own, which is not in our brain, necessarily, or our conscious mind, wherever that may be, but in and within our entire being.

The older one moves the precious cargo to the machine. He looks over, momentarily to a nearby window, and notices the faint blue of dawn. The particles are poured into a hole on the side of the machine. The motor hums higher while a slight grinding sound sputters inside. As the sound cools down and the temperature of the tools quiet the two compounds meld into one. Slowly, from a shoot on the other side, a sheer green piece of what looks like colored glass passes out.

***

Ruban slowly sits down on the stretcher before him. He doesn't want to offend his hosts. The four men raise him high while everyone follows him through the jungle to where the celebration is about to begin. As the crowd moves through the thick dark jungle, two men move before them with torches and machetes, hacking away at the thick foliage crowding their path. After about thirty minutes, the parade comes to a clearing. How they found it, spirit only knows.

A fire is burning. Conches are blown. Other strange instruments are played. Gradually everyone joins into the music. People from other tribes, Ruban is told, are joining the group and its music as well. The other tribes' music is different and their dances, which everyone is beginning to do are also different than Sascawacha's tribe's. Yet with all this supposed clash, there is harmony and a weaving of textures of colors and mannerisms and wildness in many directions all proclaiming true unpolluted art and freedom.

Ruban, who is sitting on his stretcher that is on the floor now, is not in the center, but on the side as a spectator, as he prefers. Food is brought to him. His great grandfather brings six other men and one woman to see and meet him. Ruban turns his head and tries to comprehend all that is being said. Barely being able to speak his great grandfather's tongue, Ruban can only piece together what is being said.

After several hours, the mothers are quiet with their babies, all huddled together. The fires begin to slow down. Some are still eating, and some are sleeping or talking quietly.

What was once the outer circle, is now the inner circle, all the members of Sascawacha's tribe are sitting in this smaller circle. The other tribes' members create the larger circle. Both circles surround the dwindling fire.

"There are six tribes here, Ruban. Six tribes left in the jungles of South America." Sascawacha begins telling Ruban what was said in the meetings of the tribes. He looks at the fire and says, "Many people have returned to the jungle because of all the wars and murders and hunger in the big cities and even the small villages. Their grandfathers were part of our people, our jungle."

"I don't understand."

"When the Spaniards took over our people many many years ago, they taught their slaves about power. They taught them how to take it away from the villagers with only the greed filling their hearts. Now we have soldiers whose great grandfathers or great grandmothers were once happy jungle people but are now killing and torturing their own people, or anybody who gets in their way. They torture little children because of what the little child's father might have done." Sascawacha's eyes are red and moist.

"But you can't blame the Spaniards for what they did hundreds of years ago. They are forced to do much of this. They can't be doing this on their own, can they?" says Ruban.

"No, no. You are right. They do get their orders from their leader, who is being bribed by your government and the businessmen from your country and others, all for greed. But they not only destroy our people, but they are burning down our forest. Almost all of South America was once rain forest, but now less than half is left. And every day more is being chopped down, burnt down and slaughtered...."

"So many words I am learning from you. Every day I learn new ways to say the same thing. Thank you for teaching me so much,"

"But, Sascawacha, we hardly speak my language. I've been trying to speak yours."

"My tribe escaped into the jungle when the Spanish priests tried to teach my people what jealousy and greed and vengeance were. We have always been a peaceful tribe. We had no words for the words of violence. How could we? We did know of the head hunters who killed and ate other humans. They were once our sharpest enemies. They quickly became part of the Spanish peoples. In the jungle, so great, there was always enough for everyone, even space to get away from our enemies, the head hunters."

"Until the white men came and tried to make you their slaves?"

"This is when many of us escaped. My mother did not. She was raped by the Spanish, and kept in slavery. She died a sad death of a servant girl, many years ago when I was still a boy."

"But why are you telling me all this now? What do you think I can do for you? You've talked about a special thing I have to do and how you directed me to come here. What does the past of our tribe have to do with what you want me to do?"

"Grandson, you see before you the remaining tribes of the Great Amazon Jungle, as it is known to the white men around the world. This jungle, this brush, this place, this heart, is the
loving life of our Earth. If they kill this jungle, all people will die."

Staring with an open mouth, trying to talk, trying to say something reassuring and sensible, Ruban can't believe it's the truth. He heard some commotion about all this before leaving the States, so it isn't a new concept. But somehow to hear it from Sascawacha makes it drastically true.

The low drone of the forest and slowing of festivities begins to mesmerize Ruban. He stares deeply into the fire while not really comprehending what is being said, but he has no choice. Like a child in the presence of adults, his mind trails off to another land.

Six dark-skinned men dressed with loin cloths and green face paintings scatter through the trees. The smallest and youngest hides behind the largest tree he can find. He peeks out periodically at his companions. His head turns around so his nose finds strange scents. There is perfect quiet. The young one concentrates so hard, his eyes squint but dazzle with light. He concentrates on the air, to try and find sound.

Suddenly, screeching pierces the air. The young one's companions stand trembling behind several different trees. They watch their ancient friends being yanked from the ground. One by one they're uprooted or buzzed down by blades so sharp and cold, steam seems to crystalize in the air. Mammoth tractors with buzzing blades sharply shatter the life out of the breath-giving beings till they tumble like rocks down a mountainside. Falling, falling, the once mighty giants are picked off like tiny innocent creatures, like small children being abused and abused yet continuing to trust in the face of sheer violence.

The eldest companion begins to sob gentle tears. His once-impressive back now looks fragile to the young one as the old chest heaves quietly. The long black-and-grey braid sticks with sweat trickling down the bulging spine. The other companions, dark-skinned warriors, begin darting between the trees hiding in a huddle to plan their attack, no, their rescue. They wait a few moments to allow their leader to resume his composure, and pride. They wait patiently, but carry the barely lucid energy of shock.

Loud banging and talking of the workmen holds the warriors in place as the screeching of machinery increases. Three dark-skinned men, hiding under hard yellow helmets and pale blue uniforms, carry and unroll a large spool of wire. They roll it past the hidden onlookers who scuffle to find better spots. Two other men transport a large television in and set it next to the spool. The wire is cut, and the connections are made. The switch is clicked on, and noise shoots out of the tube. Every warrior except the youngest screams and runs into the jungle. Other men catch them and drag them into a tiny tin house. They scream as they're stripped down and thrown into a large shower and scrubbed to the bone.

Soon a priest is walking into the room where the warriors are being dressed. He speaks in tongues they have no knowledge of. He talks louder and louder, expecting them to understand or stop their foolish game of ignorance. He yells, "You are bad, bad, evil demons! Repent, repent your evil ways or you will be burnt in HELL! You who have sinned will never see the glory that is to be mine! You heathens, evil, filthy, no soap or water, no clean clothes or shaved heads will win you the eternity that I have been blessed with. Go, GO, you evil fornicating heathens, go and be the slaves of these good men who labor in the name of the lord. Maybe if you die a slave of these who are greater than you, you may go to purgatory, but only maybe! Now go! Get out of my sight!" The priest walks out of the building as the dark-skinned men are still trying to escape.

The elder lays stiff and staring at those whose grandparents were his brothers and cousins. Those same distant relatives force clothes onto the old one in shock. They drag him and cut his long braid off. It slowly falls to the ground like a leaf being released from an ancient tree. The natives stare after the priest and look at each other, in a daze, at what is being done to them. One of the bravest warriors, whose face is painted with faint lines of deep purple, one who wouldn't give in to the bathing, is being forced into a straightjacket by three other workmen. The warrior is screaming and fighting all the way. He kicks them in the balls, and they double over. He yanks his body away and runs to help the others. His brother, who also fought hard and is also trying to get loose of the uniformed men trying to take him over, is almost about to give up the fight. An ambulance comes and takes both of them away.

After a few moments one of the dark-skinned workers walks over to where the young one was hiding and watching the strange box. The young one asks is his native tongue, "Why do you kill our great ancestors, the trees?"

Barely understanding, the workman wrinkles his nose a bit before answering, "The white men showed me that I need money to buy things I need. I live better. But even if I didn't, I have no choice. I need many things now. You will see what I mean...."

Ruban shudders as he is woken by the woman he

212

saw days earlier.

"Ruban, Ruban?"

"What? Who are...." He sits up quickly as he sees the beautiful face. "Where did you go? Where have you been? I've looked for you...."

She waves her hand as if to say, "nevermind."

"I want to know... where did everyone go?" Ruban realizes that the   large open area that was recently filled with celebrating, but tired people is now barren, with only a sizzle of smoke being let loose from the dead fire spot.

"They've gone to the altar to offer their freshly killed animals—their gift to the gods. But wait, we have no time for this talk. You must listen to me. If the elders know I am speaking to you this way, they would put me away again."

Ruban scratches his head and looks puzzled. "You don't mean the elders, like Sascawacha. I mean, what did you do?"

She looks pensive.

"All right, all right, what do you have to tell me?"

She looks behind her and all around. She moves in very close to Ruban, making it quite difficult for him to concentrate or stay serious.

"This thing that you are here to do—many jungle people do not understand what others are trying to do."

"So what does that...?"

"Shshsh—they may kill you. Before you go anywhere or do anything you must...."

Loud noises from the chieftains bring them down closer to the couple, so she quickly slips away. Ruban looks behind himself after hearing the chiefs, but she is gone. He contemplates his dreams and what she has just told him.

"Oh, Sascawacha, I'm so sorry I...." Ruban rises and bows to his grandfather and the other chiefs.

"Do not worry. I know you must be tired. This is

very different than a celebration you may have been in before. We have shared many ideas together." Sascawacha clasps hands with the two chiefs next to him and raises their hands high. "This night, we join together, as I told you. We are going to stop the tree murderers and land takers and slave drivers. Come here." Sascawacha motions Ruban and the others to make a circle on the ground. "What we need of you is for you to be our representative. You will go to the very important people and tell them what is being done here and you will tell them we need to be here, we need our trees. We wish to become as any country, any nation. We do not want to become like the native peoples of North America, Africa, or Australia. We want to live our way, without any changes, without them taking away who we are, our land or our trees. You will do this for us?"

"Grandfather, I had a dream just now."

"Yes, this is why we did leave you here. You did in this dream?"

"You know what my dream was?"

"I know it was a frightening dream where people, no, not real people, but machines run by machines, were murdering our trees. I know by your eyes you saw sad things happening to our people, but they were powerless. Before we left for our ritual, you had much water come from your brow as you slept."

"I think I need to be alone for a while."

"It's very dark now. We left you alone for a short time only. You must not go into the jungle alone."

"I can take care of myself."

"No, you cannot."

"Why?"

"You know there are still many dangerous animals and people here. Some people leave their country and go into the jungle, but they are very suspicious and very dangerous. If they are afraid, they will kill you, now, just now." He waves his palm over the ground with a final feeling. "Some people come into the jungle from the governments to kill deserters. They will kill women and children and even pregnant women. They will not hesitate to kill you."

"Why has all this happened?"

"I have told you of how the people were taken. But mostly, when the forests are trampled by unclean spirits and taken down by greedy beings, all people feel the pain of the loss."

"But, Sascawacha, aren't you afraid we'll be taken from here or our village too?"

"Did you not see our wall? People cannot see it so they cannot see us."

"What of the others who aren't from our tribe?"

***

I am a creative and extremely resourceful woman. Am I able to come up with solutions to the problems I make up, or am I able to be in touch with the universal mind? Concentrate. I would love a piece of pecan pie or, no, no, how about apple strudel? But maybe cheese cake will do the trick better. What kind of cheese cake? Perhaps cherry, strawberry, or rhubarb, or even chocolate chip would be best. That would be a really nice treat for the family. For Christmas dinner I could make a cheesecake and bring it for dessert. But then Grandma always brings cookies. We love them, of course, and it's the one thing that she likes to do that she can still do. They do almost seem like side dishes to the main desert dish. Like a veggie casserole is sort of a side dish to lasagna or spaghetti or tacos or whatever. It is kind of strange, though, because I'm sure people think my eating habits are strange, being a vegetarian and all. It may seem like what I eat is like eating only the side dishes. They may think that some of my main courses are secondary to the dead and putrid flesh that's been dead god knows how long and dyed to make it look fresh instead of the normal green color it would be by now if it hadn't been dyed. Oh, and what about the antibiotics and all kinds of other things that have been shot into the animals to help them survive those terribly unhealthy conditions they're forced to live in? Oh well. I still crave a sweet for now. But I can't do that to myself now. It may be some sort of brain dysfunction. I wonder if William will come to Christmas dinner at my folks' house. I wonder whatever happened to Freddy and Juanita. They were supposed to get married. I wonder if they did or will or won't or were, or if Will just failed to tell me. He's been so busy getting everything in order. He'll probably forget my name if I don't tell him from time to time. I still want something sweet to eat.

If I could only quote my deceased friend Buckminster Fuller, whom I met in a bookstore where he was signing one of his novels, which I didn't have the money for, so I bought a paperback by him that I haven't been able to get through because it's so complex.
I wish he was here. Such a fascinating man, with all his inventions. Disneyland has one of his geodesic domes in their back yard. Strange, I saw them all over in the meditations I had yesterday. That's it—we were visualizing with a group of others, trying to see what the world will be like when people will finally be at peace, with each other and with ourselves. But I saw the domes all over. One dome was in Nome, Alaska, and it had these immense flood lights outside shining in. They were actually sun lamps shining on great sections of solar panels of the dome in Nome. Inside there were plants all over, but there were children, children everywhere. They played on all types of playground equipment, upstairs and some downstairs. There was a wading pool the size of a small lake. That was on the first floor. The stairs were made of some very hard glass, not plastic because they don't use oil products anymore. Green,

green, exotic plants and birds in this beautiful new world.

What is he doing? He prances around as if the world was following him. All his plans, and here I am doing... doing what? I can't even remember what kind of job I was supposed to have had in the beginning of this story. I don't think I had a job. I guess I'm supposed to be the beautiful-does-nothing-girl-friend type. Maybe I didn't have to worry because my parents are rich or something. Are they? Well, if they aren't, maybe I can just decide they are. That's right, I have very wealthy parents. That means I can go home whenever I want, and they'll give me whatever I want, the way I want it. In fact, that's who I'll make the cheesecake for, sure. But I won't use a regular recipe, no, no. That's not my style. I'll just read a few recipes and figure out a better one. Of course, it might not turn out exactly right. So..., I know, I'll just make one and test it. If it works out, then I'll make another. If it doesn't, then I'll just have to make another. Why, before I'm through, I'll be so fat, William will never leave me alone in the kitchen again. I'm not sure he'll pay any more attention to me, but, well....

Let me see now, I see that this recipe requires gelatin. I can use agar sea weed for the gelatin. I could also use eggs instead of gel. That way, the cheese cake will be clean, the way things used to be and the way things will be again if William's plans work. I hope they do. I think I better get in there where William is because I think we're meditating in a minute or two.

I wonder if William is thinking about me or his master plan to save the world. He can be so pompous sometimes. I guess that is one reason that I love him so much. He tries things that other people were afraid to even dream of. But he does it, too. Imagine if I were walking down the street and some lady with smelly armpits walked by and tried to talk to me. I'd really like to be nice, but why should I be? I mean, why should I try and be nice? Why shouldn't I be, either? Why should I try and be nice to everyone? It's enough to make me sick! So here's the way I see it: I'll have a little shop where I'll sell lots of... no, no, not sell, I need to remember that. This world doesn't need to use money. William convinced me of that much. All we need to do is (a little of the strange but humanly possible) trust. That's right. So if someone comes across the street and takes something off the shelf, a book or an ornament in my shop then I just write down which one they took and order another one. I don't have to yell "POLICE!" 'cause we won't need any of them either. It is a strange concept.

There is a certain amount of negativity in the world, in each person, it seems. Like the universe may even be equally negative and positive, making it essentially neutral. But on Earth we seem to be experiencing both. It seems like every time I try and meditate and then afterwards experience a bit of positive stuff, then the following day or even a few hours later, and long, I get all this negativity. It could be from William one time, and another it could be from people I don't even know. Sometimes I think it's my little ego trying to fight for itself or something. I read a science book, an anatomy book to be exact, about the neurons in the brain and all that stuff. But then I realized that it was probably my body and mind and being just trying to keep a balance, or homeostasis. Maybe there really can't be a world totally at peace and passive. But then we've had such a negative first couple of thousand years, maybe the pendulum is beginning to swing the other way. In so many areas we seem to be moving toward world peace naturally, but then we still have so much really hideous violence. Hopefully the balance will come to even the scores. I guess we can't really even begin to have world peace unless we first stop the slaughter of little children. If we can't stop the molestations, the beatings, the rapes, the neglect, then how can we possibly consider having world peace? I have to look into the positive future.

I stop and sit down quietly. I close my mind to other thoughts and sights. I clear my mind and let my thoughts move into the future, where I'm in my shop putting some things in the window. One of the craftsmen brought me some wooden things that morning, and I'm trying to display them nicely. A guy walks in. He's some kind of religion peddler. He's bald except for a pony tail in back. He wears some peace-and-white-robe ensemble. I don't like him for some strange reason. He starts to tell me about his religion. I tell him point blank that I don't care about his religion. I tell him that I think religion is a personal thing, that people shouldn't go around trying to talk people into or out of. I ask him if he wants anything. He says, "No." Then I tell him I'm not interested in what he's got, either, and to please leave.

"But don't you just want to hear about the path that will enlighten you?"

"What gives you the right to decide that I'm NOT enlightened?"

"Well, I...."

"You have no right to come in here and decide anything about me. I have my own path, thank you very much, and I think mine is better than yours any day. But I sure as hell ain't gonna tell you about it."

"But...."

"Now leave, or I scream."

With that he finally leaves. Now there are all kinds of communes and communities where people can practice their own religion in peace and openness, but they don't have the right to go into any other community and try and tell us the so-called way of enlightenment. Call me a skeptic or anti anything—I don't care. Everyone has the right to practice religion as he or she sees fit, but privately or in his or her own church or community. It's probably better not to mix communities. Some do, and that's fine if everyone wants to, but that's not for me. I love everyone dearly, but that's what may have caused all the turmoil before in the first place—mixed ideas that people totally disagree with and then trying to make everyone change their ways to yours.

Some people prefer to live off the land, which is fine, too. As long as they don't come into our community and refuse to give of themselves, and only take, take, take. That won't do. It won't do at all.

A few days later I am on my way into town because I live out of town, in a little cottage. I like to walk to town in the summer and spring and fall. As I walk in my long skirts, I hear this rumbling and creaking and horses' hooves. There's this shack of a cart loaded down with who-knows-what, along with a half-dozen people or so. Along comes another and another and another, until I am passed by about four wagons of people and their things.

They're over the hill, so I can't see them anymore. I'm thinking that they're probably on their way through town and trying to get to the next one or something. It looks kind of odd, just the same, and I try not to think bad things about them. I get over the hill, and what do I see but all those people setting up a camp for the lot of 'em. There is all kinds of free territory outside the village, so why do they have to ruin our little place with their rages? But then I have to think about what this really means. A free world, I mean a truly free world means people can do whatever they want provided they simply give of themselves and never hurt anyone. So if I apply that, they aren't hurting anyone right now. I guess I just don't like to see people living that way. They made their camp on the place that Doc Jones made his claim a number of years ago. He grows apples for our village and for a few others. But what do they do? What do they offer? We can't have them here now, because they give nothing, they do nothing. We can't let them just take, take, take.

I tell the village people at the very next village meeting the following Friday about how I feel.

"They're not really hurting anyone." says one boy.

"You may be right, Roger, but how are they helping? They leave their trash and human waste all over the place, near the trees that Doc Jones planted years ago. How's that going to affect the apples? How is that going to affect the community?"

"Yeah, what can they offer us? We can't have any freeloaders here. We all work hard to live here, and we share and share alike. What are they gonna share, fortunes?"

"That's pretty racist, Roger. We can't go back to that now. We need to show them how they can share, like, yeah, the fortunes."

The next morning about a hundred or so people from my village go down and surround the wagons. We have a few dogs who are just a bit mean when they need to be. We begin our gentle but effective wake-up song. Slowly and quietly we begin. Then we wait a few moments. A few people come around by stirring everything up in the tents. We start to sing a little louder.

After a few moments, someone starts to come out of one of the tents. He practically jumps when he sees our group. I think he was about to take a leak. He runs into his tent and yells at his wife, and the other tents start rustling around. The weekly leader walks up to the first tent.

"We mean no harm! We just want to talk with you. Can you join us for coffee?" There is silence. "We have brought some breakfast biscuits. Please join us, won't you?" There is a little grumbling and speaking in a foreign tongue. "Are you going to come out? We mean you no harm."

Finally some voices pierce the morning air with

words heavy with accents.

"I—I can't understand you. Speak more slowly, please?"

A large hairy man pokes his head out of his tent and yells the same words in some strange language. It's obvious that we have a problem on our hands. The leader, Mark, tries to show him with his hands that we mean no harm.

One lady from our group makes her way over to Mark's side and tells him she thinks she understands and may be able to speak the other language.

"Give her a shot," Mark remarks.

Some schpiel slurps from her lips, and the man from the tent nods once quick, responds with a few chosen retorts and then closes the tent flap. Shortly after, he comes out with his wife and child. He calls to the other tents, and they finally join us. Strange things happen during the morning, like hundreds, well, maybe just a little over a hundred people, and all of us communicating in two languages. But we all sing and laugh and play music together and we end up with a rip-roaring party.

At the end of what seems like a few minutes, and is actually about five hours, we all come to an agreement. Oddly enough we agree. These strange people and their even stranger language are from some far-off tribe from the outskirts of Russia. But they are just as good even after the party. So we just decide to have them pick another piece of land that's outside the village, and they can become part of our community or they can stay on their own. I guess I'm from the old school, though. I'm kind of a loner, and I like people who are like me, I guess—in some respects at least, you know? The way I think, without any of the voodoo type stuff, if you know what I mean. Just, down-to-earth people, doing their share and not tryin' to mess around with my head. But these people are really way out. I can't understand them at all. Frankly, I don't really care if I

never see them again. It's not that I hate them or
something, like some folks I know and actively dislike do,
but I mean they aren't demons or something, but I can't
even say that for sure, knowing some of them. It's just that
I don't see eye-to-eye with them, and really I just don't
know what they would have or do that they could possibly
share or even get down to trading with me. I suppose that's
not exactly what all this is about, but I sure don't
understand everyone all the time, and I can't see spending
my time and energy on people who aren't willing to give
much of their time and energy to me, either. I guess
everyone has their own people they do business with.
Maybe I just complain too much, but I guess someone has
to, to keep this world a little more balanced than in the
never-never land some people pretend it is. If this world was
too peachy keen, we'd explode with so much sugary joy.
But the truth is, it's hard work, maybe harder than the lazy
days when people used to explode with anger and kill each
other at the drop of a hat, or, make sure they were the only
one who had more than enough and that there were always
starving people. Yeah, it's hard work making sure we all
have enough. It's even harder being a slave to some bullshit
job and some idiot boss who never gives a damn about his
or her employees, unless it's gonna hurt the job. It's hard
having a world at peace where everyone really pulls his and
her own weight, but I wouldn't trade it for the world.

***

What does it take to get that guy outa here? I'm
willing to compromise but when he takes and keeps a little
kid up so long, well, it's obvious that he's a drunk. I just
wish he'd think of all these sweet things to say when he's
sober instead of just when he's had a few. I don't know if I
really like him when he's drunk. He thinks he's so sweet and
funny when he's drunk, and I'm happy for him in a way,
but then I also wish he'd realize he can be just as funny and

sweet when he's sober. Oh well, what the hell, we're all human. I don't know why he affects me this way. Maybe I'm wrong. I think I need to breathe some positive energy into this manuscript. It isn't just this fairy tale fantasy like the other mediums seem to be. They're just words. Words and strange sounds against other strange sounds that all mean some one thing to one of us and something else to others. Wherever you've been or wherever you're going, I'm walking on the deck of the ship when Kent sees me and smoothly sprints toward me.

"Where you off to on such a balmy day?"

"Is it balmy? I hadn't noticed."

"Come on, Sascha, don't play games with me. Where you off to or rather, what're you up for? A game of gray tennis? Badminton or perhaps the legendary croquette?"

"Jeepers, Kent, don't you own a watch?" I say while smiling.

"Why sure, Lois, but what does that have to do with the price of whale meat in December?"

"Don't you take part in the daily visualization of the Big Change every day?" I'm sure he'll say yes, to be in vogue, and then canter off to the stage where the sun is setting.

"Gee, kid, didn't think it was all that important. Other folks is doin' it, so what do they need me for?"

"Kent, you're kidding. Don't you realize how vital your part in all of this is? Visualization is part of that part. I mean, visualization is really important for all of us to do. Now go and be a good boy and do your part."

Kent stands staring at me in slight uncertainty. He almost says something but then stops himself. He looks almost hurt, but he rarely feels that, I'm sure. Then almost suddenly, he turns without a word and walks away.

"Wait a minute, Kent, do you know how to visualize or meditate or anything like that?" Kent turns round and scratches his head a bit.

"I didn't say that, now did I?"

"You didn't have to."

"Well, I'm off, okay?"

"No, it's not okay. Come to my cabin, and I'll show you a few ways to visualize and stuff like that there. But no tricks, okay?"

Kent nods shyly. We make our way to the upper deck and down the corridor to my cabin, #518. Kent politely tries to open my door for me, but it's locked, of course.

"Oh, of course, where are your keys?"

"It's all right," I open the door without a key.

"But, I just tried that. I thought it was locked."

"Well, it was. It was a little trick of the trade. You'll learn it in time."

"But I—I don't understand. How can you do things like that?"

"You'll find out—in time." I open the door wide and open my palm to allow him to enter first. "Don't ask too many questions about it now, though. We came here for you, remember? You said, in not so many words, that you didn't know how to meditate or visualize, right?"

Kent hesitates but then concedes. A man of patience and strength is easy to work with and easy to communicate with on and in other dimensions.

> When I gaze into my past of long lost friends,
> I wonder where they've gone.
> Where have I gone wrong?
> What drew us together?
> What bond kept us close for so long?
> Why did we part, as enemies or friends,
> Why can't bygones be gone?
> What bond kept us close?

What flung us apart?

For those of you I've known and loved,
        those I've devastated
Many of you have cut out my heart,
        though innocently,
Those of you who shunned me,
        when I was down,
Any of you I'd known,
I don't blame you for avoiding me
        or forgetting the closeness we had,
Hating no one, not the worst or the best,
        I can never hate you.
Come to my door
        and I'll bless you.
Come so that I can see the face
        God made in his image.
Forget my name and I forgive you
        and bless your way.
I will not give up our memories
        of peaceful times, and
I'll never forget you.

"Who wrote this?" Kent asks as he looks away from my mirror where it hangs.

"Oh, an old friend of mine."

"Who?"

"Oh, just an old friend. You don't know him. It's kind of sappy, but it helps me when I go on long trips and stuff."

"Yeah, but it's pretty close to the truth—for how a lot of people probably feel about old friends, don't you think?"

"Well, I guess so, but I think I plugged you wrong."

"What'd ya' mean?"

"Well, ya know, I figured you were the type who pretty much forgot your old pals and chums. You know, you probably have people you'd never look at again."

"I suppose. I know that people probably don't intentionally do shitty things to me, or if they do, I don't think they really, I mean, really know what they're doing. Ya know?"

"I know that. But most people think that when someone does something wrong to them, they are totally aware and doing it on purpose."

"Tell me about it. But I know that I used to feel that way too. I mean, really, you wouldn't believe some of the things that people have done to me. They've lied and stole from and cheated me. I've been tortured by a couple of different military regimes."

"Tortured?"

"I have no toenails left. They ripped them from my feet."

"But why! Who could do such a thing?"

"Some people, well, not people, but animals who thirst for violence."

"But they must have had a reason."

"Oh, they said I helped some prisoner escape or some such bullshit."

"Did you?"

"Sure, I did. And then he carne back and helped me."

"But why didn't they just kill you?"

"That would have been too easy. No, there are some people who are raised on violence. Savages, they are. They are more savage than the native peoples of the world. Once they get the taste for violence, they lust and thirst for it, like a drug."

"I think I know what you mean."

"No, you don't really. You've had a sheltered life,

you have. You have never known cruelty."

"What makes you say that?"

"I can see it in your eyes."

"Where I've come from you do not know. I am from a different—no, I can't."

"Can't what?"

"I—when I was a little girl, I was taken from an orphanage."

"Taken?"

"I was stolen by a man who believed me to be his. But then when he found out, he raped me and nearly killed me."

"I'm so sorry, I didn't know."

"It's all right. I forgave him."

"That sick thing? How could you ever forgive someone like that. I think all molesters and child torturers should be killed."

"That'd really teach 'em a lesson."

"Well, ya think they'd learn a thing sitting in prison, if they ever get caught."

"No, at least it doesn't seem to work. If it did, there wouldn't be any prisons left, because everyone would've learned by now. So that's what this big change is all about, isn't it?"

"I hope we can come up with some plausible alternatives to prisons and death penalties—although it'll take quite a bit to change my mind about those sickos that molest children. One guy showed me a magazine once with kids doing sick things together."

"What'd ya do?"

"I tore it from his hands and punched him a few times."

"You could've found those kids and helped them."

"I thought of that later."

"And what if he wasn't even the one who liked the

stuff?"

"He was all right, he just wasn't careful about it. You know that junk just makes these sickos so horny for those poor kids that they just go out and steal them."

"You're really getting worked up about it. It can't be that bad can it?"

"It's really bad. Lots of supposedly good wholesome Americans fly to other countries and buy children for sex, 'cause it's so hard in the U.S. Though you wouldn't know it by how many milk cartons flash with scenes of missing kids."

"You're, um, I mean I know it's bad, Kent, but I really don't think it's that bad. I've never seen a man get so worked up about it. It's usually women."

"Yeah, yeah. I know."

"So what gives?"

"Well, I." Kent sits on the bed and wipes his brow. "Some years ago I worked at a daycare center see?"

"Yeah, go on."

"Well, Sascha, there was one little girl who I got along well with."

"So?"

"Well, there was one day when I was coming out of the store, and I saw her sitting in a car parked out front. And she was crying really hard. Well, I tapped at the window, and she looked at me and reached for me. 'Course the car was locked, but I still didn't like seeing her like that, ya know?"

"So what'd ya do?"

"Well, I tried to make funny faces at her to make her laugh 'cause I figured that her folks had just left her there for a bit and she wasn't too pleased. Not that I was pleased, either. I mean I figured at the time that it was pretty stupid leaving such a cute kid in the car by herself."

"Well, what happened?"

"Well, a man came out and practically shoved me aside to get into the car. Audry, the little girl tried to reach for me, but he shoved her into the car further and took off real quick."

"Well, I just thought that it was her dad and that he was pissed off that some guy that he didn't know was by his car and little girl. So I went home."

"You didn't do your shopping?"

"No, I felt so sick, I couldn't think straight."

"Is that it?"

"No, that's not it. What's it is that the next day when I got to work I found out that she had been stolen from her own back yard and hhhhu, hugn. I—I couldn't help her." Kent heaves and I put my arms around him.

"Oh. my God, I'm so sorry."

Kent sobs for a while and tries to pull himself together.

"Listen I—I can't stay in here now. I—I'm sorry I—I didn't know that would come up. I just...."

"No, wait. Go into the john for a bit and calm down. I'm going to go down the hall for a minute and check on something. I'll bring you back some tea or something."

"How about a drink?"

I look sadly at the floor.

"You're right. It'd make things worse. See ya."

I walk out after eyeing Kent's very red face and wet nose.

Never saw a man so upset and obsessed with guilt. Never knew. I walk down to the kitchen and ask for some tea. They set up a pot and some cups. They fix up a plate with some pretty little cakes and plates near it. I tote the tray up to the room. Kent is sitting in a chair looking out the window. He looks a little hollow. I'll save my trip to the captain till later.

"You know, Kent, people don't always realize what

they've done until later. But when people hurt other people, I don't think they can even feel what the other person feels. It's like they go into another level of consciousness or a wave like a storm."

"Is that supposed to make it all right?"

"No, Kent, but killing everyone for their sins isn't either."

"I know that, Sascha." He pauses. "If I told you some of the horrible people I've known, you'd wonder who I was, and maybe you wouldn't want to know me."

"You're joking."

"No, I'm not."

"Kent, we haven't known each other very long, so we're not too close yet, but I don't think I could throw it away now anyway. Besides, you are William's brother."

"Now you're kidding. I can see that stink-eating grin."

"No, really."

"You mean you can honestly tell me that you base your friendship with me and others upon who they and I know? That's really weird. I mean that sounds downright stuck up. That's more stuck up than me—that's pretty bad."

"Geez, Kent, I thought you'd take that comment differently than you did. But no, I'm only kidding. I think I'd be a real hypocrite if that were the case. What with the poem I have so conveniently posted where anyone who enters must see it."

"Sascha?"

"Ya?"

"Do you have any idea how beautiful you are?"

How can he say that to me? I am floored. But I can't fall in yet. I have to hold up for a while, so I can show him what he should soon be remembering. "Don't say that to me now."

"Why not? It's true."

"But that's not why I invited you here, and you know that."

"That's true."

"Right, now, I invited you here because you expressed an interest in visualization. So let's get started. Okay?"

"Right."

"You do want to learn, don't you?"

"I—I do but I thought you might be scared by me or something."

"Scared? No, now just take off your shoes."

He looks at her with a slight, curious smile.

"No, no, now you'll just sit right over there with your back against that wall, and I'll sit over here with my back against this wall." The two get up, find their places and become comfortable. "Now close your eyes and relax. Try and gently push all other thoughts out of your head. Every time something tries to interfere, tell your mind to stop it and that you'll think about it later. Feel your feet and legs slowly become relaxed. Then feel your back, stomach, bottom and chest relaxing, very slowly. Take in long, slow breaths. Feel your breaths completely fill you. Your breaths' slowing allows you to completely relax and concentrate. Your breaths are those of the spirit. They show you how to move to the very center of your being, to where the light is waiting. You are now in the presence of your higher self. Quietly a vision of a town where you and your brother will be living comes into view. You see your brother and some of your other friends going about their business. You may be doing something very different from what you've ever seen yourself doing before. What are you doing, Kent?"

With a dry mouth he says, "Packing."

"What are you packing?" I ask.

"Packing my equipment—my mountain-climbing equipment."

"Are you going to climb a mountain?"

"Yes. I'll be going up to my friend Ralph's house. I'll be seeing him and his wife. We'll be getting on a sled, a sled with lots of dogs."

"So the three of you are going climbing? Where?"

"No, no, the three of us are not. Silva is not coming with Ralph and me. No, she plans to use the quiet time for finishing her paintings for her show next week."

"Where are you climbing?"

"I, I.... Oh, yes, it was once Colorado."

"Do you climb frequently?"

"Yes, I do. I climb every week. I keep a notebook with me and draw or write down what I've seen or felt. I publish it in the little news rag in town, and they all love to read about it."

"Where is William?"

"Teaching."

"Do you have to lock up all your doors at night?"

"No, no. Sometimes people fight. That's especially true with the ones who drink a lot. But people don't put up with too much. When someone is causing too much loudness, and stupidity, well, people stop 'em, or they get thrown out of town. They have a choice."

> Do you hear the sounds of voices?
> Do you hear the talk of trees?
> They jibber in my ear at night.
> They wail like babies
> till I'm cold with fright that
> shatters the grey clouds
> till they wrinkle like
> a dirty beggar's sheets
> thrown cross an empty

sidewalk.
Can you smell the
wind of green things
in the Arctic?
Do you feel the music
of my tears?

"It sounds very controlled."

"We all control ourselves and respect each other's privacy and wishes."

"Aren't there any police?"

"There is no need. We all take care of each other."

"Yes, yes, but what about the other countries? What about the other religions, like the ones who keep women under cover and shawls?"

"Everything is very different now. There are no people forced into any religion or way of life that do not want to be part of."

"You mean the little baby girls' clitorises aren't cut out at birth?"

"No, the sacred scriptures were reinterpreted into very peaceful and loving ways. They do not require the murdering of people for disobeying the religion anymore. No one can do that anymore. The only surgery performed on children now is that to save their lives."

"But what about the aboriginal tribes of the world. Are they all gone?"

"No, they are not gone. They have all been allowed free choice, first choice of the land around the world."

"It sounds like a perfect world."

"Many things are close to perfect, except a few strange ways that people have not overcome completely yet."

"A few strange ways?"

"A few sick ways. Oh, someone is hurting a child!

She screams, oh, someone come and help her!"

"Look for someone who hears her, too."

"Yes, yes, here they come. They're banging on the door. He tries to jump out the window in back. But someone is waiting for him and stops him. Yes, yes! They crash in the door an—
save her!"

"Is she safe?" I try and hold my emotions in so I don't wake him.

"Yes, a woman is holding her, a doctor, yes, she holds her and comforts her and helps her feel safe. They have the man out back, and they're taking him down to the square to decide what's to be done with him."

"And the baby?"

"The doctor is carrying her out to a horse and buggy. The nurse drives the buggy as the doctor holds the child steady, in case of any internal wounds."

"How old is the child?"

Kent begins to whimper, "Fifteen months."

"What did he do?"

"He raped her. Oh god, let her be all right—she's got to be all right, she's just got to be.... But where are her parents?"

"That wasn't her father?"

"He, he was the babysitter's son."

"But where is the babysitter?"

"She'd gone out for a bit. Left the child with that wretched creature. She was crying for her mother." Kent's voice cracks. "He couldn't make her stop crying, so he took her and tried to force himself inside her, and she screamed. But people heard and came running, and they saved her, they saved her! They should kill him."

"What are they going to do with him?"

"They'll keep him locked up for a while, in a straight-jacket. After a few days he'll have to go before the town and directly in front of the parents. They'll decide how long or what type of psychiatric help he'll need."

"Not the doctors?"

"No, of course not. Everything is decided upon together with the entire group. Everyone has an equal say, and they don't stop the discussion until everyone agrees."

"Won't they kill him?"

"They'll want to probably, just as I do. But there are those who would remind the group of the kind of higher development that they have attained and that unless they want to go back to the barbarian societies where governments and police and pieces of paper and metal controlled the masses, then they must cool out and think like higher-order humans, the type we claim to be."

I wipe my forehead. "Is the girl safe?"

"Yes, yes, she's all right now. She'll have to have some treatments, maybe acupuncture or possibly surgery, but she'll be all right. But if it had been like the society of the past where people turned their heads and maybe called the cops, she would be dead right now."

"Why don't you go over to the next town, now. It's daytime."

"The next town?"

"Yeah, it's the next day, the girl is safe, and everything is all right. But you're going over to the next town to get something."

"The next town...."

"Yes, Kent. What are you going to get there?"

Kent fades off for a moment before answering, "I'm going to get a pot. A special clay pot. They make the very best there."

"It's daytime, isn't it?"

"Of course it's daytime. It's very hot. Seems hotter than my town. The kids are all in school. But they're being cooled by fans powered by the sun. The shades are closed, too, so the heat stays out. They have little lamps for each table. It's so very hot here. At this hottest time of the day the children take naps. The adults take naps, too. Many trees live here now, forgetting that this used to be a desert, a wild desert, full of angry animals. But they moved over a bit to let people live there. Irrigation makes the waters flow into the jungles and wells of the town. The buildings are sort of dripping."

"Dripping?"

"Yeah, they're made of clay or sandstone or something the people just patted down while wet. The stuff is dripped onto the wooden structures and then patted down and then left to dry. Weeds and bugs and stuff are mixed into the liquid before it's poured on—for added strength. But when the houses are done, they're pieces of art. The whole town, or village, whatever it is really moves around shifting and changing while staying put. A paradox."

"Where do you have to go for your pot?"

"Just up these steps to the top spot. Madame Swaysee should be here now." Kent knocks on the dry wooden door. He waits for a few minutes and then turns to walk away. When he is close to the bottom (54th step), the door opens slowly. He turns around and sees a little girl, about five, rubbing her eyes. Then a woman opens the door and says to the girl, "I told you there was nobody th— Kent?"

"Buenos dias, Madame Swaysee." He hops back up the stairs.

She opens the door and he enters. She apologizes for the delay and offers a mat for him to rest on so she and her family can finish theirs. She wonders how he could travel in such heat. Then she offers him a cool glass of water from a pitcher in her fridge, which is also run on solar power. After his drink and a little freshening up, he lays down on the mat and rests. As he rests, he dreams about Alaska.

The air is cool and dry. "I climb into my glider, which also changes into a solar-powered jet when the wind dies down. I fly northeast to the cold region, interior Alaska. There are no more oil tankers, like twenty years ago. I'm glad they decided to save the oil for the future, when and if the sun burns out. Such a strange thing, calling this place Alaska, or Canada or Russia for that matter. 'Cause they aren't anymore. They are just regions on maps. Nobody is ever gonna try and shoot me down if I go over their country. Because there ain't no' mo' contrees. Oh, yas, oops, I'm coming close to the air strip. Kent to flyer airstrip, come in, air strip."

"Tower to Kent, tower to Kent, come in, Kent...."

"Kent here—is there a place for me to land?"

"Well, we've got several planes trying to land, but we've got ice on the strip. The ground crew are trying to clean it up, but it'll take a while."

"How long we talkin' about?"

"Not sure yet. It's pretty heavy stuff. There is another strip about twenty miles northwest from here. Would you like to try that one?"

"Well, I'm pretty tired, and with the wind dying down and the sun pretty low for the past few hours, I better land soon."

"Well, unfortunately I've got ten of you up there with the same situation."

"Do the best you can, and just let me know when I can get down, Wilco?"

"Sure thing, Kent. Just keep circling with the wind, you know? Try and catch it as it drifts up."

"Roger." I wonder why people use Roger to signal adios. Must be something from a hundred years ago. I should look that up sometime.

Solartrucks are salting the strip, and probably throwing sand down there too. I circle round and round holding onto the wind as much as possible for this weather. But the wind seems to be incredibly strong at one level and cuts off just below it, so if I don't stay just up there for the necessary amount of time, I'll lose it. Off in the distance I see what look like caribou crossing a little stream. I'm so glad—as hard as it is—that people decided to give up burning fuels... even after only twenty years the air is so much cleaner. It's just incredible.

After about half an hour the control tower radios me, "Kent, we're ready for you to take runway 4 from the north."

"Thank you." I circle round once more to get at the right angle so I can just lower my nose, so slowly and put down my landing gear so I begin to roll down, down, straight and slow, like a long angle carved out of icy air till I hit and put on my brakes. I'm pushed back into my seat, held back by force yet with almost equal energy I push down on that brake for dear life, while steering so I don't go off the runway. Man, I can never get used to landing. I get the thing stopped all the way and use the last of my solar reserve to taxi to the corral. I stop it and hop out in front of the flag guys. I have my crash helmet in my hand along with my duffel bag in the other. I set them down a minute so I can grab my really warm coat from the back seat. The flagman walks over.

"How's your reserve of light?"

"Oh, she's pretty close to blank. Do you have a reloading station nearby?"

"Over in that blue barn, just beyond the red one."

"Right, the one that says 'solar reloading'?"

"You're sharp." He smiles.

"Say, where can a guy get a cup of coffee or something stronger?"

"Well, up in these here parts I'm afraid we basically banned any and all alcohol. It caused so much shit back twenty or more years ago that we decided to just ban it for good."

"Everyone agreed?"

"Well, the drunks, I mean the ones who only wanted to spend their days sucking on bottles, no. They didn't agree. But then again, they didn't want to contribute to anything, either. But we convinced them."

"How?"

"We gave them a choice, either detox or get out."

"Did they leave?"

"It was kind of split. But there were so many of us just waiting to go back to the old ways, or at least close to the old ways that we weren't gonna even consider taking those problems with us when we got our freedom, after about a hundred years of white supremacy."

"Well, you don't have to worry. I'm not a boozer, if that's at all on your mind."

"Ya couldn't get anything anyway. But we do want to see inside the cab, if you don't mind."

I scratch my head, "I guess I don't mind. There might be a little pint of whiskey or something, but that's just for the flying."

"You drink and fly? Oh, man...."

"NO, no. It's for like if I fall or something. You know if I get grounded or something and like, crash? I wouldn't drink and drive. Whew, that's nuts."

"Well, just the same, mister, we'd like to hold on to this until you leave, if you don't mind."

"I understand. But I'd like it back when I leave, please."

"Sure. You'll get it back. It'll be over at that little blue house next to the blue reloading barn. Old Sam Snyder is the fellow what lives thar. He'll be holding on to it."

"Thanks—ah, what'd you say your name was?"

"I didn't. But it's Johnny."

"Thanks Johnny. Say, you got any word on where a fella can bed the night down, maybe get me a team a dogs and a sled for a while—or a horse?"

"Horse don't take too kindly to this here weather. They slip and slide too much."

"I thought they was okay in the snow."

"You from the Southern parts?"

"Sure, but we git snow and really cold weather down there. Sometimes, I hear, it gets colder down there."

"For more than half the year?"

"Ah, well, no, sir. I don't think so."

"Well then, Mr. Kent, I reckon that's why."

"I don't know how long I'll be in town. How long can I keep my plane in your hangar?"

"Probably not fer ever, so you best be calling in every few days. You got any family or friends up here?"

"No, thought I'd just try and make it on my own for a while."

"This is awful bad season for making a home ya know—less'n yer part native er somethin'."

"No, I sure am not, mister. But I was hoping to meet with some and see if I can learn a few things. I understand they're one of the most successful groups to get back to their old ways—with little or no problems. Is that so?"

"Well, first of all, they who? There are hundreds of tribes up here. In the old days, them anthropologists tried to categorize and hypnotize and waiver any due causes and effects that they might have brought on through their blind ignorance. You ain't one a them, are ya?"

"Me? No way. I just want to learn. Could you tell me a bit more about what's going on up here?"

"Listen, now, it's getting kind of late, and the other flag folks have taken over for me all this time."

"Oh, sorry, I didn't mean to get in the way."

"Never mind that now. I was wondering if you'd like

a place to spend the night, an' then we kin talk more 'bout the folks up here."

"Thanks. That'd be great. Where should I go?"

"Go on over to the waiting area, in that green building over there."

"That one with the round humps on the roof?"

"Yup. I'll be done from my shift in about an hour. You can get a coffee or somethin' ta eat there. But don't eat too much or my old lady will be disappointed."

"Disappointed?"

"Sure, she's from the old school where she gets ta feelin' good when people like her food. Just between you and me, she is a master chef. Funny thing, I mean, being a gourmet like she is, people come from all over the world to eat her food. Never met another woman like her.... But anyway, I gotta get on. So leave some space. I'll see ya in an hour."

"Sure, thanks!" They run off in opposite directions.

Waves begin to hit the ship pushing it from side to side like a toy. Kent falls over and shakes himself back into this consciousness.

"What's going on here? Are we being attacked? What happened to Johnny, I mean, never mind."

"No, now calm down, Kent. It's only the waves. It's getting a bit stormy out there. I'll go and check on the captain—find out what's happening, all right? You just relax. I'll be right back."

I lock the door so Kent can't get out. I think his crew would try and mutiny if they saw their fearless leader in such a weird state of mind. I can't take that chance. I hop up the stairs to the captain's chambers, where I hope he's not. I open the door to find him lying on his bed, passed out. From what I wonder. I turn his head to make sure he's all right—not dead or something. Whew, he smells like he just drank.... I look at his hand to where he dropped a bottle, an empty bottle, on the floor. I pick it up to check how much he drank, but of course it's empty. I knew I should have insisted that this be a dry trip. Oh well, what's done is— "Aah!" I fall from the whipping waves, batting us like flies.

The captain's eyes open a little from the jerk. So maybe he's not totally passed out. "What are you doing?!" I jerk his collar and head up.

"I—I can't steeeeeer zis bot' no, no, e' jus can' do it."

"But why? You said you could when you were hired. I heard you. Now get up, and let's go!"

"I—I jus' cannnnn't. Serry." He passes out again. Who's steering the ship? I run upstairs to the bridge and crash open the door. It's the first mate. He's steering the ship, thank god, but he's shaking like crazy, and his face is quite grey.

"Where's the captain?" he yells at me. "I can't take this much longer. We're going into the straights soon, and I just can't do it like he can."

"You're doing great! Keep it up."

"BULLSHIT! Where's the captain?"

"He isn't feeling well."

"TOUGH SHIT! I haven't slept since about two days ago. He said he just needed a rest but that he'd be back in a few hours to get us through the straits. So I don't give a flying f—"

"He's passed out drunk. So you're the better helmsman now."

"Holy shit, I never did this kind of stuff before. These straits are the worst in the world! There's rocks and waves as big as skyscrapers, and I can't see the back of the boat or the sides to even know how the hell to—"

"Watch out!" He turns the wheel just in time to miss

a massive rock. But we're clear for a moment.

"Just relax now. We're gonna be all right." I massage his neck and concentrate on seeing us move easily through these stones. "We're gonna be all right. You're strong and brilliant, and I know you can do it. You're gonna save all these people, and you're gonna be a hero. I will help you." I feel his relaxation coming through until he thinks for a moment.

"You're gonna help me?"

"Yes, me."

"Get away from me, woman. Who the hell do you think... OH SHIT." A five hundred foot pyramid of water rises up like a serpent and tries to swallow us. "HOLD ON!" He steer clear of the monster and stares intently into the future. Slowly he turns the ship around waves, through waves and under waves. Sharp boulders jut out from the water like mirages about to disappear. But they don't disappear—they get bigger.

"I'm going to help you because I want to survive this trip, and I can help you anyway you tell me. Just tell me!"

"Sister, I can't think of any way you can help 'cept by prayin' an' prayin' real hard."

"What if I watch the sides or something, or direct the engine room from the com...."

"Shut up, yer spoilin' my concentration! Go on, get me coffee or somethin', but shut up!"

"Okay, okay, I'll be right back, but just try and relax and try and become part of the ocean."

"You crazy lady. You wanna end up in the ocean, you pretend you're part of it. Get me coffee before I pass out from lack of rest! Get goin'!"

"All right, all right." I pull my flowing red hair all together and stuff it into the back of my jacket to keep the knots from undoin'. I pull my jacket together and zip it up the best I can while hanging onto the stair rail. I concentrate real hard on the stairs—the wet, salty stairs—and air. I hold onto the rail so tight my hand is numb from cold water and metal. A king-size wave comes rolling toward me. I know it wants to swallow me whole! "NO!" I shout at the wind and water.

"MY WORK'S NOT DONE YET!" I'm left holding the rail with my body soaked and limp. I've got to get into some cabin where I can be alone and relatively safe enough to meditate, my last resort, though it should be my first. I follow myself as I search for an opening or someone who may see me and open up for me. I bang on windows and doors and walls. Why don't they hear me? Another wave rises up beside the ship, and I climb onto the rail with all fours so the ocean can beat on me like I'm dirt or sand. I cling to the cold metal for safety so I'm not swept into the constant waves. Over and over and over me they come and cover and come and cover, and I'm wet. My mouth feels like it's filled with the salty water and fish. A bang hits my shoulder till I just about collapse. But I can't let go. I must get through this. I must stop thinking, stop reasoning and just concentrate on the waves, the feeling of water and blackness. I must breathe fully when I can. I feel the white light fill my lungs and exhale out over and around this boat and me and the good first mate who's steering the ship. No fear needed, just breathe in hard and long before the next wave curls over me like a frog's tongue trying to swallow me or a vampire trying to drink the life out of me. No, no, the parallels are too foreboding. I must think and see and concentrate on the good. That's the only way we're going to survive.... I see the white light filling my entire body as I become encompassed by its love and peace. I exhale this—oh, I cough water out, but I must see the white light surrounding the ship, with me, too.

The waves paw at me as I see the light come and fill

me and my mind and all the darkness around me. The light seems to fill the sky, and I see my dear friend the Sun come and greet me. I see a glimpse of you as the sea slowly begins to relax, like a bad dream fading into something more pleasant. The ship is slowing and becoming steady in its rocking movements. The sky is actually becoming a peachy glaze and bluing at dawn.

No judgments on time or space or miracles that we always try and ignore. It is over, it is over, it's... o-ver. And I think I can rest for a moment. But the rocks still look jagged, so the boat begins to rock again with fear. No, no, I need to go back... the feeling of peace when I see calm water. I have my eyes closed again as I focus on that feeling, that feeling of steady waves coming in and out, in and out. Now I can't judge this or even decide how bad things should be when they're good, but enjoy them and use the light again and steady. I'd like to live in this light forever. Forever I'd live with this barely cool ocean and salty breeze with this view of calm over a glossy finish. I can finally let go and let down my body. I calm down and relax. I thank the universe that I am part of the consciousness that is universal and part of that which is life. I sleep.

***

It must have been days that I've been sleeping. When I wake, I am back in my cabin asleep, no, awake, because I am not dreaming anymore, I don't think. A woman brings in tea and biscuits with raspberry jam. Juice, too. Very continental. How do these ships keep their kitchens intact through storms, let alone find cooks who are willing to clean up and cook during a surprise attack, as a storm like that one can be called? I should hire one to clean my kitchen and cook for me in my apartment sometime. If I ever get out of this place. But maybe, if our plan works, I won't have to hire anyone at all, just ask someone who does it for a living, someone who enjoys doing that sort of thing so much that they just do it. What would I do? I won't have to worry about money or guilt.

It's amazing when we think about all the buildings and projects and munitions and everything that is not a work of art, or native living off the land, that was made for the purpose, the sole purpose of making money. I suppose almost everything is like that now.

It probably didn't start out that way. But the car, the airplane, boats, houses, food, are all things made for the purpose of getting money. What would the world be like if money had never been invented? Churches wouldn't have demanded it. Gold would not be the most important commodity. A monetary value would not be placed on every person or animal or object. We would be living with everything having a special place, instead of bulldozing the world to try and find wealth and fame and shit! Oh well, I can't think about this forever... money was invented by a white man—though wealth and power were measured in other ways before money came onto the scene. This, according to my old anthropology teacher, became easy for people who could stay in one place and accumulate food and land instead of having to move camp every day or every week or month. I guess people all over the world try and pack away things like squirrels or rats so they don't have to worry about tomorrow. Very odd behavior. The very thing that makes them do certain things is what they are trying not to be... if they could only see....

"Hey, can I come in?"

"Is that you, Kent? Don't you know how to knock?" I smile as I speak.

"Knock, knock."

"Who's there?"

"Apple."

"Apple who?"

"Knock knock."

"Who's there?"

"Orange you glad I didn't do the whole joke?"

["Sure, but are you saying that to me or to Sascha? I mean I am not just the writer but the reader, so I have to fathom this too."

"Well, I thought I was just part of the paper, this character that you've got in your imagination and on this white stuff here. Except that I can't tell what color it is really because I am not really here..., or am I?"

"Oh, enough already. I get the point. Now blend in again."

"Blend in?"

"Yes, yes, you know what I mean, become part of the paperwork."]

"I don't quite understand your joke, Kent."

"Did you ever hear that joke before—ah, but I mean any version even similar to it?"

"Where were you just then?"

"Just when, Sasch?"

"Just a little while ago, right after you told me—"

"Oh, then. Ah, well, I think it was just an imaginary place where some people are trying to focus in on us here."

"Do you mean another dimension?"

"Yeah, Sascha, that's right. It was like someone looking into our lives and trying to think or, I don't know, like talk or, or...."

"Or write about us?"

"Yeah, that's what I mean. I mean I know it sounds funny, but I just get this feeling sometimes."

"I do, too!"

"No, really?"

"Yeah, Kent."

"I thought you'd think I was crazy or something for saying that."

"No way. I've had thoughts like that for a long time. I think that it's very serious, and we should try and do something about it."

"Well, I don't know, Sascha. I think I've reached my peak of seriously deep thoughts for now."

"Are you serious?"

"Yeah, if I think too hard, I get a headache."

"A headache?"

"Really, I get so bored of thinking about things I really don't have to worry about that, well, frankly, I get headaches."

"I suddenly thought of how little we have in common."

"Well, that's what I told you in the first place."

"It was not."

"Hold it, hold it, why don't we do this differently? I'll start over here, all right?"

My mouth opens slightly. This guy is, I mean, I can't believe him sometimes. He is really out of this world. Is he really the one who is my twin light? I mean there are so many differences between us, and I keep feeling like I'm supposed to teach him all this stuff, which by rights, I mean if he's my twin light, he should know this already, shouldn't he?

No, not really.

Oh no, it's the writer again. Forget what I said. I know what you're going to say.

What?

That, he's my twin light and that I'll probably have to just remind him 'cause he's been almost swallowed into this crummy earththought.

Close.

Close?

Yes, you see I no longer think that it's the crummy earththought, or rather Earththought, anymore because I have changed my ideas about certain essential beliefs.

And what's that?

I'll tell you later. Just get the idea into your head that things aren't necessarily the way people have led us to believe. I mean if you think about it, most of our belief systems come from the interpretations of philosophies hundreds of years old. Are they accurate? Or have all the interpretations discolored and altered the truths people may have access to?

"So how ya feelin', girl?"

"Ah, all right, Kent. How about you? I mean after being locked in my cabin for half the night—hey! How'd you get out of here last night?" I pull my knees close to my chest till my red hair covers my knees under the sheets and my arms that are wrapped around them.

"Easy, Sister Suzie, I waited till the sky calmed down. Then, when one of my boys was checkin' out the deck, I opened the hatch and yelled at him."

"But how'd they get you out? I have the key—how else could I have locked you in?"

Kent reaches into his pocket and pulls out: "Masters... always have 'em for just such emergencies."

"You mean to tell me you've had keys to my room all along?"

"Sure. That was the agreement I had with Will."

"To have keys to my room?"

"No, now, don't go popping a gasket, dearie," he sits closer to her on her bed. "I have masters to all the rooms." He wiggles his eyebrows up and down.

"Get outa here!"

"Out? But I just got here and I wanted to hear what happened to you last night after you locked me—"

"Me? What do you mean? Oh, me...."

"You were a sorry sight when we found you out there. "

"Cut the crap, Shakespeare. What or where did they find me, and how did I look?"

"Well, I can't say you needed a shave, dear girl, but I wouldn't put it past you."

I can't help but laugh at your comments, Kent, but I'll be damned if I admit that to you now. So I throw a pillow at you before you make another comment. "Stop that now, Kent. This is serious. I need to know what happened—I was working on something." I try and listen to my inner voice so as not to get totally flustered.

"What? What were you working on?"

"Oh, um, well, um, er, working on? Well, let's just say that I'm not exactly just a pretty face."

"What are you talking about, girl? Did you fall or something?"

"No, I don't think so, but to tell you the truth, I was hurting so much this morning that I may have. But I honestly don't remember."

"Is that what this is about?"

"Is what what this is about?"

"I don't know. You're supposed to be telling me. What is going on here? What were you working on, and why do you think you fell or something? You silly girl." You say that as you touch my face and give me a look that pierces my heart. But I can't let on, not now, not yet. This is too important for a flash of sudden love. I grab your hand and take it sort of like a friend before it leaves my face. I'm turning a few shades of red, I think, but I have to work on keeping it cool and friendly, very friendly, but just friendly.

"You're pretty funny yourself, you old coot. But hey, it's real important for me to know where and how I was found. Will ya tell me, please?"

"But why? I mean, I'll tell you, but I just would like

to know why it's so important to you."

"Please, remember what I said before?"

"What's that?"

"Don't ask questions."

"Hoh," you drop your hand discouraged, "right. The catch-all. Thanks, Urma, for the advice."

"You will find out later."

"When later?"

"When the time is right."

You slap your forehead. "Now don't that beat all! What do you take me for anyway, some sort of idiot?"

"No, of course not. Quite the contrary, Kent, my dear."

"What?"

"Trust me, will you? You will understand, okay?" I give him a sort of sorrowful look, with a smile on the end.

"Oh, how can I refuse you?" Your eyes are oozing with desire, and I just have to look away because I'm feeling the same way. I can't stand this anymore. it's just too heavy for me to bear.

"So, what's my answer, wise guy?"

You pull up a chair and sit down before telling me, "They found you clutching a rail that you were half under—you know, like hanging off the ship.

"Oh."

"It took them half an hour to pry you off the rail so they could carry you into your room. And on the stretcher, you still looked like you were holding on."

"You've got to be kidding."

"How did you get out there, anyway?"

"I thought you might know. I mean I went to help the captain, but he was drunk. So I went up to check on who was at the helm. It was the first mate, and he was really freaking out. I tried to calm him down, but he apparently didn't appreciate my help, I don't blame him, though. Anyway, he ordered me to go and get coffee. How is he doing, anyway? Were there any casualties from that cyclone or whatever that was that hit us last night?"

"No," you say absently. "The first mate announced last night that everyone should close their hatches and bolt their doors. He said everyone should stay calm, but to pray. He said the prayer part in a very low voice, as if he didn't want anyone to hear him really, like he didn't know the loud speaker was on or something."

"Is he all right?"

"He's been sleeping all day, too."

"Who's at the helm?"

"I guess the captain felt better this morning. I think that after that storm last night, he's feeling better now."

"A part of me was very tempted to get very mad at him last night when I saw him lying there, but I don't like to use that part of me."

"What did you say?"

"Nothing. Did the captain say why he collapsed when we needed him the most?"

"Well, I guess I can tell you that. It seems that he really did think he could get through it, but something inside him told him not to take the helm."

"Any reason?"

"Well, Sascha, I guess he really hasn't flown this route in years."

"That's why?"

"Well, no, not really. But it was just that few years ago that he did, and the captain was steering the boat at this same place when his wife died."

"They had a wreck?"

"Well, the ship was knocked around a bit. It's just that his wife was pregnant at the time, and she was sick with a fever. And she was seasick."

"But if she was pregnant, why was she on the trip?

It's so dangerous."

"I think they had just found out a few days earlier from the ship's doctor, so they had no real way to avoid the journey."

"This isn't a common route, is it?"

"I don't think so. I think that's why we chose it."

"Well, I think I get the picture: she was sick with fever, delirious and she left her cabin to find her husband, and fell over from the violent waters. What a tragedy. Why would he even think to make this trip?"

"Well, I didn't ask him that one. But I'm sure you can."

"When I can see him? What's next, Kent?"

"Well, we're supposed to be avoiding trouble and at the same time, trying to locate Ruban somewhere around here."

"But we're almost in Antarctica. Did he really get this far south?"

"I don't think quite this far, but about half will end up going this way. Well, I think I'd better get going. You need your rest. Oh, except that I was going to ask you what happened when we doing our visualizing yesterday."

"Wait, what do you mean about half?"

"You know, about half of the ships we've got."

"So they're not all taking the same route?"

"No, but listen you, you really need your rest."

"But the visualizing—"

"Oh, right. Well, I know from my watch that I was under for about two hours."

"Under?"

"Listen, don't play coy with me. I know you were hypnotizing me then."

"I really didn't mean to. I mean, I was sort of helping you move into an idea, and you just slipped right in. I was kind of startled by it myself, but we just went with it."

"Honestly, I'm not trying to accuse you."

"Well, Kent, I'm not guilty anyway."

"Right." You smile.

"But how did you know anyway that you were hypnotized?"

"I felt different. I don't know how exactly. There was just something that opened up for me. It's hard to explain."

"Well, as far as answering your question of what happened, it was pretty weird, 'cause you really went into the future. I mean that. It was spooky."

"How?"

"Well, it was like everything that you were describing was actually taking place now and in the future. It was like you were seeing a vision, but stronger than that. Have you ever been able to see the future before?"

"Get outa here." You grab the pillow I'd hit you with and put it over my face playfully.

"No, I'm really serious. I was spooked. I mean it was really weird for me, and, frankly, with all my experience in strange paranormal phenomenon, I mean, I really didn't know what to do. And I didn't know how to deal with the fact that I was hypnotizing you either."

"You're nuts, lady."

"Really, I got goose bumps to prove it, then and now."

"Let's see." I show him my arm.

"Besides, I'll bet all them folks is still there. Here, I'll show you."

We laugh and understand.

"So, when do we arrive, Kent?"

"I really don't know. I'll have to ask the captain later when I check in on him."

"All right, I guess I won't die without the info now.

But I will need to get up soon."

"No way, José. You ain't gettin' up till the doc tells ya. Capiche?"

"Sure, sombrero head."

"Thanks, rattlesnake breath."

"That's getting kind of low, don't you think?"

"All right, dearie."

"Just remember, that I'm a big girl now. You don't have to treat me like a child of ignorance."

"Well, I—I'm not trying to, but I do want you to stay in bed for a while."

"What's a while?"

"For today or tomorrow, or so."

"Today, tomorrow or so? You nuts, man?"

"Well, sweetheart, I'm afraid you have no choice." Kent picks up his keys and dangles them far enough away from me so I can't grab them by reaching. He stands and then walks to the door. "Sorry, girl, gotta lock you in."

"Very funny, Kent, but you can't cage me like some bird."

"We'll see about that."

"What if I have to get out, like for a fire or something?"

"There's someone outside most of the time checking on you and the others."

"Aw, isn't that sweet. Now leave my door alone!"

"See ya later, Sasch." He walks out and locks the door. I wait to hear him walk away. I think he's gone. But wait, this is ridiculous! Doors can't be locked JUST from the outside. Otherwise what would be the point of a lock? I'll bet my keys do unlock this door, and he was just saying that because he wanted to trick me. I climb out of bed, but I feel pretty groggy. I guess I wouldn't mind staying here all that long if I wasn't locked in my own room, or am I? I open my dresser drawer and quietly remove my keys. I walk

over to the door, if you call it walk, but I hope it's worth it.
I pull out the key and insert it, hmmm, where do I insert it?
I've been just relying on my chain lock before. But what did
I use the key on? The handle lock. But then shouldn't there
be some sort of button? I try the handle again by just
turning it. It's no use. It is locked from the outside. That's
wild.

"Why in hell doesn't my key work?"

"Because we had them changed, Sasch."

"You little eaves dropper you! Let me outa here,
oooh." I begin a coughing session and sort of collapse onto
the ground.

Kent quickly unlocks the door and has to, as gently
as possible push me away from the door, with the door. I
can't get up. I can hardly catch my breath. Geez, I musta
breathed in a lotta water 'cause most of it's still in there.
Kent lifts me up and onto the bed.

"Dan! Go get the doc!" I guess it's the guy waiting
outside. I hear him run away down the corridor. I'm so cold.
How could I feel so great one minute and so crummy the
next? I can't stop coughing. Wow, am I getting hot. I feel
sweat pouring out of my pores. What is this itch? Kent has
me over his shoulder soothing my back. It feels good. I
think I'm stopping coughing. I take a slow, easy breath.
The doctor runs in with a little black bag and Bermuda
shorts.

"What is it, what is it? Dan said it was an
emergency."

"She's been coughing the entire time since Dan left
to get you, but up till now, oddly enough."

"Well, why don't you lay her down and get on out.
I'll examine her. My nurse should be here shortly too."
Kent and Dan do as they're told. The doc begins a sort of
chest/lung exam.

"I'm," I cough, "I'm fine," I cough again. "Man! I'm

really—" I cough and cough and cough and cough, oh, about fifty times. But then I start to shiver again, and then I start to sweat again along with all those coughs. Pretty soon I'm totally exhausted. The nurse comes in looking pretty spry, too, and then the two of them talk a bit, quietly. The doc makes a call. He gives me

a shot of something after a bit. I feel drowsy. I don't feel like coughing as much. I feel very relaxed. After a little while somebody brings in something like a tent with some strange machine attached to it. They set it up over my bed, and breathing begins to get easier. I can see myself from the outside of the tent, looking at myself inside the tent. A strange white tent around a bed. I watch for a while. I feel great now. No cares in the world. But I can't stay here forever. I meditate for a while. I'm quiet and peaceful with my legs crossed on the floor and a candle in front of me, burning. The room is quiet now. The nurse is gone, and so is the doctor. But someone comes in. I move out of the way, but he grabs the candle and blows it out.

"How in hell did that get there?" He opens the tent zipper quickly. "Sascha?"

"What?" I say to him.

"But she's asleep. I gave her a sedative. She couldn't have."

"What do you want?"

The doc feels her—my head. "Burning up with fever."

"Why doesn't he hear me?" I am Sascha Jarlston, aren't I? No, that's not who I am, that's my name, or at least the name my Earth mother gave me when she adopted me. But is my name or any name part of the person because that's the vibration the parents feel or sense from the child? Sounds are merely vibrations, and words are really just sounds that a group of people agree mean something. And then they pass the agreements onto their children or grandchildren. Still, I can't help feeling that this name is a fragment of what and who I am. I am an adventurer, explorer, stock broker, woman with long red hair, a woman or female considered by most to be quite beautiful, but even that seems transparent. Are not the curves of my face and body merely reflectors of the light given off by those who look? Who am I then? Am I what I am as an Earthling? Or am I what I am as a Brongonite? But what, what? I'm not some teenager trying to figure out the mystery of life, which is supposedly never answered, but I am trying to consider what this I who thinks about another I actually knows or could possibly know about this self that has really never left the ocean... the ocean. I stand and gaze out the window at the blue and green. It's really green. I walk to the door. My eyes are closed when I put my hands on the door and feel the warmth coming from my hands. I hear tiny clicks in the cylinder. I walk away for a moment and change clothes. Then, I walk out the door. I told Kent he couldn't keep me locked up.

***

A group of ex-soldiers sits watching movies of strong images in a large room. They sit around at tables with coffee or beer.

After a movie they break down into groups and talk with their facilitators. You sit back trying to absorb what's been going on. He calls on you for the first time. You know that unless you're ready to face a world without violence, you will have to stay and continue the deprogramming. You try and listen to what he's saying you're supposed to do here. He wants you to role play with someone trying or pretending to be your father. "Can I sit here?" You ask him. No, you have to go to the center where everyone in your group can see you. You and the other guy playacting like he's your father. You don't want to do that. You don't like your father. "Why?" he asks. You don't want to say. How about if you play your father, and the other guy plays you? But the other guy and you don't really know each other. "He doesn't know your father, either," says the shrink. "Just try and pretend." Pretend what? "Pretend that you—he being you—are about ten years old and that you want this toy, some toy that you really liked, and that you want your dad—or you—to get it for you."

"Sure that's easy," you say.

"Yeah, that sounds easy," the other guy says.

"You start," you say.

"All right. Hey, Dad, I really want this toy."

"NO. Shut up and go to your room. I told you what you can do if you want something. So forget it, and shut up!" You start to hit the other guy, but then you realize that it wasn't your father. It was you. You You You YOU YOU YOU!

"Why'd you do that?" the shrink asks.

"I—well, ya told me to pretend like my dad. So I did what ya said."

"Good. Now, ah, with that same situation, ah, why don't you pretend you're you." I give him a little sneer like he's not so smart after all.

"Well, you know what I mean."

"Right." I look at the other guy and proceed. "Dad, I want this toy I saw last week—"

"I told you to leave me alone about that crap! Get outa here before I beat you bloody!"

"That's really good acting, guys. Now what if you changed your father a bit and pretended he was the way you wanted him to be."

You try and think of how you wanted him to be. Maybe you think of how he still could be, but isn't.

"Ya mean like understanding and like listening to me most of the time and not yelling or beating me all the time?" You feel sad, very sad. "Your dad hit you, too?"

You ask the other guy.

He nods. He starts to look sad, too.

"Can you two do that?"

"Ah, well, I don' know man. I just know that I never wanted to be like him, but I think I am like him."

"Why?"

"Oh, come on, Doc, I just know that—"

"Show me how you'd like him to be to you now."

"This is—" you stammer.

"How about if I try and be your dad for a bit. Can we try that?"

"Oh, all right. Dad, I saw this toy I wanted."

"What toy?"

You look at me a minute and then to the ground. "Well, it's a train."

"An electric one?"

You can see it in your mind's eye. "Yeah, it's a beaut."

"Well, I think you've been pretty good these last few months. You probably deserve it. Let's go get it."

"But what about the bills and the rent and—"

"We're gonna be in a new age soon. We don't have to worry about that kind of stuff anymore. And even if we did, I'd try and get it for you anyway."

***

"How's it going, Ralph?"

"All right, William. We've been working on the pieces for almost a month now. Nobody has noticed yet, I think—none of the bosses. But I think we'll have to start installing these things soon or someone may consider squealing on us."

"Do you know of anyone in particular, Ralph?"

"No, I can't really put my finger on it, but I have a feeling it may be Brutus, the plant spy."

"A spy? You mean you have a spy for the plant who

knows and is part of our plans?"

"No, no. I've told all the people on this project that he's a spy. But I thought maybe one of the others may have mentioned it to him by mistake and was too embarrassed to tell us. It was just now for this project that I had to let them know one of the company secrets."

"So you think one of them might have forgotten or might not believe you?"

"Ya."

"How can you tell? I mean, maybe you're just frightened about the whole thing. Our minds tend to play tricks on us when we're afraid, you know."

"Yes, yes, this is true, and I have experienced this before, like in England when I was trying to help the British against the Nazis and I was afraid they were following me. Yes, yes, I know this feeling. But maybe it is this, and maybe it is not this. Brutus has been acting very strange toward me lately. Avoiding me and looking at me when I don't know until I turn and he is there. I don't want to take any chances."

"All right, I trust your feelings. When should we get started?"

"I think the day after tomorrow will work nicely."

Underneath the scientist's coffee table where he and William have been setting their cups, there is a tiny black bug, stuck but getting fat on every word. Meanwhile three men listen in amazement at their dear honest little employee.

"Right under our noses!" A man with a grey-and-maroon striped suit wipes his forehead.

"It sure sounds like him."

"Yes, well, I just can't believe he'd do this to us after all these years of working together. If he had only come to us with his needs. What are we going to do?" a deeply

262

tanned man with a red pullover sweater and designer jeans says while tossing a manila folder across to the other fellow.

"I really don't know Bernard, but I do know one thing. We one can't have him on our staff anymore. We'll have call him right away and fire him.

"But there's only one problem with that."

"What's that Bernard?"

"What if he's got information about those shady deals we made a few years back?"

"What shady deals? I didn't hear 'bout no shady deals."

"All those dumping sights we sort of forgot to report."

"You mean the times we dumped on our own land? We can do that."

"On our property, sure, a bit, but what about all the electric lines we have and all those scarecrows. The metal ones that are what holds all the power lines up?"

"You're joking, aren't you. Why didn't you tell me? Wait, though, it may be legal now."

"No, I doubt it. But even if it were, I don't think the public would allow us to stay open any longer. They may shut us down."

"You can't be—how? Why didn't you think of this before?"

"Oh, man, and now Brutus here knows about it, too."

"I ain't gonna tell no one, Boss.... Why should I?"

"For the right price, my ignorant friend," Bernard says as he doodles on a yellow pad and then stands and jerks at Brutus's collar, "you'll do almost anything."

"Hey, boss, I know where my loyalties stand. I ain't no squealer or nuttin'." He pulls himself loose.

"Ah, what d'ya think you do for a living? You squeal! But that doesn't have to be true for everything. You can keep your mouth shut, because for every one of you there's twenty guys that will shut you up for good, see?"

"Bernard, leave him alone. Brutus was the one who helped us find the real traitor anyway. What're ya gettin' on him for?"

"Holy Toledo, Brutus, I—I'm sorry, real sorry, I—I—I'm just real sorry for doubting you. Of course, you're right, Joe. I guess I got ahead of things a bit."

"A bit? You just threatened his life—Brutus, a good trustworthy employee. We should give Brutus a nice big fat bonus, don't you think?"

"Well, now, come to think of it, that's a wonderful idea."

"Well, thank you, gents." Brutus smiles, and they all begin shaking hands.

"But let's not get carried away again now, Bernard. We still have to figure out what we need to do with Mr. Chop Chop, yes?"

"Don't you worry about a thing, Brother Joe, I have a master plan to capture the culprit."

"Yes, yes?" Bernard begins to rub his hands together, drawing his head closer to his brothers.

"We need to trap him at his own game."

"Yes, yes."

"Well?"

"Oh, of course I think you're right, absolutely right brother—absolutely."

But outside the door is another spy. The oldest employee in the company. She's had her ear glued to the door now for twenty minutes, ever since she saw Brutus go upstairs to talk to the bosses. After she hears their plan, she heads downstairs to tell the others. She whispers to one woman, who goes and whispers into another ear and on and on and so forth and so what?

But how can you the author say that, write that?

Well, I haven't exactly heard much more of how our heroes are going to get out of this mess or even of how they're going to hear about it, and so you folks are just sitting around whispering and collecting hours on the clock while those demons upstairs are saying who knows what. For all you know, they've changed their plans.

The whole plant (except, of course, the bosses upstairs and anyone else who isn't supposed to hear, of course), whispers in unison, "Changed their plans?"

Well, sure, I mean, after all, this ain't no Payton Place, ya know. This here is life, and shit happens.

"You mean, isn't a Payton Place, young one," says Molly Hatchet, the one who's the snooper.

"Who's calling me a snoop?" she yells.

Well, I made you.

"But you can't call poor ol' innocent me that, the one who's trying desperately to enhance this here plot."

Watch it, woman. You can be replaced, ya know.

"You can't do that. You've worked so hard on my character. It would change the ENTIRE PLOT AND THEME AND EVERYTHING!"

No, it won't. Not in the least. But I don't want you to feel bad, I just want you to remember that I can pick you up and shake you out and speak with you or through you or around you and through you and the next guy. I can pick you up and make you fly or make you die.

She lies on the floor and sobs "Please don't do that, I was only doing my best. I didn't mean to criticize you. I DON' WANNA DIE!"

All right, all right already. Come on, now. Just get up. You're making a mess of things. We don't have time for this! Get up! You remind me of my nephew when he was two.

She looks up from her sobs—there ain't no tears, except the fake ones that actresses on soaps wear as jewelry so they never wipe off like in real life. Molly never wipes them off either, but she does ask me in a babyish whimper, "You gonna make me die?"

No, Molly, now will you please get up? This is really getting tedious. I want to know how you're gonna get this mess fixed.

"You don't know?"

No, this is an adventure for me, too—to some degree. I mean you're the characters, and I'm flesh and blood, I think.

Everyone in every scene who's anyone waiting for a line says very loudly, "YOU MEAN YOU DON"T KNOW WHAT'S NEXT?"

No. But neither do you until it's your turn, or at least until I finish this book. So relax for God's sake, and trust me. Everybody back in place now? Everybody is still—trembling for now, but as still as people made of black lines on white paper can be.

A little bird hops onto Molly's shoulder and whispers. She smiles and goes over to her manager. She tells him her dog is sick—very sick, so she has to go home and take care of him. It's only ten o'clock, but her manager smiles and pats her on the back and tells her to go home. She skedaddles but fast.

The pages and paper have become numb to my touch, or so it seems as I observe these characters moving delightfully across the page. The words find their place in space. A space for every word, and every word in its space. But now the time has come for someone to take more action than words. So good ol' Molly is going to serve her duty.

She jogs to her car and forces the key into its hole, bending it slightly in haste. She slams the car into reverse. She just misses the boss's car. I wait for her at my home where I've been talking to William—the instigator of all this.

"If your plan doesn't work, William, I don't know what I'll do. Fifty years with a company all down the drain."

"What do ya mean, Doc, you're not goin' nowhere."

"Well, then, does that mean I'm already washed up? It was your plan."

"Oh, what are you talking about, Doc? You're not going anywhere."

"What do you mean by that? I'm a scientist. If word gets out that I've gone against a company, I'll never get work again. And that I can't afford at my age."

"What does being a scientist have to do with anything?"

"I can't believe you're saying this."

"To tell you the truth I can't either. Are we reading the right script? This doesn't seem like me."

No, it doesn't sound like you. I've never heard you sound so ignorant. You have such a respect and admiration for the sciences. But I can't say that out loud. "Well, let's be thankful this isn't a screenplay yet." I tell him right out. But maybe I wasn't playing this scene right. Shouldn't I be a bit more mellow? The old brain type with the sweet wife who adores him and will do anything for him, that's what I'm supposed to be like. All except that I have no sweet wife. I have no wife, in this story at least. But then, who needs a wife? Freedom is better than listening to a nag, a hag, a rag, or a dog. A floozy, a Jezebel, a... there are so many many names for women in the English language. There are probably thousands of words for women: chick, bimbo, Amazon woman, etc., etc. And each of these words works like magic. You use them once, and they destroy the woman. It's like a hex or something. But we men never have to worry, for there are fewer names, laws or rules that really govern us. Except those placed upon us by other men.

And even if we do become something horrid, we can always reform. But a woman? No. Once she's been used up as a slut, a whore, dried up old maid, bimbo, floozy, tramp, bitch, easy lay or the good ol' dumb blonde. And we can't forget the wonderful phrases of stupid broad or OVER THIRTY! Forget it. She might as well jump in the lake. Yet, seeing as how I am a man in this scene, I'll have to use my more positive abilities and become the honest and innocent scientist—the absent-minded professor type who takes all the time in the world to explain every little thing, but only in the most complicated term possible. I can lose things often also. Like my car, dog, keys or house, or even my slippers and laundry detergent, ha, ho, hum.

KNOCK KNOCK KNOCK!

"Are you expecting anyone, Doc?"

"Of course not, William, are you? Unless, of course, we're in the wrong house or something. But, William, why are you looking at me that way?"

"Oh, ah, don't be silly, Doc. Now, don't you get mail here?"

"That's true. We mustn't leave that person out there then must we?"

William's steps echo across the oak floor. His reflection glimmers in the shine of the large mahogany fireplace as he passes. I do love cleaning in my spare time. I do so enjoy making everything look as if I have servants. William shines in the mirror in the foyer now, while leaning to open the door. I don't hear anyone in the den. Who could that be? Could it be the police? I grip the chair handle. I can't breathe. Who is at the door? Finally, William slides over to the doorway and looks at me. He has only his head looking in at me. He then reaches his hand in and points and bends it I'm assuming in the universal signal of "come here." I walk to the door, cautiously. Who is at the door? I hear my shoes loudly echoing across the ceiling. I see my fear in my mirror. The shine manipulates my reflection. The hall's shadows paint two large figures. One is William's, and the other's is... MOLLY! But suddenly my face is covered, I'm being overcome! I fall onto my red velvet chair—making sure not to crease it.

"Doc!" William leans over me, still covering my mouth! Then he whispers, "There's a bug under your coffee table in the living room. Molly overheard us talking—through the bosses' door!" I pull his hand away. I grab his handkerchief and wipe the river off my forehead.

"Let's go outside and handle this." I take one set of keys from a flower pot near the front door, and we walk outside. The day is empty. The sun is bright but colorless. The shapes outside are square and round. A fat lady wearing a pink polka-dotted purple dress crosses the street with a black baby carriage. I lock the door and look around. No one else can be found.

"Come on. My car's out back."

"His car's out back?" Molly asks. William shrugs, I smile.

"So nice to have you with us today Miss Molly. How's your dog?" I try and be pleasant. We walk around to my gorgeous back yard, which I've been dying to show someone all summer, since my noisy nephews don't come anymore and ruin it for me, it is such a shrine to the planet. We walk down the sidewalk and under a yellow rose covered arch and pop! The green shouts from every direction. The flowers bloom in every direction. Trees fill the air. Fountains spring up as we walk.

"Who is your gardener?" Molly asks as she gapes at my fruit trees.

"I do it myself." I smile.

"How can you do all this? When do you find the time?" William asks.

"My garage is just beyond that wall." I point.

"What wall?" William throws up his arms.

"Oh, it's covered with the ivy there."

"Why don't we talk out here?" Molly points to my natural wicker settee on the limestone patio.

"It may be bugged too, my dear." I whisper in her ear. She smells delightful, like an orchid.

"Did I tell you how I used to raise orchids?"

"How did you do that, doctor?" Molly stops for a moment to smell the lilacs.

"I have a green house on my roof." I point. "I developed a new variety."

"Why did you stop?" William puts his hand on his brow to cut the sun.

"We became so busy at the plant with all the new inventions I and others were developing that I couldn't continue. Now I only grow the hybrid that I developed, and one or two others. I was so sad to part with my friends."

"Your friends?"

"Yes, William, have you ever thought of a plant in terms of thou?"

"Thou?" he asks as I pull my keys out and open the door, holding it open for them and they wait by the car. I unlock the doors for them and switch off the alarm very quickly.

"I hope the alarm didn't go off. I always forget to turn it off first." We sit comfortably in my luxury car while I pull out of the winding driveway. They look at the grand houses with wide eyes. "They're not really mansions, just large homes with big lots. Mine is about average size."

"How do you keep your home and garden so clean? I didn't see any servants." William fiddles with his hat.

"Oh well, they're my hobbies." I smile.

William and Molly look at each other in amazement.

"But, sir, when do you have time to do all that?" Molly leans forward so I can hear.

"Well, I don't work at the factory all day, you know. I design for a few hours and then oversee some of my inventions, and then I come home and relax for a bit before I clean and tend my green friends."

"You're amazing, truly amazing." Molly sits back and stretches. They are silent for a few moments before we turn into a forest preserve. We get out of the car and walk along the path toward a small lake.

"Sometimes I imagine my car blowing up while I walk away." I scratch my neck.

"I'm sure you don't have to worry about that yet, doctor." Molly folds her arms. The group sit down at a picnic table under a willow by the water.

"Well, now, Molly, what is all this about?" The doctor brushes off the table a bit and then takes his seat again. "Birds are such a nuisance—at times."

"Yes, I see." William scratches his head.

"So, getting back to you, Molly—you've been working with us all along, haven't you?" "Yes, sir. I felt it was a brilliant idea almost from the start, so I've been behind both of you all the way."

"Then what is the problem?"

"The problem is that your house is bugged."

"Bugged?"

"Yes, sir. I heard you and William talking from outside the bosses' office, with them talking about your punishment and all kinds of things."

"I don't understand. How could all this be?"

"Well, I was on my way to the restroom upstairs—because the one downstairs was filled, and well, I had to get back to my post in a hurry. But anyway, I was walking past the big bosses' office when I heard your voice, William." William shakes his head slowly. "Well, naturally, I was suspicious because of, well, I thought you had, well, sold out or something. But then I heard the professor, too. So since nobody was around, I, ah, snooped, and very carefully, too. Then the three men who were really in there just started yelling at each other, while you two kept talking quietly and carefully. Bernard, I think, started yelling about you and then at Tony, and almost choked him, or at least nearly. But then they stopped and ended up giving him a bonus. But then they also said that, and get this, they heard your plan to move out the night after next—so, well, they'll be waiting for you, with the cops, I think."

"Oh no, what are we going to do? What are we going to do?"

"I don't know, Doc."

"Wait a minute now. They can't arrest us, necessarily, because I have lots and lots of photos of them and their bad business practices. I could ruin them. But they're gonna try and... ohohoooo."

"Wait now. Wait just a minute, Doc. I think we're missing an easy exit to this here deal."

"What's that then, pray tell? Here I am on the verge of losing everything, my house, my car, my garden, all because of—"

"Wait, now, don't lose your cool again." Molly folds her arms in front of her, waiting for William to explain.

"Doctor?" Molly tries to be very sweet, and the doctor is touched deeply by her voice and tone.

"Why yes, Molly?'

"Don't worry, I'm sure William has a way of solving all this, after all he has been managing all the other projects around the world for this thing. Would you like to hear his idea?"

The doctor smiles at her and nods slowly. "Ah, why yes, of course I do. What is it, William?" The doctor forgets his troubles and thinks only of the big brown eyes in Molly's gently aging face and proud stature.

"Well, Doc, we simply get everything out tonight.

See I told you it was simple."

The doctor smiles.

As midnight emerges, a hundred employees of the plant assemble about two blocks away. They're armed with flashlights and a walkie talkie for every three people—or every group. They wear ski masks. Wearing sneakers, they follow a quiet path to the factory and wait in the darkness while a few others check the grounds. Two pit bulls are with them for protection.

The large electric gates surrounding the buildings are switched off with the professor's special computer keys. Three large men walk in and inspect the grounds before signaling the others to follow. As the three creep in quietly, their hearts pound louder than their feet. The rest of the group stands in the shadows with their black clothes and masks and switched off equipment while night hums in the city some twenty miles away. The air is cool and dry for August.

Each group had been given a plan as to how and where to retrieve a portion of the necessary materials. They all sit down to await the time for entrance and consider their plans of attack.

Finally, the door opens. The group cautiously enters through the gate and then through the fire door of the plant. Two of the forerunners scout for guards. Finding two on duty, they overpower them with chloroform, tie them, gag them, and lock them in separate closets near large machinery so they can't be heard easily. In a few days or less, one of us will get them out. I'm wearing my sneakers as I was told so little or no noise could be heard from my moves. I go quickly to my section with the other two in my group. We quickly assemble the parts as our map indicates. We carry out three large boxes as on the map. Finally, after beeping our current leader to let her know we're ready to depart from the plant, we make our way back to the holding area where she'll meet us and where we can rest till everyone is ready. We set our delicate boxes down in the corner of what is actually the coffee room. We are the first ones to be ready. I know that we had the easiest load at the closest location to the exit. I go over and make a pot of coffee for everyone. We don't talk. We can't. We don't want to know who is actually on this caper so we can't name names or have to tell lies. The walkie talkies are for emergencies only. We move our caps off our chins to take sips of black from white. Our gloves are kept on the entire time—even if we have to urinate. Well, I can't go that far as to guess what the other guys are doing. But I have to go right now. But how do I tell them without giving them the wrong impression. I start to walk away from the area. The other two try and block my exit. I shrug my shoulders and point my index finger to let them know I'll be right back. I walk down the familiar hall to the familiar door where the can is unusually empty. I sit down and release my waste. I start to pull at the roll of unserrated paper, pulling at a hundred parts to try and get a wad going. They're gonna think I'm in trouble or need some help. I pull some more, and after a bit I get hold of a stronger piece while my right hand turns the wheel. I roll it onto my left and then yank a big honkin' piece in revolt against the roll.

When I return to my post I casually retrieve my cup and sip the cold black. The others look at me and jerk their heads back in amazement, open their arms in wonder, and with every other conceivable antic, signal their dismay. I shrug. I'm getting pretty tired and I have to be back here tomorrow and pretend I don't know anything at eight in the morning. I thought the others would be done by now. I look at my watch again. My heart begins to race. I wave at the others and then point to my watch. They look at their own. Theirs are closer. They get up from the table and act really nervous. The one with the red cap pulls out his walkie talkie and covers it and his head so he can't be heard.

"What's goin shcrummigen poindeicneiozdjhdhdh?"

"Who sefsnzdhkdh?"

"Theimldjflasfkjsljglfjgkfjgljlkjljuwr."

"Wlhkjdthjtugldfgdlgltlutjrltjeljlj."

He puts the toy away and kind of signals that it'll be soon and that everything is okay. After just a few minutes, two short raps but with a three-second lapse between each are let out on the door. The loading guys are ready and waiting outside. They must've been notified. Then almost suddenly people start filling the area with boxes and bags. The one in charge—for now—opens the door, and we begin loading things onto a truck waiting right outside. We know they're with us because they're wearing a red scarf around their neck. But this isn't just any scarf. It has as its emblem, the flag of the future free world. Purple with a stripe of deep forest green to depict the peaceful purple sunset and the free life of the Earth. Someone said it reminded them of Christmas while another thought it gave them a Chanukah feeling. One person is counting everybody. Then he/she beeps the others in the outside to have the vehicles ready. Soon we're filed out of the very stuffy room. Two guys or gals stay and see that all the materials are loaded on safely. A leader—for now—tidies up the place and covers our tracks. We walk out into the darkness and through the gate, like a file of soldiers.... I shudder with the thought. I ain't no soldier, I ain't never gonna be no faceless mindless follower of death, killer. But we are walking single file quietly down the road in black without light to the waiting trucks. We climb into the dark holes and hope nothing jumps out at us. As each truck fills, it pulls off into the night to a waiting warehouse. The trucks go through the bumpy alleys to get to it and then enter through a large door. We climb out still wearing the infamous ski masks, sweating underneath. Everyone who gets out of a truck is checked for the scarf of the New World. Anyone without it will be brought to the center of the crowd for questioning. Three trucks have entered and expelled their cargo with no snags. Stepping out one at a time, I hear them jump down. Our truck is in, and I'm next in line. Like having i.d.'s checked at a rock concert, I pull out my scarf. But the flag's not on it! I pull it off only to find it on the other end. I walk away like I'm cool. I look around for anyone who looks like they know what's going on and can tell me what to do and when the hell I can go home. Now we wait around for a bit till all the people have been checked before the trucks with the stuff pull in. Finally they pull into the large room where trucks are parked and the air is really beginning to stink. People begin pulling the boxes off the trucks and handing them down the line and into the storage room where shelves and tables are waiting. I start helping by just stepping into the line. Some people are even in there unpacking the boxes, but they're probably people who really know what they're doing.

"Excuse me, dear people!" a woman's voice breaks the hum of many. We look up at her. "If you will be so kind as to gather over here so we can take roll? Come on, gather round."

"What about our code of silence?" blurts out a gruff male voice.

"You were all given code names, so there should be no problem."

That guy should know that. Maybe he's a spy or something. I notice several eyes planting themselves on his head. His eyes are turned down staring at people's feet. We all walk over to her, and she begins call out code names. We raise our hands, but keep our eyes on him. I think there were over three hundred names on that sheet, and not one of them was his. But I notice him gradually moving away, so every time someone's name is called and s/he looks away for a second, the unknown guy moves back just a little, trying to get out of the crowd. But the crowd stays around him till he tries to take a run for it and a bunch of us just grab him. He's tackled, all right. Someone blows the whistle, and we get off him before we crush him. Someone yanks off his cap. But it's Tony, of course. They warned us about him.

"Tony, right?" the lady asks as if she doesn't know.

"That's right, Delilah, and I know your voice anywhere, since you were the one who told me to come."

"I thought that little pip squeak would find a way here!" yells a burly voice.

But to prove him wrong the lady pulls off her mask and says, "Guess again, Tony."

"What? I thought you were Delilah!"

"There's nobody here with that name, Tony. Maybe you got the wrong group." They take him into a back room for questioning and waiting until this portion of the operation is complete.

"For those of you who would like to stay and help with the assembly, breakfast will be served. If you'd rather go home, that's all right. You can take off your masks now because Tony's gonna be kept in the back until we're done with all this."

"What if he's got a homing device on him or what if they say we kidnapped him? He could have the cops on us right now!" says a very small man. Three people run into the back room and search Tony head to toe and do find a device in his shoe. One guy dashes for side exit and is gone far about twenty minutes before returning and saying he's thrown it into the water.

"I don't think we can let anyone leave the warehouse," says a man entering the main area from the office.

"Excuse me, everyone," says a woman who walked in with him. "But we have a little snag here. Now I know you all want to go home, but look at this situation here. We've caught Tony in our midst. And as far as we know, there is no way he should've known about our change in plans tonight. We don't know who's been leaking information to him, or the owner, if that's who it was. Is there a Delilah in the company who just isn't here or something, because if it's one of you, then all we have worked for, all we believe in will go up in a puff of smoke so fast, we won't know what hit us."

People begin looking around at each other, as if wondering.

"I know a Delilah. She's on part time, evenings," says one woman.

"I didn't know anyone was working in the evenings," says the doctor. "Maybe she saw us working on the parts or something."

"That could be, Doc." says the man that walked in. "Well, I think we should all take off our masks and see who's underneath."

"I don't understand all this, man. Some of us gotta go home and get some rest. We can't stay up all night. We gotta work tomorrow," says an older woman.

"Yes, I know this is difficult, but we have a dream that I thought we all shared, and without knowing who each other is, how can we trust each other?" William takes off his cap and then looks at the woman who's standing next to him. Mary takes off her mask and shakes her long, beautiful hair down.

"Now you see who we are."

"I don't know you, lady," says an older man.

"You don't? I was there at the first party where we talked with William and the doctor. Now will you all please take off your masks so we can know for sure who you are?

As far as you know, you don't know anyone here. But after you take off your masks, you may know some people, but not everyone. But that doesn't mean that everyone or anyone here was even working on the same project with you. You worked with two people on a project, but only William, the doctor and I really know who worked on what. You see there were several projects going on tonight, and not everyone worked at a place they knew. Everyone received a map that only you in your group saw, but you really don't know who was in your group because we all wore about the same clothing. Now as far as the maps, I think we should all throw them into the incinerator, and then nobody will ever know who did what, unless you tell. And at this point, I'm not really sure you would want to."

"That don't make me want to take off my mask," says the same older man.

"Why not?" asks William.

"Because once we see who is doing what, I mean, who's here, then we are all up shit's creek. Ya know what I mean?"

"As I told you, there were five different projects going on tonight. Only about five percent of the group came from each location, and we mixed everyone up so you wouldn't have to worry. Only those who are worried now can actually be pointed at. But before you take off your disguises, walk around and mix yourselves up so you don't know or remember who was next to you." They all walk around and get confused for a few minutes and then gradually everyone stops. One by one they take off their masks. They look around, half afraid. But they realize they don't know everyone.

"All right, then, those who want to leave can line up by the door, and then we'll check you out. The rest of you, come on. We need your help," says Mary. Some people line up by the door, and William and the security guards help to check them out before they leave. They're warned to leave cautiously because the cops might be waiting nearby because of the beeper Tony had on him.

The rest of the group follows Mary into the other room. Three people roll in tables of coffee pots, donuts, cups, bowls of fruit, hot plate containers with steaming foods underneath, and more. Chairs are brought in by everyone available, and people begin sitting, relaxing and eating.

William and Mary go into the corner and start talking. "What do you think we should do about all this?"

"Well, I—"

"Well, I—" They interrupt each other. Then Mary says, "I thought you should know what the problem was, and then we could ask everyone for help in figuring it out."

"Why should they come up with a plan when it's our thing?"

"Isn't that what this is supposed to be about? I mean nobody taking over your problems, and the group taking care of the group. Instead of one or a few solving the problems for the whole?" Mary scratches her head.

"People are watching us, Mary."

"Well, don't you all know what this is about?" she looks at each one of them.

Molly, who's been sitting next to the doctor, speaks up, "I think I know what it's about."

"I thought you would, Molly." Mary smiles.

"You mean about how the time has come when we all need to, I guess, become completely responsible for our lives. We can't blame a government that we've empowered. If we want things to be better, then we have to make things better, right?" She looks over at the doctor, who is smiling at her lovingly.

"What about the children?" a middle-aged man says.

"Well, we're responsible for them, but I think we're

responsible for all children who aren't getting what they need," says Mary as she leans on a chair. She then sits down. "Would you like to have more control over what they see and hear on the telly, or at school?"

"Sure, but—" The man is interrupted.

"But nothing, Jack. Wouldn't you like more control, like to know what's in those shots your doctor says he HAS to shove into your child, and why some get sick and die from them?"

"I know why!" a grey-haired lady stands up, "My son is retarded from those shots. They said the shots would keep him from getting sick, those DPT shots, HA, what a joke. Just another ploy to keep us working folks poor and always paying for doctor bills. Shoot 'em up with something and charge 'em for it, and then, well, if they get sick, all the better. Then they can charge you more money. But at least they don't get polio or whooping cough. So what if his mind is gone and the damn government don't even care or want to help or nothin', so what. That's what the government is for, ways to kill people." She cries for a while and then goes away to the washroom with a few other women.

"That's exactly what we mean. We want and need and deserve real freedom, not a cage just painted in a few colors, with maybe our choice in colors." Mary stands up again. "We need to take control of our lives and live the way we want and where we want."

Everyone claps and cheers. One man yells, "But how? How can we, just a few people, take control?"

William stands up and Mary sits down. William says, "It's not just us. We have people in every major city and many small towns all over the world doing just exactly what you're doing right now. We're all trying to free ourselves from bondage of the electric companies and the governments and the crime and the chains we have on ourselves in so many directions. We're doing it all with just a little at a time, but in many ways we are trying to take charge of everything. But right here we have literally tons of equipment in the next room that can and will change the faces of towns and cities for several hundred miles, forever. All we need to do is hold a little assembly, and then tomorrow night, the installations, simple installations, too."

"Simple installations? But ain't it illegal to put something on someone else's house without their knowledge?" Asks a large middle-aged man.

William sits down, "Didn't you think we were gonna install them? I thought we made that all pretty clear."

"Youse folks didn't tell us nottin' like dat. We thought we was just makin' em'."

"What's your name?"

"Jim."

"Well, Jim, you see, they don't do other people much good if the things aren't attached to their houses and buildings. That's why we planned to attach them. You're probably right about the installing part being illegal. But isn't it probably just as illegal to dump toxic waste on public lands?"

"Who's doin' that? I ain't doin' that. Who's doin' that?"

"The owners of the plant and many others like it have been dumping their radioactive and plain toxic wastes on public lands for the past fifty years," the doctor states quietly but with a firm voice.

"So what does that have to do wit' all' this?"

"Don't you see, Jim, and all of you," begins Mary, "the only way for people to stop all the bull that's been going on for so long is to just take the bull by the horns and make it so nobody needs that type of energy anymore. Then they have nothing more to say. Meanwhile we're building our world in other directions so people will not have to go through the chaos and confusion that people who are being taken over go through. Do you know what I mean?" People look around at each other for a while and whisper here and there.

"I know what ya mean." Jim smiles. "It's like pulling the rug out from underneath 'em, right?"

"That's right, Jim. Exactly. We're pulling the rug out from under them while at the same time we're like carpeting everyone else's houses with the most plush carpet we can, and it's all for free."

"I guess if we told everyone that we're doing it first, they'd laugh in our faces or something," Molly says. The doctor smooths her back, and then they smile at each other.

People grumble and rumble, talking quietly with each other.

"Wait a second... I have a home, and I sure would like one of those things on my house. Then I could just tell my neighbors about 'em, and then they're bound to want one, too."

"You're right, um, what's your name?" William asks.

"Alice." She smiles.

"We can install them on all our homes first, like you said. Then anyone who lives in an apartment could tell his or her landlord about it, and then whoever wants one could just get one installed. And then... oh boy, that's a great idea. That solves most of our problems with logistics."

"But what about the trash that's been snitching on us?" spouts an older man.

"I don't know. What do you think, Mary?"

"I guess we could question all of you privately and try and figure it out. But we really didn't take anything that didn't belong to us."

"You mean....," a young woman says.

"That's right. We didn't actually steal any of this. It was all paid for with private donations and funds. We just used the facility for some of the equipment until certain materials were assembled, so they really can't do anything to us anyway."

"We were trespassing."

"Well, I think that many of you already have permission to be on their property. Now come on there, you know we did something wrong. What about our jobs?" The woman with grey hair taps on the table. "We could all lose our jobs if this gets out, and then what would we do? We'd be dirt poor. Nobody's gonna hire a woman my age. I'd lose my pension and everything. We'd be dirt poor!" She crinkles her face and dazes her eyes till she looks like a different person.

"Wait just a minute there. Now don't worry. We won't let anything happen to you. What's your name?"

"Bridgette. But why not? I'm going to be out of work soon, and there's nothing you can do about it."

"What we can do is what we're trying to do, is to start a chain reaction here throughout the world. We don't believe there should be any money needed or used by anybody. Weren't you there either when we were talking about all this?"

"I think I heard something about that, but I don't understand really how you can think of taking all the money away. You was jokin', weren't you? The whole world uses money. How you gonna get food and clothes and stuff?"

"It's all very simple, or well, it will be when we're done with all this. You work on something for your livelihood that you really enjoy doing. I work on doing something that I'd rather be doing, and you and everyone else does the same by doing what they really want. Then we simply give and take as we need and want. Nobody really wants to steal or cheat or have more than everybody else or stick knives into the other guy's back—it's just that we're all so screwed up from society and religion and governments that tell us that somebody needs to control everything or else we have to be afraid of the next guy. Everything is totally off balance. We have to get people back on track. It's like as if all the animals were trying to be like people."

"What does that mean?" Jim asks.

"You know, I mean that's how people act, as if they were animals trying to be like people. But they aren't. They're all balanced, except the ones we've screwed up and murdered and tortured with our experiments and our so-called humane farming."

"I still don' get it," says a man with a Mexican accent.

"Well, what would you rather be?" William asks.

"I am a man, and I like bein' that."

"Right, but are you doing what makes you happy?"

"I make money for my family, and they are happy because I make lots of money."

"Yes, yes, but do you enjoy your work, or rather like, when you were young, didn't you want to be something besides a factory worker?"

"Well, mister, we all want to do different things when we are young. An' then we has a famly, an' then we have to eat. So I am happy now."

"But did you ever wonder why some people can do the things they want, and some people can't?"

"Maybe they don' need to make much money, they come from rich fam'ly or they don' really love anybody so they go on an' work."

"That's true, so then, wouldn't you rather have been the one with the rich family, able to do what you wished and dreamt of when you were younger?"

"Si, mister, but I have fam'ly."

"Right, right, but what if I told you that you can still have your dream. That that dream is what you're really

supposed to be doing. But right now you're doing what
somebody else told you was what you're supposed to do."

"NOBODY WANTS TO WORK IN A FILTHY
FACTORY!" Jim stands and shakes his fist.

"You're right! Nobody probably does, except,
maybe the people who are retarded and who actually feel
good because they are contributing to the whole. Let's face
it. Factories were designed to be able to employ lots of
people to do something faster and cheaper, but not quite as
well as a craftsman. That way, the someones on top that
own the place can make lots of money from all the things
the factory sells to all the people on the bottom that can't
afford the item when it's made by a craftsman. The
someones on the top can pay pretty low wages and
outrageously low prices for materials so they get a nice fat
profit."

"That's right! My family in Europe used to be
blacksmiths," says Molly.

"But how are you gonna change all this?" asks a
voice from the group.

"I can't and nobody else can without your help and
everyone everywhere pulling together. But most people
don't know how or even that we can. But we're still gonna
make this happen, and we're gonna start by installing these
wonderful things that you great people have done and
install them onto the roofs of houses so we can get this great
new age really started!" William pounds the air. Everyone
cheers and pounds too.

"WHAT ABOUT OUR JOBS?" a voice from the
crowd yells. "We have to live now, don't we?"

"Yes, now, of course we do. I think we aren't bad
people, and so we should figure out what to do with Tony
first." Mary folds her arms. "What do you think we should
do?" She asks the group.

"Let's search him to make sure he isn't wearing any

more bugs and then bring him in and see what makes him tick," two large biker-type fellows say. Mary proceeds by going to the other room to bring him in.

"But what is it we're really talking about here?" Molly asks.

"What do you mean, Molly?" William looks at me weird.

"You fill us with all this stuff about our dreams and your visions about world peace, but what about us?"

"I don't understand," William says.

"Well, as I understand it, most of us have probably forgotten our life's dream, and so then we can't think of anything else except whether we're gonna have enough money for this thing or that thing. But usually we don't, especially the most expensive things. But you, you're young enough and you've got enough energy and probably the means to try a little experiment with human lives, but we can't. We just can't gamble like that. What we have is, well, maybe a home and a car and maybe a little comfort. But not enough to throw it all away on a pipe dream. We've risked a lot for just the little bit we've already done. And your dream doesn't exactly sound promising, mister."

"I understand what you're saying, but I don't have a lot. I have a regular job like you all do, and I could lose it, too. This is no little thing we have here, either. It's not just my dream, either. How many other leaders or just dreamers have come and gone in the past, and they've always said the same things: we can live in peace. There is enough to go around if we all share and do our part. Now, if you're like me, you know how to share, and you don't mind. But we are not in control. But being at the top is never the solution. The only people that have been able to be happy and successful leaders are the ones who are just in charge of their own lives and their family's lives, right?"

"That's true."

"Before it was just a dream that we thought we could help you with, mister, but now the stakes are a lot higher," the woman with the grey hair says.

"You all have spent the last five months of your spare time working on materials that you're acting right now like you've never seen before. What are you saying to me? That you're pulling out now?"

The crowd grumbles and mumbles again. Some shake their heads. Some are more relaxed and try and be positive.

"We don't want to pull out, but we're also facing criminal charges."

"We'd better put our masks on now so Tony doesn't recognize us," William says.

"Here he is, boss." says the blond-haired guy with a football player's body.

"Don't call me boss, Ross. I have a name, you know. And thanks for bringing him out."

"Sure thing, boss."

"Oh, I'm not your boss!"

"Right, boss."

"You can't hold me here. I'll have you thrown in jail so fast you'll firget who you are." Tony squirms.

"Boy oh boy, what and who do we have here? It's the spy who came in from the mud. Who do you think you are crashing a private meeting like this anyway?"

"This ain't no meeting. It's a conspiracy! I have a job, and I intend to do it."

"Your job. How nice. And what is your job?"

"Private investigator, protecting my bosses' property from losers like all of you."

"You're Al Capone's nephew, aren't you?"

Tony tries to punch William but is held onto by Ross, who holds onto Tony's jacket and pulls him into the air so he can't do anything but run in the air.

"Let me go, you big dumb idiot!"

Ross holds him up higher and turns him around before saying, "Who are you calling an idiot? I have my Ph.D. from Harvard. So if you want to call anyone an idiot, I suggest you look in the mirror first."

"I, ah, this hurts, sir. Could you please set me down?"

"All right, Ross, let him down. He's just a whore anyway." Ross sets him down but holds onto his jacket.

"Who the hell you calling a whore, you thief?" Tony's voice cracks when he yells.

"I am not, and none of us are thieves."

"Ya, you just pick a bunch of honest working people and fill them with a bunch of lies and then rob their store. I don't know what you could have told them, but it's, it's like the rainmaker that lies and steals from innocent people by getting them to do the dirty work. You, you...."

"Hey, hey, that's what it sounds like to me, too!" says an older man who'd been asleep until now.

"Wait a second here now...." William holds up his hands for everyone to stop. "Before you all get excited here now...." He is silent for three long seconds. "You must realize something here now. You and I, no, none of us here now, stole a thing. Everything that is here is yours and mine. Everything has been paid for, everything. It's ours. And now you KNOW your scientist friend here is the inventor. And you know he has a spotless record as well as a fine reputation for his knowledge in the field. You know that." He puts up his hand again to hold their words. "Don't you? But this man right here who is a scientist also has irrefutable evidence that this same company that you have given to all your lives has dumped toxic waste, killed innocent people whose cancers and other strange diseases have gone on without being punished, except maybe a slap on the hand once or twice. But not stopped. Why is that?

I'll tell you why. It's because they have us snowed into believing that we need that stuff they're pumping onto and into our lives, but we don't. And a dear friend of yours and mine, the doctor here, has proven it to us." He puts his hands on the table flat down. "Don't you see? We have a chance here to start making this world a good place, maybe even a place half as beautiful as it was when we were kids— for our grandchildren." He raises his index finger. "But not if we or any of us on this planet continue to let people who do spy, lie cheat and steal continue to keep us under their thumb." He looks down. "So I'll let you decide now. If all of you want out now and want to put all this back and let this Tony fella go free to tell the boss man.... Well, it's your decision."

People mumble and whisper for a long time until Molly finally stands up and says, "Do any of you folks here remember what I was askin' this fella here first before they brought in this here cheat? Well, I knows for a fact that this little cheat here, Tony, here bugged our doctor's house." Tony shakes his head in disagreement. "Oh, no? What about what they was sayin' about that fat little bonus you s'pose t' get when you help track these folks down here?"

"I don't know what you're talking about."

"Oh, no?" Molly walks over and grabs his collar before saying, "You little pussy liar. You know for a fact that I'm telling the truth. I sat outside the door of Mr. B.'s office and heard the message loud and clear of William and the doctor here talking, during which you almost got yerself clobbered by Mr. B. hisself 'caus'n he was a-feared that you was gonna cheat him, too. In fact he almost choked you to death—see?" She pulls open his collar where some bruises of finger prints are still showing. Tony pulls away and tries to cover his throat.

"Leave me alone, you Amazon."

"Shut up there, pal," says Ross.

"Seems like you're gettin' yerself choked a lot around here these days." Molly folds her arms while Ross pulls Tony up in the air again by his coat.

"Well, she, she's lying!" Tony shakes his finger at her.

"Now everyone here knows well 'nuf that I ain't lied 'bout nothin' in my entire life, 'cept un a little white lie 'bout why Miss Katie Rosto McFigure ran off with that milkman down in Tennessee. Right?" She looks around and gets the nods and approvals from everyone in the group. "And you know he lies." She smiles as she points at Tony, "It's his job." She slaps her leg as she laughs. "Now ferget what I said before about doubting these here folks, I believe in what they're tryin' ta do here, an' they ain't askin' fer much, 'ceptin' a little hard work, and a chance for a future for our kids, a real future. What d'ya say, folks? Are you in with me here or what?"

A few seconds creep by till one man with grey hair and slightly less strong back than some others says, "The last time I took my grandson fishing to my favorite old spot... all the fish were dead and floating around.... That was five years ago... I haven't got much time...."

Suddenly several people stand and say, "I'm in," "I'm in," "I'm with ya," "Let's do it!" Then everyone stands and shouts and cheers and screams and claps and shakes hands.

After a while a knocking gets louder and louder and a little voice starts saying, "Excuse me, everyone, excuse me, may I have your attention please?"

People quiet down and look up to see a little man with white hair and glasses smiling at everyone but trying to get everyone's attention.

William whistles like a wolf, which shuts the stragglers of cheers, and then he says, "Excuse me, everyone, will you quiet down please here? I would like to introduce you to the owner of this place here, the man who's been trying to get our attention here, our one and only Doc."

Everyone claps and whistles for a few seconds while he bows a second and smiles. He pushes his hands toward the floor a few times and then everyone is quiet.

"Thank you, everyone. I'm so glad you could come and make this very important decision that you just made here. I'm so glad you could come and help us with our plan. You have no idea how important this is here, that you are getting in on the ground level. This is bigger than, oh, just bigger than, well, I can't even tell you how big this is except that I can tell you that what we are doing here will insure the future of our planet, our Earth. But what do I mean our Earth when we belong to the Earth? It's just that for many generations we've messed things up so badly, but now we're finally having some good clean people come and take over again. The pendulum is beginning to swing the other way." He smiles at Molly. "Now, now, Tony, how did you get in here? I thought we were rid of you."

"Well, doctor, we meet again."

"Ross, will you put him back where he was? He doesn't need to hear this." William folds his arms.

"After all these months and all this money we've put into this thing I thought we'd be done with the snags." The doctor scratches his bald spot.

"You're right, Doc. We've been at this thing for almost an hour now, and I think we're all ready to find out what you'd like us to do next."

"We've been at it for almost forty-five minutes, and that's long enough!" says a large woman standing by the door where Tony is being kept.

"What is your name, madam, anyway?" The doctor asks.

"Hildegard, sir."

"Hildegard? That was my mother's name. She was a good woman." Hildegard smiles and looks at the floor. "Hildegard, I just wanted to tell you that we appreciate your work. You've been a great help, and, all of you, thank you. Because without you none of this is possible." He puts his right hand out to everyone, smiles and nods and then says, "Now, let's get started."

That night the sun- and wind-powered mini generators are loaded onto the trucks and installed onto thousands and thousands of houses all over the world from hundreds of little factories like ours. When the dawn breaks, people find their ways home, and somehow I find a ride home. I wave to my co-workers. So much work for nothing? I walk around my deserted apartment. I don't think I could get one of those contraptions onto my roof. My landlord's roof, I mean. He won't even let me take down the putrid curtains his wife bought for me a hundred years ago. I keep walking alone in the dark toward the bathroom. I don't want my nosey neighbor poking her head out her bedroom window. I sit down in my great-grandmother's chair and disappear. Here I am all zapped full of energy. Fifty-eight-years old, no husband or children. Not even a cat. I'm active in my church—sometimes. It's never gotten me anywhere. I never had an inkling of where I wanted to go, but I want to go there now. I unbutton my coat for a moment, and then button it again. I tiptoe out to my old beater. I slowly open the door and climb in. I set the brake to off and shift it into neutral till I coast out of the driveway and partway down the block. I turn the crank and sail out of there too fast for the lady next door. What a plastic old building I live in. It always seemed so clean before now. But now I see how it has the same cleanliness as every other prefab building built twenty years ago on this block, this plain, white block. I'm sure that nosey Mrs.

Swanson knows I left the building now. She hears everything. When she heard the noise, she probably looked for whose car might be missing, like mine. I can practically see her eyes looking at me or thinking about me whenever I walk down the street. But I guess we all get lonely sometimes. Especially when we think we're alone.

I turn down a side street to avoid the main roads and make my way all too quickly to the street of warehouses I just left not thirty minutes earlier. I park on the side out of the lights. I quietly get out and walk into the shadows where the large doors stand waiting for me. I find a side door hiding, so I knock on it lightly first. I hear nothing. The sky is pretty with stars and clear with a tip of cold. I'm getting scared. Is this the right building? Sure. I hear someone coming. Someone is looking through the peephole. I wave and smile. The door cracks the dark with piercing white and loud music painted with the words, "Come on in and join the party."

I can't tell who it is at first because of the white streak of blind spot I have across my eyes. I'm practically pulled into the room. The hollow door shuts with an echo hammering through the place. It's an assembly line of people putting more of the contraptions together. I thought it was all done. Several people are sitting while they work. Some, or most, are still drinking coffee, soda and/or are eating donuts. Music blares all over the place. I stand there dazed because I can't believe people are still at it, and because of the complexity of the operation. They're laughing and kidding around while they're doing all this. Are they drunk? Are they doing it right? It's practically morning out there, or it will be in this hour. The doctor comes up to me and smiles nicely.

"Molly, I'm so glad you came back. This is quite unexpected. They said they brought you home."

"You kiddin', Doc, this whole place is unexpected.

What'd ya do, bribe 'em?"

"Ho, ho, you know I'm not rich, of course.

"Well, I wa'n't quite shore 'bout that, but...."

"You know me better than that, Molly. Well, never mind about that, dear, come on with me here now, and we'll have ourselves a nice talk. The talk we've been waiting for."

I smile, and my knees go weak.

"Shall we?" He offers me his arm. I smile and put my hand in the curve of his elbow. We walk into an office I'd seen him go into earlier. We sat down and talked for a good long time about almost everything, including his plans for putting the natural gas companies and the oil companies out of business. But not everything, just a few tidbits here and there. I don't know how it could be possible to change so many things all at once. He assures me that it won't be all at once. But he invites me to dinner tomorrow night.

***

William and Mary drive home late in the morning after being up all night sorting, inserting, attaching, installing, talking and packing.

"I wonder if there's an easier way?"

"Not a chance, William, unless you scrap the project."

"No way. I guess I have to keep an open mind." William smiles. They walk into the house and switch on the lights because they feel like night. The two of them mope around trying to find their assorted routines, forgotten due to lack of sight with lids glued shut. No sleep for almost thirty hours. Their senses confuse each other.

"Do I have to go to school today?"

"I don't know, honey, William. Better check your calendar." Mary lies with her negligee over her jeans and pulls her quilt up under her head while her pillow is under her feet on the floor. "William, dear, please set the alarm for about one o'clock. I have an interview."

"Today?"

"Yaaaa."

"You're asleep again. Left me awake, eh? What kind of wife are you? You're supposed to wait until I'm asleep. Silly girl. Are you really asleep? I'll bet that if I tickle your feet you'd.... Oh, never mind. I'm so dizzy. Maybe I should have a beer. Feel like I'm fifty... that's not old. Feel like I'm a hundred.... That's old... huhu. That's old, but I doubt I'll ever get that old. No, I'll... never... grow... old... because I won't stop growing. That's it! I'll grow so much I won't be able to fit into the john. Poor Mary, she's so little. I wouldn't be able to do it to her if I kept growing. Hahaha."

An hour later the phone rings. William answers, "Haaloe? Isn't it sort of, oohh, earlee?"

"No, it isn't, William. It's eleven o'clock, and you've missed several classes. What're you trying to do? Were you out drinking last night or something?" The principal spits words through the phone. William barely hears him.

"Ah, excuse me, sir. I—I—I'm sorry I didn't call in. I'm very sick, and I just wasn't able to call you, sir, I'm sorry, I—"

"You're what? Sick?"

"Y—yes—er, I'm sick. No, I don't know what it is. I—I think it must be flu, because I ache all over. It's hard for me to even hold the phone up. That's okay, sir, don't worry. No, you had every right to call and be angry. I just didn't hear my alarm. Well, no, that's all right. I'll call later on today and let you know how I'm feeling, sir, thank you, sir, thank you, bye." William's hand is locked onto the phone as he rolls away from the night stand, pulling the phone off and down onto the floor. William's hand with the receiver wraps the line around Mary as he snuggles up to her. Suddenly the recorded announcement comes onto the phone, and William whips his hand away from Mary, dropping the receiver onto the floor where it slides under the bed. As the receiver slides, it pulls the rest of the phone with it whose wire that connects it to the wall slides and gradually knocks the alarm onto the floor, conveniently shutting the alarm off. The tiny white wind-up clock clicks short into a sort of locked position at one, but not loud enough for Mary or William to hear beyond their cloudy slumbers.

After some hours the sun begins to set. Mary begins to wiggle. Suddenly she sets up and says, "Whoa, where am I?" She looks around for the clock. The broken electric alarm that tells good time flaps its mocking shutters of white painted on black squares at her, mocking the hour of 5:18 p.m.

"How can that be? What day is it? William, get up. What day is it, what time is it? Did your alarm go off?" She stands and walks across the bed and bounces off William's side. She runs around shouting at William trying to find her clothes, and at herself. Shortly she's dressed. She runs back in the bedroom yelling, "William, get up! Get up! GET up! GET UP!"

"What, what?"

"Don't you have to work or something?"

"No, no, I told the principal I was sick... go back to bed. We've only had...." He reaches over for the clock, hitting the empty table. He scoots up and sits up. "Where's the clock?" He scratches. "I think I have something else though. What day is it? Where's my clock?"

Mary looks over at his night stand and says, "Where's the phone?" She folds her arms. "What did you do here? You dropped the phone and...." She kneels down and picks up the phone pieces and searches blindly with her hand under the bed for whatever else she can. "You dropped the phone and the clock, too! Great, William. The alarm got shut off when you dropped it!" She picks up the phone and sets it on the stand. She picks up the clock and sits on the end of the bed near William's feet. "You did it again. I missed my appointment because you shut off the alarm again."

William rubs his face and head. "I didn't shut the alarm off, honest. I always remember if I shut it off, and I didn't shut it off, Mary."

"You probably didn't, I know. It must have shut off when it fell or something. Well, it's almost six. We'd better get up anyway and try and salvage what's left of today."

"Mary, do you realize we haven't visualized about the new age in two days?"

"You mean if we don't do it today?"

"Well, we're supposed to do it at noon, like everyone else around the world."

"Well, but hey, if you think about it, somebody somewhere is visualizing about world peace and the new world, because we know that it is noon continuously around the world."

"No, it's not. How can that be?"

"Because of all the time lines. See, if it's noon here, then at the next time line and that space inside of it, will be either one hour ahead or one hour behind us. So as we pass into the hour of noon, everyone else gets closer. So somebody somewhere is praying or meditating or visualizing about world peace continuously around the world."

"You are so brilliant, William."

"Gee, thanks."

"Hey, what about the television station? Don't you have to meet someone there?"

"I—I don't know, I don't know. I feel so weird. Can't we just keep sleeping? Where are you going?"

"I thought I had an appointment, or rather, I did have an appointment, but, it's too late, so I guess I'd probably like to go with you."

"I really don't think I have an appointment, dear. How was your appointment anyway?"

"I should be really mad at you. We have to move the clock. I can't be late or miss any more appointments. I should be really mad at you." She stands up and goes to the dresser. She pulls a drawer out of her jewelry box and picks out some earrings.

"Oh, rally, darling, why is that now, dear?"

"Stop talking funny. You sound like Fred Astaire or someone."

"But he's not an Englishman."

"You think you sound English?"

"Sure, don't I?"

"Well, never mind, it was probably that other, you know, what's his name?"

"I really don't know, dear, but if you want me to stop, I shall."

"Oh, do whatever you want. I can't do anything now, anyway."

"What do you mean? Come here and tell me how was today?" He pats the bed.

"William, you forgot to set the alarm. I missed my appointment today."

"No, dear, I didn't. I distinctly remember setting the alarm clock and setting it back up on the table." He leans over to snatch the alarm to prove his point when he slips off the bed.

"That's one way to get you up, I guess."

"Thanks."

"Well, I think that must be almost what happened this morning, except I'm pretty sure it had something to do with your phone call from the principal. What do you think?"

"Yup, yup. I think when he got so pissed at me, I just fell back asleep or something. I remember letting go of the phone sometime during the night. I remember thinking that I need to pick it up in the morning. Oh, yes, something else dropped, too."

"I gathered that already."

"I could have dropped it when the doctor called me, too."

"Did the doctor call?"

"No, not that I know. But anyway, anyway, here. I can't stick around here all night. I have to get out and get going, do something. I may have something to do at the studio. You want to come with?"

William leans over and picks up the phone and takes the clock out of Mary's hand. He sees that the glass of water that was next to his bed is cracked and spilled. Mary trots into the bathroom for a towel when she sees it, too. The two work on the glass and water. He gets up and grabs the broom from the linen closet and sweeps up.

"This is ridiculous, William. You just got up, and you have no shoes on."

He sweeps up the towel she is trying to wipe the water with. She pushes back and yanks it from him, and he pushes and pulls back and forth.

"Listen, Mary, thanks for bringing in the stuff."

She pulls the rags from him and he pulls back until they're just putting parts together and trying to keep things coherent when it's sleep that everyone needs including me.

The two wrestle back and forth for a while until he grabs her and tries to kiss her. "Oooh, no," she smiles, "alas for I was not born to kiss a dragon." By this time the sheets and blankets have tangled around them because of falling on the bed during their struggle.

"A what? Pooh—so solly—I fo'got, miss... but the dragon will not be able to kiss the maiden until its fire's been quenched. AHHAAA! Or the other way around." He puts his arms around her as she squeals and laughs. They hold each other for a while, mingling their fantasies together. William whispers, "I'm really sorry about your interview. Was it really important?" He sits up. He stands on the towel and cuts his foot. He hops into the bathroom with Mary following grimacing at his pain. She tries to nurse him back to health with a bandage and a kiss, but before she can reach its proper location, he kisses her again—or tries to. Before he can, she makes the symbol of the cross in front of her face.

"Sorry, sorry, I forgot, but with all this pain I'm in, but if you insist, I will." He tries again to kiss her, but with his mouth wide open like he's going to swallow her in a dragonly way.

"Oh, poor baby dragon. No, it didn't mean that much. But I would have liked to at least called them."

"So do it," William says trying to get up.

"I can't do that. Besides what good would it do me now?"

"You can explain what happened."

"What, that my live-in boyfriend and I were out all night robbin' a factory and assembling WOLAR Power Packs so we can put the electric companies out of business? Sure, that'd go over real well. Like lead in a lake."

"No, I guess that wouldn't exactly work right now, would it?"

"Nope."

"You could lie."

"Hey, now, man of such high and pristine morals, how can you of all people suggest such a thing?"

"Well, in this society and the way these things are set up it's designed for people to have to lie in order for them to allow you to have freedom and keep it."

"You really think so?" She leans on the sink.

"Well, I don't know for sure." He takes some water in and gargles a bit like a man of the gay twenties did.

"I need to settle something with you, girl."

"Yes, sir, what's that, sir?"

"You said we were robbin' a factory—but that's not true, you know."

"Well, William, what would you call it?"

"We didn't rob the place. The things we took belonged to the doc and me."

"We were still on private property and could have been arrested."

"All right, all right, so we could have been, but we weren't. And nobody's gonna connect us with all that because everyone who's involved has something to lose if they squeal. Besides, I checked the place, and it doesn't look at all like anyone touched anything."

"Look, I don't know what good it does for us to talk about this again. I think we must have talked about this for days and days, and we hardly got anywhere before, so how could we get someplace now?"

"Well, I don't know about that."

"We didn't get much done last night."

"Yes, we did. We got the support of thousands of people, and we put lots and lots of those WOLAR Power Packs together and installed a real lot, too, and put together a ton more that we will be able to install tonight. It'll be like Christmas for some poor folks."

"Interested or not, you'll have to have more than a majority of the entire world population before you can have this kind of major change actually take place."

"You can be so negative sometimes. Now don't you worry about a thing. Everything will be taken care of. And soon, very soon, we'll have a peaceful and happy planet again."

"Somehow, when you say that, I get this feeling of doom." She leans back against the door jamb with her back while her arms fold together.

"You've been watching too much telly. After all, what did that famous man say... what you love the most, you will one day resemble?"

"And what is that supposed to mean?"

William squirts white foam into his hand and spreads it onto his face. "It means that I love the images we've been working on, so I'm sure that we'll accomplish our goals. What else? Now be a good girl and high tail it outa here for a bit for this here fella, will ya? Unleshen a'coursh, ya wanna watch me cut myshelf shavin'."

"Why would you cut yourself? Oh, yeah, because you're pretty clumsy most of the time. And hey, don't tell me to be a good girl. Who do ya think I am, anyhow?"

"I think you're cute. Now I'm sorry, honey, but you do make me nervous, so if you could please get out and give me some privacy, please?"

"Oh, all right, I just wish sometime that you'd let me watch you shave. I love watching men shave."

"Then go watch a commercial or something. Now get going before my foam drips and I'm pissed."

"Some king you'll make!"

"I am not a KING. I don't want to be either. Now, oooh!" Mary shuts the door loudly.

"OW! Thanks a lot, I cut myself! I hope you're happy!"

Mary goes into the living room and sits down in front of the tube. She stands up and goes to the back door to see if the newspaper is waiting on the porch. She grabs it from the deepening evening. She cracks open the plastic bag and swipes a pop from the fridge. She sits down again and searches the want ads. She says to herself, "Maybe I can find something tomorrow. Oh, I don't know, here I am, 22 and I can't even find a real job. I don't want to be a secretary or anything like that. It takes a lot of tenacity to sit there all day long and type somebody else's ideas out. Maybe I should go back to school or something... learn a trade or something, like welding or driving those huge trucks, or working on cars."

"Mary, I think I'm gonna go now. Would you like to come with me or not? What are you doing?"

"Looking at the want ads. Maybe I can find something to apply at tomorrow."

"Find anything?"

"Not really. I'm not really trained for anything. I don't want to be a secretary or computer operator."

"Well, do you want to come or not?"

"What can I do?"

"You can come and watch. Let me teach you about television, and then if you want, you can work for me. How about it? Do you want to come?"

"Oh, let me go to the bathroom first and then I'll decide." She walks away and spends about twenty minutes locked away in the cubicle. William is watching the telly when she returns.

"I'm ready." She smiles, waiting for a little attention.

"Mary, did you see this?"

"What?"

"It's all over the news!"

"What? What's all over the news?"

"The soldiers being kidnapped and the WOLAR Power Packs and, wow! The word is out! Things are starting to pop!"

"Wow." Mary sits down next to him. "Do they know who's behind all of it?"

"I sure hope not, at least not yet. Did you hear that guy?"

"Yeah, yeah, he says it's like Christmas getting that Power Pack thing. They were just shutting off his electricity today, but last night he got this thing on and he doesn't know how or where. That's great, William!"

"Even if it all doesn't work out, at least I know I helped a few people." His throat is sore, and his eyes burn. Mary puts his arm around him.

"Well, are we ready?"

"Sure, I don't need to hear the sports now." They shut off the tube and the lights and walk out the door to her Mitsubishi. They get in and drive off down town to the studio. Mary parks the car, and they get out. They walk over to the building and open the large glass door. They take the elevator up to the tenth floor and walk down the empty, dark hallway. Their heels slap against the walls with sound, and they go. Near the end of the hall William pulls out his keys and unlocks the door of an office and flicks on the light as soon as he opens it. He holds the door for Mary.

"Go ahead." She says with a slight smirk.

"Oh, thanks." His eyes dart around. They enter the office and sit down at his desk. He pulls out some files and starts looking through them.

"When are you going to open up shop?" asks Mary quietly.

"You mean when am I going to start broadcasting?"

"Yeah."

"Well, hopefully next week, if all goes the way I plan. I've got several kids coming in tomorrow and the next day to start taping their shows, but I've got to hire a camera person, too. Oh, and all the other crew. Some of them are coming in tomorrow, earlier than the kids, to look the place over and give me an okay or tell me what they need to do or have me do. I wish I knew more about this business. Sometimes I think I bit off more than I can chew." He sorts through some papers, and scratches his head.

"What positions do you have open, anyway?"

"I don't remember exactly. They're all in the paper. I know there are at least five of them.... Are you thinking about my offer?"

"Sure. I think it'd be pretty exciting, but I don't know anything about the industry, besides what I've seen on TV, so I'd probably have to work as a sort of apprentice or take a bunch of classes or both."

"You'd probably learn as much or more by being just an apprentice with one of the people I hire here. I don't know what they'd think, of course, so I'd have to check it out first. But if they were game, you could learn the ropes and then take over a shift here when whoever it is is off or something."

"That would be really great."

"I have one guy coming in pretty early tomorrow from another station in town, WLAP. He's gonna help us get started."

"The competition? You're gonna have the competition in here?"

"Well, he's not really the competition because his station is really a commercial station and ours is more of an educational station. Hey, why don't I show you around?"

He shows her the shooting area and all the lights, turns up the volume on a few microphones and plays around a bit with weird voices.

"Wait a minute, Mary, why don't you just sit right there for a minute."

"Why?"

"Just trust me." He walks away and soon he says over the speakers, "Mary, I see you. And I think I know the best for you."

"What's that?" She smiles.

"As an actress. Now on the floor to your left is a little table with a script on it. Read it over a few times, and then we'll see how you do."

"What part should I read?"

"Oh, the part of Alice."

"Should I read them alone, or are you going to read them with me?"

"Oh well, I think it would be a bit easier if I read them with you. Just a minute." He comes out of his booth and walks over to her. "All right then here we go now."

"You're going into your English again."

"Right, right, let's not fuss about it then." William searches for his part's beginning.

"This isn't a very good script, you know."

"Well, let's try and make it good, then."

"Right. All right, then—Roger, why don't you take that ax out of your hand? Doesn't it hurt?"

"Yes, Alice, but I can't possibly find the other product on the shelf if I look this way."

"Is this punk or some such stuff, William?"

"It gets better. Go on."

"Roger, I'll just have to do it myself. Please don't get mangled there in line. I really will help you if you'll only let me."

"But, Alice, I just can't move anymore."

"Of course you can't. You've got an ax in your hand. How in the world did you make it here in time for the sale?"

"I was chopping down my uncle's peanut bush when suddenly I felt faint and then I remembered your shop was having a sale on typing ribbons this afternoon."

"How can you think of typing when you've got an ax in your hand?"

"It is my last hope of making the deadline for the school newspaper with the story of the week."

"And what's your title?"

"Well, yes, the title, I almost forgot. I can't even consider writing until or unless I have a title, no matter how poorly it defunks the story. How about this: Boy meets ax, uncle loses bush?"

"That's so, so gauche, Roger. But I think it'll sell!"

"Great, Mary, great! You were made for this part."

"You're really going to air this?"

"Well, the kid's worked pretty hard on it. You should have seen it before."

"I'm glad I didn't, I don't think I can do this, William. It's terrible writing. It's like a combination of a fifties soap opera and a horror film trying to be funny."

"Well, the kids are completely responsible for the success or failure of their pieces, and I just help them a bit."

"I don't see how you can consider putting this junk on the air."

"Well, it's not exactly the finished product, but I'm so busy that I don't have much time with the kids. I would have had some today if I hadn't screwed up the alarm or something, I guess."

"I don't see how you can say that I'm perfect for the part."

"Well, if you don't want to do this, either you can work on the script with the kid, or maybe you can be in something else we're having. We have several programs we're planning: there will be an hour or two of student-planned and produced programs. They'll include fiction, non-fiction, music, poetry, plays, etc.; an hour or two of one minute commercial splices like things on ways people can improve the planet in all dimensions; an hour or two of children's shows like cartoons and stories that are all non-violent and also nature-type kids shows; an exploration as to why the planet is in the state it's in, which'll be a sort of talk show, with lots of different guest speakers like some top scientists and environmentalists and their ideas on how to change things; as well as news spots of areas needing ideas; and most importantly, we'll have a program called *Peace Now*, which will show all kinds of ways people are working to make things better in all subject areas, from politics to cooking. There will be lists of different people who will be able to offer financial backing for sponsoring world peace and the arts. Oh, and of course there will be programs showing the arts all over the world, etc., etc."

"Woah! That's really a lot. Do you have all the material you need for this?"

"Well, no, but I'm working on it."

"I wouldn't mind working on the news stuff."

"That'd be great, I was going to try my hand at it, but I'm so swamped with stuff to do to get this place going, and none of it can go anywhere if I don't have material to broadcast anyway."

"Well, I do have an idea that I think you'll like."

Two days later as William and Mary are sitting in their living room watching their television station, channel 58, they see writing running across the frame for a few minutes and then some beautiful photos from all over the world and outer space. The writing says: One week from today there will be a new television vision being shown to you, called Station Peace 58. Right now we need help in many television capacities and in other talents such as writers and artists who are interested, seriously interested in sharing their talents in ways that will bring about worldwide peace and harmony. Music is playing during all this, sometimes rock, jazz, classical, new age, country and even pop music. After the request is run, the list of the type of programs to be showing is run, but their titles only. This message is run over and over with only a few breaks in between.

"Well, what do ya think?" Mary has her legs crossed in front of her, bent up in the air with her feet flat on the ground.

"You and Merv did this?"

"Yup, I wanted it to be a surprise. Were you

surprised?"

"Yes, this is great! Look at the phone, it's been packin' in them messages all evening. I'm glad we got that machine before now."

"You're right. Have you listened in on any of them?"

"A few."

"Any good ones?"

"Yes, and some not so good."

"When are you going to call them all back?"

"After the tape gets filled, which probably won't be too long from now. But I think I'll just have a meeting with the ones that sound the best."

Two days later a meeting is set up. William calls the doctor and Molly to join him in the selection, along with his students. Because he doesn't know these people and wants to check their ref's first he sets up the initial meeting in the main library downtown where they have large conference rooms available.

William goes to the conference room a half hour before to set up the refreshments.

"Do you think this will be enough?"

"I don't know, Mary, I hope so. But if not, they can go and get their own."

"We're going to have over three hundred people, William, and some said they'd bring a friend, didn't they?"

"Whew, that many huh?"

"That many. Are you ready?"

"I hope so. That's a lot of people that I don't know and, boy...."

At one thirty people begin to show up and Mary greets them. She asks them to sign in, she collects their resumes, shows them where the refreshments are and asks them to take a seat. People fill the room till they are just standing in the back. There are people from several peace organizations and some who are from non-peaceful groups. A security guard enters the room and looks for William and Mary. She sees him and goes up to talk to him.

"I'm sorry, ma'am, but there are too many people in this room here. I'm afraid I'm going to have to ask several of them to leave."

"All right. I see what you mean. If there was a fire or something in here, we'd be trampled. I'll notify William to ask the ones who are standing to leave. Will that be enough, sir?"

"Yes, ma'am. And if you need any help, there's a courtesy phone over there by the door."

"If you don't mind, some of these people who are standing don't look very friendly, so could you wait until we can get them out before you leave?"

"Sure, I'll stand over by the door."

"Thank you."

"Sure."

Mary walks over to where William is standing at the podium. She whispers into his ear. He announces: "I'm terribly sorry, but for those of you who were unable to arrive sooner, those of you who are standing, I'm afraid we are beyond our legal capacity to hold you all. We'll have to set up an additional meeting for you. And don't worry, there are probably as many positions available as there are people here. So we will definitely be calling you. Thank you once again for coming, and please don't feel bad. It's like throwing dice. Good bye. We'll see you soon." William sort of waves to the people as they go, and Mary shakes their hands and makes sure she notes which ones had to leave.

Soon William welcomes the group at hand and thanks everyone for coming. He explains the purpose and goals of the station and what the role or position of each person present could be. He has several students come up and explain portions of their work and what type of help they need. The meeting lasts for about an hour with an extra half hour of questions from the audience at the end. Finally, William, Mary, the doctor and Molly go around meeting each person so they can put names and feelings to faces before any of them are called back for a second interview or meeting.

A week later, as planned, William goes on the air to announce the official opening of the station Peace Now 58. For the first week they show only news programs and a few children's shows. But gradually the number and quality of shows increases.

For the student-produced show—*Stage One*—William welcomes the show with a large red bow and ribbon across the cam set and then cuts it while all the students are present, saying, "Welcome to *Stage One*, where the students of Johnson High write, produce, direct and act on all their own shows. Here are some of those participants now. Congratulations." As he shakes each of their hands, William asks each of them to introduce themselves and tell about what they did for their own show(s). After the introductions, the actors stay on the air and take a bow before beginning their skit, or scene.

Later after the hour of the first run *Stage One* show, the *Top Peace News* comes on. Professor Reinwaldt is hosting the show this afternoon. The screen is bright green and then shows the Earth from outer space, with music in the back ground. This scene fades and Reinwaldt is shown sitting at a round table.

"Today's top stories are about a hospital that has begun research on child abuse by using a pilot program in which all new and expecting parents who come to their hospital will be required to go through parenting programs and screening for past childhood problems that may lead to child abuse. With me this evening I have Dr. Philingful, the hospital's leading obstetrician. Thank you, doctor, for coming. Now, I am wondering if you could give us a little background into what prompted this program."

"Well, several of my colleagues and I were discussing the current problems in child abuse and how the Band-Aid solution just isn't fixing the problem. Then we thought maybe if we begin with the parents and adoptive parents and foster parents and gave them a very intensive training program, that would not only show them the different developmental stages of children, but several forms of discipline and the success rate for each, as well as ways to cope with their own problems so they don't take it out on the kids. Then this may help curb the violence in homes and against children."

"Incredible, doctor, and didn't you say something about screening the future parents?"

"Yes, professor. Our studies show that the rate of recurring child abuse and most child abuse is found in clusters. It's not usually just a freak. Most abusers have been abused themselves and don't know any better. So if we can find them, then we have a much better chance of helping them, through counseling and peer help, to somehow come to grips with their past and help them go beyond the pain and the horrifying experiences they themselves experienced as a child."

"Well, doctor, don't you risk the chance of people lying to you during the screening?"

"We are aware of the risk. We do have ways to ask questions that will reveal some characteristics of previously abused children/adults."

"What if an adult was abused as a child. Would you still let them have a child?"

"We couldn't stop them from having one of their own offspring, though some people have suggested it, but we can give strong proof against people who are considering giving foster care or adopting."

"What does your program do to help the new child if the parent has been abused?"

"It makes the parent aware of the reality of abuse, that it is not all right for adults to abuse children, and we give them a support group that helps and meets with them regularly for the rest of the child's life as a child. But I think one of the most important factors is that it helps those who have been abused to become aware of the fact that what they experienced was a very real pain that they did not enjoy and therefore don't want to inflict upon their own child."

"How much research have you done with this?"

"Well, this is a pilot program, so it will be the beginning of the research. We'll observe the results for several five-year increments and establish the reliability and possible success rate based upon this one and one at our cousin hospital in the next state over."

"You are avoiding saying the name?"

"They've asked us not to at this time."

"Well, thank you, Dr. Philingful, and I'm sure we'll hear some positive results in the very near future."

"Thank you."

The screen fades to a commercial advertising a health food product that will even be used on a new show, *Vegetarian Gourmet.*

Next there is a scene with William thanking everyone for their support so far, and if they would like to put their ideas online, they should call *Idea Line,* "a show that wants to hear you think."

The screen fades to black for a ten-second interval and then changes to yellow, where the names of the people who helped make the next show are being run. It is a show called, *New Age Fun for Kids.* A little girl walks past and

turns into a drawing. She walks back and forth, sort of the
way old-fashioned cartoons did. She is wearing little overalls
and shoulder-length brown hair. She has light skin. She
walks along to where a road begins. Then some houses begin
to pop up from the ground. She squeals with delight as each
house pops up like a flower in spring. The houses are
painted with beautiful pictures all over them. All but one at
the end of the block has many colors on it. She flips and
wheels down the uninhabited street to the last house. Out
walks a little girl with very dark skin from that single-
colored house. The single-colored house begins as a red
house, but then fades to pink. It slowly turns to lavender
and then to deep purple and then to blue. Then as it
changes to forest green, the little girl stops flipping and
wheeling around and watches. Other houses continue
popping up in the distance, but the light-skinned girl
doesn't continue. She instead, waits for the house of her new
friend to change to pale green and then to cream and then
grey and then shimmering gold. Just as it is doing this, the
girl on the front steps calls for her mother to come out. Her
mother comes out and joins her for a walk down the street.
The light-skinned girl watches as the two walk away. Before
they are out of sight, they turn and ask, "Would you like to
come, too?" She stares at them for a while and then does a
double flip toward them. As she lands on her feet she says,
"Who are you?"

"We are the Rubys. Where's your mother?"

"I don't have a mother."

"Well, you can come with us and live with us.
Wouldn't that be nice, Mommy?" the little dark girl says to
her mother and then does a double flip toward the other
girl.

"Then, yes, I'll be your sister, and your mother will
be my mother, too." The two girls do flips and somersaults
down the block and then rejoin their mother in walking

down the street. They seem to fade away, but the Ruby's house continues to change colors in the foreground.

William is having much success for his new little station and has been contacted by people all over the world. He is interviewed and written about by newspapers and magazines. He gives lectures at universities and schools, junior and senior. Mary goes with him and speaks about current issues, also. She speaks about how the rising peace movement is beginning to form a new reality.

William goes on a national talk show, *Meet the Nation*. Ms. Pam Ronaldson introduces William and Mary and asks them to take a seat.

"William, if you intend to create a true world peace, how would you solve the problem of world hunger?"

"Well, as we all know, the food is available. It just takes people to transport it and to make the commitment to help with this problem."

"Well, I guess it's hard for people to stop working and worry about the starving nations of the world."

"That is the problem. We've been snowed into believing that the only way to survive is to have a nine-to-five job of little or no importance to your personal life or the world. That job is supposed to take care of all your needs, from money to excitement to a social life. But it rarely does for any of us. That's usually because people work at things that they think will bring them the most money. It occupies their time and their entire life, and then what do we have? Nothing. Maybe a pension. We have nothing to show for it except maybe a house or car and maybe some land that used to belong to nobody."

"I don't understand. Are you saying people shouldn't work?"

"Oh, no, Ms. Ronaldson. Quite the contrary. I think

everyone needs to find the something that they really enjoy doing the most. If they love to paint, or build, or talk or—"

"Talk? Doesn't everyone enjoy talking?"

"Yes, but there are people who are alone and afraid and all kinds of things that, if you're good at talking, are roles that are important to a smooth society."

"So what you're saying is that everyone should find something that they're very good at or just really enjoy doing and work at that?"

"Well, that's part of it. May I plug for my new magazine?"

"Sure. What's it called?"

"It's called *Peace in Our Time*."

"Interesting title. And what kinds of things are in this?"

"Well, we have a similar format to the television station, where we have many articles about how people are changing the world right now for a peaceful future. We also look at certain problems that need ideas, and we ask people to call or write in about these problems, and this way we can come to some viable solutions. We also give reports on the environmental condition of the planet, and what is being done as well as what needs to be done. We also are going to begin offering awards for one or two people per month who have done the most for world peace."

"Sounds incredible. Now when did you start this?"

"Three months ago."

"Well, I hope it goes well for you."

"Thank you."

***

After the talk show, we go back to our hotel to relax and meditate. William pulls the shades and sits in a comfortable chair. I sit on the floor with my back against the end of the bed. We relax our entire bodies. I try and see nothing but clear darkness. I block out the sounds in my ear except the roar of my inner self, the sound that some have said are spirits or perhaps the one great spirit talking to me. I work on feeling the Universal Mind. I'll hold onto this for a little longer before I think about the future. Darkness. All I see is darkness. Stop words. Sh, sh, sh, not now, I will come back when I need you. The darkness parts into a shimmering peachy light over mountains where the sun is rising. I see my house in the distance as the path becomes harder to handle with my four-wheeler. Good thing the sun is coming up. My batteries need recharging. I'd like to get one of those rechargers that is self-perpetuating or a Solar Power Pack to attach to my truck so I don't have to rely exclusively on light. But I won't have to worry about the distance when I'm up here. Sometimes I need to carry an extra battery or two if I'm going really far, but usually it'll last about two hundred miles.

A large bear is in the middle of the road. I'll back up. Unless, of course, if he moves. I don't think he could turn the truck over, but I don't want to find out. He looks at me for a while and then makes some sort of barking noises. Uh oh, is he gonna charge? Maybe it's a mother with cubs. I throw her into reverse. I honk real loud and turn my brights onto her, too. I'm backing up as fast as I can. When I stop and look back for a minute, she's gone. Whew! That was very close. But it wasn't the first time. Good thing I keep a power bow and arrow with a snooze drug in the capsule for just such occasions. I don't want to become somebody's dinner. I can see my beautiful geodesic dome shining from the colors in the sky. I'm glad I had it installed around my log cabin. It keeps unfriendly visitors out, and it keeps my garden happy all year round. I rarely have to burn a fire anymore because my cabin is warm most of the time. But when I do have to build a fire, I use only the wood I've found dead. We've all agreed that we shouldn't cut down any more trees unless it's absolutely necessary. If fact we rarely burn anything anymore. If we are to survive the utter devastation that our forefathers created for us, we have to do everything possible to help our mother Earth survive.

I pull my truck into the little garage I have attached to the dome. There are two entrances to my house from here. One is through the cellar, which I enter at the end of the garage that goes into the side of the hill. The other door goes right in from the garage. There is one other door, in case of emergency, and that is on the other side of the house where the mountain creates a little cave. I walk into the cave and not far from the opening is a door that is really strong, metal, that I have locked in case of animals. I can get in or out that door or any other door, depending upon my needs. The sun is growing bright against the grey winter sky. It's cold out here, but very beautiful and quiet. I feel like I'm in a very holy place when I look out at the real world, the world of the earthen plants and animals. People have come and gone. We're parasites to the planet, but the Earth must not die. I think I'm going to paint outside later when the sun is highest and I can leave my lamps off over the dome. My easel is still outside from last week.

I open the thick glass door to the house after parking my truck in the garage and closing that door. My dogs and cats greet me. I feed them. I grab a snack, too. My mom used to tell me about the days when we had gas stoves to cook on. Now everything is electric, but it is only powered by wind, water or sun. Oh, and of course, by our own strength as well as our friends the animals.

I grab my tray of oils and thinners that I've used for years. I pour the liquids through filters into the jar I've had for centuries, I think. It was my great, great grandmother's. We don't mass produce any glass anymore. It's only hand-blown near the mouths of volcanoes. A very dangerous job. No more factories of any kind pouring hideous black and grey garbage into the air we all breathe and need. No more piles and piles of garbage that doesn't disintegrate. Everything is recycled. Paper, glass, plastic, what there is of it, wood, metal, and everything else that is one person's trash is another person's wealth. The restaurant in town gives its leftovers to the farmers to use as a mulch for the growing season. All the soaps are biodegradable. The diseases we are concerned with curing are the ones caused by the centuries-old toxic waste left here by our greedy and selfish grandparents.

I take off my clothes and put on an old shirt that's very big and soft. I carry my tray and clean brushes out to the yard. I walk down the stone steps to where my little stump and easel set. I set my things down on a little table nearby. The air is warm and fragrant from the lilacs and roses that bloom continuously here. I look around outside. Nobody is here, so I take off my shirt and set it on the chair. I lift one of my brushes and paint. I open my mind and being. I grab and dab and stroke and pull at the red and then blue creating a deep purple. I bring in a dark green that I've made darker with blue and place this near the front. I create an edge of a mountain with a corner of white, and I can see the sun trying to place its strange colors out on the scene, too. I see the dall sheep climbing over the rock in the distance, and I put them on the rocks of my pretend mountains near icy-looking strips of glacier and a spot of purple and grey shelter. The sun glares over the bluish mountains and forces the shadows to darken in certain spots. The sky seems to move past me as I become part of the paint and scenery. Life trails my thoughts and improves my looks but never takes my place. I live alone because I cannot move as easily when I live in the shadow of someone else. I am closer to the earth than I have ever imagined I could be. This is my secret place, my secret dream, my secret future....

"Mary?" he whispers in that sweet voice. I know he loves me. He doesn't know me to love me, I don't think. He feels my dependence upon him. He knows that I love and support his work and plans. I am like the loving wife who is always understanding and forgiving and being whatever he wants her to be. I could be swallowed into that space. But that is the very reason why I can't become his wife, at least not yet.

***

Trees are losing their leaves slowly, as they wait for the cool air and pale skies to do their magic first. I feel the bite of the winds. William and I walk down the road near the Seine River in silence. We walk near the Louvre in silence. We almost say something as we walk under the Eiffel Tower, but the words don't come from him or from me.

You startle me when you say, "This is the street here." We turn. I follow his steps to the front door of a small house. You ring the bell. Three times you hit the little black button. Then you wait about five seconds before just lightly tapping it. The door opens fast. We're dragged inside—gently and quickly. Several people stand in the front room, waiting by the way they're standing and talking. Also by the way they look at us when we enter. Almost as soon as they see us, we all walk upstairs into a large attic room.

The room is dark, without a window. Only tiny grates cover the ends of the highest peak, as vents or something. The room is full of chairs. Wooden, cushioned folding chairs, with a few odd overstuffed chairs of several different choice colors. We all take seats. Shuffling across the hollow wooden floor as we try and become comfortable in this dreary place. One little lamp sits next to the speaker's chair. After we are seated, the speaker introduces

William and me to all the people. There are people from Germany, Sweden, Japan, Denmark, Poland, Russia, Serbia, Croatia, Hungary, England, Israel, Armenia, Turkey, India, Pakistan, China, Lebanon, and many other countries. Not many people from each country, since these must be select representatives from each, but still, there are about fifty people. How can so many people fit inside the attic of such a small house?

Gradually, each person speaks on the current state of global peace as it exists within his or her own country. Each government has its own problems of how this idea, this dream could and will take place. Why would a government, which is simply a group of people who are currently in power over the masses, even consider stepping down, unless they had no possible alternative. William explains his plans of how to systematically destroy each government. By beginning with the guns and munitions plants as well as how to destroy the money making plants. Some of the people in the room breathe hard when they hear some of the ideas. The stock markets crashing in each country for the purpose of people learning to become more self-reliant, is one that receives the most attention—negative attention.

"But what about the trust? How are you going to develop the integral part of this new society?" The Swiss woman sits back.

"That's an excellent question. This comes about when the heads of state are talked to and convinced that they should step down from their positions. They will at that time also explain the future plans of the planet to their people. The most plausible way for everyone to move into the new stage of consciousness."

"Bloody how are you going to convince these power mongers who themselves have to report to others we don't even know of? Not to mention the fact that they are under the strictest security." The Englishman sits up straight.

"Well, we've come this far, and we've had very few hang ups. We just have to find a way. That's all there is to it."

"This is an almost impossible task you've asked of us." The Japanese man folds his hands and looks at William's shoes.

"Have you all been visualizing as I suggested several times?" Some look around and scratch their heads and arms and move around in their seats.

"That means no, I take it. Will everyone please close their eyes and relax. Relax your feet and arms. At this time I want to bless this Earth, and I'd like to ask all the powers that are within and with-out to help all the people to become at peace with who we are so that the world will be happy and balanced again. Picture a place. A very special place that may be in your own country or one you'd like to see. Imagine all the factories fading away. See the trains and cars and busses dissolving and becoming trees and flowers and a few small self-contained villages with a few horses trotting by. No matter how large the city is now, it will become peaceful and calm with the loudest noises coming from children playing or the people laughing and singing. There is laughter and excitement at all the new discoveries, all the new forms of art and music that will be coming of the new age. There will be no more poor houses or jails. The freedom will come from within and will be demonstrated as a result.

* * *

Ruban lies near a waterfall listening to the jungle's music. His hand dips into the warm waters of the pool below. Everywhere is green and the breath of the purest air he has ever tasted. He considers the girl who tried to warn him. He wonders where she has gone. He becomes tense for a moment and begins to walk toward the camp. Nothing looks familiar, so he becomes afraid. Something cracks behind him. Ruban whispers out loud to himself as he begins to walk more quickly, "What was that? I see nothing back there. I need to walk even faster. But there's another sound I hear coming from somewhere else. I can't tell, and I can't see except that I thought I'd be back home by now. Where I am? Branches get in my way and splinters jut out before me as I move faster and faster through the green. A sound like a leopard! I heard something that wants to eat me, I think, and I see it now! YYYYEEEEEAAAAAAAA AAAAHAHAAAAAAAA!"

The thing that hits him grabs him and then drags him without teeth but with hands and arms.

"My eyes are closed. Do I dare open them?" He slowly and slightly opens his eyes, so only the slightest bit of light escapes them, and he only sees the green of the jungle as it passes over him. His eyes open a little wider, so he sees a girl in front and a girl behind, or at his head. Shamans. A large mask covers the face and head of the one behind him. The mask is carved deep and covered with brilliant feathers, except for a portion of the mouth and nose that looks sadly mangled. Where is the leopard, Ruban wonders. Where did these people come from?

Sleep seems to come over him as these words move through him.

Sleep, sleep lay your dream-swept hand cross my slowly closing
    lids,
Time will turn your ever wandering lips toward my
    ear,
Where sights of the morrow once
    sat.
Sleep, don't lean, for I do not stay away.
But sit quiet near my thoughts where I may

sneak secrets to
>   you
>   During
>   day.

Ruban rests for a short time though he is not tired. Maybe it was the gentle way he was carried or the energy expended and the fear released when he wasn't eaten by the leopard he thought he saw. Perhaps he sleeps because the day is so hot, or maybe he sleeps because of some inner change that is taking place. Something inside him is changing that only his higher self knows of and which will enhance Ruban's mission.

Ruban wakes in the arms of the same girl who's been resting with him. In his hut there are two jungle doctors who dance around him, singing to help take away the evil spirits or bad feelings Ruban is still harboring. The music is screeching, loud and nonmelodic, which reminds Ruban of the music he used to listen to. He has a fever and feels the sweat he lies in and that pours from his body. He struggles to raise himself, which startles the doctors for a moment until they become curious and come closer to examine him. The girl is still asleep. Ruban tries to wake her.

"OOh, na, na," she mutters.

"It's all right now," Ruban replies. "You are here. We should be married, for you have slept in my bed."

"You cannot marry one of our women," Ruban's grandfather whispers as he enters.

"But I am of this family, too."

"That is of no concern. Soon you will return to your people in the world of hate and destruction. She cannot go into your world."

"But, Grandfather, you know that my friends and I are working hard to change this world from hate to—"

"We summoned you here. We have heard of your

plans from our brothers the trees."

"Then you know that my request to marry her is honorable."

"This is true, but the world is not yet peaceful, and your ways are very different from ours. There is much to do."

"Yes, but we will get there."

"Lenbia cannot go into another world. Many people have tried this, and it only causes anger, resentment, and sadness. This is part of the struggle of the modern world that they have gone too far from the Mother Earth. This is a great source of grief to the souls of all people who are not connected with the earth anymore, or not that they know of. To be with mother is always the most happiness anyone can have. Mother gives all, produces all and rejuvenates all. Mother Earth is not ours, but we are hers."

"So you're saying that I cannot marry her because I would not be able to take her back to my world?"

"This is true. But you are very ill. You must not concern yourself about this now. I have come to take her back to her mother's house before she wakes. You must rest and listen to the doctors here."

"But what if I want to stay?"

"You have much to do back in your world. If you have completed all your tasks and still wish to return, then you may. But she is of the age for marrying, and I am not sure that her path will be with another before you return."

"But I want to marry her. I love her."

"We must go now." He gently lifts her from the bed and carries her like a baby out into the quiet.

Ruban rests and waits. Gradually his shivering and sweating slow to a halt, and he feels cleansed. He thinks of his grandfather's words. "You have much to do back in your world."

But why then was I summoned here? I must find the

answer if I am to stay. I can't just keep going on blindly. If I can't marry Lenbia, then why am I here? The night is getting dark and the drums are beginning again. The shamans must have left when I was asleep because they weren't here when I woke up. They must have known I was better. Amazing how I could feel so good now. What was I doing when I talked with Grandfather? I felt so horrible, but so good to be lying next to the beautiful Lenbia. I put on my clothes, my cloths, that is. I walk out into the night toward the fire where the elders and other tribal leaders are waiting.

I find a spot near Grandfather. I eat and listen. I ask questions and listen to the translators for the answers. Those who I speak with somehow lose their fear and anger with me because Grandfather explains finally why my spirit has been summoned.

I wake with enthusiasm. I walk out, and everything is the same as every morning except that this morning I will be leaving. Two men escort me and my little bag of things to the edge of the forest, where the bulldozers are hard at work. The walk to the edge is almost twenty miles, so I am very tired. My escorts disappear into the green. I walk up to one of the tractors and ask them if I can get a lift into town. The guy I talk to looks at me like I'm a ghost or something, scratches his head and asks, "Where in hell did you come from?"

"Oh, I was hiking around and I got lost. I really don't know how I ended up here, but I sure am glad to see you. Can I get a ride? I sure am tired."

"Ah, sure man. But you'll have to wait till my lunch hour, and that's in about twenty minutes. I also have to check it out with my boss."

"Fine. I'll wait."

On the way into town, we're both pretty quiet at first, and then he begins asking all sorts of questions like

327

why I was out there and how long I was out there. I tell him that I'm an anthropologist and that I was trying to study the people of the jungle, but they're quite hard to find and get close to. I ask him if he's seen any. He says he's seen a few, but they run away pretty fast. He asks me if I'll need another ride, or if I need a place to stay. I tell him I'm going to be leaving soon and that I only have to type up my notes for my paper and then I'll be off. He gives me his name and number in case I need anything. I thank him as he lets me off.

"Ciao," he says.

"Ciao," I say, while thinking, I thought that was Italian.

I walk on over to the airport and get a ticket to the States. When I step off the jet, I'm in New York. I hop a cab to the most important building for me now, the United Nations building. I practically jog upstairs to a foreign relations office. I explain what I need to the receptionist, and she finds someone for me to talk to.

After about twenty minutes, a Miss Pinot comes out and asks for me. I follow her to her office and am directed to sit in a chair with a very low seat, while hers is very high. I explain to her what my work has been for the last six months and just outline our ideas on the subject.

"Have you had lunch?" she asks me.

"Well, er, no. I forgot about it."

"You look like you've spent a month in the jungle. What kind of sandwich would you like? There's a great deli downstairs that delivers, and if I'm going to help you with this, we're going to have to be here for a while."

"Oh well, I guess I'd like just something simple like Swiss cheese with mustard on rye with pickles and lettuce."

"That's not too complicated. No meat?"

"No, it makes me sick to eat flesh that's been dead for very long, or been dead at all."

"You prefer to kill and eat your meat raw? Or perhaps while they're still walking around?"

I smile and lean my head to the left.

She smiles and says, "Never mind, I'm only kidding. I don't eat meat, either."

Soon after she orders the sandwiches they arrive. Miss Pinot discusses with me in detail a plan for helping my ancestors. She has asked many questions about the statistics of the people and how they live. I tell her as much as I feel I can, but some things are personal and private, for tribe members only.

The next morning at eight I walk through the doors of the United Nations building again. I'm really shaking. I wish I wasn't, for it just makes things like this more difficult. I meet Miss Pinot at her office and go over the outline of things to come this afternoon during the meeting. In about thirty minutes, she asks, "Are you ready?"

"Sure. Do I look all right?"

"Sure. Here." She straightens my tie, my only tie right now. We walk down the hall and enter a tremendous meeting room where several dignitaries from many nations are waiting. I shake hands with several of them, and the others I am too far from I tip my head to, like a bow without a hat. I am prepared at this time to have Miss Pinot do all or at least, most of the talking.

After a few minutes of Miss Pinot's briefing everyone about the current affair in South American jungles, she sits down and waits. There is whispering among the people on the panel.

After several minutes of quiet discussion one older man, the Secretary General, I think, asks in a reserved manner, "Uh, so what you're are proposing here is for us to declare the jungles of South America off limits to all other governments and other businesses?"

"Yes, Mr. Secretary. This is what the tribes of the nations there would like."

"I see. And just who are these tribes?"

"I believe, Mr. Secretary, that we have outlined all the names of the different tribes in the depositions that were delivered to your office a few days ago, ah, just before your secretary set up our meeting today." Miss Pinot straightens her papers.

"Ah, yes, of course, I did note that information. But I would like to know why they were unable to present themselves and why you have been chosen as their spokesman?"

"Well, sir—"

"Ah, if I may say so, Mr. Secretary, Mr. Quintero has already explained all of this in the text of the information you have before you."

"Yes, of course, Miss Pinot, so noted. However, I did not find the exact reason that entitles Mr. Quintero to hold the position as spokesman. Is there a reason, Mr. Quintero?"

"Yes, sir, there is."

"And it is?"

"The leader of the tribe where I stayed most of the time is my great-grandfather, Sascawacha."

"Your grandfather?"

"Uh, great-grandfather."

"Yes, yes, of course, but how did you find this out? I mean, weren't you a teacher in the Midwest?"

"Yes, Iowa."

"But how did you find your, ah, great-grandfather in the jungles, and how did you know where to find him?"

"Sir, I don't think you will want to hear all of those assorted details at the present time, but I can say that my parents were aware of and tried to keep track of their lineage after they left South America."

"So, the details about how you found your great

grandfather are complicated and perhaps irrelevant for this hearing, I believe you're saying. "

"Yes, sir, I would agree with your last assessment."

"Well, I think we have all that we need for now. We will go over the material and if we need to ask more questions, we'll contact you."

Ruban asks Miss Pinot, "When will they give us an answer?"

"Is there something more you'd like to add, Mr. Quintero?"

"Mr. Secretary, what my client wants to know is what kind of a time frame can we expect before you'll make a decision about this matter?"

"We will work on this matter and try and reach a decision within a fortnight."

"Thank you, Mr. Secretary."

"This meeting is adjourned."

Everyone waits until the Secretary General gets up, and then we gather our things and leave somewhat quietly. Miss Pinot and I go back to her office.

"Well, what do you think?"

"I don't know, Mr. Quintero."

"Please call me Ruban."

"Yes of course, Ruban. I can tell you that I have been one to keep my eyes open to just such an opportunity."

"Excuse me?"

"Well, the tribes in those jungles, I am sure, have been suffering a great deal, what with all the exploration and settling by other governments, not to mention all the ruining of the forests. I hoped and prayed that there would be some way to avoid sabotaging yet another nation of natives. This way the people are recognized before a total slaughter of tribes and customs."

"They almost were. In fact a good percentage left

the villages and went to live in the cities. Some were forced out, and some were tricked. But those who stayed fled and hid in the deepest parts until now, when their lives are being massacred by greed."

"Well, I'm glad we at least have a chance to stop all this. And I'm very honored to have had the chance to help with this."

"Thank you very much for your help, Miss Pinot. I guess I should be going now, then." We shake hands.

"I'll notify you as soon as I hear something."

"Thank you." I walk out. I'm not sure how I feel. Sort of good, sort of bad, sad, uncertain. I walk back to my hotel and climb the stairs instead of using the elevator. I feel like sleep from the climb up the ten flights and from the day. I lay down on the bed to rest. But wait! I sit up. The ship! Kent and Sascha and the ship were supposed to meet me down in South America! What am I gonna do? I know. I'll call William.

I go over the white cover almost pulling the pillows off to get to the phone on the night stand on the other side of the bed. Everything is on something, it seems like. I dial the school.

"Yes, Mrs. Carlisle, this is Ruban Quintero. Is William Lewis there?"

"Why, Ruban, how are you? Where are you? How was your trip? Are you coming back?"

"Mrs. Carlisle, is William there or not, this is an emergency."

"Oh, why no, he's in Europe. Can I help with anything? The students are asking about you."

"Did he leave a number to reach him at?"

"Well, no, he didn't, b-but he does call in for his messages every day or so. Would you like to leave a message?"

"Yes, please tell him that I'm in New York, and give

him this phone number: 212-555-1555, room number 1002. Could you tell him that it's an emergency, please?"

"Why yes, of course. But, Ruban, your students are asking about you. What shall I tell them?"

"Tell them I'll be back in a month or less, and send them my love. Thank you, Mrs. Carlisle. Have a good one." I hang up the phone.

That night I lay on my bed contemplating my next move. I'm exhausted, but I can't give up now, not ever. I turn the lights down and close my eyes.

I hear dogs in the distance running and panting hard. They come closer and closer until I see them in front of me attached to my sled.

"Come on!" The sled squeaks and packs the ice and snow below until we skid down over the ice and screech across the surface. The dogs' spit sometimes hits me in the face when I turn a certain way. It trickles into tiny droplets as it falls onto the ice when I've avoided it properly. I relax for a bit. This is easy running for them. They know the way up to another ledge when I have to get off for a moment and pick up the sled a bit and put it up onto the snow again.

After a few hours we stop inside a village where the old ways have returned mixed in with some of the good things they learned from the white people, however few. The life up here in the cold desert is a little easier. There's a large geodesic dome over the entire village, which keeps it warmer. They can grow some plants under the dome, berries that grow wild in the summer.

I park my sled outside, next to the dome, and bring my dogs in. An older woman with mukluks and a beautiful seal parka walks out, looking very fat and warm in her clothes. She says, "You can't bring the dogs inside here." No accent. That's odd.

"They're cold and tired and hungry. I won't keep them in long."

"No, no. There's a place for all the dogs out back of the dome. Go on look out back."

I walk away dreary and sad. Somebody who'd just caught a seal is giving treats to the dogs. Looks like fifty or a hundred dogs he's giving to. There are some little dog hutches lined up near the others without names or residents. I bring my ten dogs over and set each up with a hutch near each other. I tie them onto the hutches. I ask where I can find fresh hay or some type of bedding for the dogs. He points to an old barn. I walk over and find it half full of hay. I have no idea how they keep it so full this time of year. I grab a few arms full and spread it out near the hutches. The dogs play around and start pulling it inside to form little nests to sleep in.

"Who should I talk to about keeping charge of my dogs while I'm away?" He points to himself.

"I'm the dog keeper around these parts, er, this place. I make sure they all get fed and they get exercised. Where're ya goin'?"

"I'm on my way to Old Russia."

"Oh."

"I'm going to visit some scientists there to talk about how the rejuvenation of this part of the planet is going."

"Oh, good." He smiles wide. His eyes crinkle almost to a slit as he asks, "How's she doing?"

"A lot better. With all the factories, oil fields and refineries closed just five years ago, I guess we can't expect much."

"What of all the people recycling everything, so there's no more junk?"

"There's still a little, but I know we've kept it to things that can be buried and can disintegrate easily."

"Oh." We stand there without anything left to say.

"Well, let me introduce my dogs to you." I bring him

over and tell him all ten of their names. They greet him with some friendliness and some shyness.

"I'm glad we return the Earth to the old ways." He smiles as he pats Brenner.

"I think she is happy too."

"What of the big hole in the air, is it closed?"

"You mean the ozone layer hole they found down in the Antarctic?"

"Hmmm." An affirmative sound.

"Not quite, but we think it is closing a bit. Maybe after a hundred years of treating the planet right, then things will be as pure and clean as they were a couple thousand years ago."

"How can you tell it's closing?"

"There are some pretty complicated tests we use, but we can also tell by the trees and cloud formations, oh, and by the aurora australis."

"Hmmm."

"How could I find out when the next plane will be coming in?"

"It was here this morning. Every morning it comes about ten. You have a cabin up there?"

"Yeah, you're welcome to it. It's pretty warm with a fire going."

"No solar or wind power?"

"No, it's pretty old. We don't stay there too often, just a few months out of the year. I haven't been able to hook up any of those devices."

"Any family in Russia?"

"Yes, sir, got me a new baby girl."

"Good, er, congratulations." He shakes my hand.

"Thanks."

"Why don't you come in for a while and have something to eat. You need to rest and be ready for the plane tomorrow morning."

I am the air that travels below the plane. I am the sea that holds the waves even and pulsing across the waters, forever flowing around the Earth. The liquid that is here now was once near China and Australia and Japan. Everywhere there is ocean, there is life and the breath of spirit.

The waves crack so high that I hear them spitting at the plane. Plane, it planes across the ocean like a piece of paper gliding across the floor. Except, the floor is crooked and cracked and breaking and making walls upward to try and pull the plane down over itself. The waters want us. Us, who are here inside afraid to become dissolved onto the surface and into the ocean. The cold cold blues and blacks of things we seem to never know for certain. We are being sucked downward into and onto something we can't and don't want to see. Where is the angel that I once knew in my dreams? Where is the old spirit that holds the... I need to forget who I am and try and become the pilot I always wanted to be. And I am an excellent pilot because I pull this baby up far above the storm and into the clearing where the skies are blue and sunny and the ship can catch some extra rays of light for the solar panels. I'm a great old ace flying pilot maneuvering over and under each questioning wave, each lick from the air that tries to tickle me and my ship. I feel the plane pulling itself up and up and finally we speed up and over everything that tries to grab at us and stick its mouth onto us.

This Earth wanted to eat us for breakfast, I think, but she can't this time. We have to free our minds from this. AHA! That's it! That must be the reason why we men have always wanted to douse this Earth with our poisons and our macho ways, our heavy armor and our shining points and bullets trying to stick everyone else into the mouth of the Earth so she'll never swallow us... never, never, unless we in our old age, after many years of battle, forget our winnings and allow the fierceness of this passionate existence we've encountered on this planet—this being this creature far greater than any we could imagine or find the skeletons of— take us over. This ever-changing creature that daily threatens to consume our breath and our light and our souls if we fail to turn down the right street and instead turn down the left street. As if we were on top of the world when there is no top and there is no bottom. The South Pole is only relevant if you are north because there is no going up on this planet. It is always seeking to trick us and therefore needs to be killed. Who cares if everyone dies of radiation or toxic fumes or the loss of our brothers and sisters and plants and animals. The most important thing is comfort, while trying at the same time to trick her back! We must fool her and her children, for only then will we never die in her belly. She may take our bodies and reproduce them into her other forms by using our very bones to nourish the plants and animals that we will eventually eat ourselves, but there again we must still try and fool her by placing the human bodies into boxes and preserving these morsels of food so it is very difficult for her to digest us in her myriad of vesicles and evaginations.

We see that she tries to trick us by moving spirit across the land and water and then placing us into predicaments that are beyond our reach to figure out. We've tried to place what little we know on the table, but then it's turned around again. It seems that each place I walk to has a different vibration, and, scientifically, I can see that this is so, even as the North Pole attracts certain magnetic forces, while the South Pole and Equator attract different forces. The seas have proven that the poles of the planet have changed over the millennium. Can we ever know truly if our carbon dating has actually determined when something was actually wrought unto this Earth? What if something else was being played? We humans are magnetic, too. We're attracted to each other, to certain foods and objects like cars, because of the feelings we have for these things. Feelings WE have for these things. Do we decide through our tiny, limited senses as we believe we do? Do we decide on the basis of logical and mathematical formulas as we like to think? Or do we make our choices through some other patterns or senses that we have consistently refused to accept? Why is it so hard for us to accept that there are more than five senses? Why is it so difficult for us to prove that we are more than we have been led to believe? Why do we fight this planet? Why do we need to believe in the death of each other in order to prove our life? Can't we look at the planet from above? Like the photos of Earth from the satellites or the space ships.... If we look at these we see—what?

I am not in a separate body any more. I am a cloud of dust about to be blown away by the wind. But I will drop onto the plants and flowers or maybe be lost and found among the millions and trillions of other particles of dust in the desert. Maybe I will be food for the tiny molecules that are the food for the food for the body of some being like you. Or you see those monstrous things found in the microscopes that you can't believe would be on your body but which is essential to your body's existence. Those things are the true warriors that fight off all the evil spirits of sickness. They have claws and teeth and grotesqueness that—hey, didn't you say you saw that on the movies last week?

Which one?

You remember the horror of the lost lagoon? You saw that big old ugly thing making its way across the muck and mire?

Holy shit! I didn't know they got the idea from me, or pardon me, my residents.

It's like how they try and scare the artists. Fear is the best deterrent against artists.

Whew, they've kept that one hidden well.

"Where are we?" I sit up and wipe my eyes and touch the woman sitting next to me.

"We're almost home."

"What happened to the storm?"

"We pulled clear of it. You went into shock or something. You were talking and jabbering. I thought you were asleep at first but you were saying all sorts of things, really weird things."

"Things like what?"

"Well, I can't exactly remember what, but I'm sure it'll come to you."

"I know I was having a nightmare. Everything was dark, and I was really scared. Two people were talking, only they weren't people, I don't think, they were... I don't know." I smile and look up at you almost expecting to see something gruesome, but you have a gentle way. I can feel the peace in your eyes. "You're probably right, it'll come to me. After all what do I have to fear in this day and age?"

You smile.

Persis Gerdes was the beloved wife of Eckhard Gerdes and devoted mother of Sterling, Ludwig, and Ulysses Gerdes. She passed away from metastatic breast cancer in 2002, but left behind this novel, a screenplay, a couple of short stories, and a passel of people who loved her. Inspired in part by her well known grandfather, Seth Phelps, a long-time teacher at the University of Chicago Laboratory School, she earned a Master of Arts in Teaching and used her talents to help develop the love of music in underprivileged elementary school children. Her optimism and vision for a better future for the world were unwavering, and they live on through her work.

57054366R00209

Made in the USA
Columbia, SC
06 May 2019